ONE-WAY CONVERSATIONS

DENNIS KING

One-Way Conversations

Copyright © Dennis King 2016 All Rights Reserved

The rights of Dennis King to be identified as the author of this work have been asserted in accordance with the Copyright, Designs and Patents Act 1988

All rights reserved. No Part may be reproduced, adapted, stored in a retrieval system or transmitted by any means, electronic, mechanical, photocopying, or otherwise without the prior written permission of the author or publisher.

Spiderwize
Remus House
Coltsfoot Drive
Woodston
Peterborough
PE2 9BF

www.spiderwize.com

A CIP catalogue record for this book is available from the British Library.

The views expressed in this work are solely those of the author and do not necessarily reflect the views of the publisher, and the publisher hereby disclaims any responsibility for them.

Author's note:

This book is a work of fiction. Names, characters, places and incidents are a product of the author's imagination, or are used in a purely fictional way. Resemblance to any person, either living or dead, is coincidental.

THE AUTHOR has lived with his family in rural Norfolk for over forty years, having previously resided in South London. He and his wife currently live in a renovated country cottage with an extensive garden where they grow organic produce and raise poultry.

His working life spanned nearly forty-eight years including a long period as a director of a children's charity and culminating in several years supporting and guiding high-school pupils who struggled with both the curriculum and life in general.

Now, so-called retirement is preferably regarded as a new, exciting phase in what has always been a very full life. Four children and six grand-children contribute substantially to ensuring days are never dull and he also manages to find time to regularly play his favourite sports of tennis, bowls and golf. Interests shared with his wife include walking the North Norfolk Coast where the vast expanse of sky never fails to take their breath away.

kingdennis@gmx.com

ACKNOWLEDGEMENTS

Sincere thanks to Sue Bevan, Ian and Julia Fleming, and Susan Yaxley for your interest and input. A number of your helpful comments have been taken on board.

Lance Alexander produced the stunning photograph that adorns the book cover. Well, we got there in the end, Lance, and your humour kept me going!

I wish to express my warm appreciation to Laura, Jenni, Camilla and Haylee at Spiderwize, a publishing house with a difference - you are that difference.

Finally I am particularly grateful to Ann Wood. Your cosy summer-house in Suffolk is where this all began so many years ago.

Dennis King
2016

To Marion

Your patient support and gentle encouragement enabled me to eventually meet this fascinating challenge.

BOOK ONE : THE NOT VERY REVEREND RAYNER

"So, do you wear that in bed?"

The attractive young woman's eyes were fixed on my neck, making it feel even more uncomfortable than it already was.

"I'm sorry?"

My tinselled theological training hadn't quite prepared me for this.

"The halo that's slipped from above your head to below it. Does your god never let you go? This is a party not a prayer group."

"Perhaps it is I who needs to let go," I timidly responded, wondering who on earth this direct and vibrant person was that had so suddenly and brashly crashed into my cosy, quiet existence.

"For goodness sake take it off and enjoy yourself."

*

"For goodness sake take it off and enjoy yourself."

Those same words uttered one year later, this time not haughtily and mockingly, but tenderly and lovingly, the tears of joy glistening in her coal-black eyes and dampening her chiselled cheeks. Temporarily startled by unexpected coyness she realised how, emboldened by twelve crazy months of her sparkling and infectious company, I had remarkably usurped her position of dominance. For there I was, on our wedding night, standing to attention by a huge four-poster wearing just my dog-collar and a mischievous smile.

The collar came off but that smile stayed on for the rest of the night.

*

Sudden movement in the meadow pulled me unwillingly from past to present, from pleasure to pain. My vacant gaze out of the bedroom window absently latched onto her beloved barn owl as, on cue, he glided effortlessly around the perimeter during his low-flying twilight mission. I flung the window open.

"She's not here, she's gone....."

I welled up.

".....she's gone."

And then, only then, did the full realisation of my wretched situation swamp me. She was indeed gone and I had to fly solo now, with four young fledglings to rear. I collapsed onto the bed and simply broke down.

I looked outside again but it was pitch black by now. Had I really wept that long? Owl hadn't hung around moping - he was off for a bit of nightlife. That's what she would have me do of course - any excuse for a party. Then there were the children. They needed me to be strong, not like this.

"Take it off. Enjoy yourself."

It was as if she was there in our room, cajoling me.

I ripped the black tie from my collar and tried to think positively. Completely unrealistic, of course, just after the funeral of the one person I relied on so much - Annie, my wife. There I was surrounded by four young kids who were utterly confused by the sudden loss of their mother, a class-conscious mother-in-law who appeared to blame me for it, and a close-knit rural community all hell-bent on helping their Rector through this tragedy, when all I wanted was to be left alone.

Waking up at just before five the next morning, numbed by best malt, didn't exactly help either. As early light filtered through the semi-drawn curtains I inevitably recalled the appalling events of the last few days.

*

It was a wonderful opportunity for Annie to play with the Arcadian Consort at the Barbican. She would only be gone three days and anyway we could do with the money. Besides she would enjoy space from our hectic routine and the daily demands of my five Suffolk parishes. Annie always supported me very willingly but I knew she was exhausted and I insisted she went, bravely enlisting her mother Molly's help. I felt strongly that Annie should go. Playing professionally always challenged and inspired her and, as I said, we needed the money.

Apparently death was instant. No pain. Reassuring that. Good to know. Thank you, God. So thoughtful.

If only she'd listened to Molly and not to me. We waste so much time and energy thinking 'if only', don't we? If only she'd taken the train; if only she'd partied an extra night with Sara; if only her car had coped with that bend in the wet and if only someone hadn't planted that oak tree a hundred years ago.

I was told, as funerals go, there had never been such a turnout. Hundreds of people crammed into the church and many more gathered in the churchyard, where the service was relayed by modern technology. And yet I remember none of those people, just four. My four bereft children. Yes, I have a dim recollection of a sea of faces, glumly set, out of deference to the occasion. But let me straight away balance that very cynical comment by saying that they all loved her. Annie was adored by everyone she touched. She lit up any gathering with her effervescence and beauty. Quite why she looked my way for love had always been a complete mystery to me, and many others I expect. But I never complained! When you are dull, over thirty-five and someone electrifying and thirteen years younger sweeps you off your feet, you don't bother to think about why.

Now, approaching fifty, I saw only these four young people, my sole and precious responsibility:

Carrie-Ann, twelve, the happy outcome of that four-poster; the twins, Josh and Seth, nearly ten and bloody hard work, but worth it; and little Joanne, not quite three, yet already showing her mother's spirit. The life of the Reverend Will Rayner, for so long an easy passage, had suddenly entered severe turbulence and the day I lost Annie signalled the beginning of a dark, stormy period. A period I survived only as a result of my wife's constant encouragement from beyond the grave.

*

I drew the study curtains as the church clock chimed seven and opened the window onto a perfect April day.

Annie's orchestra of daffodils, planted our first autumn seven years ago, were tuning up. Golden trumpets practising the new composition of my life. The branches of her favourite forsythia gently waved in the breeze, the conductor checking his score in preparation for the performance. Now I had to perform. Already I could hear the early rumblings of energetic little bodies charging about upstairs. I rushed out into the hall and began leaping the stairs to make sure the kids didn't disturb Annie. By the window seat at the top of the first flight I froze, as reality engaged gear. This is how it would be for a while. You'll get used to it, I persuaded myself.

After a quick wash I returned downstairs to try and think about breakfast. As I marched boldly into the kitchen I sensed I had already been beaten to it. Sure enough Molly was bustling around, her way of coping. The table was laden with all manner of breakfast ingredients and news presenters were exchanging pleasantries while technicians hastily tried to connect them to the Home Secretary from his radio car.

"I do so enjoy listening to Andrew Egan," gushed Molly.

"I never have the radio on at this hour because it's my lull before the storm. Anyway, I prefer Machin."

"But he's a northerner."

"And Egan's from Essex."

"Yes, but he was educated in London."

"North London."

This hurt. In south-west London Molly shared her very modest flat with nobody. Long before I had met Annie, father-in-law had transferred his affections to Edmonton, and not just for geographical reasons either. This made the north-south divide even more intense for his wife.

"I shall cook you eggs and bacon," said Molly, on the one hand appearing to ignore my baiting, yet simultaneously flicking the transistor off.

"I always get my own breakfast."

"William....."

"Will."

"I beg your pardon?"

"My name's Will."

"Look, I know you're upset and I realise it's very difficult for you, but some things will have to change now. You must look after yourself for the sake of the children."

"You're absolutely right. Some things must change, but not everything. For thirteen years of marriage to your daughter I always got my own breakfast because she could never function properly before ten. As for the children, they soon learned that survival in the early part of the day in this family meant self-sufficiency."

"Hi, Dad! Hi, Grandma!"

The kitchen door took off as the twins hurtled in shoulder to shoulder, racing for the cereal cabinet.

"Boys, breakfast is on the table. I've got it all ready for you."

"We always get our own breakfast," retorted Seth, to my chagrin, but not surprise, for he was constantly likened to me.

"Thanks, Grandma."

Not only did Josh bathe the wound he also healed it with a hug.

"Thanks, Grandma," echoed Seth, rather hollowly.

Seth and I exchanged glances. We both knew Josh had the right attitude but neither of us could match his open affection. This was Annie setting us the example. Perhaps one day we would learn to follow it, but neither of us was nearly ready enough yet.

"Look, Daddy, good girl!"

We all turned to the doorway as one where little Jo proudly stood with potty held aloft.

"Oh, you're such a clever girl!" Molly exclaimed, rescuing the trophy just in the nick of time.

"Did you wipe?" I asked Jo.

Without warning her bottom lip quivered and her round eyes filled with the oncoming tide. I rushed to her, comforting, reassuring.

"Here," said Molly, returning after dealing with the potty's contents, "let's think about getting dressed. You can tell me which jumper and skirt I should wear today."

They strolled hand in hand down the hall with Jo already imparting advice.

"Not that black one, you look like a witch."

Despite my friction with Molly I had to hand it to her. She had a remarkable gift for distracting the children from adversity and they all responded affectionately to her, all except Seth that is. I daresay, however, deep down he wanted to. I made a mental note to have a long talk with Molly. Much had to be sorted out and I conceded her presence made a very difficult situation just that little bit more bearable. Until I stopped displaying such open aggression towards her, then Seth would go on copying me and hurting her even more. It just wasn't on.

As the twins and I ate, my mind turned to Carrie. The boys were eating as greedily as ever, but I had no appetite at all. Eventually I pushed my plate away and went to seek her out. From birth she had taken on her mother's sleeping pattern - very much the night bird. As I waited for reaction to my knock I smiled at the sign on her door - a cheap souvenir from our holiday last year. I knocked again. At last she responded.

"Come in, Daddy."

Not a sleepy response but the voice of someone very much awake, albeit subdued.

I was completely unprepared for what greeted me.

Carrie was seated at her dressing table wearing some of Annie's jewellery, hair swept up and back in her party style. I was so utterly stunned, and Carrie was the first to speak, quietly but positively.

"I want to be like her, Daddy, so you won't forget her."

It was an eternity before I could answer.

"I shan't ever forget her, Carrie, believe me. But don't try to be Mummy, just be you. That's what I want. I just can't handle this. Can you understand?"

Time stood still for a moment, and then she slowly nodded, as realisation grew. She took one last look in the mirror, rose from her stool and wandered over to me. We held one another tight and, as she stepped away, I teased her.

"You're nowhere near her height yet, anyway."

She smiled weakly and whispered, more to herself than me.

"I'll change back to Carrie then."

I closed her door, choking back the tears, and returned to the kitchen where the twins were already behaving very badly. However was I going to cope with all of them on my own? I probably should get them out today. We needed to be away from this highly-charged, emotional atmosphere.

*

We often had a picnic at Orford Castle. The triangular walk from our village, Great Chesney, was one the children could all cope with and enjoyed immensely. Annie always made sure walking was fun for them and I had been determined this was where we would go as soon and as often as possible. Now was as good a time as any. Molly had packed up some lunch and sent us on our way with a strained farewell. I could tell she was struggling and for the first time it dawned on me that she too had lost the most important person in her life. How thoughtless and self-centred I could be. I was so busy drowning in my own sorrow I simply hadn't given Molly any real consideration. Some priest I was. For how much longer could I keep the charade going, I wondered?

Inevitably several parishioners greeted us as we walked through the village. If they tried too hard to be sensitive neither the children nor our rogue red setter, Paddy, would let them. Beyond Church Farm the footpath to Orford, via Sudbourne Hall, beckoned, and Paddy could be let off his lead. At the stile he followed his normal habit of half squatting and panting furiously, only just about able to contain himself. Every muscle shuddered at the prospect before him. We should never have had him of course. He was maniacal and even wilder than the twins, constantly leaving bedlam in his wake. How grateful I was for his presence now though. It was Paddy who would be such a vital part of the children's gentle healing process.

Jo was at that age when any walk was stop, start, pick up, let down, but in the main she was usually quite content on my back, talking to the buntings that flitted feverishly in and out of the hedgerows as they built new homesteads. Every so often Jo's attention would turn to my head and she'd pull yet another loose hair out.

"Ouch!" I yelped with feeling. "Jo, I'll let you down and leave you here if you do that again."

"No, no, please, Daddy, don't," she sobbed.

I realised my mistake too late. Normally she chortled at this, not caring a damn, but now she clung onto my neck and it took us the mile to the park for her to recover her composure. Carrie and the twins were already clambering up to their secret hideaway deep inside the cavernous decaying walls of what had once been a magnificent beech. Jo forgot her trauma and joined them, restored again to childhood pleasure. I eased myself onto the grassy knoll and was grateful to the clouds which had finally cleared. The gentle warmth of the shy sun made me drowsy. I gratefully sipped water and reflected that no drink man had ever created quite matched the refreshment meted out by Adam's Ale.

*

"Adam's Ale! Everything in your life has to have bloody biblical connections, Will," complained Annie. "This is foul south-west London tap water and tastes like shit."

She stopped walking and leant heavily over the roof of the double buggy that housed Josh and Seth.

"I'm sorry, I'm sorry," she mumbled, before I could

begin to rebuke her.

Not that it would have done any good. It was an unrelenting sultry day in August 63. The boys were a little past their first birthday and had, to put it mildly, contributed substantially to a year of taut nerves. We were toiling up the hill toward the Rookery, a natural haven amidst ever-increasing concrete and exhaust fumes.

"Look, Will, I know you feel you have to be called, but please let's get out of London. I want our children away from all this urban development. It's choking our real spiritual needs."

She valiantly resumed the uphill struggle and I lifted Carrie onto my shoulders. Should I tell her now or wait until we rested at the top? I decided on the latter and simply practised the lines in my head.

Annie, as always, was absolutely right. My family needed space and six years for my first post was plenty long enough. It was time to move on, time to find that space. We arrived at our bench-seat beneath the scented rose arbour.

"I will have some water please, Adam," she perversely joked.

This was Annie, always able to laugh at herself - or was it yet another go at me?

"I, er, I have to pop to Suffolk on the train for the day next Thursday," the words began to tantalisingly drop out.

"Suffolk? That's a long way to go for one of your dreary old meetings."

"Yes, but I'll be back in time to help put the kids to bed. The interview's at eleven and I should be able to get the afternoon train back - might be a bit touch and go."

I was interrupted by a plaintiff cry of help from Carrie who had managed to get herself wedged under a privet hedge.

"You said 'interview'," whispered Annie upon my return.

"Did I?"

"Will Rayner, what are you plotting?"

I took her tenderly by the shoulders and brushed my lips against her cheek, flushed by the combined pressure of the heat and her mounting curiosity.

"Now stop all that. Just hurry up and tell me what's going on."

"You remember Don Alliston?"

"How can I possibly forget? He married us."

"Yes, he couldn't even remember my name when it came to the vows."

"Will, if you don't stop this dramatic smoke-screening nonsense I swear I will smack you one."

"Is Daddy being naughty again, Mummy?" Carrie piped up from behind us.

Immediately she was gone again to investigate a family of snails. I doubt they were too impressed at being discovered under that rock, after taking all day to crawl into its cooling crevices.

"Well, Don's retiring and has recommended me to his Rural Dean to succeed him at Upper Chesney. I'm to see the Dean next Thursday and, according to Don, it's mine for the asking, provided I behave myself at the interview, praise him for his choice of pre-lunch sherry and admire his petunias."

Annie wasn't listening to the back-end froth of my ramblings. Now it was her turn to take me by the shoulders. This was no gentle embrace though. Her lips met mine as I admired his petunias and they only parted as Carrie knowingly pronounced:

"You're kissing it better then?"

*

"Dad, wake up. We must capture the castle and overthrow the enemy."

I leapt to my feet, somewhat dazed, and followed my knights. Josh and Seth were always the heroes in shining armour but Carrie flatly refused to be the rescued heroine. She was, after all, the eldest and she was also her mother's daughter. So, much to the twins' lament, it was Carrie who was their leader, albeit understandably subdued today. I could tell her involvement in our pretence was entering its final phase.

Soon the fortress was ours and we celebrated with lunch. Then the twins engaged in sword-play and jousting. Poor Paddy was somewhat woefully playing the part of the handsome charger, but at least it prevented him racing out of control after rabbits. Carrie sat quietly, distancing herself, obviously missing her mother. Jo, predictably, dropped off, and I gazed out over the River Ore, to the swollen sea beyond, clutching her to me as my life raft. Let's face it children have a much more buoyant way of grieving. On the whole they seemed to be having fun today, but I was just acting, acting all the time. Like our seizing of the castle - pretence. Now our play had no leading lady. Annie had been killed off and I asked myself what sort of God had directed all this?

*

Late April's reluctant dusk brought with it the order Annie and I had always striven for at the end of each day. It had been her habit to efficiently yet lovingly pack the kids off to bed promptly. Jo by six-thirty, the boys an hour later and Carrie, with difficulty, by eight o'clock.

Tonight there had been no such problem for me. Carrie had kept herself tucked away in her room and I, with Paddy's help, had successfully worn the others out completely.

I stared into the bright embers of the fierce fire Molly had lit in the drawing-room, grateful for the tumbler of malt beside me, the embracing armchair and an inner feeling that - all things considered - this most difficult of days had passed relatively well. For the kids, at any rate. I realised though that I had made special plans for the day and it had taken a tremendous effort on my part to achieve the right result. Then I was always good at one-offs. How the hell would I keep this going?

I drank heavily from the glass and topped up. Molly had, in her practical way, dealt with all things domestic. What was going to happen when this fell to me? Perish the thought. I had always been cosseted like a valuable antique, from cradle to middle-age. I started to perspire with anxiety. On top of all this I had five parishes, each with between three and five hundred men, women and children, all expecting me to baptise them, confirm them, marry them, bury them - generally wipe their arses for them on a daily basis. I took another slug and re-filled my glass. That was another thing, even before Annie's death I was beginning to show too much affection for this stuff. What the hell! At least I had a good excuse now. Anyway, why should I care? Had God cared about me? He'd left me to my own devices, so everyone else could stew in their own juice as well. They only tolerated me anyway. It was Annie they worshipped - not me, not my so-called God. It's a good job congregations were dwindling if you asked me. Less meaningless small-talk to have to listen to at the church door as their withered hands cracked inside my restrained grip. Telling me what an inspirational sermon it was when I knew it was hypocritical and worthless.

The alcohol was beginning to bite now and fury was building inside me. This was the real man grappling with the cardboard cut-out in holy orders. The priest bit was a sham. Annie had worked it out long ago but I had kept denying it out of cowardice. I wanted our cosy existence to be protected, but this had been jettisoned by her loss, and my rage was escalating furiously. I no longer wanted to hear about Nora Stokes' latest stray she had rescued as I sat in her stench-ridden scullery, gingerly sipping from a grubby, cracked cup; I refused to plead with Lady Beckwith-Holmes anymore to increase her deed of covenant to St Saviour's as a result of her husband's latest bent business deal; and I couldn't possibly assure Bill Simmons that his Faye was now at peace. I didn't even know if my own wife was.

"Annie, why did you go? I want you back. Please come back."

Clumsily I rose from my chair and hurled the empty glass at the fireplace. It shattered on impact. I staggered to the fire, crying copiously, apologetic, desperate to make amends. I wanted to re-build the fragments but it was too late. I had lost another friend. I clung to the fireplace and shook with rage and remorse.

After a while Annie put her arm round my shoulder.

"All will be well. You can go soon."

I momentarily froze.

"Annie?"

I looked round, but I was alone.

"ANNIE!" I bellowed at the empty room in frustration.

"Bertie holds the key."

"Annie, don't do this to me. Where are you?"

"Seth needs help."

It was a one-way conversation. Annie was directing me with clipped instructions and clues. My words were futile, but I still persisted.

"How can I help Seth?"

"Be patient with Mummy. You need one another - believe me."

"I believe you. Of course I believe you. But answer

me, please answer."

The crackling of the fire was the solitary sound. She had gone. I glanced down and surveyed the smashed glass.

*

I had just finished clearing up my temper when, as if the Director was at work, Molly entered on cue, bearing a tray of coffee and shortcake for us to share. At sixty-six she was amazingly fit, but as she sank into Annie's chair I noticed the etched lines on her face. She was all in.

"Seth is in your bed, William."

"In my bed? Seth? But he and Josh are inseparable at night."

I was too aggressive, not yet adjusting as instructed by Annie earlier.

"I'm sorry. It's not my fault. I tried my best to dissuade him, but he kept saying he wanted his mummy and....."

Sitting on the edge of her seat, coffee-pot poised to pour, she suddenly dissolved. I rushed over to her, gently rescued our beverage and consoled her for the first time in my life.

"Molly, forgive me. I apologise. You've done wonders looking after all our needs today and now I must look after you for a change."

"I don't need looking after, thank you. One sugar, isn't it?"

Unable to cope with this sudden physical contact she immediately re-grouped back into her hard-glazed shell of practical efficiency.

I respected her feeling of awkwardness and returned to my armchair, thinking this had possibly been the mildest of breakthroughs.

"William, we have to talk. We are both exhausted but

bed won't bring sleep for either of us, and the children's future has to be sorted out."

"Yes, of course, you're right. We have to sort a lot out, but just getting through today was my sole objective and I'm absolutely shattered right now. I do realise there's a lot to discuss but....."

The whisky was the main culprit for my state of mind of course. My head was banging and clear thinking was currently not an easy option. However, Molly was as determined as her daughter and she persevered regardless.

"I do hope you will let me help you."

I nodded tacit agreement.

"It's all been such a shock. The whole family and community are numb, and I'm anxious that this will prevent you from taking the necessary steps to ensure you and the children can go about the normal routine daily tasks." Molly had this incredible knack of making life such bloody hard work, but I buttoned it and let her continue.

"These past few days have been very hard and it won't get any easier," she continued. "Now I know you have a lot of time for Biddy Sugden. Annie recently told me that Biddy was the only parishioner you really had any time for, apart from that awful Jem fellow from Chedgrave."

"Now Jem's all right," I interjected. "Just because he enjoys a drink or two."

"Yes, well, he's not the only one, is he?" Molly said, taking a sideways look at the empty malt bottle.

"Anyway, we're digressing. The point is Biddy needs work after being laid off at the hatchery and....."

"Oh, that's good, Molly, very good," I chortled, for the first time in a long while.

"I don't see that it's good at all. Losing one's job after so many years' loyalty?"

"No, no, I meant your quip about the hatchery - you know, laid off? Oh, never mind."

Annie had not of course inherited her sense of humour from her mother's side.

"Well, as I was saying, she needs employment. So I took it upon myself to invite her over for tea this afternoon, and she's agreed to do it."

"Do what?"

I was beginning to understand. Unknown to Molly I had already wondered about seeking a bit of help, but it was a question of money - or rather the absence of it.

"Well what will you do when I return home on Monday? The children will need constant female input."

God, she was so conventionally sexist, but probably right to a point.

"Anyway, Biddy's happily agreed to cook, clean and take care of things here during the week, and I will look after the weekends. Now, before you object, I know you're thinking I'm an interfering old battleaxe, but I employed her on the basis I'm paying."

"Molly, you're very generous, but you can't possibly afford it from your little part-time job. And as for every weekend, train fares will cost a fortune."

"William, I am adamant on this. I shall keep out of your way and just see to all the chores. What's more I can afford it. To ease his conscience, and protect his reputation, Mr Tompkins has never failed to send me my monthly peace offering. He always did spend freely and years ago I only agreed to the divorce provided I was adequately compensated. I wasn't going to let his tart have all his money, as well as steal him."

The vehemence was quite frightening, but her unexpected passion was soon quelled as she returned earnestly to the matter in hand.

"At least please give it a try, William. If it doesn't work out we can think again."

My alternatives were bleak so I concluded it would be folly to block this one. My wife's earlier words rang in my ears: 'Be patient with Mummy. You need one another.....'

I leant across the coffee table and lightly stroked Molly's sinewy hands.

"You're so very generous and I'm really grateful."

Her bottom lip quivered like Jo's that morning and, reddening, she brushed my hand aside, picked up the tray and made for the door. It was shut and she became flummoxed at not being able to open it without putting the tray down again. I came to her aid and, with eyes full of tears and anger, she turned on me.

"Annie was all I ever really had. If only she had listened to me and taken the train. If only she had listened to me and not you."

I accepted the criticism, for I had certainly insisted Annie took the car.

"Why did she let you persuade her? Why, William, why?"

I had no answers of course, and Molly knew that.

Then she was gone to wash up the coffee cups. I just hoped this new partnership would work. Biddy was no problem, but I knew the anger Molly could kindle in me and how unpredictably ill-tempered I had become. I sensed the chances of success were less than even.

Ten minutes or so later Molly returned to say goodnight.

"Oh, I forgot to give you this."

She handed me a letter post-marked Hove.

"It's from Norbert I think. No doubt he's trying to excuse himself for not attending his niece's funeral."

The piercing, bitter tone was still there, but I ignored it.

"Thanks, Molly."

Norbert - or Bertie, as we called him - was Molly's

older brother. He adored Annie, and he in turn was loved to bits by her and all our children. Not only that, but I was apparently seen by him as the son he never had - astonishing really. According to Annie I was the one Bertie constantly referred to during her frequent visits to see him and Aunt Glad on the Sussex coast.

Glad had never been able to bear Bertie any offspring. Not for want of trying, it would seem, for he often assured me Glad gave him unlimited access to what had obviously once been a very attractive body. For the last few years our family's annual summer holidays had been blissfully spent camping in the grounds of their old farmhouse where there was ample space for the kids to run riot.

Poor old Bertie had lost Glad two years ago. He was a wreck at her funeral - which I was honoured to conduct - so I knew instinctively he would be unable to bring himself to attend Annie's. I read the bold hand:

'Will,

You must forgive me for not making the journey tomorrow. I always thought losing old Glad was the worst moment of my life. When you telephoned about Annie I simply crumpled. I'm sorry, but I know you will understand. I would be of no comfort or use to you, or to those wonderful children. How I feel for you all, deeply. Are you coping? I hope so. When I welcomed you last summer I could tell you were wrestling with a crisis then, and not too calmly either. I forecast that you and the cloth were soon to be rent asunder. You won't stay now of course. It's only a matter of time before you throw in the towel. I often recall our last chat in the 'Cat and Fiddle' when you said that you didn't know what you were doing in the Church and that you didn't think you actually believed in it anymore.

Well, my boy, you can't go on with the pretence forever - she would want you to be true to yourself. I just know something will turn up for you soon. Meanwhile I've stuck a little gift in with this. As my Executor you will recall I have left my whole estate to charity, but I'm going to make sure your immediate needs are covered. It's bad enough that you have to cope with the grief so I can't bear to think of you struggling financially as well. Anyway, I hope you can see what I am clumsily getting at, old chap, so accept the enclosed with a good grace and let's say no more about it. I think it should see you through the next few months. Then I'm sure things will take a turn for the better. In fact I know they will.

Hold tight, Bertie.

By the way, I talked to Annie's dad on the blower yesterday. He's terribly cut up of course, despite not seeing her for years.'

The 'little gift' was for five thousand pounds!

First Molly, now Bertie. I racked my foggy head for the third person Annie had talked to me about earlier. Ah, of course, Seth. 'Seth needs help'.

Well, I would have to deal with that another time. Right now I needed to try and sleep. I clambered up the stairs with no enthusiasm, only to find poor Seth had saturated himself, and my sheets. It took me an age to sort out and Seth was bitterly upset.

Even before the tragedy Annie and I both felt something was troubling him. I suppose if anyone should be able to understand him it would be me, being so alike, but I just could not get to the heart of what was bothering him. Josh was also perplexed by Seth's occasional withdrawals into himself. Well it was back to school for them all after the weekend and perhaps that normality would settle him down a bit.

I slumped into the empty, lonely bed and wept. Tired as I was I couldn't sleep of course.

My mind returned to Bertie's letter. What unforgettable holidays he had given us. Perhaps I should take the kids again this year.

*

August at last and the first Monday of the month we were off to Barton Green for our favourite three weeks of the year. Our old estate wagon was bursting with canvas, tent poles, billy cans, buckets and spades, lilos and rucksacks, each stuffed with shorts and tee shirts. Carrie and the twins could hardly contain themselves, their little bodies pulsating with the anticipation of another Bertie and Glad holiday. It was our third one in a row and the nature of our luggage indicated our total faith that this year would be as sweltering as the previous two - it was never in doubt. It followed the twins' first full year at school, adding even more excitement. The journey was long for Annie, forever trying to entertain the kids, but she too was looking forward to a complete change.

*

I glanced across at Annie whose outward glowing radiance matched my inner contentment. It was a Sunday morning and we were stretched out alone on a screened plateau of lawn adjoining Bertie's orchard as we soaked up all the ingredients of holiday bliss. He and Glad had taken the kids out on a ramble. I hoisted myself onto my elbows and studied the delicious contours of my wife's half-naked, sun-drenched form.

"It's nearly time for morning service, isn't it?"

"Well, Rector, perhaps just one lesson? The congregation will be back soon though."

Her voice had thickened.

"Oh, it won't be a long sermon today, I can assure you."

*

Bertie was wheeling the twins up the drive in his barrow, with Glad and Carrie skipping behind. Their labrador Tramp barked with confused delight. He was beside himself, not knowing which group to be with, solving that problem by charging from one to the other.

"Hello, you two," bellowed Bertie, "no rest for the wicked."

Their walk to Rowley Mill had obviously not worn them out at all, unlike me from my recent exertions. The boys tumbled out of the barrow on top of us. Bertie saucily winked at me as I winced from Josh bouncing onto my sunburn.

"Bit sore are you, Will?"

He gave a knowing look as he towered over us, burnished arms on hips, his whole weather-beaten countenance oozing cheeky innuendo.

"Uncle Bertie, you're an old devil!" Annie admonished him, leaping up to greet him affectionately. "Now, it's time for the beach I think."

I nodded my agreement, and the kids needed no second invitation.

Annie, as usual, had cleverly deflected another of Bertie's saucy comments. His outrageous language and manner was designed to provoke people, but I was getting used to it now. In fact I found his bluntness refreshing, if a little over the top on occasions. You knew just where you stood with Bertie, but he did purposely push it a bit sometimes. Annie had the measure of him though, and often gave him a severe wigging for his behaviour in front of the kids. He took it well and seemed to enjoy the public example she made of him.

For any trip out I never had a choice of vehicle. Bertie insisted on driving me in his rust bucket of a mini, and Glad took my place, Annie driving and the children leaning out of the back windows screaming ecstatically. Every journey with Bertie was hell on earth. It wasn't that he was fast, just arrogant. Back at the bridge of his ship, navigating the middle course, with all other vessels having to give way. How we avoided collisions I shall never know.

"Look at that!"

He bawled at me above the engine and wind noise.

"Silly bitch wasn't going to give way, was she?"

I glanced back, heart in mouth, only to see this poor little Morris Minor picking its way gingerly out of the hedgerow.

On arrival at the beach the twins were gone in a flash, little brown buttocks zooming down to the sea until they were swallowed up by the white froth at the water's edge. Another bit of Bertie's influence. He would have gone in naked too but for Glad's very firm threat. His naval background constantly caused him confusion when it came to civvie street and he genuinely could not understand why everyone didn't bathe as nature intended.

"Well I shall jolly well have them off when I'm out there."

"Yes, dear, of course you will, but at least I won't have to know about it."

"Will he remember to put them back on?" I asked anxiously.

"Oh, he never takes them off. He just has to have a grumble. All puff pastry he is."

Glad was Bertie's perfect foil, and sharing their company was a privilege and enormous fun. A perfect holiday. Little did we know Glad was to soon part company with us and holidays would never be quite the same again.

Mercifully that evening the journey back for Bertie and me was on foot. Glad drove Carrie and Annie took the twins, all energy extinguished by numerous exhausting dips in the sea. The walk was only a mile and a quarter but I was ashamed to struggle alongside Bertie's strident frame. Despite the corpulent waistline and his seventy-eight years the daily habit of long-distance walks with Tramp was a fine example to us all. I was always inspired by his athletic life-style and was determined to try and take a leaf out of his book one day. We could never walk past the 'Cat and Fiddle' though.

"Seems so ungrateful when the landlord goes to such trouble to open up," ventured Bertie.

We were allowed two pints and one hour, while our ladies sorted the kids out. That hour was nectar for me. I learnt so much from that outstanding man. I had led such an impractical, dull existence before meeting Annie but this uncle of hers had seen and done it all. He was a giant - so worldly-wise, so unpredictable, yet so endearing. He was the master and I the apprentice when it came to perfecting the art of living a real life. I wanted to mould myself on him for I envied him his ability to create something from nothing, his two fingers to the establishment, his down-to-earth realism, outrageous bawdiness and frank honesty. Sensitivity was not on the agenda with Bertie, otherwise he would strip you naked and crucify you.

"Annie looks radiant, old boy. Hard to resist, I bet!"

"Bit like your Glad, Bertie," I retorted cheerfully.

"Yes, only trouble is I've got nothing to show for it."

His reply brought a brief cloud but he got through it and was resigned to the situation.

"Do you think you'll have any more children, Will? The more Annies we have in this world the better."

"Phew, I'm not sure, Bertie. Besides, they could turn out as dull as me."

"Nonsense, you're not dull. I've seen life, my boy. I've met a lot of men - and women - and I'm telling you straight, you're the brightest thing that ever happened to

Annie."

"Thank you, Bertie," I whispered.

"You've got to let it all out though. This bloody job of yours is stifling you, for God's sake."

"I've not got much choice at the moment," I meekly responded.

"I see that. I'm not so damn stupid I don't realize you've got responsibilities. But it doesn't suit you. You don't sit comfortably in that black and white uniform. I want you to have an escape route. You're a clever bloke, Will, talented - don't waste it."

This was typical of Bertie, genuinely and passionately pointing out the obvious, but wisely leaving it there, not telling me what he thought that escape route was. But he meant to motivate me, set me thinking.

"Money's always the stumbling block, Bertie."

"You can't have it all, damn you!"

His sudden bark startled me.

"You've got that angel and her babies. What more do you want, you greedy bastard?"

I was getting used to these unexpected vicious outbursts, but I coloured up as I became aware for the first time that the pub was getting rather populated.

"Sorry, my boy."

Immediate regret, as always.

"Lost my head. Uncalled for. Here, let me get you another."

"Now, Bertie, we've had our ration for today."

"What? Oh. Oh, yes. Better not, eh?"

"Let's make tracks."

He hesitated, his grey steely eyes bathed now in heavy dew.

"Ask your god this, Will. How can he have denied Glad one little nipper? Just one. He lets millions breed like rabbits and then pays them benefits. Benefits? It's the snip I'd give them. On the National Health of course."

One defiant finale brought the show to an end. We bid the landlord a hearty farewell and linked arms for the last quarter of a mile home, which was completed in comfortable silence.

At the gate he hugged me.

"I've made my will at last. Thought I'd better. Done it myself. Language any fool can understand with no legal claptrap. Be my Executor there's a good chap. I want someone I can trust, someone who understands me."

He noted my frown.

"Look, Will, it won't cause you any work at all. Say you'll do it, please."

I cautiously nodded my assent.

"Jolly good. Thanks old boy."

He turned as if to open the gate and then hesitated.

"And don't think any of you lot are getting a penny either - it's all going to charity. With conditions of course. We can't have them squandering it on bloody admin can we?"

No mention of Glad.

"Now, I think it's time for the 'Hornpipe'."

Bertie loved to bring his violin out to our tent last thing at night. His final routine of the day was to play the 'Sailor's Hornpipe' for the benefit of the three sun-kissed faces that peeped out of their sleeping bags while Tramp performed a demented jig at the tent entrance. He relentlessly chased his tail on the same spot until Bertie's bow completed its melodious dance across the strings. Then Bertie turned to the children.

"Ship's Company - dismissed!"

With that they were all gone - Bertie to his beloved Glad, Tramp to his kennel, the kids to slumber.

As the day closed Annie and I sat on one of the garden seats, spellbound as we watched shooting stars dart across the night sky.

"It couldn't be better," I ventured.
"Well it might be in our sleeping bag....."

*

Two months since Annie's fatal accident and I suppose I was just about coping. Midsummer already, but this year the weather seemed to match our mood. Substantial rain reflected our deep sorrow and Carrie insisted that nature was also grieving for her mother. Sentimental nonsense of course. Or was it? Carrie earnestly believed it and I encouraged Annie being talked about by all the kids in whatever way comforted them. It helped. It helped me. Molly struggled with it, but then she always brushed awkward matters under the carpet.

On the whole we all seemed to be slowly making the adjustment, but it hurt. It hurt every day, in every possible way. I must admit that the presence of Molly and Biddy was a huge relief. We ate well, I drank rather too well, and we ensured plenty of activity kept the kids focused. But nights were killing me. It was at night, cold and alone in bed, when everything fell apart, when there was no Annie, no sleep, no real desire to go on. Yet I had to keep going, and Annie sorted most problems out with her one-way conversations.

Bertie's astonishing cheque had been invaluable. It replaced Annie's income, and more, and without it I would have panicked. The car insurance had yet to be settled, we had not bothered with life cover - couldn't afford it - and I had no idea whatsoever where our money had ever gone. Annie had dealt with it all. So it had been a shock realizing the cost of our fruitful lovemaking - never-ending clothes and mountains of food which were demolished in seconds, as well as books and equipment for school. However, it did me good to have to face up to these fundamental facts of life. Once Bertie's money ran out I needed to know how to juggle everything around. The car claim certainly wouldn't be much so I couldn't rely on that for long either.

My mind was flitting through weighty financial matters one morning as I dried up the breakfast things. The older children had left for school and Molly had taken the bus to market with Jo and Biddy, both of whom were very obviously helping Molly through her personal tragedy. Rain, torrential until now, gave way to rays of sunshine that peeked through still-threatening leaden clouds. I stood at the sink and listened to the silence. I knew at once she was there.

"Will, Glad's here."

I froze. I couldn't cope with this.

"No she's not. Don't tease me. Please. I can't bear it. Stop this. Do you hear me? STOP IT!"

I picked up two glasses, smashed them together and felt no pain as the blood seeped from my trembling hands into the dirty washing-up water.

"Glad says you must go and see Bertie. Soon, Will. Very soon."

I turned round, fell to my knees and pleaded.

"Where are you, Annie? Where are you?"

"Seth needs help."

"You keep saying that. Show me how. Show me. SHOW ME!"

I collapsed in a heap and whimpered like an abandoned dog for the rest of the morning.

Somehow I was able to pull myself together by the time Molly and Jo got back, managing to casually dismiss Molly's concern about my hands. She probably went to check the level of the whisky bottle.

So, Annie and Glad were together after all, still trying to organize Bertie and me. In the calm of my study I was pleased about that. As for Seth I was none the wiser really. He seemed himself most of the time, but when he withdrew his sullenness was impossible to break down. No one could reach him and I had to hope time would sort this out.

I'd actually sought advice on Seth, and from a surprising source really. The Rural Dean Tom Hargeson. Despite me doing the necessary sucking up at the interview - I actually disliked petunias, and sherry was the one drink I could happily pour down the toilet - we never really got on. I saw him, a bachelor, as married to the Church, rather wet and very uninspiring. Yet, to be fair, he generously offered to continue teaching music to the twins at no cost. My restrained objections had been discarded and I was actually very grateful.

As for Bertie? Yes, of course, I had to go. I knew that. I wanted that. Come what may I needed to make the time - probably three or four days in the following week. I'm sure Bertie needed some cheerful company, and I could certainly do with a change. I would have to clear it with Molly of course, but I suspected she would jump at the chance of a completely free hand here, which I normally doggedly resisted.

*

By my reckoning it would now take me just over an hour to reach Barton Green, Bertie's village. It had been a strange and difficult journey, throwing up so many different, deep emotions. On the one hand it was essential I took a short break but of course many aspects of the trip were bound to be painful. For a start I had to pass the spot where Annie crashed. I had managed to avoid it up until now, but decided it was time to face it. The experience was perhaps less difficult than anticipated, that is until I slowed down slightly beyond the tree. I wasn't going to stop, but something had caught my eye. I pulled onto the grass verge, wandered back and picked up the card propped against the gnarled oak. Beside it was a single white rose.

'Missing you so much, Mama'.

I guess I stood there several minutes. I don't know how long. Finally I lumbered back to the car.

A young woman passed me on the road and smiled, murmuring "Bertie's waiting....."

I turned round sharply.

"Annie?"

But she was gone. The lane was deserted. A sharp breeze scattered the card towards me, now torn up into small shreds.

*

The sun was gradually and reluctantly sinking as I hit Barton Green. The journey had taken a good part of the day, with several hold-ups. During one jam I recalled a conversation on the phone from the previous day.

I had rung Bertie and spoken to his housekeeper, Kath Simmons. I was surprised she had answered so late in the day, but she was preparing him supper. Unusual, for he normally cooked for himself, or dined at the 'Fiddle'. Kath kept him spick and span but he avoided her at all costs.

'If she thinks she's going to take Glad's place she's got another think coming. Follows me all over the house, the old fuss-pot. I only have to sneeze and she's on the blower to the bloody doctor.'

Bertie had told me this so many times and he certainly didn't like her answering the telephone. Anyway traffic was moving again and I'd soon be able to rescue him from her clutches. Having said that she was a lovely person. Hard working too.

I swung into the lane that led down to Church Farmhouse - an amusing name for such an irreverent old man. Stopping at a five-bar gate, I gazed fondly over undulating fields where trees whispered flirtatiously to one another and my favourite beasts chewed their last meal of the day ensuring Jimmy Weatherall could deliver our daily milk. This would suit me I thought. A few cows, a couple of pigs, some chickens. But Annie had been the practical one and always done the work in the garden. What use would I be on my own? Anyway, time to see Bertie.

Pulling up in the drive I sensed something familiar was missing. No Tramp. No barking, no rushing to leap all over me, no tail wagging. Even when I knocked on the door all was strangely quiet from within. Then it was Kath, not Bertie, greeting me.

"Kath, what are you doing here so late? Where's Bertie?"

"Oh, Will, I'm so pleased to see you at last. I thought you'd got lost." A huge hug accompanied her relief.

I returned her greeting in equal measure for, despite our uncle's frostiness towards her, Annie and I had always got on well with this genuine woman.

"What's going on, Kath?"

"Well, just go into the kitchen, then I'll tell you. Now, have you eaten?"

"But where's Bertie, Kath?"

She guided me into the cosy room.

"Will, he's in bed. Now sit down and I'll put you in the picture."

I sat at the table while she made a hot drink.

"Now, for the second time, have you eaten?"

"Yes, thanks. Molly provided more than enough. I hope you haven't gone to trouble on my account?"

"No, I thought she would have done. There, just a dash isn't it?"

The coffee looked comforting.

"You always remember, Kath. But, come on, what's

up with Bertie?"

She sat opposite me to break the news I was already half-expecting.

"The Captain took to his bed more than a week ago, Will."

Local folk had always referred to Bertie in this way and of course he was more than happy to let them.

"He hasn't touched his food for three days, he won't talk to anyone - least of all me - and he was so rude to Doctor Ogilvy. Refused to co-operate and when the poor man tried to take his temperature, the Captain told him to.....well.....er....."

"Put the thermometer somewhere else?" I offered.

"Yes," replied Kath, blushing, "I'm afraid he's just letting himself fade away."

"Where's Tramp?" I asked.

"In the Captain's bedroom. He won't eat either. All I've managed to get both of them to do is drink water."

"Well, that's something I suppose. I'll go and see them now."

"I'll put your things in the front bedroom. Your bed's all made up."

It was quite distressing to witness Bertie in the state I discovered him. He was propped up against pillows and staring blankly down at Tramp, whose head lay on Bertie's left arm. No recognition from either as I entered the room - not a murmur. I drew up a chair on the opposite side of the bed to Tramp. Sitting quietly for a moment I did actually wonder if I was already too late.

"Good of you to come, old boy. Tramp, I said he'd be here, didn't I?"

Bertie spoke with great difficulty and - uncharacteristically - so quietly.

"I can be myself again now you're here, Will."

"I'm pleased to hear that," I replied, taking his hand in mine, "and I presume that will include eating will it?

You've got that dear Kath so worried about you."

"Bloody woman," he croaked, "won't leave me in peace."

"Bertie, that is so unfair. She cares about you."

"I know, I know, but all I want is for Glad to take care of me."

I couldn't say anything to that so I simply squeezed his hand then gently stroked Tramp's head. The poor animal's sad eyes didn't flicker and remained intent on Bertie.

My gaze returned to Bertie and tears had begun to quietly moisten his pallid cheeks. Tramp lifted his head and tried to lick the salt water from his master's face but Bertie turned towards me, smiled, put one arm round Tramp and closed his eyes.

Later, in the gathering gloom, I said a silent prayer for the Captain and his Mate.

*

Like most people, I had experienced several surprises in my life. None quite compared with what greeted me as I went downstairs the next morning though. My eyes must have jumped out of their sockets at the sight of Bertie tucking into cereal and a stack of buttered toast, and Tramp licking his special bowl clean, then demanding a re-fill from a totally bemused Kath.

"Will, what's been keeping you? You're normally such an early riser!" Bertie exclaimed, ejecting bits of muesli which Tramp gobbled up.

"Captain, please, where are your manners?"

"Oh, be quiet, Kath, there's no pleasing you, is there. All bloody week you've been telling me to eat, haven't you?"

Like water off a duck's back Kath ignored him and warmly greeted me.

"Normal service has resumed, as you can see, Will."

That day was surreal. After his hearty breakfast Bertie barely allowed me time to drool over Kath's breakfast efforts for me. Soon we were off on his favourite local walk with Tramp barking incessantly and Bertie greeting the villagers like never before. Their responses were amusing, chins hitting the deck and quite obviously unable to cope with the Captain's uncharacteristic friendliness.

"Can't understand everyone this morning, Will. They all look so damned miserable."

"Well, I don't think they've ever seen you so, er, how can I say - convivial?"

"Nonsense! People have got to start looking beyond the packaging, my boy."

He stopped abruptly.

"Look at me."

I did so, but obviously not to his satisfaction.

"Into my eyes, man, read my eyes. There's life buzzing there, real life. I'm going to grasp it today, and I'm going to live it forever."

We had reached the gate I'd leant against the previous evening, and he enjoyed looking down at his undulating field, the brook beyond and the bare remains of what had once been a magnificently productive small-holding. Wisps of delicate blue smoke indicated Kath had lit a fire, ensuring a revitalising warmth for him once he had eventually run out of steam. That moment looked light years away though.

"Glad and I planted every single tree and plant here you know. Such happy times. Nature freely gives us all so much, yet it's abused. Everyone on their own agenda, in a hurry, not aware you can't keep taking from life - you have to give back. That's what trees are about. They weren't planted for us, but for future generations - the likes of your children, Will."

He was momentarily lost in thought, but then we continued walking up the hill, Bertie striding out as never before.

We reached the 'Cat and Fiddle' six miles later, with me literally on my knees. Bertie burst boldly into the snug and declared to the bemused barmaid that drinks were on him and what did she fancy. I believe his saucy wink might have embarrassed me more than her, as she hastily fished for the lunch-time menu.

"You're extremely generous today," I ventured.

"Not that bloody generous, Will. It's hardly packed here, is it?"

And for the first time I looked around and noticed that Jimmy Weatherall was the only other customer.

"Obliged, Captain," said Jimmy, doffing his moth-eaten cap.

A man of few words it would seem.

"Meet my nephew, Will."

A froth-covered mumble accompanied a second disturbance for the moths as Jimmy made the most of his unexpected bonus drink.

"You'll be seeing a lot more of him in future."

Well, that was news to me, but I was used to being bowled along by Bertie like this.

Having devoured pie and mash we somewhat stuttered back home, Bertie's energy finally sated by one pint too many.

At the front door he thumped me on the back.

"Marvellous, Will. A wonderful finish to the day."

"Well, not finished yet," I said, "it's only two o'clock."

"It's finished for me, Will."

He surveyed all about him.

"It's been perfect. It's all been perfect, but now I need to sleep."

He lumbered off, shouting a final order.

"Put Tramp in his kennel, there's a good fellow."

*

Kath and I had chatted for a couple of hours on my return from the pub. Bertie had taken himself off to nestle by the fire because even in June the drawing room was decidedly cool for him.

Strangely it didn't surprise me that Kath had found him gone when she took him a cup of tea. We agreed, looking back, there had been an inevitability that death would pay its visit just when it did. He had certainly known.

There was much for me to arrange of course, phone calls to make. Molly received the news stoically. I had to leave her to tell the children of course, which might not be easy for her. Quite tough in fact because I knew that the hurt would be deep in all of them. Their emotions were certainly getting a hammering lately.

After supper, picked at really, I walked round the garden and grounds and ended up crossing the brook to wander amongst Jimmy's quiet herd. Looking back down at the farmhouse, it had an air of complete and utter desolation, but of course that was merely a reflection of my inner feelings - absolutely empty.

"Mr Youngman."

Annie's voice. I was momentarily thrown.

"Who?"

"Kath can help."

"How?"

"Go to him. Tomorrow."

And that was it.

Well I guess I'd better find out who this Mr Youngman was. Kath might know by the sound of it so I plodded back to the house, despondent, yet oddly resigned to the whole situation.

I had the most miserable night. I tossed and turned continually for my mind was all over the place. Over a very short period of time I had lost the two most influential people in my whole life and I was far from sure I would cope.

*

I had eventually tracked down the cob-webbed offices of Youngman Foulkes in a back street of Brighton, the one British coastal town that, for me, defied every argument for choosing Spanish package holidays. I was now fidgeting about on a lumpy leather chair that had seen better days.

Eventually, having again familiarised himself with Bertie's file, Mr Youngman wearily dropped his reading glasses onto the paperwork and sighed. It was not, as I first suspected, with frustration, but what appeared to be genuine sadness.

"Mr Rayner, f-f-forgive me, but I should initially explain I do have a sl-slight stammer. I like people to know. Your uncle used to say it was so I could take longer and ch-charge even more. I hope you don't sh-share this view."

He smiled benevolently and I warmed to his friendliness.

"I'm sure it was just his joke," I replied.

"Of course it was, of course, and I'm going to m-miss him pulling my leg every so often."

Another smile, this time more wistful.

A comfortable quiet embraced the room as I allowed the senior partner time to mourn his client.

"I was of course aware Mr Ewing had originally chosen to ignore convention. Yet even he f-finally realized we dull old lawyers sometimes have our uses. I was so relieved when he instructed me two months ago.

His well-meant earlier will would have caused you, as his Executor, so many p-p-problems you see."

This was a major surprise. So Bertie had swallowed his pride after all.

"Thank you for seeing me so promptly," I said.

"Not at all. Life has to go on for the rest of us and you, I gather, have more on your plate than most. Anyway, I have little to do here these days, now that I have made Mr F-F-Foulkes a p-partner."

It occurred to me that he could have chosen someone with a name that helped his impediment more.

"A very capable young solicitor and someone you can trust implicitly, Mr Rayner."

"Does that mean he, not you, will be handling Bertie's affairs in future, Mr Youngman?"

He looked somewhat thrown for a moment, then confused.

"One step at a time, Mr Rayner. Let's get everything in the right order, shall we?"

The professional was taking over and I took the mild rebuke in the spirit offered.

"My apologies. I guess I'm just anxious about this executor business."

"No need, I assure you, no need."

All very well, I thought. Piece of cake for you, a mountain for me.

"Now, first things first."

There was no pulling him off course.

"Here is a letter from Mr Ewing to you, which I am instructed to ensure you read before I declare his will."

He rose.

"Will Darjeeling tea suit, Mr Rayner?"

"Er, yes, um, yes, by all means. Thank you."

He stole out of the room with due reverence, leaving me with Bertie's envelope shaking in my surprisingly unsteady hand. The mesmeric, soothing tick of

Youngman's French mantel lulled me into thinking fondly about the dearest friend I had just lost.

*

"I find this particularly refreshing on such a warm day," Mr Youngman commented, as he re-entered his office armed with tray and Darjeeling.

"Oh, I'm too soon I see. F-forgive me."

He glanced at the unopened envelope.

"No, no, I just got lost in thought I'm afraid. Please stay. I'll look at it now."

"Good. Meanwhile I'll pour, shall I?"

"Er, what? Oh, yes. Yes, please do. Thank you."

I tore open the letter and once again read Bertie's hand:

'Well, old chap, I've been thinking of you today. Made a couple of minor changes to my will. Don't be offended but I have decided not to give you the onerous task of being Executor after all. You've enough to deal with. I've also sought advice from a solicitor. Didn't want to, but needs must. Charles Youngman's someone I've used from time to time. He takes ages about anything - fee justification - but I believe him to be a very decent and honest person on the whole. By the time you read this I hope to have seen my Glad again.'

I hoped so too.

"Mr Rayner?"

"M-M-Mister Rayner?"

The stutter brought me back.

"Yes?"

"More tea?"

"Oh, thank you. You're right. Most refreshing."

"Good, now are you ready for the will?"

"Yes, where there's a Will there's a will, eh?"

"Quite."

I shall never know if he had a clue what my feeble joke was about because the glasses were perched on and we were back in business.

"Now I may look old and crusty, Mr Rayner, but with your permission I shall simply read out the main j-juicy bits - if you'll forgive the phrase - rather than sit here wading through unnecessary legal jargon."

"Please do, I much prefer it."

Bertie was obviously wrong about the fee justification.

"Right. Now the f-farmhouse and all nine and a half acres are donated to the Oak Apple Trust."

No surprises there.

"The Trust will also receive a capital sum to cover the set-up costs of renewing and expanding the small-holding activity, to include livestock, f-f-fencing, buildings, m-machinery, plus one year's running costs."

Well it was really good to know the place would be productive again. I wished old Youngman would put a sock in it though, the Darjeeling was making me soporific, or maybe the heat had got to me.

"The Oak Apple Trust to create an open-ended lease which will enable Will Rayner and his family to live there, free of all cost, on the con....."

"What? What did you say? Did you say we can live there? Live there for nothing?" I shouted, leaping out of the chair and knocking the teapot onto the desk. "But what do we live on? I can't just up sticks and leave everything. I can't, I just can't."

"Listen to him." Annie was back.

"I've been listening, believe me. Do you know all about this? It's your doing, isn't it?"

"Mr Rayner, I can assure you it is nothing whatsoever to do with me nor will it be in f-future. Mr F-F-Foulkes has been appointed Executor by your uncle, on my advice. That's my only part in all this."

"I'm sorry, I wasn't talking to you. I mean I was just, well, you know, thinking aloud again. There's a catch isn't there? I just know there's a catch."

"Well if you'll let me continue you will see there are conditions certainly."

"Will, sit down and shut up!" Annie again.

"Yes, darling, of course."

"I beg your pardon, Mr Rayner?"

"Sorry, I wasn't talking to you. Please, do go on."

The poor man took a long deep breath, found his place again and prepared to continue. Hesitantly he looked up over his glasses and spoke in a bare whisper.

"You know, if you prefer, we can do this another time. I expect the shock of....."

"No, no, I'm fine now. Please go on."

"Very well. So you can live there free of all cost, on the condition you r-resign from the church and m-manage the small-holding."

The old boy braced himself for my next onslaught, but all I could do was burst out laughing, shaking my head in utter disbelief.

"You old beggar, Bertie," I muttered good-naturedly.

"Well, certainly your uncle was never short on surprises, Mr Rayner," said one obviously very relieved solicitor.

"He certainly wasn't."

"There are various clauses that pr-protect you from a f-financial viewpoint but....."

"Mr Youngman, thank you. I don't need to hear anymore if you don't mind. I know my uncle would never make life easy for me but equally neither would he ever let my family be put at any insurmountable risk. It's for my family. I see that."

"Well it's interesting you should say that because there is one more extract I would like to read, if I may?"

"Very well, if you think it's necessary."

"I feel it is relevant at this stage."

He cleared his throat.

"To my sister Molly, the regret we never really got on, but my solemn declaration that everything I have set out here is in m-memory of her daughter and for the b-benefit of her four grand-children."

I guess that finished me. I tearfully collapsed on his desk, knocking the teapot onto the floor this time. He was round to my side of the desk like a shot, consoling me. Well, I like to think it was me he was concerned about but I noticed he did quickly pick up the teapot and carefully examine it.

"I'm sorry. I'll pay for a new one," I muttered.

"Out of the running costs for year one, Mr Rayner?" He smiled as he spoke.

"Yes," I laughed. "Take it out of there."

"No need. It's intact."

And then we both roared with laughter.

"The Axminster broke the fall, and you didn't like the Darjeeling anyway, did you?"

"It's certainly unusual," I replied, as I gathered up Bertie's letter and made for the door.

"How long have I got to decide?" I asked.

"As long as you need. Please take your time. It's a big step."

I nodded, headed out again then hesitated. I opened the letter and looked at the date.

"Mr Youngman, you never did tell me the date of this new will."

"Oh I'm so sorry, I simply f-f-forgot. Let me see. Ah, yes. April the twenty-fourth."

I looked at Bertie's letter again. It was the same date. April the twenty-fourth - the day of Annie's funeral.

*

A few days later our uncle's wish to be buried at sea was realised. It was, for me, a sobering experience by virtue of its simplicity, and it felt absolutely right for him. So natural, so practical. The captain and his three crew, all ex- Royal Navy of course, welcomed me aboard and we caught the early evening tide on a most beautiful, warm summer's day. I was certainly grateful for the calm weather.

On the short dignified journey out, a solitary black-headed gull persisted in swooping before the launch as if showing us the way. Waves lapped lazily around us once we had anchored at the chosen spot, and on the captain's bidding I proceeded with the service. Then we laid another captain to rest, his body to feed the ocean life and his spirit dispersed to enrich our world.

No tears this time, merely a swelling of pride and real gratitude in my heart for knowing such an astonishing man.

On the gentle journey back I experienced a sense of balance restored to me for the first time in a very long while. I really had no idea what I was going to do. I had always found decisions difficult, but I didn't let it bother me this time. Somehow I just felt Annie would guide me, although it was still me that had to actually make things happen. I needed time. Too much drama had unfolded in such a short while. The children and I had to be given time. I missed them. Perhaps tomorrow I should return home.

*

"Your poor father," protested Molly. "Let him drink his tea, Seth."

"Don't worry, he's fine. I've missed him too. I've missed all of you very much."

"Can I sleep in your bed tonight, Dad?" Seth pleaded.

"Oh don't be silly, Seth, you....."

"Er, excuse me, Molly, but I think that just this once won't hurt."

"But....."

"No, please. I would like it."

"Well, if you say so I suppose," she sniffed, picking up the tray and heading for my study door.

"Now go and explain to Josh," I said to Seth, "and if he's unhappy about it, I expect you to let me know."

"Thanks, Dad."

He shot off, nearly sending his grandma flying.

It really was good to be back. Molly had of course run everything like clockwork and only Seth had still been up waiting for me. He had refused to budge from my chair. Despite his initial excitement his face looked drawn and his general demeanour was actually edgy. That's why we needed time, and what better way to start than let him be with me for one night.

"Seth's music lessons."

Annie's voice broke my train of thought.

"You don't have to worry about Seth," I replied, "I've got him in my sights. Trust me."

"Seth's music lessons."

This time she was more insistent.

"Now, Annie, give me a chance. You know I've only just got home. I'll catch up with all that sort of thing over the next few days."

"Seth needs help."

"Look, I'm giving it."

I was getting slightly hacked off now.

"Dad, Josh says its fine," Seth shouted from upstairs.

I rose from my chair, went to the open door and acknowledged him.

"That's good, now get into bed and I'll be up very soon."

I returned to my chair.

"See. Now give me some credit, Annie."

But she was gone, so I shrugged my shoulders, put out the light and went and made Seth's day.

*

Summer was quite abruptly displaced by autumn, with unseasonable cold weather and high winds. Molly and I had managed a few days with the kids in two caravans up at nearby Southwold and things could certainly have been a lot worse. Since Bertie's demise I had definitely mellowed and especially towards Molly. Tolerance had been replaced with an immense respect for her, so there were some months of reasonable calm and order while I came to grips with what to do about Bertie's will. In all that time I had no contact from Annie.

Mr Youngman thoughtfully applied no pressure, just a couple of very brief letters, but I knew I could not delay it for much longer. One problem I tussled with was Molly's position in all this. I kept recalling the words Bertie had used - 'enabling Will and his family to live there.'

Sometimes I felt this excluded Molly, and yet Molly was family, and Annie had said Molly and I needed one another. But then Molly would hardly want to live in her brother's old place, would she? No love lost there, ever. It was a conundrum, so, in typical fashion, I forgot about it and simply got on with parish business. There was certainly plenty of that, with harvest festivals looming.

Our own service at Chesney was the last one, in the middle of October, and it was then that my newly-found calm began to fray at the edges.

I had gone into the vestry to disrobe after the service and discovered Seth being consoled by Tom Hargeson. The Rural Dean had attended in an unofficial capacity as the twins' music teacher. They had both played short solos, and equally competently. However it appeared that

Seth - rather a perfectionist already - was unhappy with his own performance for some reason.

"Ah, Will," said a slightly embarrassed Hargeson, "Seth says he wants to stop having music lessons."

"Oh that seems a pity," I replied, comforting Seth. "I thought you played really well."

"I didn't," he muttered. "It was rubbish. I'm rubbish, and I hate music. Music killed my mum, and I hate it." He pointed to the Rural Dean. "And most of all I hate HIM."

With that he burst out of the vestry, tears streaming down his face.

"I'm sorry, Will, I don't know what to say."

"Well you have to understand that all of us are still raw, and out of all the kids Seth's the one who appears to have felt Annie's death the worst."

"Yes, well, he's a very sensitive boy. Let's hope he will change his mind when he's calmer. The offer remains there."

"Thank you, I appreciate it. Now if you'll excuse me I'd better go and see what else he has to say for himself."

"Will, he says some strange things at times. I think he fabricates a lot."

I immediately saw red.

"Really, well I'll be the judge of that if you don't mind. I can't see you as having had much experience with children."

I too stormed out, leaving a red-faced, blustering Hargeson in my wake.

"Supercilious, stuck-up twit," I muttered, as I approached our church-warden, Lady Beckwith-Holmes, who was at the font.

"It was a beautiful service, Rector."

"Good. I'm glad you enjoyed it, Beatrice. But please excuse me. I've got a minor family crisis to deal with."

"Poor Seth is it? I could see he was upset. He played

so well too. I don't understand it."

"No, I don't either, Beatrice. He doesn't want to have any more lessons with the Rural Dean."

"A pity, such a pity, but then perhaps Tom Hargeson is not the most suitable per....."

She trailed off as he came out of the vestry.

"Yes, well, Rector, I'll just finish putting all these hymn books away and then help my husband load the produce into the land rover. We're taking it to St Faith's Nursing Home in the morning."

"Good, good. Er, thank you."

I really wanted to quiz her but obviously couldn't so I continued homewards to try and get to the bottom of it all.

*

It was over two weeks later before I got any further with Seth. The music lessons had very much been given on an ad hoc basis so it wasn't unusual for such a period to lapse. Tom Hargeson had a very full diary.

Shortly before Guy Fawkes he called round, just as I was reading to the twins in my study. All our parishes traditionally gathered at the Rural Dean's every November 5th for fireworks, bangers and mash. The children loved it, especially the twins. Molly showed Tom in and I immediately felt Seth tense up.

"Sorry to barge in like this, Will, but I just wanted to check you and the children were coming on Friday. I've also extended the invitation to Mrs Tompkins, but she insists she must look after your dog."

"Listen to Josh, Will."

I was then thrown completely as Annie came out of the blue.

"What was that?" I asked her.

"Your dog Paddy gets very nervous I understand,"

said Hargeson.

"Oh, yes. Yes he does - it wouldn't be fair. But I'm sure we shall all be there, eh, lads?"

At this point Josh stood up, beckoned to Seth, took him by the arm and stopped by the door. He then calmly addressed the Rural Dean, while Seth stood head-bowed, hiding behind Josh.

"Thank you for asking us, sir, but Seth and I won't be coming."

With that he pulled Seth out of the room and they disappeared upstairs.

An uneasy silence was broken by the telephone ringing in the hall.

"Sorry, Tom, but I think you see how things are. Now, if you'll excuse me."

"Yes, of course," he mumbled, and uncomfortably made his way out.

The call was parish business, so I sat down and went through the agenda for the next day's P.C.C meeting with her ladyship.

The boys were asleep by the time I'd finished and it wasn't until the weekend that I got an opportunity to follow up Josh's astonishing comment. Saturday was typically misty and dreary but after lunch Molly nevertheless took the girls for a walk, while I played cards with the twins. I was just about to deal another hand when Annie joined us.

"Listen to Josh, Will."

"Right, I'll do that."

"Do what, Dad?" said Seth.

"Oh you know what I'm like, always talking out loud."

"Yes," laughed Josh, "Grandma thinks it's too much communion wine."

Two months of high school and already so knowing.

"Oh she does, does she?" I chortled back, playfully

punching him.

"No, to tell you both the truth I don't want to play cards right now. Can we please talk about music lessons and firework night and why you have turned away from it all?"

They looked at one another. Josh raised an eyebrow and Seth nodded to him.

"Well," Josh began and, in a remarkably adult way, painted me a disturbing picture.

"The Rural Dean treats us like babies, fussing around. He's really weird and says odd things, and does creepy things."

I was on the edge of my seat now, trying to keep in control.

"What sort of things, Josh?" I whispered.

"Well whenever we want a pee he comes with us and stands outside the door. He asked Seth to keep it open once."

"You said you wouldn't say that!" Seth shouted, pushing the card table over.

"But it's true," said Josh.

Seth crumbled, ran to me, and threw himself into my arms.

"Seth, it's good that I know. Now we can sort it out and things will get better, believe me."

"I'm sorry, Seth," mumbled Josh.

"No, Josh," I said, "you were right to tell me. Look, here are Grandma and the girls. You go and join them. Just tell Grandma that Seth and I are having a chat. Don't say what about, please."

"Still pals, mate?" Josh asked his brother.

"I guess," Seth murmured faintly in reply.

Josh and I exchanged glances and I gave him a reassuring smile.

After what seemed an eternity, during which time I tried desperately to decide how to deal with this situation,

I finally broke the silence. There was never any doubt what I would ask I suppose. Whether I was right or not, I don't know, but it had to come out.

"Seth, I have to know something."

He nodded.

"Did the Reverend Hargeson ever touch you in a way you didn't like?"

"Yes."

"Do you want to tell me about it?"

"It was the day of the harvest. Josh had his lesson first and when it was my turn he was allowed to watch tv in the study."

"Go on," I gently encouraged him.

"He sat next to me at the piano and when I'd finished playing, he.....he....."

"It's alright, Seth. Go on. What happened?"

"He took hold of my hands and said how beautiful they were and kissed them.....and.....I didn't like it, Dad. It was horrible. I don't ever want to see him again."

Empty of tears now, he simply panted in my arms like a wounded animal. I had heard enough.

After more words of comfort and assurance I then persuaded Seth to join everyone else in the kitchen.

Half an hour later he seemed much more himself and I left Molly preparing supper with the boys while Carrie bathed Jo.

How I maintained my self-control during that half-hour I shall never know. Nor can I remember any single part of the drive to Hargeson's house, taken at break-neck speed. I was also completely oblivious of the patrol car parked at the southern end of Knotts Way.

*

Bishop David tapped his pencil on the ostentatious, inlaid desk surrounding him. On his right hand, the Dean of Bury St Edmunds, Mike Jarvis, and on his left, the Bishop's Chaplain, Rod Lewis. Interesting that David Llewelleyn had chosen a fellow Welshman.

So the Bishop had his two protectors and the strongly built Dean, a Suffolk man born and bred, certainly looked as though he would stand no nonsense. In fact he looked more like a nightclub bouncer, with his broken nose and craggy features. I could just picture him punching the lights out of some poor drunken punter on a Saturday night in Ipswich.

Eventually, David rose from his seat, encouraging us to do the same.

"Perhaps this is too formal. May I suggest we sit in more comfort?"

He pointed to the array of luxurious chairs surrounding the glowing fire.

When we had settled, he continued.

"I feel a short period of quiet meditation would be appropriate before we proceed."

Three heads bowed in unison, while I simply studied the beautiful ash logs burning brightly in the grate.

It was late afternoon, two days after my maniacal drive to Hargeson's. I had been summoned to Bishop's Hall and now it was just a case of going through the motions. The Rural Dean was still in no fit state to attend, having severe lacerations to his throat, a badly bruised and cut-up face, two broken ribs and suffering from a state of great shock. This was as a result of me bursting in on his quiet Saturday afternoon and knocking hell out of him. That is, only until Sergeant Jim Bailey had charged into the house and breathlessly hauled me off, assisted by his surprisingly tough female colleague.

Jim was a very supportive and loyal member of my congregation at Upper Chesney, still living in the old police house with his wife and three energetic children - all of whom were good pals to my brood.

Looking back, had it been anyone else my future would have been more than a little bleak. Jim certainly saved me from myself that day, so thank God it was him in that patrol car. I wouldn't have just been done for speeding. For sure, I would have killed Hargeson - absolutely no doubt about it.

David cleared his throat.

"Will, I find myself in a very uncomfortable position."

"Well perhaps if you move the other side of the Chaplain? You're obviously too close to the fire," I retorted.

"Will, show respect," Annie barked.

I held up my hands.

"Sorry, just my little joke," I submitted.

"Will, it's far from a laughing matter, you know," interjected Mike Jarvis.

They obviously all thought my last remark had been intended for them.

"Thank you, Dean," snapped Bishop David, "I'll handle this."

Then he returned to me.

"But Mike's right. However, it would seem there is a reasonable chance that neither Tom Hargeson nor the police will take this matter any further. If that is the case you can consider yourself very fortunate indeed. At least we shall stand a good chance of keeping everything low-key."

"That's it, brush everything under the carpet."

"Will, stop it!" Annie burst out.

"Okay, okay. Have it your way."

"In the circumstances there is no other way," continued the Bishop.

"David, may I say something at this stage?"

The Bishop's Chaplain spoke for the first time.

"Please do, Rod."

"Will, we know what you've been through these past

eight months and....."

"Oh, you do, do you? And how could you possibly have any idea? Let's stop all the platitudes, shall we?"

"Reverend Rayner."

The Bishop practically whispered the bark at me.

"Rod was my curate in Carmarthen when, three years ago, his wife died from a terminal illness."

He turned to his Chaplain.

"Forgive me, Rod, but it needed to be said."

The Chaplain continued, as if neither the Bishop nor I had intervened.

"I would say the last thing you need is the niggling worry of all your parishes. You need so much more time than life has allowed you so far. Picking up the pieces is a painfully slow process."

He looked gently at my pathetic features which had creased upon Bishop David's last comments.

"Rod, I'm so sorry, I had no idea. I just don't know what came over me. I often just simply snap."

The man shrugged his shoulders and the Bishop picked up the reins again.

"How do you see the future now?"

I didn't reply.

"Look, I know it's a tough question, but I have to make some decisions here, I'm sure you can see that. Equally you are very important in all this, and at least deserve a say on what route I should take to try and solve what is, after all, a complex and tricky situation."

I began to appreciate his difficult task and slowly realised the time had come to stop any further prevarication.

"Now, Will, now," urged Annie.

"I just don't know where to start."

"We've got all the time you need, Will," said Rod.

"Tell them what you really feel and believe. Our children will be fine, whatever you say or do."

Annie said more than she had ever done before.

"I.....I....."

Stumbling, I bowed my head and then took a few more minutes composing myself.

To my complete surprise I realised I wanted to go right back to my childhood and talk about my parents.

"My mother was very shy and did her best to avoid social situations. She was happy to quietly observe life and guide me gently through its puzzles. But Mum had a surprisingly short fuse and her temper usually erupted whenever elitism became evident. She was East London working-class and, being in service the early part of her working life, had cause to feel a strange mixture of fearful respect and burning resentment towards her employers. As far as Mum was concerned so many more opportunities were available to the upper classes, not as a result of talent or hard work, but because of birthright. This stung her, and it certainly didn't help when she realised my father had put in a transfer request and been sold to the opposition."

"Sorry," interrupted Mike, "but what do you mean by that?"

"He worked in a factory but later trained for the Church."

"Right."

"I don't blame him in some ways. Like so many of his generation he had a goal of his own, to better himself and his family - but primarily himself. He saw going into the ministry as a way to gain respect from the higher order in a way he could never possibly attain in any other walk of life - however hard he tried. There was of course in his day an aura that surrounded men of the cloth. They say ladies melted at a uniform and men showed respect for it, so he chose the uniform we're wearing now. He didn't have a calling, it was simply a carefully-crafted career.

"My mother didn't like it, I could see that, but we had

a roof and security and back then a wife deferred to her husband. But she found it difficult and could not bear listening to him from the pulpit, labelling him 'the pompous preacher'. Hurtful, because he was kind and generous, but sadly very near the truth.

"So I was, I suppose, a perfect hybrid, although I have always wanted to think I was far more in the style of my mother. Like father though I enjoyed the standing we had established, the comfort. He was a good man but I definitely inherited my mother's passion and intensity, bottling it up most of the time, but shelling gunfire on the class system at every opportunity. This constantly created conflict between my father and me, although ironically I could rarely do any wrong in his eyes. My mother understood me better I think and certainly gave me a harder time. She often harassed me into actually saying what I really thought - not what I tended to say in pursuit of an easy passage. If I had shown her brand of honesty I would never have chosen this mockery of a job."

"That's harsh, isn't it?" Rod suggested.

"Possibly, but there you have one of the reasons I fell in love with my wife, for she too was loyal to her roots. Annie was dragged unwillingly into middle-class virtue by a doting mother. The difference was that she rebelled, whereas I usually submitted to my father.

"For thirteen years Annie enriched my life. We laughed so much, lived so much, loved so much. She and my mother helped me realise that the real meaning of life is love. It's not about improving ourselves because someone else will doubtless be pushed aside in order to fulfil our ambition. We must never forget that alongside so-called success probably walks failure for someone else, and none of us easily retain confidence after experiencing setbacks.

"I have had more setbacks in the last few months than the whole of my life. Thirteen years of blissful marriage I had, just thirteen. Long enough to become so reliant on her and yet so frustratingly short. But now I have four amazing young people to consider. I must not let them down. I have to be able to live honestly in order to maintain their respect and their love. I can no longer be the fraud you see before you.

"You see, I believe Jesus lived. He was obviously a man born with extraordinary gifts and was certainly ahead of his time, but as for his resurrection? No, I'm sorry."

Bishop David nodded in apparent understanding but couldn't match the gesture with the right words.

"We all have the Doubting Thomas in us, Will."

"I'm not a Thomas. I simply do not identify with any of this organised religion. We are all so far off the mark. Look at us now. How do we possibly relate to the people out there?"

"Will, I think I've heard enough to realise you currently feel unable to continue your clerical duties. So, what do you propose we do?"

Even now, for some strange reason, I hesitated.

"Say it, Will. Say it and go home," pleaded Annie.

"I tender my resignation, Bishop David."

I gave him a long, hard look before continuing.

"I am quitting the Church. I don't need it, and it certainly doesn't need me."

All three exchanged significant glances - enough to tell me it's what they had anticipated all along. Even Rod seemed relieved I had finally got to the point. But then I had rambled on. I therefore sat quietly and listened dutifully to the Bishop's sensible and reasonable suggestions for my departure. I felt a sense of calm, something that had eluded me for a very long time.

*

As I drove home from Bury I looked forward to tucking into one of Biddy's cracking suppers. It would be gone nine, but I was starving. Perhaps I'd open a bottle. Yes, celebrate with claret.

"Mummy's job," Annie whispered, as I hit the outskirts of our village.

"What about it?"

"Mr Youngman," she continued.

"And what about him?"

"Mr Youngman!"

"Very well, I'll contact him. I'm sorry you seem so stroppy all of a sudden though."

"Carrie....."

"I'll look after her. Don't worry, she'll love living at Bertie's."

".....so lost.....so vulnerable....."

I usually tried to take everything Annie said on board but I felt remarkably high-spirited to let anything get me down at that moment. Maybe, just maybe, I could even get a decent night's sleep for once.

*

A couple of days later I contacted old Youngman. You know how you hear something, can't believe your luck, go away, think about it and, eventually, act on it? Well at this point you then wonder if you did in fact understand everything correctly. The die was now well and truly cast, so I had to double-check I hadn't got anything wrong.

"Mr Youngman? It's Will Rayner."

"Ah, M-M-Mr Rayner, how good to hear your voice."

"Er, Mr Youngman, well, er, I thought I should let you know that I've resigned from the Church."

There was a very worrying pause and an even more worrying response.

"Oh, I see. Well, dear me, I don't know wh-wh-what to say."

"Mr Youngman, nothing's happened to change Bertie's Will has it? I mean, about the family and me living there and managing the smallholding?"

"No, no, no, not at all. I just find it difficult to respond because leaving your calling m-m-must seem such a wr-wrench."

"Oh, please don't concern yourself. It's fine. I'm actually very relieved."

"Well, that's good."

He returned to more positive mode.

"So you've decided to come down here. How wonderful. I'm so p-p-pleased."

"So what happens now, Mr Youngman?"

"Well I do know that a representative of the Oak Apple Trust has p-p-popped over to your uncle's a couple of times during the last few months. Just to check things out, you understand. I gather your uncle's housekeeper has kept an eagle eye on the place. It's p-p-pristine."

"Dear Kath. She must miss him so."

"M-M-Mrs Simmons is really hoping you will all come down. I dealt with her husband's affairs, as you know, and we've become, well, er, good f-f-friends. We often enjoy afternoon tea together."

Well, well, Kath and old Youngman, up to a bit of hanky-panky!

"I'd be grateful if you don't confirm it to Kath yet, Mr Youngman. I've got to break it all to my family first."

It was the wrong thing to say of course and he was quite affronted.

"M-M-Mr Rayner, p-please never doubt my confidentiality in these matters."

Oh, dear, why couldn't I keep my mouth shut?

"I'm so sorry, Mr Youngman. It's been a difficult time and I guess I'm still a little tense."

"Not to worry. I do understand. Now, when do you leave your post?"

"Well, my last service is on Christmas Eve, but we've been allowed to stay on in the Rectory until the end of March next year."

"That's splendid, a p-perfect p-piece of timing. So, er, I suggest you and Mr F-F-Foulkes get together here in, say, early January. M-meanwhile he can alert the Trust and everything can start moving forward. It'll be tickety b-b-boo."

He seemed so excited it was infectious, and I began to realise how much he'd probably been waiting for a call from me.

"But, Mr Youngman, I know you did say your partner would be dealing with my uncle's estate. Won't you be involved at all?"

"No, Mr Rayner. I'm retiring at Christmas. So, you're not the only one. But, rest assured, you will still see me about."

I bet I will, I thought. No doubt you'll be tidying up Kath's rambling rose in your spare time.

"Well, I'm very pleased to hear that, Mr Youngman. Meanwhile I wish you a very happy and contented retirement."

"You are very kind. Thank you. And I wish you and yours every p-possible success for the f-f-future. Now f-forgive me, I have to go. I have another client waiting, so au revoir."

Well whatever had his secretary put in his Darjeeling that morning?

*

Molly would not be coming up the following weekend, which in some ways was a blessing. I could concentrate on explaining our move to the children.

Molly seemed defensive on the phone - something about too much on her plate and things to think through. I didn't pry. I had been lucky for the magnificent support she'd given me these last few months. I could surely manage one weekend? After all, once we'd moved, it would all be down to me - or would it?

*

The weekend arrived to the accompaniment of high winds and the resulting chill factor made a long walk on Saturday rather unattractive, but I was determined we would at least enjoy some air before I settled to the task of explaining our future.

Biddy had very kindly insisted she sorted out lunch, so I gratefully left her to it and we braved the elements.

I was so pleased to notice Seth's old self gradually creeping back. I had decided to keep the details of my visit to Hargeson as brief as possible where the children and Molly were concerned and a letter had arrived only that morning from Bishop David confirming acceptance of my resignation. He also intimated that the Rural Dean would be moving on, whatever that meant. Of course I still felt strongly that, like me, he should play no further part in the life of the Church, but I was hardly in a position to even attempt to enforce that. It still frustrated me though. How could the Church maintain credibility protecting such people?

After lunch I felt the time was right to put all the children in the picture.

Josh and Seth were over the moon and Jo immediately went and fetched her little suitcase.

"I'm ready, Daddy," she announced, dragging the case into the study. "Will I need my wellies?"

The boys and I burst out laughing and Josh gently explained to Jo she was just a little premature. On being told we had Christmas to get through first she then decided to go and find her stocking for Santa. I encouraged the boys to go and help Jo write her letter to him. I wanted to talk to Carrie, because she appeared to have taken my news rather badly.

Once we were alone I tackled her.

"Carrie, you don't seem very pleased about our move. Can we talk about it?"

"How can you think of leaving Mummy like this?"

Oh, so that was it. This was not going to be easy.

"We won't be leaving her, she....."

"But we are. You just said we're going to Sussex. I can't leave her on her own."

Carrie began to shake. It was not like her to interrupt like that.

"Look, Carrie, Mummy isn't just in the churchyard....."

"Of course she is, don't say that. I visit her every day. I talk to her."

"Mummy's body is certainly in the churchyard, of course it is. Her spirit, though, is everywhere. She will be in Sussex with us, believe me."

"She won't!" Carrie screamed. "She'll be here, all alone. I'm not coming. I'll, I'll.....I'll stay with Biddy."

I put my arm around her.

"Carrie, please try and....."

"I'm not coming. I'm not!"

With that, she wrenched herself away from me and ran out of the house, obviously heading for the churchyard. I put my head in my hands in utter exasperation. Was everything I tried to do going to be so full of drama? I decided I had to follow her and sort this out.

On arriving at the church gate I could see she was already talking to Annie. And at that moment I knew I had to let go. It was unreasonable of me to expect immediate acceptance and co-operation from everyone. She obviously needed time, and perhaps support and encouragement from someone like Biddy. I would have a word with our friend and, in time, Carrie should come round. Meanwhile I would just have to dig in and sweat it out.

*

It was in fact well into December before Molly visited us again. Luckily Biddy very happily and competently looked after us at weekends too. She and Carrie spent a lot of time together I noticed, especially cooking. To all intents and purposes my daughter was her normal self towards everyone else, but there was constant anger and coldness in her manner towards me. She was certainly making me pay but I knew Biddy would respond to my plea for support, so I left well alone. It all made me very sad and down though.

Molly was a bit of a puzzle. Following my collision with Carrie that Saturday I had decided to write to my mother-in-law rather than be on the end of yet another argument. It was the Bertie connection that troubled me. I was concerned she would not be happy with her grandchildren living in his shadow. But actually I was quite wrong.

Molly too had been sorting her working life out. In my letter, with tongue in cheek, I had suggested that she was more than welcome to come and live with us. As luck would have it, she quickly declined this offer, saying she had already begun to make special arrangements at work. This meant she would in fact be staying with us occasionally, but on a different basis. Rather mysterious but I knew she would explain when it suited her and not before.

A second letter from Molly revealed all. She had

secured a new contract at the library. As she succinctly told me it didn't actually matter where we were living. What was important was the fact that she had, for a long time, been negotiating not to work over any of the school holidays. It had been difficult apparently, but she eventually persuaded her line manager. Broken him probably, for after just a few minutes of her badgering I'd have certainly relented. I pictured him crumpled at his desk, whimpering, with Molly towering above him in triumph.

I felt that holidays only for Molly would probably work very well, provided a second option I had in mind went to plan - persuading Kath to stay on at Bertie's. Then all I would have to sort out was the Carrie situation. I fervently hoped for Annie's help with that one for I sensed it was going to be far from straightforward.

*

St Saviour's was packed for our carol service on Christmas Eve, and it was the last time that I would officiate in any church. Parishioners seemed genuinely sorry we were leaving, but then this happens, doesn't it? All of a sudden people try to make you feel emotional and that you're doing the wrong thing. But I was unaffected by all the handshakes and pats on the back. I knew that this was merely the occasion getting to certain quarters.

I kept reminding myself of that for I now firmly believed my children and I had to get away to face fresh challenges in a new environment.

So, to my immense relief, the Reverend William Rayner could finally be consigned to history.

*

"Will, come and m-meet Gerry. He's our Club Captain. I'm just going to have a word with the Pr- President."

"Good to see you at long last, Will," said Gerry, shaking my hand warmly. "Charlie has often mentioned you and your family."

"Well he and Kath have certainly looked after us these first few months so I really don't know how he's managed to find much time for golf."

"Oh, he'll always find time. You don't play I suppose?"

"No, but my twin boys are learning."

"Now that'll be Josh and, er, Seth?"

"That's right."

"W-W-Will, let me introduce you to Roger Murdoch." Charlie was back. "R-Roger is very interested in hearing about your plans for the smallholding....."

*

It was late summer and Charlie Youngman had generously invited the children and me to his golf club's annual barbecue. Kath was there too, which helped enormously, but he seemed keen to introduce me to so many people and I was hopeless with names. Since our move to Barton Green he had certainly devoted a lot of his new retirement time to us all and I was very grateful for his friendship. My family were clearly having a great time and Charlie and Kath's support in the first few months had resulted in the transition from Suffolk being remarkably smooth.

Looking back I suppose I didn't really have a clue as to what to expect when we arrived here, or how any of us would react, especially to small, but important things, such as sleeping arrangements. But that, along with everything else, had worked out pretty well. I had my usual room; the twins grabbed Bertie and Glad's great big bedroom; and Carrie had insisted she wanted Jo in with her. This had been a relief to me because I had been worried about Jo in particular. She was delighted to be with her older sister.

Even Carrie had settled - especially thanks to Kath. School and new friends had helped her and the twins a lot and Jo usually seemed to enjoy nursery. As for me, well, I had been very determined to make it all work. I realised the many changes in my life would obviously take some getting used to but continuing to feel sorry for myself was no longer an option. I was intent on repaying the debt I felt I owed Bertie.

The only tough moment leaving Chesney had been at Annie's graveside on the day of our departure. Ironically I began to feel emotions like Carrie had expressed - that I was deserting my wife. I was desolate and wept copiously. But suddenly, in a remarkable moment, her strong presence gave me the resilience I needed. It was to be her last conversation: 'Goodbye, my darling.' Although in itself heartbreaking it was at that moment I had to finally accept our children's well-being was now completely down to me. I had to try and pack the sadness of the past right away.

*

Money was tight. But then I knew it would be. Although Charlie's successor, Liam Foulkes, had dealt with all the legalities, it was Charlie who actually helped me understand the financial aspects of our situation. To make the smallholding viable would take three or four years but a clause in Bertie's will ensured an allowance would be available to me during that time for our basic living expenses. However I wanted to try and pay my way whenever I could so I started looking for part-time work soon after we arrived. Within a couple of months I had got a job as a clerk with a small import/export company near Newhaven and the hours enabled me to be at home when the kids got back from school.

Kath had readily agreed to carry on as Housekeeper but I didn't want to be too reliant on her and so I was determined to try and learn how to cook. Yes, cook! And to everyone's surprise - not least my own - I became rather good at it. Even more amazingly I enjoyed it - especially the compliments.

"Wow, Dad, that was great!" said Seth, after one particularly successful supper. "Much better than Mum's pasta."

We all laughed because Annie's culinary expertise rarely extended beyond reading the instructions on the frozen food packaging or tin.

"To be fair I had a lot of help from Carrie. Your cookery lessons are paying off, love."

"But you did most of this, Daddy," she replied, "and all I've cooked at school is scones."

"I liked them," piped-up Jo, "cos once they made my tooth come out and I got a present on my pillow from the fairy."

"They weren't that hard," protested Carrie.

"Well, the chickens enjoyed them anyway," said Josh.

"You beast!" Carrie replied, but she took it all in good part.

At long last fun was creeping back.

*

The Oak Apple Trust was certainly quick off the mark setting everything up and for the first couple of years their Project Manager, Tommy Barnes, was a godsend. He helped me a lot at weekends when I worked alongside him as much as I could. It took a very long time but eventually I just about got to grips with managing the place productively. But I especially welcomed the school holidays when Molly came to stay. We seemed to be able to tolerate one another more and so she took on the cooking again, looking after Carrie and Jo, while the twins and I spent long days working outside in all weathers. I still had to juggle my part-time job of course but with careful organisation it worked. An added bonus was I usually fell asleep the moment I hit the sack.

In fact everything appeared to be going so well at one stage I even began to hope that perhaps I had at last won back Carrie's complete trust. Sadly the more relaxed atmosphere of that initial period gradually seeped away as her teenage years seemed to take a hold. Out of the blue her hostility towards me returned. I was so dismayed and it all rather alarmed me. Just as I had thought a sense of balance and order was being restored to our family we were fighting again and she didn't hold back.

Past habits returned, and one in particular. For the more we argued the more I sought solace from a couple of old friends - a bottle and a glass.....

BOOK TWO : AN ELDEST CHILD'S REBELLION

What a party! And what a night it's been for my beautiful sister, Jo, serenaded on her twenty-first birthday by the rather gorgeous night-club singer. Not only that, he's monopolised her ever since. Part of me wants to protect her from someone I suspect is just looking for one thing, but I learnt long ago that you need to experience the knocks in life to survive. Anyway men always let you down in the end. Good for only one thing and usually not that good, though they like to think so. Oh, yes, they can be fun, useful even, but they all work to their own selfish agenda and can never be trusted. Let them get a foot in the door and you've lost everything. Although I admit to believing that my current guy was actually an exception.

I used to love the men in my life - my brothers Seth and Josh especially. Still do, I suppose. But they always listened to my father, did as they were told, hung on his every word. Jo was so young she couldn't be expected to have understood but she would have been on my side, she wouldn't have left our mother behind. My father did and then war broke out between us.

"Carrie, take care!"

Mummy was back, warning me again.

"Don't worry, I'm fine. Jo and I are leaving now and we shall walk to my flat - it's not far."

"Take care!"

Oh, there she goes again, always trying to look after me.

"Taxi."

"No, we won't bother, we'll walk. The fresh air will sober me up. Anyway you know what some of these taxi drivers are like - eyeing you up in their mirror, undressing you. Cretins."

"Taxi, watch out for a taxi."

Jo disentangled herself from her new man and tripped over to me, looking serene.

"Carrie, thank you. Thank you for the most wonderful day."

"Titch, you deserve it. Now have you finished with our friend over there because I need a walk, then my bed, although I'm tempted to invite him along to share it?"

"He's not for sharing, thank you very much, and anyway he has an early rehearsal in the morning."

"It's the morning already, half past two, and I had to get through two bottles of seriously good white while I waited for you to devour him."

"I had no idea it was that late. Let's get back to your place and reminisce over strong coffee."

"Coffee? I've got something better than that." I swigged out of a champagne bottle. "Come on, let's start walking."

"You sure you don't want to take a taxi?"

"You sound like Mummy."

"What do you mean?"

"Oh, nothing. Let's go."

We began walking - well, in my case, lurching - and chatted, giggled, sang, jigged and wolf-whistled at amused road sweepers. We were back as little sisters again, recalling the good times we had shared. They were my only completely happy moments back in those dark days of the seventies. Then suddenly, there she was. My mother, waving to me from across the street, calling me.

"Look, Jo, there's Mummy!"

"Carrie, what on earth are you saying?"

But I was off, shouting at the top of my voice.

"Mummy, you've come back at last!"

I saw the taxi out of the corner of my eye and heard

the plaintive screams of my sister, accompanied by screeching tyres and distant warning shouts. All to no avail. There was a sickening thud as mobile metal tossed my mini-skirted frame onto the pavement, garbage ready for the refuse collectors.

"Carrie, Carrie, don't die, please don't die. Not you too. Not today of all days, not any day. Please....."

"Can you see her, Titch? She's waiting for me over there."

"No, no," Jo whimpered, tears cascading down her lovely face.

"It's alright, my darling, we shall be together again."

And pitch black pervaded me.

*

There followed a period, I cannot work out how long, when I drifted from place to place, memory to memory, one despondent family face to another, each anxiously hoping the life-support machine would do its job for me. I wanted to respond, to tell them all I was fine, even Dad. But he had a look of anguish, despair, almost envy perhaps. I guess he knew I was going to her and of course that was probably what he wanted to do. Well now he knew what it was like to be abandoned, what it was like to watch at a distance, existing on the periphery.

*

There can be nothing harder to bear for a young girl of twelve than losing her mother - her confidante, her example, her friend.

Yet when my father first told me about Mummy's fatal accident I am sure I simply did not believe it. For I had no concept of her not coming back; of us never again talking through my latest tiff with a friend; of us no longer playing music together; of her not being there to explain my developing body to me; of me being unable to weep in her arms for no reason whatsoever. Suddenly, although I did not realise it at the time, all that was over.

Even when she was lowered into the ground and my flower fluttered down with her, I still earnestly believed she would return. Foolish of course, but at the time I was so naive. That is why I was shattered when my father told us we were leaving to move south. How could he do that? How could he even contemplate abandoning our mother like that? But I was so immature at the time, and completely unable to accept the situation.

Dad was obviously totally stunned and the day of the funeral must have been so hard for him. At the time I still thought the world of him and I wanted to soften the blow, ease his pain. Naivety again, and of course I fell flat on my face. He spent the night downstairs drowning his sorrows in malt - I know because I got no sleep either. I took the opportunity to slip into their bedroom and procure some of Mummy's jewellery. I wanted to wear it so he would remember her. But in his eyes I obviously did the completely wrong thing. He couldn't handle me trying to look like her, he made that quite clear. And from that moment on we were never to be the same again.

I, perhaps petulantly, felt an overwhelming sense of rejection. In my childish way I felt I had just lost my mother and father in the space of a few days. Looking back I was probably harsh on him, but I never felt, apart from the occasional hug, that he showed me any true sense of affection. Always it was the twins or Jo. I don't resent them at all for that. He was the problem. Why was I so ostracised? The astute of you might say I simply reminded him too much of her. But that wasn't my fault. So, with such bitter resentment in my heart, I set out to make his life even more difficult than it already was, even blaming him for her death. That was Grandma's influence of course.

It was bad enough losing Mummy in the first place, but for me it got far worse when we moved to bloody Sussex. The boys had one another, Dad clung to Jo and I tagged reluctantly along, with only Grandma for company. She was the one adult I gravitated towards in the early years following Mummy's demise, and I guess that did little to help the relationship with my father. She had always made it clear where the blame for the loss of her daughter lay. Now he had to fight that on two fronts. In Grandma I may not have found a confidante or someone able to guide me through tricky situations but she at least listened. So many people want to give advice when all you want is their time. She was good at that, always there for me, despite her old-fashioned ways, and so, so generous.

*

"Well, Carrie, the older you get the more you remind me of Annie. You do look very beautiful but I really think that dress is, how can I put it, well, perhaps a little skimpy?"

"But, Grandma, all my friends wear far skimpier than this."

"In that case they deserve what's coming to them that's all I can say. Though I must admit the colours are lovely and the material is a good quality....."

"So please can I have it. It's just what I want. I really adore it."

"In that case, what can I possibly say? After all it is your birthday. Go on then, get changed again while I settle up."

"Do you mean I really can have it? I thought I'd have to work much harder on you than that. You're getting a soft touch in your old age you know."

"I've still got time to change my mind."

"Too late, I have a witness", as I pointed to the sales assistant, "and she's already spending her commission."

"Carrie!" She turned to the smiling lady behind the counter. "I do beg your pardon, she isn't normally as outrageous as this."

"Oh yes I am," I retorted, as I shut the changing room door with a flourish.

"Well, yes, she is, if I'm honest," I could hear Grandma stuttering, "but she doesn't mean to be rude, it's just....."

"I know. It's just her age, madam. Let's see now, seventeen is she?"

"Yes, tomorrow."

"Well, please don't worry. I've got two daughters at home so I understand your grand-daughter is just excited."

"I'll say I'm excited!" I exclaimed as I burst out with my prize, having got changed in express time.

"Party tonight?"

"Yeah, at 'Fresh'. Do you fancy coming?"

"Carrie, enough!"

"I would, but I have nothing to wear."

"Borrow one of these for the weekend. I won't tell. They'd never miss it."

"Now, come along" interjected a very flustered grandma, "I need a coffee."

"Black and sweet, madam?"

"Yes, very black and very sweet."

"Your receipt and change, madam."

"Thank you, thank you so much."

I waltzed to the door to open it for Grandma, and as I looked back the lady gave me a wink.

"Now why couldn't you show that lovely lady some similar good manners and respect?"

"Oh, she loved it. I wouldn't be at all surprised if she turns up tonight."

"God help her if she does. Now, let's find a restaurant because I need to talk to you about tonight."

"Don't worry, I shan't lose my virginity. Not yet awhile anyway."

Grandma stopped in exasperation and embarrassment, shaking her head, but I ignored all that and hugged her.

"The dress is gorgeous and you are lovely. Thank you."

"Let's hope your dad thinks the same - about the dress that is."

Her smile told me I was forgiven. But mention of my father changed my mood. Only the previous day we had played out one of our all too frequent slanging matches which ended up with me unfairly hurting him yet again. He frustrated me, simply because I felt he just was not prepared to look at the pathetic argument we'd got into from my viewpoint. As always it centred round my mother.

I have already indicated that my mother's death shattered me and I guess I never really recovered. Just a few months after she had died my dad obviously went through great distress and had to make difficult decisions about our family's future. In the cold light of day I am prepared to go with the theory that he made these with our welfare in mind but in darker moments I feel he selfishly proceeded with two-fingering the Church, and dear Bertie's extreme generosity simply made it so very easy for him. Oh, yes, I can't argue he worked quite hard when we got to the farmhouse, but we became total strangers, his temper got shorter and nastier, and the drinking increased substantially. It could become quite scary, especially for my twin brothers. But at least they had one another. Jo could never do any wrong and always got by that way.

I was simply the defiant one, constantly challenging him and always standing my ground. He didn't like that. He didn't like it because I refused to be won round by his empty assurances that we were in the right place. Well, he was, and perhaps the others were, but I certainly never felt settled from that awful day we left our old home. It harboured such poignant memories of my mother. I knew at the time that my father worshipped her - and me too. But from that point on I kept pushing him away, enjoying the hurt I was inflicting on him, childishly paying him back. You see, he was actually a good man when sober - kind, fun, giving. Sadly, as the years progressed, he wasn't sober very often.

*

"So, you two, did you manage to find anything suitable?"

"Well we found something, Dad, but of course you won't think it is at all, that's why I chose it."

"Now, Carrie, what did you promise me?"

"Sorry, Grandma, but it's that word 'suitable', isn't it? So pompous, so boring."

"But that's me, as you so often point out. Now come on, Carrie, I certainly don't want another fight, not after last night."

"No, you're not ready for one because you're not tanked up enough yet."

With that I flounced out of the kitchen, stormed upstairs and locked myself in my room. Tears flowed again and then I didn't want to go out with all my mates - or that lovely lady from the dress shop. I just wanted Mummy. And suddenly, magically, she was with me, doing her level best to calm my stupid temper.

*

The first time had been by her graveside on the day of our departure from Suffolk. I had picked some of her daffodils and they reminded me it was nearly a year since her accident.

Her voice pierced the stillness surrounding me and initially I felt very scared and confused.

"Carrie, go willingly."

I looked around, trembling, expecting to see her. But I was disappointed.

"Go, please. Daddy loves you but can't show it."

"Mummy?"

Silence.

I felt bewildered and frustrated, and I started to weep.

"Go!"

"Where are you? I want you back here."

There was no further response and I ran home sobbing.

*

So, over three years on, I had come to terms with what to expect from Mummy's visits. But it was still exasperating.

"Carrie, be gentle with Daddy."

"I want to be, but he just makes me so angry all the time, never supporting me, never....."

"You'll meet a new friend tomorrow."

"Oh, that's exciting."

"Daddy, be gentle.....gentle....."

After a while I had calmed down and decided I would go out after all. I felt great in my new dress and knew I looked good in it, so I put the upset behind me. My mother seemed to have had a soothing effect so now I needed to find Dad and attempt some sort of apology.

He was in his study struggling with a pink bow on what was obviously my present for tomorrow. He hadn't heard me enter and he buried his head in his hands.

"Annie, you should be here to do this. I'm so clumsy, you know that. Tell me how to do it. Why don't you talk to me anymore?"

"She talks to me now, Dad."

He nearly jumped out of his skin, turned round, looked me up and down, and simply crumpled. I hesitated and then crossed the room to console him. No spoken apology was going to be needed. We hugged briefly and awkwardly and then I did as I was told for once and tried to be gentle with him.

"Mustn't crease my new dress," I said, as I released my tenuous hold on him.

"It's lovely. You look fantastic. So beautiful, so like your....."

"Don't even go there please, Dad. You always wanted me to be myself, not her, and that's what you will continue to get."

"Be that as it may, we cannot continue to ignore the obvious."

"Got your temper though, haven't I?"

I tried a weak smile.

"Yes. Sadly, yes. But as long as you keep off this stuff," pointing to the glass of red on his desk, "you may be able to control it better than me."

"Why, Daddy?"

"Why what?"

"Why do you drink so much? It's not good for any of us you know."

"So, what's this about you having chats with Mummy?"

My question blatantly deflected.

"Well, it first happened the day we left Chesney. I was by her grave and she spoke to me. I couldn't see or feel her, which frustrated me - still does - and she would only speak to me, not really with me."

"One-way conversations," whispered Dad, as if to himself.

"Yeah, that's about it. But it's her voice, clear as a bell, and I'm not making it up, honestly I'm not."

"No, no, I know that, Carrie. I know exactly what you're saying. You see, it has happened to me."

Only then did I recall what he was muttering as I had first entered his study.

"You mean she speaks to you too?"

"Used to, but not anymore."

"When did she stop?"

"Can't you work it out?"

"No, I can't say I can actually."

"The day we left Chesney."

There was an awkward pause, but I knew I was going to ask.

"Can I ask what she said please?"

"Oh, I guess so," he sighed.

"She said....."

He faltered.

"She just said goodbye."

And with that he swallowed back more grief and forced a weak smile.

"Daddy, I'm so sorry, I had no idea. It must have been really horrible for you."

"Yes, of course, there's no denying, but at least now I am comforted that you are hearing from her. Actually it wasn't doing me much good you know. Unexpected visits, frustrating chats - if you can call them that. No, in truth I'm better off not hearing from her. Now, if you don't mind, let's not mention it again."

There was another silence as he tried to pull himself together.

"So, at the end of today you will become a precocious

seventeen-year-old. However will we all cope then?"

"Not very well in your case, but I'm glad we had this chat because it will help me to be more....."

"Gentle with me?"

"Pardon?"

"Will you become gentle with me?"

"Gentle?"

"One of your mum's phrases."

"I know."

What I didn't know was whether his comment was just a coincidence. But I wasn't given time to dwell on it.

"Now then, young lady, as you can see, I have been wrestling tortuously with this present. The ribbon is a nice touch, don't you think? I would actually like you to have it now though before you go out."

He handed me the scruffy package with a sheepish look and pecked me self-consciously on one cheek. I gingerly opened it and immediately recognised the long, thin black box. Inside was Mummy's beautiful white gold watch glistening up at me in the evening light. He took it from its resting place of close on five years and carefully placed it on my wrist, gently squeezing my hand as he did so.

"You asked me about my drinking. Well, I just can't help myself. Your mother has gone and sometimes, just sometimes, drink is the only way I can handle it."

"Well, I shall follow your example tonight and get hammered."

"Please don't do that. I won't have you talk like that. Just have one or two. We want you to be able to enjoy your day out with all the family tomorrow."

"Don't worry, I promise I'll be sensible."

"Now look, I have let you have that watch because, again just like your mother, you never have a clue what time of day it is. When should you be leaving for this den of iniquity?"

"We're all meeting up at eight."

"Correction, everyone else might be. It's ten past already."

"Shit!"

"Hey, hey, what's that sort of talk?"

"Sorry, Dad, Sixth Form College."

"But you've only been there a week."

"A week's a long time."

"Well just temper it in front of your brothers and sister, please. Oh, and Grandma especially."

"I'll try."

"Now, get your coat on and I'll drop you at this 'Fresh' place. Might even come in myself."

"Fine, I'll get you fixed up with the lady from the dress shop."

"The dress shop?"

"Not important. Let's go then.....and.....Daddy....."

"Yep."

"Thank you for my present. I shall treasure it always."

*

The nightclub was packed when we arrived and as soon as Dad saw all my friends descend on me raucously and already rather drunkenly, he changed his mind and vanished, reminding me he would pick me up at midnight, together with my friend Emma.

"Twelve o'clock and not a minute later, and watch out for all those charming princes."

"Don't worry, Dad, I can take care of myself. Just you make sure the wheels don't drop off your pumpkin."

He was about to say something else but obviously thought better of it. We both took a step or two backwards that day, but how long would it be before we resumed hostilities? My sharp tongue couldn't be trusted for very long.

*

Voices again. Strained voices, hoping for the miracle I knew wasn't going to happen.

"But she opened her eyes last week, Doctor, I didn't imagine it."

"I am not suggesting you did, Mr Rayner. All I am trying to explain is that we do not believe that you should hold out any real hope. It would be wrong of me to mislead you."

"Well, thank you for being straight. I know, deep down, there is an inevitability, but it's only a week since her accident. I just can't make a decision this early."

"I understand. We shall of course continue to do all we can."

I felt my dad's clammy hand as he tried to urge me back to life, but I knew it was to no avail.

Another, cooler hand now. My sister Jo was there too. Oh, Titch, I'm so sorry I spoilt your party.

*

I was determined my party wasn't going to be spoilt though. Half an hour into the company of a dozen or so college friends and my empty promise to Dad was, well, empty. By ten I was in a bad way and I was in the ladies being extremely ill when Emma came in.

"Oh dear, Carrie, you look so pale."

"God, I feel absolutely awful. But don't worry, it'll pass. I'll sit out here for a while - it's cooler."

"Well I shall wait near the door and when you do come out I'm not letting you out of my sight. I promised your grandma I'd take care of you."

"Is Mark Palmer still draped round that cow Felicity?"

"Worse than that, they disappeared, and rumour has it they're under the pier. I doubt they're looking for seashells."

"Now I really do feel a whole lot better."

"Carrie, don't beat yourself up about Palmer. It's high time you realised what a smooth operator he is. Mark's decent enough but he's like most of them deep down, just desperate to see our knickers. If the likes of Felicity want to end up in trouble that's her problem. Anyway, Kevin and Barry have both got the hots for you so why waste your time on Mark? Barry's a great bloke when you get to know him. You could do a lot worse. See you in a bit."

Why waste my time indeed? Emma was right of course. She was far more street-wise than me and I was secretly grateful for all she had taught me about the opposite sex, even though I doubt she realised it. Dad and Grandma had not been able to match my mother's very liberal upbringing so such matters simply passed me by at home. Only by listening to Emma and picking up occasional useful guidance from magazines was I able to cope with it all.

Surprisingly, I soon felt a whole lot better. After extensive road-works to my dress and make-up I was back in full swing, less the alcohol, courtesy of Emma who sampled all my drinks first. For the next hour I gyrated to the brilliant rock band that had started their session during my absence. I flirted outrageously with Kevin and Barry and virtually every other male in the room. I noticed Mark return, alone and not looking at all happy.

All too quickly the evening was coming to a close. Suddenly Mark approached and whispered in my ear for a dance. The band was playing out with a slow number and I seemed to be the target for him now. Insolently I pushed past him and dragged Barry onto the floor, draping myself provocatively around him, much to his surprise and obvious pleasure.

Whoops and cheers erupted around us and Mark

eventually left, head bowed. And then, like a complete bloody imbecile, I was excusing myself from Barry with an apology and rushing out of the door after Mark.

"Mark, don't go. We're not finished yet."

"You seemed to have finished with me," he responded, continuing to walk off.

"And you've finished with Fancy Pants have you? I suppose that's ok, is it?"

"I only went off with Felicity to make you jealous."

"Well you had me seriously considering suicide for a minute there, I must admit."

He seemed to appreciate my off-beat sense of humour and a slow smile spread across his craggy face.

"Come back here you idiot," I goaded him, attempting to put on my most provocative pose. "Come here and really wish me a happy birthday."

Our hug was long but our kisses awkward, and very forgettable if the truth be known. We locked arms, crossed the road and began to wander towards the beach when there was a familiar shout from out of the shadows. It was Dad parked, waiting to pick me up.

"I thought it was Emma you were bringing home?"

"Oh, Buttons, is it midnight already?" I retorted mischievously.

"Five to, so bid Mr Charming farewell and leave him a slipper or something, there's a good girl."

We went off to find Emma, with me feeling a mixture of anger and embarrassment at being spotted by my dad in such a situation.

*

"Seth, I can hear you. Don't weep for me, my darling. Oh, if only I could communicate with you. I'm at my seventeenth birthday. We had such a fantastic day, didn't we? You and Josh had your first taste of champagne, do you remember? And Joshie fell for Emma.

*

Despite my alcohol intake of the previous night I was buzzing the next day and bounced down for breakfast with excitement at the prospect of my birthday celebration. We were meeting two of my favourite people, Charlie and Kath Youngman, at the 'Mermaid' in Brighton for coffee, and then all of us would be trooping down to the beach to spend the day there, followed by supper back at the pub. This was Charlie's treat and typically generous of him. He had even asked me to bring a friend.

'A female, of course.' So old-fashioned, bless him.

With Emma in tow, plus Grandma, Dad, Jo and the twins, I was going to be in my element for once.

Charlie Youngman and my dad had become firm friends during the period when we inherited Bertie's place. Although Charlie had retired just before we moved he had more than a passing interest in the farmhouse, in the shape of Kath Simmons who had stayed on as our housekeeper. Kath had looked after Bertie following Glad's death and we all knew he wouldn't have survived as long as he did had it not been for her loving care. She was a lonely widow for some years and so it was perhaps no great surprise when she responded very happily to Charlie's pursuit of her, which eventually ended up with him popping the question. I can just imagine the scenario though, with his unfortunate stammer underlining his nervousness:

"K-K-Kath, m-m-my dear."

"Yes, Charles."

"I've b-b-b-been w-w-w-wondering."

"Wondering what, dear? It must be worrying you because I've never known your stammer so bad."

"W-W-Well, it's not every day that a m-m-man, that a m-m-man. Oh, bugger."

He would have sunk to one knee.

"Charles, I do believe you're asking me to marry you."

Charlie would have nodded.

"Thank goodness you went on your knees otherwise we would never have got to the shops today. Oh, and yes, of course I'll marry you."

And that's how dear, shy old bachelor Charlie and no-nonsense Kath would have sealed their sweet romance. I loved them both dearly but I just wished that Charlie didn't encourage Dad so much on the drinking front.

*

"So, my present has obviously had the desired effect," said Dad, checking the kitchen clock. You've only slept a few hours."

"I'm just too excited for words. Now where on earth is everyone? It's all so quiet upstairs."

"I can't imagine," he twinkled.

Then, from under the table, came the sweet voice of little Jo, accompanied encouragingly by Grandma and gruffly by Josh and Seth, as they greeted me in the traditional way.

Each family member proceeded to shower me with gifts and cards, and my lovely day took off.

"Carrie, we've got croissants and honey, your favourite," piped up Jo.

"Our own honey," interjected a very proud Josh, who had taken a real interest in bees over the last couple of years.

"The very first crop," he said, as he handed me a gift-wrapped jar labelled 'J's Bees'.

"Oh, Josh, thank you so much. I really....."

"These are from me, Sis," interrupted Seth, determined not to be outdone by his twin.

And so it continued, everyone bursting to make my day a memorable one.

*

Emma and I were stretched out on the beach while the early afternoon sunshine caressed our tanned bodies.

"Hey, Carrie," said Em, "I'm too hot again, let's go for another dip."

"Not yet, it's just divine lying here. Let's wait a bit."

"Wow, talking of divine, look who it is!"

I raised myself onto my elbows and noticed that her eyes were trained on a couple approaching with two small children and a very wet labrador.

"Who is it then?"

"Are you saying you don't know? It's Mr. Jamieson. You're doing Art, can't you recognise him? He's the Head of Art."

"Well I'm being taught by Miss Locke this term."

"Poor you, dear old Lockers with the droopy....."

"Emma, stop it."

"Oh, my God, they're heading this way. Watch out, their bloody dog's charging at us."

Skidding to a halt by our towels, he covered us with sand and then proceeded to shake the remnants of his last dip all over us. A very concerned Mr. Jamieson ran up the beach apologising profusely. He certainly was startlingly handsome, with tanned rugged features but he didn't seem to have realised we were students until Emma blurted it out.

"Don't worry, Mr. Jamieson, we were just going to have another dip anyway, weren't we, Carrie?"

"Oh, I'm so sorry, I don't think I can place you. You're at St Joseph's are you?"

"Yes, sir, I'm Emma Taylor studying English and Philosophy."

"And you?"

His attention suddenly turned to me.

"Oh, Carrie Rayner, sir."

I blushed.

"What are you trying to learn at our dear old establishment?"

"I've only just started, but Art actually."

"Art? What a coincidence, that's my subject. Well I expect we'll be bumping into one another before long."

"I'm with Miss Locke, sir."

"Right, right. Well, look, I am really very sorry about Oscar. I hope he hasn't made too much of a mess."

"No, no," Emma quickly assured him, "we love dogs."

"Good. Well, I'd better get back to my family so enjoy the rest of the day."

"We shall, sir. It's Carrie's birthday."

More embarrassment.

"Oh," he said, turning to me, "many happy returns. And I'll look out for you at college."

"Thank you, sir," I replied, but he was off racing Oscar back to his family.

"'I'll look out for you at college'. Just my luck to be out with you. No interest in me whatsoever."

"Em, he's a happily married man for goodness sake."

"No charge for looking though is there?"

"Come on, let's swim, then we can have a final sunbathe before it's time for supper."

As we sauntered down to the water's edge I recalled my mother's words:

'A new friend tomorrow.....'

*

The September sun was slowly setting and I shivered slightly as the temperature began to drop. We felt it was time to change and Emma and I agreed with Kath that we would meet them all at the 'Mermaid' around six. The pub was located directly on the promenade quite near the pier and Charlie had booked the only table in the conservatory, so we had a private situation and an uninterrupted view of the sea. Perfect. As everyone excitedly perused the extensive menu I simply gazed out at the amazing vista. I thought of my mother and hoped she was with us in spirit. As if reading my thoughts Dad's comforting smile gave me reassurance that she was indeed there.

"Now then," said Charlie, "ch-choose just what you like everyone while I go and discuss the champagne with my friend P-P-Pierre."

An excited ripple went round the table at the mention of champagne. A first for us. Pierre was the swarthy Frenchman who owned the 'Mermaid', one of many chefs, come entrepreneurs, who had begun to glance across the channel at that time and detect rich pickings.

Deciding what to eat was always easy for me. I could not eat meat. Watching our sheep and cattle going off for slaughter was just something I could never come to terms with. Fish I could enjoy, but of course I got endless ribbing from my brothers for this and even today was obviously not going to be an exception.

"So what will it be, Carrie, scampi and chips for the vegetarian?" Josh shouted out.

"Now then," cautioned Dad, "I don't think we need to go there today, thank you."

"Oh she stuffed a sausage roll last night," Emma mischievously joined in. There was a gasp of disbelief around the table.

"Some pal you are," I replied with a smile.

I turned to Dad.

"What she's trying to tell you, Daddy, is that I needed to balance out the alcohol at one point in the evening. I had no idea what I was eating and promptly brought it back up anyway."

Dad smiled.

"I'm a vegetarian too," said Jo, "so I'm going to have a sausage roll....."

The twins burst out laughing.

".....with chips," she relentlessly continued, and we all joined in.

At about eight o'clock the meal drew to a close and Charlie called for attention as he rose, somewhat unsteadily, to his feet.

"F-F-Firstly, to this p-p-pretty girl on her special day, K-K-Kath and I wish you all p-p-p-possible happiness."

"Thank you, Charlie, but should we order breakfast now? This is obviously going to take some time."

"Carrie-Ann," said Grandma, "respect please."

Stifled giggling from the boys.

"Molly, you mustn't w-worry. Carrie and I have the m-measure of one another, don't we, Carrie?"

"Are you a size 36B too then, Charlie?" I asked.

Dad and Kath both choked on their cheddar.

Charlie chortled and then continued.

"Now I want to take this ch-chance to say how well you have all done on your smallholding over these last f-four or f-f-five years. As you know you m-made a very small p-profit last year and I was told by the accountants a few days ago you will m-make quite a decent one this year."

"Darling, it's not the golf club AGM. Put a sock in it, there's a dear," pleaded Kath.

"Yes, of course, K-Kath's right. You've got school tomorrow and I talk too m-much with my extra syllables. So let me f-finish by saying how m-much you have all lightened up my life and what a delight it has been to be with you today."

The cheers could have been heard on the pier I should think, and Daddy spoke briefly in reply. I am sure, at our different levels, we all concurred with his words, that Charlie and Kath were true friends and we loved them dearly.

*

Later I gazed out of my bedroom window at the countless stars as they heralded a new year for me. Given the opportunity I had a feeling Charlie would have gone on nonchalantly to list all that we had achieved in our relatively short time here. Clearly I had not contributed with much zeal. My only interest was the kitchen garden really. I enjoyed experimenting with more unorthodox salad crops, and actually was quite good at it. We didn't sell more than the odd lettuce at the farm gate but I gradually managed to keep our family going from late spring to early autumn.

Josh, as well as his bees, worked tirelessly on a huge allotment as soon as he got home from school each day, in all weathers. As a result, this year we had virtually become self-sufficient, except for a couple of winter months.

Seth on the other hand had a very sensitive way with animals and helped my father with all the livestock, milking, mucking out, even sheep shearing this year, although some of them looked rather a mess after he'd finished.

Even Jo had her own special tasks, feeding the chickens and collecting the eggs. She loved it too, talking to her hens at every opportunity and scolding the young cockerels when they were greedy. I smiled at more than one memory of her finding a juicy worm, assuring it that all was well, and then throwing the poor little sod into the run.

Yes, it all did seem to be working out, but I usually felt I was on the periphery, not really part of things in my heart. I wanted to be a sculptor. Nothing else seemed to matter.

Thoughts of sculpture brought me back to the day's events and our chance meeting with the Head of Art. Miss Locke was the expert in the area I was most attracted to, but the course was such that we would have to study many formats over the two-year period and that would mean being taught by the handsome Mr Jamieson. I was already looking forward to it.

*

The next few months passed quietly enough. I was really enjoying my course and Miss Locke constantly inspired me - a huge improvement on my previous teacher at high school. Suffice to say I had retained a great interest in Art despite her.

Everything was a lot calmer at home, with only the odd flare-up between Dad and me, and the boys were very busy helping him prepare for next year's crops. Beds were roughly dug to help them welcome the frost into their midst; well-rotted manure from our own cattle was liberally spread and seeds ordered. To Jo's confusion young pullets were purchased and installed, which meant that, unknown to her, the older hens had to be knocked on the head and then discreetly buried when she wasn't around. In his well-meaning way Dad chose not to be too open with Jo about it and had rather unconvincingly tried to fob her off with some garbled tale about them escaping one night. However she clearly wasn't settled about it and in the end Seth spent the early part of one October evening explaining it more honestly. All five of us had been in the sitting room enjoying the log fire and Jo was very excited about the fact that her new birds had started to lay.

"The eggs are so tiny though and fall through the holes of my egg-rack."

"Don't worry, Titch," said Seth, "soon they will lay them as big as your old hens."

"Perhaps the old ones will wander back one day."

Glances all around the room.

Following a raised eyebrow, Seth to Dad, and a nod from Dad in return, my brother then proceeded to put the issue to bed.

"Well, I doubt it. They're not here anymore and that's it. Forget them. You see, after three or four years, sometimes sooner, chickens just don't lay as many eggs as when they were younger. That means we still have to feed them, which costs money."

"And they're not feeding us so well at breakfast anymore," piped up Jo.

"That's it, you've got it."

"Daddy, did you know that?"

She jumped on his lap.

"Well, I er....."

"So you see, it's a jolly good job they did escape. Saves us having to feed them. No point if we don't get eggs out of them."

Dad and Seth exchanged thumbs-up as Jo shot off to go and shut up her new treasures for the day. Josh, who had followed her out to do a final bit of tidying up outside, later enjoyed telling the rest of us how our little sister had marched up to her pullets and told them in no uncertain manner to pull their fingers out and lay larger eggs.

My friendship with Emma grew stronger, although she did spend a lot of time trying very hard to lose her virginity. Eventually, just after Christmas, she achieved her goal and the guy was a good mate of mine from the art class, Gary Blake. I had Em on the phone to me for an hour or more a few days after Boxing Day and she was absolutely beside herself.

"Carrie, I've done it with Gary."

"Em, you haven't!"

"Two nights ago, at his place."

"But what about his parents?"

"They were away overnight with relatives. He didn't fancy going, too boring, so they let him stay behind on the condition he looked after the cats."

"Overnight? Does that mean.....?"

"Yep, I stayed the night."

"You what? However did you explain that away to your mum?"

"No problem. I just let her assume Gary's parents would be there. Anyway she met a new bloke at her Christmas staff party and was only too pleased to have the place to herself."

Her mum was divorced and apparently rather sociable with the opposite sex.

"And what's more, Carrie, she's going away with this Brian for a couple of days over the New Year. Gary's planning to stay here. And, Carrie, I've told my mum I'll be staying at yours - is that ok?"

"Em, you haven't! You could get me into hot water you know."

"Course I won't. No-one will find out. Trust me."

"Well, I'll try and deal with it if I have to I suppose. Now, come on, I want to hear every detail."

"Carrie, even I'm not that brazen. Let's just say it was pretty damn good and I can't wait for New Year's Eve."

Suddenly I panicked. It was that all too familiar feeling of loss again. Emma and I were such pals and I was going to lose her to Gary, I just knew it.

"But you'll still be coming to Mark's party won't you? It wouldn't be the same without you both."

"Of course, but don't expect us to stay that long. We shall want to see the New Year in by ourselves - and guess where!"

"Oh, Em, I'm pleased for you, really I am, but I shall miss you. I thought we would get drunk together."

"Sorry, love, but this is too good an opportunity to miss. You know you really must go for it with Mark. I highly recommend it."

"It's not through lack of trying on his part. I just.....oh, I don't know....."

"Come on, Carrie, he's just plain boring, that's the truth of it."

"Yeah, he certainly can be at times. I do like him though."

"Take a tip from me my darling and make him jealous. Go for someone else more exciting. That should do it. It's not as if you and Mark are even going out together."

"We've been bowling."

"Along with half a dozen others. Oh come on, Carrie, take my advice and you really will have more fun. Anyway, I've got to go. It's my turn to cook supper."

I felt fed up and lonely without really knowing why. It was moments like this I so missed my mother.

Curiously, after a long period of having heard nothing, she visited me later that night as I read in bed. But she relayed so much disjointed information I just got confused and tearful with frustration.

"Carrie.....new friend....."

"I don't want a new one, I'm happy with Em. But now she's got Gary and....."

"Be careful."

"Why?"

"Your art.....surprising direction....."

"Miss Locke is great. She thinks....."

"Art.....a true friendship....."

"Mummy, you're not making much sense and now you're fading. Oh, please don't go."

"Love.....wait....."

"You're confusing me. I just can't make head or tail of what you're saying."

"Beware.....butcher....."

"The butcher? Whatever do you mean?"

But I just knew she was gone.

I furiously hurled my book at the wall and childishly sobbed. Nothing added up - new friend, art and friendship, love, the butcher. So I simply turned off the light and tried to let sleep take over.

*

"Come back, please Carrie."

Josh by my bed.

Dear J, you lost Em too, didn't you? But she was always far too old for you. Huh, listen to me. I could talk.

*

It was the best part of three months before my mother's latest remarks began to make any sense, and she didn't return in all that time. This was her way - she just let other people in my life sort it out. Yet I still saw her as the orchestrator. She had never once been wrong when I thought back, but strangely her comments never seemed to actually affect the way I led my life. I didn't go around thinking that I ought not to do this or that, or tread carefully because she had warned me about something. But then that's the whole point isn't it? So many parents try to smother their offspring and control them. They look to protect them from the mistakes of their own lives, but it isn't the way of course. Kids have to trip up, get back on their own two feet, repair the damage and learn the lesson. In a perverse way perhaps I was fortunate to have no such controlling experience. My situation with my mother was such that she hinted without demanding, suggested without giving opinion, loved without smothering, made me independent without being too reliant. But then she always had been like it, so why take her away from me? It hurt, having no mother, and I could sometimes see how much of a struggle it was for my siblings, especially Jo. But I had to stop all this negative thinking. I had my Easter 'A'-level art review in a few days and I was certain Miss Locke would be able to give me a very good report.

*

"Come in and sit down, Carrie,"

"Thank you, sir."

I had never seen Mr Jamieson in his office before and it was just as untidy as all the art classrooms, cluttered up with stuff and, for the next forty-five minutes, Miss Locke and me as well. He appeared flummoxed as he desperately searched for my details under all the miscellaneous papers on his two desks.

"Now, Moira, I know you gave me Carrie's report but did you put it on the right desk?"

Miss Locke sighed, gave me a wink, and rescued it from under his chair.

"Oh, however did it get there?"

"I just can't guess, Paul," she said, winking at me again, "it was certainly in the correct place yesterday."

"Carrie, I'm sorry, but, as you will have worked out for yourself, this part of my job does not come very easily to me. I would be utterly lost without dependable Miss Locke here, just as I would be with all the bills at home without my wife."

Their casual informality, and obvious friendship, emboldened me to speak up.

"I understand, sir, my dad is just the same and I help him out all the time with his paperwork."

"Well, thank you for being so lenient with me, but I am supposed to be head of this department and sometimes I think they made the wrong choice."

"That's a load of nonsense, Paul. Now, you vain man, for goodness sake put your glasses on. You are obviously struggling to read Carrie's review and we would all like some lunch today."

I glanced at my watch and noticed my allocated three quarters of an hour had already dwindled to thirty-five minutes.

"Yep, well, that is, I would if I could find them too."

"Try your hair."

He fumbled in his locks, located his glasses and self-consciously perched them on the end of his roman nose. They were of the type sported by John Lennon at the time and suited him.

"Right, now, let me just refresh my memory."

He studied my report as I grew more and more nervous, then he put it down rather absent-mindedly, glanced at Miss Locke, and finally addressed me.

"Carrie, let's start by you telling us how you think everything's going for you here. I really only know what Miss Locke has reported back to me and don't see you myself until next term. So, put me in the picture from your perspective, and, um, please forgive the awful pun."

"I really have enjoyed every minute of Miss Locke's lessons and I think my work is going well. I feel my planning is thorough, my sketches pretty good and, although the finished product has flopped once or twice, sculpture is what I have always wanted to do, and I'm, well, doing ok."

Another glance from Mr Jamieson to my tutor.

"You do realise that this course is not just about sculpture. We want to see development of your artistic skills in other significant areas."

"Yes, sir, I do know that. It's just that, well, as I've said before, sculpture is what I want to do for a career."

There was a pause and my words hung in the air without any immediate response from either teacher.

"Miss Locke, I'm sure you would like to say something here," he eventually, and perhaps rather pointedly, suggested.

"Yes, thank you. Now, Carrie, you have shown yourself to be a very meticulous student and I agree with you, your planning is certainly well thought through and I do appreciate your sketches. In fact, they suggest to me that there is untapped drawing talent ready to come out - something I have suggested to Mr Jamieson he could definitely work on when you join his classes next term."

"Thank you, miss."

But this was a rather edgy interruption because I sensed something was coming I might not like to hear.

"Carrie, I never try to pretend to any student of mine. I am afraid that I have always had to be perfectly honest because, in the long run, it is not being fair to people if you dress up the truth."

I began to feel queasy and clenched my hands tightly under my chair.

"You have yourself admitted that your finished work has occasionally let you down and I have to agree. You see, when we admire the work of any artist, sculptor, whatever, we are appreciating what's immediately in front of us, not the preparatory sketches, not the planning, but the finished piece of work. You tend to prepare painstakingly and you are, as I have said, meticulous. But this commendable talent that you have restricts you when it comes to the practical work in hand. You say you want one day to be a sculptor but, Carrie, I'm sorry, right now

I simply don't see it happening. You haven't shown the qualities I was hoping to see, that is to boldly confront the materials and create, without hesitation, without excess preparation. I'm sorry, but, as I say, I like to tell the truth. Nevertheless you have shown other skills as I have mentioned, and I have no doubt you will go on to complete our course with much success."

I was gutted and the backs of my eyes were stinging.

"So, Carrie," said Mr Jamieson, "as Miss Locke has said, we don't make any pretence to any of our students. Therefore, while I have no doubt the news is a disappointment to you, I hope you will also believe us when we genuinely say you have a great deal of promising artistic talent, and I for one am determined to bring that out of you for the remainder of the course. Please do not go away disheartened. It is after all early days, and we admit we do make mistakes."

Miss Locke's sideways look at him suggested otherwise in my case.

"I'm sorry my work's not been good enough, miss. I have tried so....."

And then the bloody tears dropped. I felt such a fool.

"I know, I know, and your hard work will reap its reward one day I am sure."

"But not as a sculptor," I sniffed.

"Sadly, at this juncture, I think not. But, as we have both said, you have talent, and if it's there we shall get it out of you, don't you worry."

The lunchtime bell signalled the end of my review.

"Carrie, just before you go," said Mr Jamieson. He turned to Miss Locke. "Can you let me have Carrie first period after lunch, Moira? I haven't really covered everything I want to this session."

"By all means. I'm sure you will be very pleased not to have to help clear up Room 8, won't you, Carrie?"

I nodded and managed a weak smile.

"Good," said Mr Jamieson. "So, Carrie, meet me in Reception at half past one and we'll talk about next term and the hopes I have for you. Oh, and bring your coat if you've got one."

"Yes, sir. Thank you, sir."

I rushed out of the door before more tears embarrassed me.

*

"Sarah, sign out Carrie Rayner and me for this period, will you, please. We'll be down at the playing field. Don't want you worrying about us if there's a fire drill."

He looked at me.

"Oh good, you're wrapped up. It's a sharp old breeze out there today. Here, grab hold of these."

He gave me a sketchpad and a couple of charcoal sticks.

"One of your educational trips is it, Paul? Or just an excuse to watch the rugby match?"

The receptionist was obviously quite used to his unorthodox teaching style and little trips out.

"A match?" His deep blue eyes sparkled. "Is there an actual match then?"

"You know very well there is." She turned to me. "Our 'A' team is playing a travelling French youth side from Dieppe. Some very handsome young men for you to sketch, my dear."

I blushed and Mr Jamieson smartly responded.

"No, sorry, only landscape this afternoon."

With that he led me off and I was completely bowled over in his wake as I became aware of envious glances from fellow students who were dragging themselves to endure a boring hour of lectures.

"Mr Jamieson," shouted the receptionist, "don't forget your heads of department meeting at two-thirty."

"Would I?"

My feeling was, given the chance, he very happily would.

*

"Right, Carrie, stop right here."

We were approaching the rugby pitch down a wide path that led us through beds of daffodils and other spring flowers.

"Look around you. What is the first thing you see?"

"Daffodils, sir?"

"Yes, ok, well expand on that."

"They are mainly yellow, some are cream, almost white and, er....."

"Good, so we've brought in one important element - their colour - what else strikes you?"

"Some are in full bloom and others just in bloom."

"Excellent, yes, and some are beginning to fade. They are ever-changing. Nature is constantly on the move and we artists need to take note and move along with nature. You could choose just one of these flowers and depict it many times over. Your picture of that flower would be totally different every single time. Initially its tip peeps above the soil, then, green leaved, it might slightly sway in the wind. In time buds appear. Soon the flower partly opens then it is in full bloom. Finally, the plant gradually fades. Now how many stages have I mentioned?"

"Six, I think, sir."

"I'll take your word for it. We're not having a maths lesson, are we! The point I want to make is, all around us there is constant change. Look up. Those clouds weren't there a moment ago, and they are moving and changing shape even as I talk. As artists we have to try and show things moving and changing, and it's a challenge we shall confront next term. There are techniques I can show you and your class that hopefully will enable you to meet that challenge. So, choose a flower, sketch it and then join me on the touchline."

He began marching to the pitch.

"And no longer than 5 minutes. A quick sketch, no preparation, no ripping spoilt pages out. Just let it flow in a carefree way and do it from your heart, Carrie."

With that he was gone, whistling merrily, and, upon reaching the match, exuberantly cheering on St Joseph's.

I chose my daffodil and, squatting down, did my utmost to quickly sketch it. My effort took about four minutes I think and it was reasonable, but not quite as I'd hoped. I was pondering how I could improve it when a voice from the touchline bellowed:

"Time's up."

I shrugged my shoulders and walked the fifty yards to where he stood, blasting an unfortunate member of our team who had just dropped the ball a short way from the French line.

"Look at that. Luke Butcher, clean through and dropped the pass. Mind you Hargreaves did him no favours. He threw the ball far too high."

"Sorry, sir, I'm afraid I'm not that sure of the rules. I know a bit because my brothers play at school, but only a bit."

"Right, well, it was a knock-on you see. When you drop a pass from a team-mate and it goes forward, there's an unfair advantage if you manage to retrieve the ball, so the referee has to call play to a halt and they go back to where you dropped it and the other team have the put-in at a scrum. Follow all that?"

He didn't seem at all interested in my sketch.

"I think so, although it does seem a complicated game to me."

"Ah, there's nothing like it. Wonderful game."

"Do you play, sir?"

"Used to. Turned out for my Old Boys up until two seasons ago at outside half. Quite reasonably my wife put a stop to my antics. Too many injuries, you see, and what with the responsibilities of parenthood and all that. Anyway, come over here."

He gestured to a muddy, leafy area a little distance away.

"Don't you want to see my sketch, sir?"

"Are you an honest person, Carrie?"

I was a little taken aback but was able to give a firm reply.

"Yes, sir. Very."

"Yes, I believe you really are. So, did you alter that sketch of yours at all?"

"No, sir," I replied, rather relieved I'd run out of time back there.

"Then, no, I have no wish to see it, thank you. But keep it in your portfolio." He firmly pressed his foot into a yielding mix of mud and leaves.

"Now then, you see my shoe's imprint? Sketch that too. Ten minutes this time," he continued, glancing at his watch, "then you must go and do your bit for Miss Locke and finish clearing up her room. And, sadly, I must tear myself away from here and go to my meeting. Pity, just as our boys are getting on top."

That day was quite extraordinary for me. I had never experienced a lesson like it. This teacher was totally unconventional. He seemed to possess the kind of natural gifts that enabled his students to learn calmly without feeling pressured, but which then got them fired up and inspired to produce the goods. As with the daffodil, he didn't want to see my interpretation of his footprint; that day he simply wanted me to just do it, without any judgement. I believe he felt I had taken enough knocks and needed my confidence restored. Well, it certainly seemed to do the trick. I was still a little fed up about the morning's review, but the afternoon had definitely eased the blow. Perhaps I was just his excuse to see some of the rugby, but I wouldn't have minded if that was the case. As a result of his little lesson I was now more determined than ever to change my style for next term and I actually found myself wishing the Easter holiday away. I also realised I was thinking about Paul Jamieson rather too much.

*

Just over a year later, with my course and 'A'-levels behind me, not for the first time in the intervening period I thought back to the day of that rugby match. My mother's words also still buzzed around in my head. She had mentioned a new friend, told me to listen to people and that art would take me in surprising directions. Well, I had listened and, following the day of my review, my drawing and painting blossomed and excelled under Mr Jamieson's inspirational guidance.

At the end of June every art student was invited to a midsummer barbecue at his home. Other members of staff were there and we were allowed to take a friend. Mark agreed to come with me and Emma was still in a very strong relationship with Gary, so she went too. It turned out to be a night of very mixed emotions for me.

The Jamiesons lived in a three-storey Edwardian house full of character and not at all what I expected. I anticipated a complete muddle, like his office, but his wife was obviously a very different character and the place was surprisingly ordered. Yet it had a good, homely feel to it, and their two children, who were up the whole time, were friendly and lively without being precocious. They were on front door duty and confidently directed us through the house to the back garden where the rest of my class were already gathered, greedily tucking into burgers and hot dogs and knocking back the alcohol that seemed to be in plentiful supply. Mr Jamieson was covered with perspiration as he energetically cooked and served from the barbecue.

"Ah, Carrie, you're here. That must mean everyone's arrived now."

He winked at Mark, whom he had already met.

"I gather you've quite a bad reputation for your timekeeping."

"Well, all good things are worth waiting for, sir," I cheekily retorted.

"Absolutely, and, as I have told everyone else, it's Paul from now on. I've done my bit as your tutor and I hope, in future, we can all be more informal when we meet. I don't want any more of this 'sir' stuff, especially tonight."

"Now, Carrie, we all know you are not going to be an enthusiastic customer of mine, and there's one other too. So, Sara has prepared an asparagus quiche. Mark, keep an eye on things here for a moment will you and I'll find Carrie her food."

With that he guided me by the arm towards the back door to the kitchen where his wife was calmly organising bowls of strawberries. Paul nicked a couple of fruits, dipping them into some thick cream.

"Wow! First of the year. Wonderful."

"And possibly the last for you," said Sara, playfully punching him in his midriff.

"I've seen you wolfing all that meat, Porky, and we have guests to feed you know."

"Loads for everyone. All except, that is, for this young lady," pointing to me. "Carrie, this is my wife, Sara. She has got something special for you."

Sara looked momentarily puzzled.

"Carrie's the other vegetarian, along with Catherine."

And he was gone, back to his meat.

"Oh, right. Carrie, forgive me. I've popped it back in the larder for safe keeping. Won't be a minute."

She quickly disappeared, returning moments later with a beautifully latticed tart.

"Take it through will you, and don't let my greedy husband, or anyone else, get hold of it until you've had enough."

With that she was back focusing on the dessert and I felt dismissed, not necessarily in an unfriendly manner, but certainly firmly. I had felt slightly uncomfortable being with her anyway so I wasn't sorry to get away.

When I returned to the garden I noticed Mark lighting a cigarette for this Catherine. They obviously knew one another rather well.

"Carrie," shouted Mark, "you're in for a treat according to Cathy here."

She smiled warmly at Mark.

"Thanks for the ciggie, darling. Now where's that wine glass of mine?"

And she wandered off towards the house casting another flirtatious eye back at Mark as she did so.

"So thanks for my cigarette then," I said coldly. "Haven't you even got me a drink yet?"

"I had to look after the barbie."

"That's what you call her is it?"

"Oh for God's sake, Carrie. Cathy simply cadged a fag, that's all. She's always doing it. Why do you always get so niggled?"

"And why do you always have to chat up every bit of skirt the moment my back's turned?"

"Carrie, I really don't need all this. I came this evening because you invited me, so what am I supposed to do, stand here like a stuffed lemon? Cathy and I are good mates, that's all."

I knew that of course. I also knew that Mark only had eyes for me, but I found him so uninspiring all the time.

In a cruel way I was behaving aggressively towards him because I'd grown tired of him and actually wanted him to move on from me. It was of course very selfish of me. I had used him several times for a lift or just to make it look like I had a partner at social events. Tonight was just one of many such situations. I realised I had to stop hurting him like this. Nevertheless I couldn't help putting the boot in one more time. He was choking me and I needed him out of it.

"Good mates, eh? That's what you say about all these girls I find you draped around."

"Draped around? Here we go again, same old pointless and pathetic row about nothing. Grow up, Carrie, it's becoming very boring."

"And you're boring, Mark, very boring, so why don't you just sod off!"

With that I flounced off towards Emma and Gary in search of more entertaining company.

As the evening wore on I drank more than my fair share of wine and smoked heavily. My alcohol and tobacco consumption were both now increasing significantly and, worryingly, I seemed generally unaffected by the excessive intake. Admittedly I usually got very high but that was about it. Ironic that I still berated my father for the same habit.

I could flirt too. Oh yes. And that night I hurt Mark time and time again. Eventually, about nine, he left.

Towards the end of the party Emma, Gary and I were part of a very raucous group on the Jamiesons' patio. Also present was one Luke Butcher, the butter-fingered rugby player. He had arrived late with our mutual friend Neil Burton and became increasingly flirtatious with me as the evening wore on especially after I had made it abundantly clear I was a free agent.

"Quiet now, please, everyone!"

It was Paul Jamieson trying to make himself heard.

"Sara and I hope you've had a great time but, regrettably, we shall have to wind it up shortly. Kids to put to bed and all that. You'll all know about domestic bliss one day. Even you, Wilding."

Much mirth at this.

"Before you go however there is an award to make. Each year Miss Locke and I make sure there's enough left in our measly budget to buy some art materials for the student we feel has shown most enthusiasm and improvement during the course."

All the students whooped.

"Somehow, this year, we've even found enough to purchase a foldaway easel too."

"But I've got one already," shouted out Sam Wilding.

More mirth.

"I know, Sam, so that should tell you something."

Mass jeering at poor old Sam now, who took it in good part.

"No, I'm afraid the award does not go to Sam Wilding, but Moira and I are delighted to give it to Carrie Rayner. So come up and claim your prize please, Carrie."

With cheers ringing out around me I walked up to Paul who handed me one of the packages and kissed me lightly on each cheek.

"Well done, Carrie, you deserve it," he said, to a background of whistling and catcalls.

I felt my face burn up in response to his contact, garbled a shy thank you and returned to my friends who proceeded to pull my leg relentlessly. But I didn't mind. I was so thrilled to have been chosen and I was already looking forward to throwing my newly acquired treasures into the back of my car and driving off to quiet spots on the coast where I could paint to my heart's content.

"There's only one problem," said Em.

"What's that?"

"Well, how are you going to get them home, let alone

yourself? You came with Mark, remember? We can't help because we've come on Gary's motorbike I'm afraid."

"No, good point."

"Perhaps you'll let me take you home, Carrie?" It was Luke Butcher.

"But what about Neil here?"

"Oh there's plenty of room and we can drop him off on the way."

"Well, if you're sure, then, yes, thank you very much."

I quickly found my stuff and got in the back.

*

The water was cool as it barely touched our outstretched feet. The surrounding darkness embraced us on this sultry June night, the balmy air cosseting us like a blanket. Distant seagulls were squawking at late theatre-goers as they sat on the prom devouring fish and chip suppers. And further away the Newhaven ferry would be completing its last trip of the day from Dieppe.

After we had dropped off Neil, Luke had driven to this deserted cove. I was clearly not the first girl he'd brought here but that didn't bother me. Nothing was said and nothing needed saying, for we both knew what we wanted and why we were there. As we walked from the car we held hands and talked easily. At the water's edge we dispensed with shoes and lay down. Without hesitation we embraced with a fierce passion, his hands deliciously exploring my trembling and willing body.

I was moaning now, guiding his hand down.....

'Beware Butcher!'

From nowhere my mother's words rang out loud in my ears.

'Butcher'. Oh my God! Butcher. She'd meant Luke

Butcher. Of course. How could I have been so dumb?

I froze. My whole body came to a sudden halt as I realised the risk I was taking. I really should not be doing this. And luckily the message got through to Luke. He sat up and asked what was wrong. This was the crucial moment. If he understood, fine, but what if he didn't? What if he insisted we continue? He was a strong rugby player. I wouldn't have much choice.

"First time is it, Carrie?"

I nodded and mumbled an apology as I straightened my dress.

"We can wait if you prefer."

Thank God, I thought. My relief must have been pretty obvious.

"I don't understand it. I really thought you wanted to....."

"Luke, I did, but....."

"I'm not the one for you am I, Carrie? There's someone else."

"No, no. Mark and I are not....."

"I'm not talking about Mark, Carrie. Any fool can see he's not the man you're interested in. But then nor am I."

"Luke, I think you're great, really I do, but we've only just begun to get to know one another."

"Carrie, I understand, really I do. I may be sitting here, but I'm betting there's someone else we know that you'd rather be with, isn't there?"

"Well, I really don't know who you mean."

"Oh, I think you do. But it's none of my bloody business, so come on, let's get ourselves home."

"Luke?"

"Yep."

"I'm so sorry."

"I'm the one who should apologise, Carrie, for thinking you were like so many others. You're not. I respect you for that."

"Thank you. Thank you very much."

We walked back to his car in silence and nothing else was said until we reached home.

"Last year, Carrie, we played a French rugby team around Easter. My tutors all agree that I'm not much of a scholar but that I am lucky in having quite an amazing memory. I remember that match well. Paul Jamieson came down and watched most of the first half."

"Oh yes," I responded, trying to appear casual, but wondering where this was all going.

"That was you with him, wasn't it?"

There was a long pause while I blushed and tried to work out what to say.

"It was, but what are you getting at? It was an extra art tutorial. I had to do some sketching for him. I didn't really see any of the game."

"Mm, I thought it was you. Here, I'll give you a hand with all your stuff. That is after all the reason I gave you a lift, wasn't it?"

"Yes," I laughed nervously, "I suppose it was."

As we hugged goodnight he whispered in my ear.

"Be careful, Carrie, be very careful."

*

Two days later and it was the beginning of what would be a very long holiday, July right through to the end of September. That was of course assuming that everything went to plan and my exam results were good enough in August for the provisional place I had been offered on a degree course at Camberwell Art College in London. It was for three years and I couldn't wait to get there. I was desperate to step out on my own and live in the capital. Besides, Brighton wasn't that far away by train, should anything go wrong. But I didn't even entertain that notion because I firmly believed nothing would entice me back home. It was a big world out there and I wanted to sample it. I'd be in Halls for the first year and I was sure that would make life a lot easier. I was really looking forward to new pastures, new friendships and new experiences.

I had risen early, excited at the prospect of so much time to myself. The weather was set fair, temperatures were forecast to be in the low eighties later, and I had thrown my easel and paints into my mini the previous night so that I could get off quickly and enjoy a full day by the sea. I had decided to make for a lonely spot I knew near Peacehaven and was just about to leave the house when the phone rang. Everyone else was busy outside. I didn't want to be delayed but took the call in case it was important. It was important.

"Hello, this is the Rayners."

"May I speak to Carrie, please?"

I knew the voice and sat on the stairs, just a little shaky.

"Speaking."

"Ah, Carrie, I thought it was you but wasn't sure. Paul Jamieson here."

"Oh, hello, sir."

"Paul, remember? No 'sir' business."

"Sorry, couldn't help myself. Er, how can I help, I'm just off out."

"Right, well I won't keep you a minute. It's just that you left two items of your prize here the other night and we're away from tomorrow so I'd like to somehow get them to you today if at all possible. Pointless them sitting here doing nothing for weeks."

"I thought Luke and I took everything."

"Not so. You were both in rather a hurry to get off and forgot these. Are you out for long?"

"I plan to make it all day."

"Oh, somewhere exciting I hope?"

"Well, I'm actually aiming to drive out to the Chines near Peacehaven to paint there."

"Fantastic. Study the cliffs. So many shades, breathtaking. Hold on a minute would you, Carrie?"

I could clearly hear a conversation he was having with his wife, so I was prepared for what he said next, although still taken aback.

"You there, Carrie?"

"Yes, I'm here."

"Look, after lunch I've got to get our dog to the kennels at Rottingdean. I can drop down to the Chines afterwards and let you have these oil paints. Bound to spot you. That ok? Oh, sorry, hold on again. Sara's trying to say something."

This time he must have covered the mouthpiece. But he was soon back.

"Carrie, Sara quite rightly has pointed out you may be with someone, Luke perhaps, so it's probably best you give me your address and I'll drop them off at your home."

"No, no, I'm going by myself," I hastily replied, "so the Chines will be fine."

"Splendid. Well I should think it will be about, let's see, half two, so I hope to see you then. Bye."

And he was gone.

Phew, my pulse was certainly racing and so I sat for several minutes pondering. Finally I went upstairs and reviewed what I was wearing.

*

It was a long, winding route down a path to the beach below but my equipment was easy enough to carry. The cafe owner recognised me and we exchanged pleasantries before I began the descent. I could not remember such hot weather and was glad I had changed into shorts. It was still before ten yet already I could feel the sun's warmth on my arms, legs and neck. Halfway down I stopped to take in the view. Gulls swooped up and down the cliffs, briefly visiting their neighbours, a quick hello, then off again. Using the slight breeze in their favour they then glided elegantly in its wake so as to conserve energy, before spotting another friend and popping in for another little chat. Out at sea their mates were greedily searching for some late breakfast. Beyond, on the horizon, I could make out the ferry, pretty full no doubt, even though the majority of families still had three or four weeks for school holidays to start in earnest. Not a cloud in sight and the water was almost devoid of any movement save gentle lapping as the tide began to turn and make its way out again. I decided I might concentrate on the cliffs as Paul had mentioned. Their jagged contours created a rugged backcloth to the gently sloping beach and I wanted to capture the vivid contrast nature was creating.

I could see only one other person about and so choosing my spot was easy. With the tide about to go out I set up near the water's edge and made sure I could be easily spotted later on. Confusing thoughts kept crossing my mind as I began sketching and no matter how hard I tried I constantly thought about the afternoon visit I was to receive. I kept telling myself he was only dropping off some art stuff, but perhaps I was hoping for a bit more. Maybe he would stay for a while and let me know what he thought of my morning's work.

However after a couple of hours I realised I just would not be able to paint well that day. I was too pre-occupied and the midday sun was beginning to beat down so fiercely I decided to cool off in the sea. I had already put my bikini on at home so I was quickly in the water, but it was very shallow and I had to wade out a fair distance before being able to swim. It was heaven on earth.

"Carrie.....new friend....."

"Mummy, how lovely, I've been thinking so much about you. But you're very faint."

"Art.....friend.....misinterpret....."

"Oh, please make more sense. Art, friend, what do you mean?"

"Mummy.....heart....."

Gone again. I was beginning to feel tired now, and a bit peckish, so I swam lazily back to shore to lie down for half an hour before grabbing a snack at the cafe. I was displeased with my frustrating morning's artwork so I had hauled my equipment back up to the top of the Chines and slung it all into the boot of my car. One or two older couples were having lunch and I took a small table a little apart, just picking at a salad which I didn't really want. I checked my watch - twenty to two. Not that long to wait now. So I paid my bill and wandered back down.

Two young mothers and their toddlers now occupied the area I had previously chosen but it was still very quiet and I found a beautiful spot about a hundred yards away. I double-checked I could be seen from the steps and tried to bury myself in my book. But it was hopeless. I was beside myself with ridiculous nervousness and totally unable to concentrate on anything. To make matters worse it reached a quarter to three and I became convinced he was not going to show up. He definitely hadn't got here and missed me because I had checked the slope and steps every other minute. Then, all of a sudden, he was there, cheerfully chatting to the two mothers. He must have walked along the beach from another path further down. He waved his hat to them as he spotted me, and then jogged towards me.

"You seem to know everyone, sir. Sorry, I mean, Paul."

"Well I certainly do seem to bump into people

wherever I go. Don't really know them. Two friends of Sara's, part of the ever expanding kids' network she's mixed up with."

I felt quite uncomfortable but tried to remind myself his wife knew he was here and he'd just give me the oils and jog off again. How wrong I was.

"In fact Sara's taken the boys with her to some other friends this afternoon. Thomas's hamsters have to be taken care of while we're away, so she's dealing with that. That means I have some unexpected time on my hands this lovely sunny day, and what better place to be."

He sat down next to me and gazed out at sea.

"Very tempting but, like an ass, I've not got trunks or a towel. Good book?"

"No, afraid not. I don't really read much. And today I can't seem to paint either."

"Yes, I wondered where all your stuff was. Have you not had a crack at those cliffs?"

"I did a couple of hours this morning but it wasn't, oh, I don't know....."

"Flowing." He answered for me. "I know the feeling and it is hopeless continuing when you feel like that. Look, why don't we take a walk instead."

It wasn't a question. He was up again offering his hand to help me up. At his touch I felt self-conscious and confused and found myself nervously glancing down the beach to see if Sara's friends were watching. To my added consternation he guided us in that direction.

"Don't get too much sun, will you," he cheerfully suggested to them as we passed. "It's too hot for us to sit in that's for sure."

Luckily my deep tan covered my huge embarrassment.

"So, Carrie, tell me all about yourself. Your real self I mean, not the one I've had to put up with at college."

We had distanced ourselves sufficiently from Sara's

friends for me to relax more now, so I was able to be more myself.

"Oh, 'put up with'. That's nice."

"Don't get me wrong. It's not your fault. No, I just find school rules and social decorum so frustrating. I believe teachers would get much better results if we really knew our students and dug deeper to discover what makes them tick. Sadly I'm in a minority of one. Well, that is, apart from Moira Locke. All my other colleagues draw the line much higher up than I do and I am often mildly reproached for over-familiarity towards our charges. Such nonsense! It's not that at all, just genuine interest. God, they are so pathetically old-hat."

I had never experienced him having such an outburst and obviously showed surprise.

"Sorry, Carrie, no need for that. It's very unusual for me I must say. Now, please tell me about you and your aspirations."

"Aspirations? That's tricky. I do have hopes but I dare not build them up too much. I want a career in art of course. It's just.....well.....impossible for me to ever believe that the future will pan out as I want it to."

"Why ever not? Carrie, you have the world at your feet. I can't see anything but success for you in the future. I'm sure your parents believe that too, don't they?"

I stopped walking and simply could not stop the tears. Paul put his arm around my shoulders.

"Hey, hey."

He comforted me and handed me a red-spotted hankie to use.

"Sorry," I muttered, "it was just the mention of my parents. Well, my mother really. She died you see....."

He released his hold to allow me to sort my eyes and nose out.

"Sorry, I've rather ruined this lovely hankie."

"Please don't worry. Keep it."

"Thank you."

"It must be painful for you."

"It is painful. It's very painful and I've never really been able to talk about it properly to anyone. I simply dare not look forward to anything in my life for fear it's taken away. Like she was."

"Carrie, I'm here if it helps at all. But I'm just as happy to carry on in silence. Conversation is like music, all the better for the quiet bits."

We walked on deep in our own thoughts for a while but, eventually, I finally found myself able to outpour, releasing the pent-up sadness and frustration of my last six years. I recounted my mother's fatal car crash, my desolation following her death, and my ongoing problems with my father. Paul just let me get it all out and we must have walked well over a mile before I dried up. Then he gently suggested we turn round and make our way back. We were both hot and thirsty so he treated me to a coke and ice cream at the kiosk and then he fished in his rucksack.

"Mustn't go home without giving you these," he said, handing me two packets of paints. "Mind you, Sara wouldn't be at all surprised. I've got a memory like a sieve you see."

Mention of his wife made me feel a little uncomfortable again and, if I'm honest, rather envious.

"She won't.....well, that is, does she not, erm, mind.....?"

"Mind what?"

"Well, you being here.....with me."

"Why should she mind? Sara and I are individuals, Carrie, as well as a partnership. I know it's probably difficult for you to understand because you haven't been there yet but our relationship is based totally on trust. I can never see myself breaking her trust in me and I'd like to think she would behave in the same way. Sara and my kids are the world to me. Now I'd love to stay longer and talk more but it's time I got back. We're off early tomorrow."

"Where to?"

"We shall put the estate wagon on the ferry to Dieppe then drive south to Orange. Sara's got a distant cousin there and we are staying with him in his rambling chateau. He's absolutely stinking rich, but very generous apparently. We'll be there about two weeks then he's taking us to stay on his yacht at Cannes."

"You'll be gone some while then?"

"Over a month and we're really looking forward to it. Anyway, bye for now, and enjoy the rest of the summer, Carrie."

He disappeared in a flash, as always, and his departure left me feeling drained and a little disconsolate.

"I'll send you a postcard," he shouted over his shoulder.

Well I didn't believe that for one moment. He didn't know my address for a start and by his own admission paperwork was not his strong suit.

*

I was wrong about the postcard. A month later I crawled downstairs for some late breakfast after a particularly heavy night's drinking with Luke and his rugby club mates. My hangover was the result of my determination to show everyone a girl could knock back pints as well as any bloke. My father entered the kitchen without any acknowledgement. True we didn't get on that well but he never completely ignored me. On top of that he relentlessly started banging cupboard doors and saucepans about.

"For God's sake, Dad, ease up, I've got a foul headache as it is."

"What do you expect if you drink so much?"

"Huh, where do I get it from?"

"Don't you cheek me!"

"Dad, whatever's wrong with you this morning?"

"Wrong? I'll tell you what's wrong. No. On second thoughts, you can read this first."

He angrily flung a card onto the table. It was a postcard from Cannes addressed to me at Barton Green, Sussex. No other clues for the postman.

"It's a wonder it got here without our proper address," I said, as I read the short message.

"Is that all you can say?"

"Well, what else do you want me to say?"

He noisily drew a chair up opposite me.

"Now you listen to me young lady. There were only two art tutors that taught you at St Joseph's, and one was Miss Locke."

He snatched the postcard and read:

"Monet's Garden. Remember from my History of Art lessons? I travel back with the kids tomorrow."

"So?"

I felt myself reddening up.

"This bloody card is from that arrogant shit Jamieson isn't it? Unless Miss Locke has little bastards I don't know about."

"You have no right to read my personal mail. And how dare you call him that, or talk about Miss Locke in that manner."

"I'll call him what I damn well like. He's a married man, Carrie, so what's he doing sending a nineteen year old ex-student of his stuff like this?"

"It's just a card."

"Yes, a card to let you know when he'll be back. What's been going on, Carrie?"

"Nothing's been going on. Since college we've come to know one another more as friends, and he knows I really love Monet's work."

"I'm warning you, Carrie. Don't have anything more to do with him. You can't go round breaking up marriages. It's wrong, and I won't have it."

With that he stormed out and I held my throbbing head in my hands, shaking and sobbing with untold anger and hurt.

Later that day, when my brothers and Jo had gone to bed, I went downstairs to grab a coffee. Grandma was staying with us and I thought she and Dad were both in the sitting room, so I would hopefully avoid him. I reckoned that they had probably been having a long conversation and it didn't take much to work out what, or rather who, the subject matter was. Dad was however fixing some cocoa when I entered the kitchen. I went as if to go out again.

"Please stay, Carrie."

I hesitated.

"I want to apologise for my outburst."

"Only because you've been lectured by Grandma."

"Yes, she has tried to put me right on one or two things. But she's upset too."

"What have you been saying to her?"

"Look, Carrie, I needed her advice so I just gave her an outline of our argument, that's all."

"But, Daddy, she suffered a broken marriage. Surely you didn't tell her everything you said to me?"

"No, no, of course not, but I confess it might have brought a few old issues up for her. Anyway, I'll give her this," pointing to the mug in his hand, "then I suggest we talk a bit more because all I want is for you not to get hurt."

He stopped at the door, looked back, and with obvious difficulty muttered - almost more to himself than to me.

"I do care about you. I know it's probably hard for you to believe, but I do."

Well, well, affectionate words from my father. But no further thoughts were possible. Dad was shouting for me.

"Carrie, come quickly. Quickly!"

He was bending over Grandma's crumpled figure as she slumped in her chair.

"Look, take over here, loosen her clothing. It's her heart I think. We need to call an ambulance."

Dad rushed to the phone once I had relieved him. The ambulance arrived very promptly, but the heart attack was too severe. My Grandma died on the way to hospital.

*

Grandma Molly was buried in Barton Green churchyard. As I knelt by her grave a week later I remembered my mother's words while I swam on that day at the Chines.

'Mummy.....heart.....'

It also dawned on me that I would be leaving Grandma here in much the same way as we left my mother at Chesney. Only this time it would be my choice. Of course this sort of thinking was simply temporary misguided emotion and I was older and more realistic now. There was no way she would have wanted me to postpone my degree, especially as my exam results had been so good. I had subsequently been granted my first choice course at Camberwell. The rest of the family were older too and could cope, especially since Kath could always be called upon. I must admit I was anxious about Jo though. She was still only ten and, when I left to go to London, she would have no female company at home. That was quite a concern, but I was not really in a position to be able to do anything about it.

*

In the aftermath of Grandma's death the rest of my summer was very sombre and I concentrated all my efforts on rallying my family, increasing input into domestic affairs and giving Jo as much time as possible. She was upset, no doubt about it, but was able to project a surprisingly stoical air, reminding me of the time she was very matter of fact about her old hens.

It was therefore with rather more mixed emotions than I had anticipated that I left home for the first time. I confess the tears fell again. The hard part was saying goodbye to Jo but she seemed ok and, once I was on the train, I tried to look forward rather than back. This became difficult as we passed through Rottingdean. Oddly I thought of the Jamiesons' dog, Oscar, and wondered if he had enjoyed his holiday in the kennels there. His master hadn't contacted me again so that was that I guessed. It hurt though. Life had been so hectic I hadn't really had much time to think about him. Now, as I did, I began to face some harsh facts. For all his rhetoric Paul clearly saw me as just another of those many people he bumped into in life, whereas I had rather fallen for him. Yes, Carrie Rayner had a bit of a cracked heart at the moment, but of course I should always remember he was a very settled family man.

As my train left the familiar Downs behind I recalled our walk. He had, as always, been his usual very open and naturally friendly self. It was obviously me that was beginning to allow some inappropriate feelings in, even though I knew I ought to resist them.

As I have said, I had off-loaded to him on the first part of our walk, to the point of emotional exhaustion. Then, after a period of silence, Paul started extolling a few of his fundamental philosophies on life. And, in the main, it was about love.

*

"You see, Carrie, we men are odd animals. Take your dad for example. You and he, by the sound of it, are constantly fighting, whereas the relationship you had with your mother was obviously very close. And yet I'll warrant your dad loves you just as much as your mother did. Unfortunately you aren't in a position to know what your relationship with your mum would be like now. There's a chance it could have been her you had fights with the older you got. Then you might have shifted the prime focus of your attention to your dad."

"No way," I interrupted.

"Well, anything could have been possible, and you'll never know. The point I'm really trying to make is that different people handle love in contrasting ways. It's almost like looking at bold colours on the canvas as against more subtle ones.

"Some of us, like me," he continued, with a grin, "can be forthright and talk about our feelings and demonstrate our emotions with great boldness. Perhaps your mother was also like that? Whereas other people, like your dad, need to stay quietly in the background, unable or unwilling to talk at such a level, where they may feel vulnerable. But, to complete a satisfactory picture, you need boldness and subtlety, light and shade. They are of equal importance. I am certain your dad loves you. He simply cannot show it very well, if at all. And you've got to try and remember he lost the most important person in his life in very tragic circumstances at a particularly awkward time. I'm not sure how I would have held up in his position."

"I do realise that, but it's tough when he loses his temper with me. I don't feel much love then. Anyway, what is love?"

He stopped and gazed out to sea.

"What is love?"

He paused.

"Probably, love is doing the best possible thing for the other person."

"I don't really understand that."

"Carrie, love is complicated because there are so many different forms of it, but I believe that you really love someone when you do what's best for them, not what feels best for you."

"But it's so hard to do when that someone else is making life so very uncomfortable for you."

"I know, but we all have to remember that it is never just the other person's fault. By our nature we contribute to the situation. You react in a feisty manner to a lot of things your dad does or says because that is how you are. It is hard, very hard, but the next time your dad is losing it with you, just try and hold yourself together. It won't do him any good you hurling insults back at him, so do what's best for him, even if you feel hard done by. Stay calm, keep quiet. Love him."

He resumed walking and I followed, still somewhat confused, but wondering again if this was my new friend my mother had kept mentioning. I reckoned they would probably have got on like a house on fire if they'd ever met.

*

"This is London, Waterloo. We terminate here."

*

 "It's all right, Dad. I'm ok, really. Do what's best for me and let me go - it's meant to be."

His hand left mine as if hearing me, and his sobs

faded as he went out of the door, mumbling unintelligibly to the nurse as she came to check me on her evening routine.

*

I stepped onto the platform, temporarily dropped my two bags onto the concourse and drank in my new environment. People hustled and bustled around me, charging off to tubes, buses, taxis, but I was not in any hurry whatsoever. I wanted to embrace this moment, the moment when my lifestyle would change dramatically. I was already loving it. The hectic atmosphere, the anonymity I could now adopt. Like a filing cabinet my first nineteen years were locked away. Perhaps it sounds heartless but I was totally focused on enjoying that moment, completely able to leave everyone and everything in the past behind me. No-one was going to get in the way of my next three years, for I was determined to look after number one from now on and hit life running.

*

For the first six months at College I became totally absorbed in my course and I actually grew fascinated by the history of art. At lectures I began to discover the works of so many artists who until then had, apart from Monet really, merely been fascinating names.

The really exciting bit was that I could follow up lectures with visits to all the London galleries, viewing these remarkable people's talents, seeing their original work first-hand. It absolutely absorbed me and I found myself wanting to one day visit all the places that inspired them, where they grew up, and imagine myself in their shoes. It is so easy to just look at any work of art- it can be a very ordinary amateur landscape, for example - but we all tend to give it insufficient time, not even bothering to consider for just a moment how much effort went into its production. I like to think I did, and Moira Locke and Paul Jamieson could be thanked for that. I was taught to appreciate an artist's feelings, even if I felt the outcome was poor.

'We all see everything from different angles and therefore always need to be respectful of others.'

Miss Locke often brought us down to earth if she felt we needed it. This stood me in good stead now. I began to be able to positively criticise work instead of tearing it to pieces if it simply did not appeal to me. Criticism is viewed as a negative word, but it really shouldn't be. And this new trait of mine was to be significant in the future - to be able to look on works from two important aspects: what the artist was saying and what an admirer, and perhaps potential buyer, might be hearing.

As my new life unfolded so my circle of friends expanded. And parties? Well, life suddenly became one long one and I had no conscience about it. It was there and I took it. I simply wasn't prepared to take any sort of advice. My father, at my first and only return home, tried that and, totally ignoring Paul Jamieson's suggestions, I proceeded to engage in the most explosive argument we'd ever had. It ended with me blaming him for Grandma's death as well as my mother's.

I didn't go back for years and just wrote very occasionally to my brothers and sister.

I drank everything put in front of me. I absorbed it all in huge quantities but, amazingly, without too many ill effects. No doubt certain relevant internal organs might have suffered abuse, but what did I care?

Drugs? Yes, but only minimally. I smoked twenty or thirty cigarettes a day and they seemed to satisfy me sufficiently. Besides I witnessed first-hand the appalling devastation certain drugs created on a couple of my fellow students and, thankfully, I managed to desist - other than the odd social puff of grass.

I had a nasty experience at the beginning of my second year. Three of us had rented rooms in Stockwell, about all we could afford at the time. Stuart and Georgina were together on the second floor of a rambling terraced house and I had an attic room directly above them. Not ideal, especially when Stu and Georgy decided to copulate, which was pretty often actually. Sadly though they became more and more fuelled by drugs and therefore more reliant on them. Not just gentle stuff, but increasingly high toxic mixes which one night sent Georgy into rapid decline. God knows how they financed it all, although I noticed they barely ate.

I was finishing an essay on the Renaissance when the hubbub increased from down below. Oh, God, I thought, one o'clock in the morning, I'm dog-tired and those two are going to be at it for another hour. Suddenly the excited tumult ceased, to be replaced by Stu shouting in panic. I became aware of my name being yelled out a couple of times, followed by silence. I charged down the rickety staircase to their door.

"Stu, Stu, it's Carrie. What's up?"

I got no response so I tried the handle. The door opened grudgingly and the scene I witnessed was ugly. Both of them were on their bed, scantily clad, Stu completely out of it now, mumbling incoherently and pointing vaguely at Georgy who was shaking and foaming at the mouth with a glazed look.

"Ambulance.....quickly.....police on the way....."

My mother was suddenly there, urging me into action.

Fleetingly recalling Grandma Mollie's heart attack I didn't hesitate another moment. I rushed out of the room, practically fell down all the stairs and sprinted barefoot down the road towards the telephone box. On the way I passed our lovely Jamaican neighbour, Aloysius, as he trundled back home from work which comprised cleaning the toilets at Stockwell tube station.

"Lordy, Lordy! Carrie Ann, whatever.....?"

"Phone, ambulance, Georgy....." I gasped.

I left him in my wake, as he removed his trilby and scratched his head in confusion. Well, when I thought about it later, I must have been quite a sight in just my tee-shirt and knickers.

When I returned, limping from a cut heel, it seemed as if the whole neighbourhood was out and I couldn't believe the ambulance was there already. But the flashing lights outside our house actually belonged to a police panda car and one of the two officers was talking to Aloysius who pointed to me as I breathlessly leant against his front wall. At the same time I heard a siren in the distance heralding the arrival of the ambulance and I was grateful all the services were operating so efficiently. Grateful, that is, only momentarily. One of the policemen had gone indoors. The other, who had briefly interviewed Aly, immediately turned his attention to me. Attention I could well have done without. He must have been in his late thirties, early forties, thick-set and rather mean looking. His eyes went up and down my shivering body, a leer covering his countenance. My hackles went up straight away.

"And you are?"

The sneer said it all.

"Carrie Rayner," I responded coldly. "I live here on the top floor. My two friends are on the second floor below me."

"Carrie. Nice name."

He gave me another up and down glance, which caused me to try and cover myself as best I could.

"Yeah, Uncle Tom over there was telling me about

you."

He jerked his head in Aly's direction. That did it. I wasn't accepting racist shit like that.

"His name is Aloysius Grant," I spat out.

"Yeah, yeah, well they all look the same to me. Dirty."

"How dare you!"

"Easy now, love, there's a good girl."

The ambulance screamed to a halt and we both moved to one side to let the men through.

"You see, my mate and I are here to investigate a little breach of the peace. One of your other neighbours, a....." He referred to his notes. ".....that's it, a Mrs Webster, called us because she's had enough of your student antics at all hours God sends. Apparently her old man is doing early shifts on the buses and can't get his beauty sleep."

He paused and leered again.

"But you're obviously getting yours, love."

"Don't keep 'loving' me."

"Wouldn't mind, I must say."

"Ignore.....Carrie, don't retaliate....."

Mummy was certainly on the ball at the moment. I just about shut myself up as the ambulance crew returned for stretchers. And luckily the seedy copper left to assist them.

One of the crew threw a blanket round me as he hurried past, shouting to a bystander, telling them to wrap me up, sit me down, and be aware of the cut on my foot that, amazingly in all the commotion, he had noticed.

"Then we'll get her to Casualty with the others."

Before I could argue, and in no time at all, I was whisked away in a blaze of blue flashing lights, to St Thomas's, sat next to the driver while his mate tended to Georgy and Stu in the back.

It was like a horrific nightmare but I grew up quite a bit more that early morning. Fortunately I was later interviewed by the other policeman who showed greater manners and understanding. My foot had been cleaned and bandaged and a hot mug of sweet tea was slowly bringing my senses back. The constable tapped on the treatment room door and asked the nurse if he could have words with me.

"Of course. She seems more settled now."

"Thanks."

He pulled up a chair.

"Well, miss, I expect you're wondering why the police are involved."

"No," I replied, cautiously, but more comfortable with this one, especially as the nurse continued in the background tidying the room up, "the other officer explained that."

I put as much venom in 'officer' as I possibly could and it was picked up.

"Did my mate give you a hard time then?"

"Careful, Carrie....."

Mummy again. So I hesitated and thought better of what I intended to say. Best if I tried to keep calm.

"Well.....not exactly, it was just, erm, well, I was upset, worried about my friends and I.....well, I didn't like the way he referred to my neighbour, Aly."

"Would that be Aloysius Grant, miss?"

Like his colleague earlier he had referred to his notes.

"Yes."

"The West Indian gentleman at number 38?"

"The gentleman at 38, yes."

"I'm sorry if you object to my detailed description of this person, miss, but that's what he is, no offence, and perhaps you might understand our position and feelings a little more if you saw what we have to deal with these days. The constable that talked to you outside your place is my new partner. I lost my old one in a stabbing incident three weeks ago. A gang of black youths - you may have read about it?"

I did vaguely recall the headlines on the newspaper hoardings so I nodded.

"Luckily he'll survive but he won't be able to continue in the force. Legs are useless you see. So please try and see it from our point of view."

I nodded again, deciding not to expand on my other feelings about his new colleague, the way he looked me up and down. So I buttoned it and just answered his questions. Ironically this Mrs Webster was our landlady. Her husband was at the end of his tether and they just wanted to get to sleep. Apparently Stu and Georgy's night-time activities had constantly prevented that, something I could actually sympathise with of course. On top of that, they were a long way behind with the rent. Now I understood how my friends managed to fund the drugs.

As it happened, in the end neither Stu nor Georgy returned to the flat, or indeed to college. Stu decided it wasn't for him and got a job as office boy, in a solicitor's of all places; poor Georgy went home to Sheffield where her mum and dad could take care of her. I tried keeping in touch but got no response other than a terse note from her dad saying he wanted Georgy to have no further contact with 'people who had ruined her life forever'. I was very upset but realised she was in a bad way and needed protection. I just found it hard to be told I was someone she had to be protected from.

However I took it on the chin.

As a result of the whole experience I had to quickly learn some harsh realities of life and the incident firmly made my mind up about certain social issues. For a start it helped me steer clear of drugs totally from that moment on. The experience of seeing two young people like me ruin their lives so dramatically was warning enough. Additionally I had seen and heard at first hand examples of severe racial tension. Despite the second policeman's testimony I simply could not accept his colleague's inflammatory and derogatory language directed at Aloysius. There was no place for any such discrimination in my heart and these strong feelings of mine were soon to be sorely put to the test.

The room below me obviously became vacant and, within a month, one of Aloysius's nephews moved in. Ironically he had heard about it not just from Aly but Stu as well. Lawrence was a trainee clerk at the same legal firm where Stu had found work. Aly introduced me to Lawrence as soon as he moved in. His manners were charming. He was also very handsome.

*

For three months I went out with Lawrence. He was my first lover and really good company. But the relationship was never destined to last. For the short period it did however we had some great times. Lawrence was an avid fan of the cinema and so we went to the Brixton Clifton at least once a fortnight. He also wrote poetry and I was frequently the subject material. Initially I was quite embarrassed but grew to enjoy his flattery and expressed devotion towards me. Sadly two things stood in the way of a long-term connection. His family in Kingston, Jamaica were constantly in his thoughts and I knew it would only be a matter of time before some situation or other would cause him to have to return. His father became very ill and could not cope with the family hardware business. Consequently Lawrence's mum, quite understandably I suppose, began putting pressure on him to go home and run their store.

I caught him reading a letter one December evening, tears dampening his beautifully chiselled face. I knew at once what it meant.

"Bad, Laurie?"

"The worst," he whispered. "The very worst."

We said nothing more that evening. I hugged him through the gathering gloom and kept my own counsel but we both knew that was it. In the morning he went to seek out Aloysius and together they made swift arrangements for his passage home. The boat wouldn't get there in time for his father's funeral but at least he could eventually get home to support his mother and sisters. That's what mattered to him more. As he said in his brief note to me once he had left, presumably written on the boat:

'I'm going where I should be, not where I want to be. You see, Carrie, I love my family so much I must do what is best for them. However much I enjoyed being with you and living near Uncle Aloysius, I struggled so much with the issue of my colour in your country. Wherever I went I was cut dead by the majority of people. It also hurt me to witness you suffering insults.

I shall never forget you.

With so much love, L.'

No, and I guess I would never forget him. Well I had to face facts, it would have been almost impossible to keep it going in the atmosphere that pervaded that particular part of London at the time. Lawrence was right. I did suffer a lot of taunts when we were out. And if nothing was said the unfriendly looks and poorly concealed whispers spoke volumes.

Ironically on our last date there was an uncomfortable incident at the 'Kennington Arms'. For a final treat Lawrence took me to a matinee at the Odeon, Leicester Square and we saw 'Dr Zhivago'. We caught the tube home but, as often happened at weekends on the Northern, the train stopped at Kennington, so we decided to walk to Stockwell. I fancied a drink or two and, much against Lawrence's better judgement, I persuaded him to drop into the 'Arms' where I admit I downed more than one or two. Towards closing time I needed the toilet.

"Won't be a mo, I'm just off to the ladies."

"I'll come with you."

"Don't be daft."

"Well steer clear of those noisy fellahs by the bar, they look like trouble. I can tell a mile off."

"I'm a big girl so stop worrying," I replied, kissing him affectionately.

But he was right. I got provoked by one of them as I passed, although the rest of them, to be fair, told him to cut it out. They seemed decent guys actually and harmless enough, but this one was nasty.

"Little slut", he ventured, as I passed by again on my return from the toilet.

I know I shouldn't have reacted, but I noticed Lawrence was no longer in the bar and must have gone to the gents at the other end of the pub. So I stopped in my tracks and turned round to face the speaker, who was short and weedy with a permanent juvenile sneer on his face. His mates went very quiet. I guess they all knew he'd gone too far. They certainly made him look rather isolated and turned their backs on him to continue drinking.

"Slut, eh?" I responded, striding angrily back towards him.

He actually looked rather sheepish at this point, which gave me more confidence. Encouraged by this and fuelled by my alcohol content my big mouth took over.

"Well I expect you enjoy sluts so come outside with me now."

I could deal with this little shit - I'd grown up with two very strong brothers after all - and so I grabbed his collar and literally dragged him outside to a chorus of whistles and cheers from his so-called mates. Looking round quickly I noticed that Lawrence was still nowhere to be seen. I wanted to deal with this myself and not involve him.

I engineered the slob against a wall at the back of the pub. He couldn't believe what he thought was his sudden good fortune.

"Slut, you said. Well, if sluts do this then, yes, that's me."

To his disbelief I covered his mouth with one hand and his crotch with the other, squeezing with all my might. His muffled scream of anguish was very satisfying.

I returned to the bar, spotted Lawrence and we left. As we passed his mates I bid them a cheerful goodnight.

"Your mate was such a disappointment - no balls at all when it came to it."

*

Although the immediate period following Lawrence's departure was flat, I soon put a positive face on things and my second year at college saw me in many short-term relationships as I gradually began to realise the power I seemed to have to attract. I have to admit I probably became a rather shallow teaser. Certainly I enjoyed sensing blokes becoming attracted to me and I played up to it. But I didn't find that the physical, beyond petting, was really enjoyable. I even unwittingly found myself in a tight situation with a third-year student who befriended me to the point where I suddenly realised she wanted my body as well as my company. I didn't have a problem with it. I simply put her straight and she accepted I wasn't of a like mind. We therefore continued our friendship, but at a comfortable distance. In those days it was happening more and more and people of both sexes began to gain confidence in making more public their previously secret sexuality. I was happy to mix with anyone but I always made my position very clear. What I didn't make clear was which man I really wanted. But then he was cosily wrapped up in Brighton with his wife and kids, wasn't he?

In the New Year I began to get interested in CND. Well, let me be a bit more honest, a guy I rather liked the look of persuaded me to go and listen to a debate on the organisation at our college theatre one evening. I certainly was most definitely against nuclear weapons and the increasing preparedness of so-called super-powers to play with such dangerous fire. However I admit the chance of a date with Adrian was initially of more importance at the time than CND.

After several months of Adrian's influence I may well have got more involved with the setting up of the Greenham Common Women's Peace Camp. But I had finished college and a good career opportunity had arisen. However I read about the policies of our government with mounting fury and frustration. They led to some very unsavoury incidents and particularly frightening were the race riots in Brixton.

*

It was mid-April and my new flat-mate Laura and I were returning from Brixton Market late one Saturday afternoon with weekend supplies of wine and crisps. At the end of my second year I'd moved in with Laura to a reasonable flat in Shakespeare Road. I had to ensure I did well enough in my finals and Laura was a good, steadying influence (although she could match me in the drinking stakes).

The whole area in which we lived was very tense that day. Apparently the trouble could be traced back to the previous night when a black youth had been stabbed by criminals and the gathering crowd turned their anger on the police, I think because they felt more should have been done by them. Anyway it all turned nasty in nearby Railton Road with police presence substantially increasing. Railton was at a junction with our road and that's where I, about ten hours or so after the stabbing, got into bother and yet again ended up in Casualty.

Misunderstandings cause more trouble than anything, don't they? It would seem that an element of the local community had now decided that the stabbed youth - by now dead - had actually been the victim of police brutality. So we were unfortunate to be trying to get home at this point. We thought we had left the worst trouble behind us in Brixton High Street where we witnessed police cars being pelted by bricks. That was not the case. Ahead of us, close to the access to our road, an ugly mob was beginning to loot a couple of small shops and a police van had been set alight. The fire brigade were having a very difficult stand-off. They had got as far as the junction with Shakespeare Road when a large crowd of youths appeared and started to approach, armed with bottles and bricks.

"Jesus, Carrie, we're going to be lucky to get home," screamed Laura.

"Well we just might if we can get to the junction before that lot. Come on."

I grabbed her arm and we ran, but just a bit too late. We did make it, but not before I managed to get in the way of a beer bottle.

Luckily it was a minor, glancing blow, but bloody painful, and it made me even more determined to get home.

"Carrie, you're bleeding!"

"It's nothing. Keep going. We can make it."

And we did. But I have to admit anything could have happened. Sadly far nastier things did happen to a lot of people that day. Pubs in the district, along with businesses, schools and other buildings, were set on fire throughout the night as rioters went absolutely berserk. Eventually, in the early hours of Sunday, the police had managed to quell the riots. But the situation was so tense that the fire brigade apparently refused to come out again until the Sunday morning. So, really courageous men were not even prepared to risk it.

Laura and I just about coped and, like all our neighbours, got by with the theory houses would be left untouched. And so it turned out, but I likened it to a storm when you were a frightened kid. We occasionally glanced out from behind our curtains during quiet moments, just like, as children, we peeked out of the bedclothes between the thunder and lightning. As for my injury, well it stopped bleeding and I felt shaken but ok. Anyway I certainly wasn't going out again. Once Sunday afternoon had arrived however, and relative calm restored, Laura rightly insisted I got looked at.

"You must be careful with head wounds, Carrie."

"Do as she says....."

My mother underlined Laura's sensible advice.

"Oh, not you as well, Mummy....."

"Pardon?"

Laura looked at me in alarm.

"Er, nothing, I was just muttering to myself."

"You said 'Mummy'."

"Oh, did I?"

"That does it. We're going to the hospital. Now."

And with that Laura prepared to march me off to Casualty.

"Don't worry, I know where it is."

"Stop being stubborn....."

"I'm not being stubborn. I'm letting her take me, aren't I?"

Again very puzzled looks from my friend and by this time she was absolutely convinced I had a serious problem, but of course I was not going to enlighten her, and anyway she would have a lot of fun recounting all this to our friends for weeks to come. Yet, as it transpired, we were both put off going out much for a long time from then on and so we began working in earnest for our degrees.

*

"Still nothing I'm afraid, Mr Rayner."
"Thank you. Please thank everyone for being so patient with us....."

*

"Carrie, wake up. Wake up, you dope. It's our big day."
"Oh," I groaned, "surely not yet. I'm so tired."
"It's ten o'clock. We have to be at college by midday," Laura persisted. "It's Graduation Day, my darling. Have you forgotten?"
"Shit!"
I leaped out of bed.
"I have to meet my sister off the train before then."
"That's why I woke you. But don't worry about any thanks."
I grabbed a towel and rushed for the bathroom before stopping at the door.
"Thanks, Laura. Thanks for so much. We must never lose touch. You've been such a friend."
"Actually, not that much of a friend. I've used all the hot water I'm afraid."
"You little sod!" I yelled.
I soon yelled again as the freezing water rushed from the shower-head onto my shocked torso.

But it woke me up and I could now enjoy Graduation Day. Wow! I was so looking forward to it.

*

The problem of whom to invite had been on my mind for weeks. I really wanted Jo there, but of course she was only thirteen and, being July, she would have to get time off school. I didn't see that as a problem so much as whether she needed to be accompanied on the train. There were only three seats allocated per graduate and I knew who else I wanted to be there. Sadly that didn't include my father. However, despite our intense friction of the past, I felt a bit mean-spirited about my attitude towards him and so I tried to present him with an olive branch in the form of a letter a couple of weeks before the event:

'Dear Dad

This letter will no doubt come as quite a surprise to you in view of our last meaningful communication stretching into years. I cannot apologise for my outburst at you because I meant what I said. We were never destined to bowl along easily, you and I. However I do recognise your love for me and I am sorry if I have caused you so much pain in the past. Perhaps we can try and at least be civil to one another in future.

As you may know from Titch I have amazingly managed to scrape a 2:1 despite my hectic social life and a similar taste for alcohol to my father. I expect you and the boys are very busy harvesting so I am wondering if you can agree to Jo attending my Graduation on July 12? Obviously she will need to get the day off school but it would mean a lot to have her here and they do precious little at that time of term anyway. I would meet her off the train and take great care of her from then on. If you're unhappy with her travelling alone I could ask my old college tutor, Miss Locke, to accompany her. I know she wants to be here as well.

I wait to hear from you. C.'

Of course what I conveniently omitted was how I was carefully engineering who actually attended. I didn't really lie to my father but there was, I admit, some serious massaging and omission. I knew for sure who I wanted as my third guest. Anyway my dad's response made it easier. Never a great letter writer he helped me proceed in my undercover direction:

'Dear Carrie

I am very proud of your achievement, and I know Mummy is too. Yes, it is a pretty hectic time here, but we can organise Jo to come if you can get Miss Locke to co-operate.

Keep in touch please, Dad.'

Well, I was halfway towards getting what I wanted and so I immediately penned a letter to Moira Locke and sent it care of the college with fingers crossed:

'Dear Moira

Remember me? Well, thanks to you, and a few other tutors, I've got my degree. My graduation day is July 12 and I would like to invite you as one of my guests, as a token of my gratitude. As usual with me however you will realise there's a catch! If you would like to come could you possibly accompany my thirteen year old sister on the train please? Cheeky of me I know, but my dad and brothers are busy with harvest and Dad will not be keen on Jo travelling alone.

My very best wishes, Carrie Rayner.

p.s. I have a third ticket if you feel Paul Jamieson might be interested. Just a thought.'

'Just a thought'! It was a rather pathetic ploy really and doubtless Moira would see right through it.

However the reply was actually very enthusiastic, warmly accepting my invitation and only too pleased to look after Jo. She even indicated that Paul might also attend but he would only get to the evening reception because one of them had to be at college until early afternoon.

So my conniving bore some fruit and I was certainly delighted to be seeing my little sister. It had been too long.

*

"Jo! Jo! Over here!"

I was waving and shouting frantically as, duly accompanied by Moira Locke, my sister daintily stepped off the train in a very pretty lemon dress, which set her amazing tan off so beautifully. My goodness, what a stunner she was turning out to be.

The day progressed very happily for me but, by six o'clock - an hour into the reception - still no sign of Paul Jamieson. So I gave him up.

"Carrie, we have to be going very soon. The best train to get is the 7.25. and we need to get the tube first," said Moira.

"Of course. I understand. I will just say some farewells then come with you to Waterloo."

"No, no. Unless Jo here feels differently, we'll go alone. You can be responsible for getting us there, Jo. It'll stand you in good stead if you ever have to come to London for your own degree. And if we miss it there's another an hour later."

"Anyway, Carrie, you should stay and have fun here with your friends," added Jo. "I like Ben. He's just your type you know."

"You cheeky madam," I laughingly responded, and then I turned back to Moira.

"Dad will meet you at the other end, will he?"

"I think it's more likely to be one of your brothers, but

we can ring as soon as we are at the station and someone will certainly be there, so please don't worry."

"Well it's really kind of you."

I gave Lockers a brief hug and my sister a long, tender one.

"Thank you so much for coming, thank you both. It's meant so much to me. Pity my other ticket was wasted, but never mind."

"Actually," replied Moira, pointing behind me, "I don't think it has been totally. Look, he's just arrived."

The new arrival accepting a glass of champagne was, initially, barely recognisable, but it was Paul and the sight of him made me somewhat flustered.

"Is that Paul? I, erm, well, I hardly recognised him at first."

"Yes he has changed over the last two or three years, what with one thing and another. Anyway, Jo, we'll slip away, shall we? I see enough of Mr Jamieson at work. Bye, bye, Carrie, and keep in touch."

"I will, I promise. Thank you."

I turned to Jo, who already was beginning to follow in Moira's wake, and we silently held out our hands to one another for a final embrace.

Moira moved towards Paul, exchanged a few pleasantries, and then turned round to point me out. I gingerly waved and he nodded recognition. He said a couple of things to Jo who then gave me a smile and a last wave.

Paul obtained a re-fill for his glass and carefully made his way through the throng towards me.

It was an awkward initial exchange, a formal handshake and stuttered greetings. But I too had armed myself with a drink, then I introduced him to some friends and we both seemed to relax more after that.

By about ten o'clock the celebrations began to cease as the majority of people left. Paul, who seemed to have been chatting to virtually everyone in the room, came up to my group again and asked if I needed a last glass of something.

"Well, I've rarely been known to refuse, Paul, but actually even I have had enough, thank you. Don't let me stop you, though, or have you a train to catch?"

"No, I won't either. Otherwise my day in London tomorrow might be dull and cloudy."

"Oh, you're staying on then?"

"Yeah, just for a couple more days. I've got special leave of absence so I can attend to a few personal matters and I thought I would do some sightseeing at the same time. Thank you very much indeed for inviting me. It was a big surprise to receive it via Moira and I haven't had so much fun in a long while."

"Knowing you, I find that pretty hard to believe. You always seemed to me to have a very full social life."

"Ah, that used to be the case. Less so lately, I'm afraid, much less so. In fact I was actually wondering whether you are busy tomorrow afternoon."

"No, no, far from it," I replied, rather too quickly perhaps.

"Would you like to come to the Tate Gallery with me? It's a while since I've been and I need to keep up with things really."

"I'd love to. Thank you."

"Look, I have some business to attend to in the morning. Why don't I treat you to lunch? You name the place."

So we arranged to meet at one o'clock in Crank's, one of my favourite whole-food places. He grimaced once he knew it would be a meat-free menu but insisted it must be my choice.

"You're as bad as my brothers. I bet you'll love it."

"We'll see. About one then? I shall give you until three. I remember your time-keeping reputation."

"Huh, you can talk. And who rolled up today just for the food?"

He held his hands up in mock submission.

"Fair point. See you tomorrow then."

And he was gone in his customary speedy manner, dropping off, I noticed with some jealousy, to have a final chat with two very attractive friends of mine on the way. He had taken a while to become himself though and something wasn't right. What was it Moira had said? Oh, I couldn't remember. The wine was blocking serious thinking. Anyway, I was seeing him tomorrow and I felt very excited at the prospect.

*

"Your friend needs help.....understanding....."

I was on the tube the next day, heading towards my lunch date, and I didn't respond to my mother. Too many times in the past year or so I had managed to embarrass myself in similar situations. No, I was not going to attract the attention of fellow passengers and she wouldn't reply anyway. Instead I gazed at the blackness outside and started thinking about Paul. My mother was usually right so perhaps he did need some help. And if I could be the one to give it I most certainly would. Whether he would accept it was another matter.

*

There had never been a day in my life to match that one with Paul Jamieson. When we met again all previous inhibitions at my graduation reception had evaporated. He greeted me warmly and the day just got better and better. Once we had finally finished a very lazy lunch he suggested it was too hot for going indoors and how about a river trip. And I was very happy with that. He knew I loved the water and it was a spectacular day's weather - hot and cloudless. Being on the boat gave us a welcome cooling breeze.

Afterwards we just walked, ate, drank, and, more importantly, talked. This was when I discovered what had happened since I last saw him. His business that morning had been with an old friend of his from his own college days who was now a very successful solicitor. Paul had asked Rufus to start divorce proceedings against his wife, Sara. Initially I was stunned but he carried on as though unaware of my reaction. Astonishingly the trouble between them went back to their holiday in France not long before I left for college. Apparently Sara showed Paul nothing but coldness the whole month they were there and made up to their host to the point of embarrassment. In the end Paul could take no more humiliation and travelled home a week earlier than intended with his children. Sara flew back only a couple of days later. She assured Paul nothing was going on that need worry him, apologised in a very roundabout way and then proceeded to carry on with life as if everything was rosy. But it wasn't, certainly as far as Paul was concerned.

"Our so-called happy family life had suddenly become a sham, Carrie. Our very special bond had broken. I was broken as well. Once the kids were in bed it became one long argument, always picked by Sara and so hurtful. It's ironic because I recall telling you how we trusted one another implicitly. After that ill-fated trip I found myself on edge, constantly worrying about what she may be up to, who she might be with, or even just talking to. At parties she behaved outrageously towards a couple of my closest friends and of course it all got noticed and comments flew around."

He hung his head and I put my arm around him. After

a while he squeezed my hand and perked up.

"This is ridiculous. I'm sorry, Carrie. I have no right to hoist this onto you."

"Please don't say that. I want to help."

He thanked me and we continued walking until we reached Covent Garden tube station.

"My hotel's just around the corner. What are your plans now?"

I looked at my watch. It was only eight o'clock, still light and I was actually very hungry.

"I don't have any, although all this walking and lovely air has made me famished."

"The hotel has a really decent menu I believe. Let's eat."

And the old Paul was back, taking hold of the situation and guiding me along the busy street to his hotel. It was quite small, but very attractive and welcoming. We had dinner on the terrace and, when the light started fading, the attentive waiter lit candles. It was a trigger for Paul to get depressed again and he needed to get a few more things off his chest. Basically it was his children that he talked about, especially his little boy. Yet again however he eventually was able to admonish himself in deference to me and apologised once more for his miserable company.

"Paul," I said, taking his hands in mine, "don't say that. I'm sorry for your situation too. But actually I'm not that sorry because today I have felt so close to you, and that's what I have wanted for so many years."

There, I'd said it.

He looked at me, somewhat bemused.

"You mean.....?"

I nodded and put my finger to his lips, directing him to be quiet.

"Now, enough of this. I need to book myself a room here. I'm certainly not going to spoil a perfect day by returning to bloody Brixton."

"Here." He jumped up. "Allow me. You're not to pay for it."

And he was off, organising it all.

We spent an hour in the comfortable bar but at around midnight Paul decided it was time he got some sleep.

"Perhaps we can go to the Tate in the morning? I checked with the manager and our rooms are both vacant for tomorrow night as well."

"That would be great. Are you sure you don't mind?"

"Mind! You've brought me out of myself, Carrie, and I am so grateful for that. I'd love it if we can share another day together."

We walked to my room, which was on the ground floor, and at my door Paul took me by the shoulders and thanked me profusely. Then he was gone, bounding up the stairs to his room, which I had made it my business to find out was on the second floor.

After a luxurious shower - such heaven compared to my lodgings - I lay in bed trying to get to sleep. By one o'clock I gave up. I had tossed and turned thinking about Paul and his situation and thinking of him two floors up. My mind was made up. I crept out of my room and, seeing no-one about, tripped up the stairs. Without hesitation I knocked on his door, tried the handle, and it opened. His bedside light was on and he was reading.

"Carrie, whatever are you doing here? Is something wrong?"

"I'm here to look after you and nothing, absolutely nothing, is wrong."

I climbed into his bed.

"Now, switch off that light and love me. Love me, Paul....."

*

We were obviously never destined to get to the Tate Gallery.

We spent all morning in one another's arms and, following a brief afternoon outing and an early dinner, resumed our lovemaking, this time in my room. The parting the next morning was difficult but he had to get back and sort his life out while I needed to begin to concentrate on my forthcoming career at Sotheby's.

*

I had been very fortunate in landing a post with the famous auctioneers. It was an administrative role but gave me the opportunity to be involved with a fantastic range of famous and valuable paintings about to be auctioned at the House. It would be my job to draw up the auction details, post them off to relevant potential buyers, and then assist with creating notes for the auctioneer.

It proved to be very exciting and challenging and I was really getting into the full swing of it when, three months into the job, I got some very sudden and unwanted news. The baby was due the following spring.

Obviously I knew something was up when I started feeling so rough before work, but it was a hell of a shock and I was angry. I was angry with myself for having unprotected sex and I already very selfishly resented this life growing inside me. I blamed myself totally, but I was at the point in my life when my career was all-important to me, virtually at the exclusion of everything. The thought of nappies and a tiny child being totally reliant on me was not something I even wanted to try and cope with. My future therefore suddenly looked bleak and I simply did not want this baby. But I was only too well aware it really was my own stupid fault. I couldn't possibly let Paul take any of the blame. Let's face it I had always yearned for him. I definitely took the lead at the hotel and I really didn't give him any opportunity to resist.

Anyway I had satisfied my five-year desire and, although it was good at the time, it wasn't an exceptional experience. Then it never had been for me, and I sensed that he was constantly just a shade edgy all the time we were together. So, I needed to face practicalities. And I decided that only Paul and I would ever know. Getting hold of him was tricky because we had mutually agreed on parting that there would be no further contact until his divorce was through. I therefore rang Moira at school during what I estimated would be her lunch-break.

"Moira, it's Carrie, Carrie Rayner."

There was slight hesitancy, then.....

"Oh, Carrie, how are you? How's the job shaping up?"

"Brilliantly, thanks."

"Excellent. Now, how can I help?"

"Well, I need to talk to Paul Jamieson about a little matter" - how appropriately put, I thought afterwards - "and I would be grateful if you could ask him to ring me. I'm in a new flat and I've got a phone as well now, so I'll give you the number."

"No, Carrie. No, don't bother to do that."

Her mood had a definite chill to it now and it reminded me of the time she told me in no uncertain terms about my lack of creativity as a sculptor.

"Oh? And why not?"

"Look, I'm sorry, but I shall have to keep this brief. I have a student waiting outside to see me. Carrie, it would be a bad time for Paul. You see, I don't obviously know any intimate details but he did tell me you became very close after your graduation. On his return he discovered a few things and he's called off divorce proceedings. Paul and Sara are trying to make a go of it and it's going to be tough, the way she is, so please leave him be. Make no more contact. They have to get through this."

I was shocked. Shocked only because Paul had not had the decency or courage to let me know. But shock immediately erupted like a volcano and I simply couldn't help myself.

"Well stuff you, Locke, and tell Jamieson to go stuff himself too. He's shit, just like the rest of them."

I slammed the phone down, sobbing.

There were copious tears after that of course but more of anger than anything. It was a Friday and I had been instructed to work at home that day in order to be able to compile notes for the following week's auction. This often happened and, as always, I'd completed the task that morning which gave me a free afternoon and, I had hoped, a long weekend to enjoy. Now I simply spent the rest of the day experiencing every possible negative emotion going. I became unaware of anything else going on in the world and stayed on my bed for over twenty-four hours.

By Saturday evening, having ignored the phone every time it rang, I had formulated a plan. There was no way now that I could even share my news with Paul, so I had to deal with it myself. Whatever happened, I was even more determined my career would not suffer.

That night however I stupidly drank myself into a stupor at Kenny Holt's party. At around midnight I came out of his bathroom, missed my footing at the top of the stairs and hurtled down to the bottom, blacking out as I did so.

I was in hospital for ten days, very bruised and battered, but towards the end of that period I was in reasonable condition. The only serious physical damage was internal.

Losing the baby in this way had not been part of the plan but at least it saved having an abortion. However I was affected emotionally for some while and of course I felt I would never again be able to trust any man, or anyone else for that matter. On what turned out to be my last day in the ward I managed to ignore the noisy activity around me and write a letter:

'Paul

I'm glad I managed to find you out before it was too late. Firstly, I confess I did go all out to sleep with you on my graduation weekend. Yes, unlike most people, I am always able to admit the truth. It's a pity you are so gutless that you haven't been able to be more open with me. I understand completely that you had to go home and sort everything out and I know we agreed we would lie low for a while. But it was on the clear understanding we would be together once your divorce was through.

I needed to talk to you about something that is totally irrelevant now, yet all-important at the time. I would not have tried to bother you if it hadn't have been.

To be told by Moira that she knew about us and that I should leave you alone was not only a shock but insulting. I then learnt that you haven't even been bothering to seek a divorce as you'd told me but are working at your marriage instead. Well, thanks. Thanks for showing me just in time what a heartless bastard you really are underneath all that shallow charm.

You certainly had me fooled, but then I expect you've had plenty of practice at deceit.

Enjoy your new-found tranquil domesticity.

Carrie Rayner.'

When we are deeply upset it always helps to get everything out, but of course, after I had posted this vicious piece of writing, I immediately regretted it. Paul Jamieson might have been all the ugly things I had slung at him but nobody's perfect and, by my own admission, I had definitely done all the running. So it was no surprise that I received no immediate response. In fact it was nearly a month later before I heard anything. I was back at work with Sotheby's and just beginning to regain total equilibrium when his letter threw me slightly off balance for a while:

'Dear Carrie

I won't insult you further by raising excuses. I shall simply give you the facts.

On my return from our weekend together I discovered Moira at my home looking after the kids. Sara was in bed and later that day admitted to hospital with a severe problem. Things quickly escalated and she became seriously ill. It was touch and go for a long time but she survived and now I nurse her and look after the kids as best I can along with help from Social Services. Her medication may eventually enable her not to be totally bed-ridden but it is likely she will never walk again.

You have every right to sound off at me as you have, but my place is here not with you. Sorry, but I hope in time you will come to see that's how it has to be. I wish you all possible future success in whatever you do, Paul.'

As usual with me after an emotional scenario I was consequently in a confused state, but I had no choice now. Paul had to be part of my past. I understood to a point. He had a sick wife and two kids on his hands. But I also realised I meant far less to him than he did to me, something I had known right from the beginning. I could still justify my anger though. Surely a quick note of explanation from the outset? But, as he said, he was absolutely useless at putting pen to paper. However, I could never completely forgive him. That way I would finally get over him. And that is exactly the case, although it took over six years.

*

Looking back, the whole experience really hardened

me and work became the focus of my existence. I was prepared to do anything, and tread on anyone, to further my career. That was all that I was concerned about and woe betide anyone who tried to get in my way. I threw myself tirelessly into every project and, within two years, had become something of a high-flyer. In my third year with Sotheby's I was head-hunted and persuaded to work for a consultancy specialising in sourcing major works of art for wealthy collectors. As a result I got to see many European countries. But I worked very hard and the rewards for many thirteen or fourteen hour days were fast cars, fabulous apartments and hotel suites, exotic food and cocktails, and rich men, who thought their wealth bought them your body. Well it worked with some women, but never me. That is until I bumped into Hans - literally.

I had been sent to Milan to service one of our English clients who had extensive business interests over there. Italy was my favourite location and so it was a very welcome assignment. Our chief had a luxurious penthouse apartment on the edge of the city centre where staff could stay and I was studying my notes in the lift one morning after an exceptionally late night. The doors opened and, without really paying any attention, I walked slap-bang into a very sharply dressed, six foot-plus male, probably in his late thirties. As I discovered later, he was hurriedly and rather absent-mindedly trying to take the lift back up to his apartment on the second floor, having forgotten important papers for a meeting.

"Oh, I'm so sorry," I said, as my papers dropped everywhere, "I wasn't paying attention."

His response was in carefully crafted English, with that charming odd grammatical lapse which I found so attractive in a lot of Europeans. He had obviously immediately realised my nationality.

"No, it is I who must apologise. I am doing always

this sort of thing. Here, allow me."

He bent down and gathered up my scattered notes.

"You are most kind. Thank you, but I must bear some of the blame."

I noticed his eyes taking in my bare legs as he rose from the floor.

"It is why they give me this name, my English colleagues. Let me introduce myself. I am Daisy," he said, with the most mischievous and captivating twinkle in his eye.

"Daisy?" I replied, one eyebrow arched, with equal mischief.

"Oh, please, no, no, I am not, how you say, um, homosexualist."

He smiled and I burst into laughter at his comment.

"Ah, now, you laugh at my very inadequate mastering of your language."

"Not at all," I said, "but why 'Daisy'?"

"Look, this is perhaps not the best time and place," he continued, as he checked his watch. "I must get to a meeting. Please, allow me to buy you dinner tonight. Let us say, nine o'clock, at 'La Boheme'?"

"Why not? But only on condition you explain 'Daisy'."

"But of course. No problem."

He headed off, and then added, over his shoulder, "I know you English have to solve these mysteries, yes?"

He disappeared round the corner and I continued on my way to work, already looking forward to seeing him again. The restaurant was probably one of the three most outstanding eating establishments in Milan and very expensive indeed.

*

"So, how did you get your English nickname then?" I

asked, as our meal was being served.

"Oh, it is quite simple, yes? I work for Ferrari and often I visit your country, so I have made many friends in England. They tease me because I am never looking where I am going. So, if I tell you my real name, you, Carrie-Ann, have to work it out from there."

He seemed to like using my full name and for once I rather liked it too.

"My brain doesn't do teasers this time of day."

"Oh, it will be easy, you'll see. You have humourous, I sense that already. Now, my mother was German and my father a Dane, by the name of Nielsen."

"Right. Interesting. With you so far."

"Yes, a good mix I have always felt. Well, my parents, how do you say, christened me.....?"

I nodded.

"They christened me Hans. There you have it. Now you will have to work it all out."

"Hans Nielsen?"

"Yes."

"Hans Nielsen," I repeated, "and Daisy. Whew, must be this wine. Not getting it, sorry."

"Say it very quickly, my real name."

"Hans Nielsen."

"Well?"

And, with a fork poised to enjoy another mouthful, realisation suddenly dawned.

"Of course!" I exclaimed, as everyone in the restaurant turned their attention to me.

"Hands, knees and boomps-a-daisy. Hans Nielsen.....boomps-a-'Daisy'!"

"She's got it," he shouted to everyone, most of whom then burst into spontaneous applause, as was the custom in this beautiful country when two people were clearly having a significant moment.

"I knew you would," he said, returning his attention to

me.

"Carrie-Ann. Please, you will however do me the honour of calling me Kurt, my middle name, yes? That is my preference, please."

And Kurt it was from then on.

I had never met anyone who, in one glorious evening, made me laugh so much. He admitted to enjoying playing practical jokes on people whenever he could and his sense of humour was so infectious I just ended up in tears. It got to the point that I simply found myself hooting at everything he said and did.

"Kurt, I really ought to call it a day."

"You mean call it a daisy, no?"

And we both collapsed in laughter again, to more applause from the remaining customers.

Kurt was a perfect gentleman that night, although part of me wished he wasn't. Common sense prevailed however. I needed to learn some more about this lovely man first. And in time I did, and it was all positive. Just over a month later we became lovers.

*

"Go home.....Kurt.....Daddy.....bury differences....."

It was nearly a year later, a beautiful early summer's day, and my mother had made one of her very brief appearances. Kurt and I were still together and saw a good deal of one another, despite our busy working lives. I had never before met a man that made me enjoy life so much. In fact we spent the majority of our time together wiping the tears of laughter from each other's cheeks. Kurt was different from any man I had known, even Paul Jamieson, and surprisingly I trusted him implicitly. So one Sunday when we were lazing around, I found myself opening up, as I did once with Paul, and telling him about my fraught past with my father. I almost mentioned my mother's little conversations with me, but drew the line, even with Kurt.

"So you are saying you have not seen or contacted your father for years?"

"Virtually. The odd phone call, a card at Christmas perhaps."

"That is so sad. I do not like to hear this. We will visit next weekend, no?"

"No, Kurt, most definitely, no."

"Oh, my feisty English wench, don't you see? Life, it is not for making this hatred. It is for loving between people, yes? Carrie-Ann, come on, swallow the pill and take the headache away."

I sat in my chair in absolute amazement. This wonderful man, a foreigner, was able to use our language in such a way that was so clever and blindingly obvious.

"What is it? I have said the English wrong, have I?"

"No, my love, you have just taught me an English lesson."

"It is nothing. A gift. You have either got it or you have not!"

And he smiled as I realised he was pulling my leg yet again. He was in fact turning a phrase round I had taught him to his advantage. And I enjoyed it. I hugged him and covered his mischievous face with endless kisses.

And there was no debate from that moment on. The following weekend did indeed see us eating up the miles in his Ferrari to Sussex. Back home to a welcome I was dreading yet which turned out to be astonishing. They all loved Kurt, my dad in particular. He hogged his company for most of the Saturday evening while I enjoyed catching up with Josh, Seth and Jo and then started organising Jo into coming to London in a few weeks to celebrate her twenty-first birthday with me. As we all chatted in the sitting room round the fire every so often there were peals of laughter from Dad's study.

Then, on Sunday, my father and I found ourselves alone for an awkward moment in the kitchen.

"Bury the past....."

Significantly my mother was also there.

".....not much time left....."

I took the plunge.

"Do you like Kurt, Daddy?"

"I do. He's a great guy, very funny, just what you need. I like him a lot."

"That's good."

"Does that mean you've got something to tell me? Is he the one, Carrie?"

"He is the one, but I've nothing to tell you."

"No church bells ringing then?"

He smiled nervously, knowing I had reacted badly in the past to any sort of intimate questions.

"There might have been if there was time. But, no, Sod's Law. That's the phrase isn't it, Dad?"

He walked up to me with desperate sadness in his eyes.

"Carrie, I don't understand."

"You will, Daddy. You all will one day. Quite soon in fact."

I held out my arms to him. He filled them, and we both wept.

*

"Carrie-Ann, I'm here. It's Kurt. No-one knew how to contact me. Now wake up. Wake up for Daisy."

He pressed a small posy of flowers into my left hand.

"I picked these from the park. You know me. Last of the big spenders, is it?"

I smiled to myself. Always able to make me laugh. But he wasn't joking anymore, nor was he laughing. I had never seen him cry before and he obviously knew.

For what seemed like an eternity he clutched both my hands and kept pleading with me to come back. But I was too far down the path. And anyway someone else was waiting at the gate.

*

"Time to go, Carrie. Come on, darling. You're always so late."
"Coming, Mummy....."

BOOK THREE : TWIN OF THE SOUTHERN HEMISPHERE

'Would all passengers for British Airways flight BA212 to Singapore report now to Departure Gate twelve. British Airways passengers for Singapore to Gate 12. Thank you.'

"I guess this is it, Seth," said Josh, rising clumsily from the cafe table and spilling the remains of our cups of coffee.

"Oh, there you go again, knocking things over as usual. No finesse, that's your trouble."

"Yeah, well, you always were the one with all the niceties. Not sure you'll need them where you're going though. Bunch of roughs by all accounts."

Josh playfully punched me and grabbed one of my cases.

"Now then, Josh, that's no way to speak of my Australian relations," interjected Bill, with a wry smile. "They may not have many of Seth's good manners but they've got plenty of style you know. Roughs indeed."

"Sorry, Grandpa, just my joke. Guess I'm rather jealous of Seth if the truth be told."

"You could have gone too you know."

"I know, and thank you for the very tempting offer, but Dad needs me at home. Jo simply wouldn't cope, what with his, well, you know....."

"We know, Josh," said Rosie, "and it's good of you to look at it that way. So, Seth, you're ready?"

"As ready as I possibly can be thank you, Rosie."

Turning to Bill I held out my hand to bid him farewell.

"Grandpa, I can't thank you enough.....I just don't know what to say....."

Shamefully I gulped and pushed back emotions that had threatened to embarrass me.

"Seth, it's the least I can do. I have the means and, God knows, I've not exactly been much of a grandfather up until now, have I?"

"You know what they say, better late than never, Bill," said Josh, trying to keep things cheerful and at the same time putting a consoling arm around my shoulder.

"Bill told me he thinks this is the first time you two have really been apart. Is that right?"

This question was too much for me really and Bill gave his wife a sharp look. I noticed her mouth 'sorry' at Grandpa and then she came up to me and gave me a long hug.

"I'm afraid I don't do 'goodbyes' very well, Rosie. What a wimp, eh? Twenty-nine for God's sake, and getting in a right old state."

"Just be grateful the boys at the rugby club can't see you," jested Josh, as he took over from Rosie, "then you'd get a right lot of grief. But then you always were the sensitive one. Even took that fly half that you laid out last season some grapes in hospital."

I managed a laugh in agreement as I recalled that event, and imagined just what my team-mates would be putting me through if they saw me now.

"Now come along or you'll have me at it soon," Josh continued.

"That would be a first," I retorted, determinedly trying to sort my embarrassing emotions out.

'British Airways passengers for flight BA212 to Gate 12 please.'

"I'll be away then," I continued, pulling myself

together. "It's only across there so don't bother coming any closer. And, thank you, thank you all.....you know, for seeing me off."

With one final hug for my brother I hurriedly grabbed my case from him, gathered everything else up and began threading my way through the crowds to Gate 12.

At the gate I turned for a final wave and could tell that even my strong twin, Josh, was struggling. He knew and felt the pain I was experiencing - it was the unique bond twins had apparently - but the difference was he would never show it, always proudly camouflage it. I would miss him so much, he was part of me, but I was determined to take the wonderful opportunity my grandfather had granted me, however difficult this part of the adventure was proving.

I watched them move away. They would be going up to the departure viewing area to try and see me take off. But I wouldn't be able to pick them out of course, and they probably would end up waving at the wrong plane anyway.

*

"More chicken, sir? We have a little left."

A very attractive air hostess interrupted my thoughts as I gazed into space.

"Er, thank you, yes, I will."

"We have some roast potatoes and gravy too, sir, but no other vegetables left I'm afraid."

"No worries, that's great. Thanks."

"Practising your Australian lingo already I see, sir."

"What's that?"

"You used one of the Aussies' favourite phrases, sir, so I wondered if you're en route to Melbourne."

"Well, yes, I am actually."

"It's a great place. You'll love it. Would you like the

steward to bring you another drink, sir?"

"A beer would be great, thank you."

"I'll make sure you get one as soon as possible."

"Very good of you."

She gave me a beaming smile and I felt my face reddening up. This young lady was certainly a beauty and I persuaded myself she was beginning to flirt with me. But of course she was simply doing her job. I was hopelessly naive in the company of attractive women. Bit like my dad apparently. Mum was his one and only, as I understood it, and he was way into his thirties before he met her. So, time for me yet. Oh, don't get me wrong, I'd had many opportunities, but I was painfully shy about the other sex, unlike my twin, who just took every young woman he wanted. He had never had anything approaching a serious relationship though and boasted at the rugby club that 'no woman will ever trap me'. I envied him his self-confidence with them.

The rather camp-looking steward gave me my drink with an unnecessary flourish.

"Thank you."

"My pleasure I'm sure, sir, and do let me know if you need anything else."

I immediately felt uncomfortable. Josh was the rugged one out of the two of us but we were both often assured how handsome we were. However, I was conscious of always looking, well, almost too much so, to the point of 'cute', as a couple of Josh's old flames had labelled me. My mum's blonde, curly hair didn't help. Therefore I was ultra-sensitive when effeminate men like the steward appeared on the scene. But then I knew it all went back to that horrendous experience with my first music teacher years ago.

"May I clear away, sir?"

The lovely hostess was back.

"Yes, thanks, that was really good."

"It's not bad considering we're thousands of feet in the air, is it, sir?"

"Better than 'not bad' and much appreciated, thank you."

"Thank you, sir."

My embarrassment was heightened as she leaned over to relieve me of my tray, flashing me another radiant smile.

Later I settled as comfortably as I could in my seat and started to think about my Grandpa Bill. He was after all the sole reason I was here. In the short year I had known him he had taken such a genuine interest in my future - and Josh's too - so much so he went to our dad and put an unbelievably exciting proposition to him on our behalf. Bill had distant - very distant, literally - second or third Australian cousins who farmed in Victoria. To cut a very long story short, he was prepared to bear all the cost of sending Josh and me over there to experience farming on a far bigger scale than we could ever imagine.

Well, for some reason, it just didn't interest Josh. He always gave Dad as the excuse, and that was fair enough to a point. Our smallholding venture had grown, with a modicum of success, and Dad would certainly have struggled without us both. But actually I knew Josh simply wasn't that interested. He was completely content and carefree as he was. Whereas I had wanderlust, yet to find exactly what I wanted in life. This was an amazing opportunity and one I didn't intend turning down.

Of course Dad found it difficult to swallow such generosity at first. He was a proud man, and although I knew my older sister had always felt differently, I believed he had barely coped with all that Bertie had given us. But Dad and Grandpa had a very important thing in common, they had both struggled with Grandma - to put it mildly - and this seemed to bring them together.

They got on really well and Bill was obviously enjoying getting to know his son-in-law.

So, after many hours discussion between them on separate occasions, either in the 'Cat and Fiddle' or Dad's study, Bill eventually persuaded him round to his way of thinking, although I knew Dad would probably have preferred Josh to be the one leaving. Dad had always seemed to get on better with me and cosseted me a bit, if the truth be known. Once he realised how Josh and I had reacted to Grandpa's offer though he seemed to appreciate what I could gain from the trip and he finally relented.

It was a mind-blowing package that Grandpa set up for me. Initially I would live on a ranch within an eight and a half thousand acre station owned by one of his cousins in Warnock, a town about three hours drive north-west of Melbourne, the Victorian capital. There I would be part of the working team, learning the ropes of Australian-style cattle and sheep farming. A friend of Bill's cousin owned a thriving and expanding vineyard in the Yarra Valley. I would get to work there too. Another relation owned a fruit farm, specialising in blueberries and strawberries. This was in a small suburb of Melbourne. The vineyard and fruit growing were what Bill had, quite reasonably, thought would be of real interest to Josh, but, luckily, I was to benefit from all three situations.

With customary military precision Grandpa had set up a bank account for me, with a generous allowance to start with, and he had also organised every little detail with his contacts at each location. My food and lodging would be down to my hosts and in return it was made very clear I would be expected to work very long days for them. At my first port of call there would apparently be occasions when I would work away from the ranch and experience existing in the outback.

Well, I was never afraid of hard work so it all sounded pretty damn good to me. Grandpa did lay down one or two stipulations however. As a result of his own experience, and obvious success in life, he insisted that I was to commit, and commit for quite a while. For reasons best known to him he had suggested, very firmly, to Dad and me that three years was the optimum period for what he termed my 'apprenticeship of life'. Coming from a military background he was used to postings of that nature and the disciplinarian side of his character was very strong. So, if I was to do it, then that was the deal. One year, or thereabouts, at each homestead, and a minimum three years away from home - take it or leave it. It was never quite put like that but Dad and I drew our own similar conclusions.

"Make a man of him, Will."

I once caught him talking to Dad, so I eavesdropped from outside the study.

"Lovely fellah, but he obviously needs toughening up, and there's no better place, my cousin at Warnock assures me. They don't stand on any ceremony there, and they won't make it a cakewalk for him. Besides, he and Josh need time apart. I can see Josh carries him on occasions. So, even though I offered it to Josh too, I'm glad he turned me down in retrospect."

In fact, from the moment I overheard what Bill had to say I wanted to go even more. I had to be honest, he was right. I was too sensitive, required roughing up a bit and, no argument, this experience would allow me the independence both Josh and I doubtless needed from one another. It was important to try and become two real individuals.

Three years it was then. No turning back now. It may well prove tough and a bit lonely, but I vowed to work flat out to repay my Grandpa's generosity.

*

I woke up with a start. We were experiencing some turbulence which lasted a rather uncomfortable twenty minutes, during which time we were instructed to put on our seatbelts.

Eventually the Captain came on to advise all was now well and we could revert to normality.

I released my belt. Darkness had fallen quite swiftly during the turbulence and we were still four hours short of Singapore. So I snuggled down as best I could with yet another book. My eyelids became heavy as my brain couldn't cope with the complex storyline and my thoughts again turned to my family. I began to recall a traumatic weekend of about a year ago, a weekend that had all started out so happily and boisterously.

*

"Come on, Rosie Lee, come on!"

Bill was beside himself, urging the mare on. Dad was equally animated, having backed her as well.

"Seth, ours is making a late run. Look!"

Josh frantically grabbed my arm as Rough Pasture, switching to the outside, came under pressure from his eager jockey. I didn't really like the way the horse was being driven - I would never push mine like that - but even I was caught up in the excitement.

"Come on, number eight, you can do it," shouted Josh.

And at the line none of us knew the winner. It was a photo.

"What do you think, Grandpa?"

Josh looked doubtful as he asked the question.

"I think 'Rosie' got it by a short head," Bill replied.

Josh and I groaned. Grandpa was apparently rarely

wrong on four-legged matters, and, sure enough, this was no exception.

"First, number twelve, second, number eight and third, number three....."

"Bugger!" Josh exclaimed. "Do you always have such luck, Grandpa?"

"As soon as I saw the name I had to back her, didn't I?" Bill responded, glancing warmly at his wife Rosie.

"And I'm glad you did, Bill," said my dad, "I think I've won about thirty quid."

"What about you, Grandpa?" I asked.

"Well, Seth, I stuck to just a thousand, so at 6-1 that should pay for the day."

Josh and I stared open-mouthed at one another, totally speechless.

"Now, let's get some champagne in and toast Jo's twenty-first, Will."

Our grandfather and his wife left the box with an equally bemused Dad in tow. Bill had treated us to this luxury at Brighton racecourse in celebration of Jo's special birthday. She, ironically, was in London however with our older sister, Carrie.

I turned to Charlie Youngman who was engaged in tearing up his betting slip, much to the chastisement of his wife, Kath.

"No luck either then, Charlie?"

"I'm afraid not, Seth. I p-picked F-F-Free Sp-Sp-Speech, and I do believe he came in second from last."

"I told you not to tempt providence with a name like that, Charles," said Kath.

"Well, you know what my w-warped sense of humour is like, my dear. It seemed a sign! Anyway, we're still up on the day, thanks to your grandpa's w-w-w-wise counsel, Seth. Though I must add, my p-p-pound each-way habit has not amassed the considerable sum Bill appears to have done today."

"He's astonishing," said Josh, "I simply can't get my head round the amounts of money he seems to deal in."

"Yes, well, money's not everything," Kath chipped in, "but I must say, in the very short time we have known him, Bill does seem to turn all he touches into gold."

"I believe from what I've seen of him that he's very generous too, dear, and not m-many w-wealthy people like him are."

And Charlie was so right, although Kath was very cool about my grandpa. Rather like his first wife, my grandma, probably had been towards him.

Anyway it was good to be getting to know him after so long.

Our family reconciliations had been down to Carrie's guy, Kurt. He was obviously a great bloke and had taken Carrie by storm, bowling her off her feet with continental charm, clipped humour and straightforward commonsense. Like the company he worked for, Ferrari, he did everything at great speed and his way of operating actually did the Rayners (and me in particular as it transpired) a big favour. Carrie apparently kept all family matters from Kurt right up to a couple of months before those Brighton races. Then, not only did she explain her division with Dad, but she also admitted it was her fond wish to meet our maternal grandpa, whom Grandma had divorced and cut off early in our mother's life.

It was frustrating that Carrie had taken so many months to tell Kurt about our family, but I suppose she had her reasons and of course her enmity towards our father went very deep. I was sorry that, as a result, Josh, Jo and I lost out with her though. It would seem that Carrie and Kurt were both so busy in their high-powered careers that she had previously always been able to conveniently put us on the back burner, not giving him any chance to ask too many awkward questions.

Once Kurt was brought into the family circle, one

unforgettable weekend, we all instantly took to him and no-one more so than Dad. They had an immediate rapport and this went a long way to healing a couple of Carrie's wounds. I was particularly relieved because I had always been fond of my father, although he often scared me too. He fought my corner on so many occasions and that meant a lot to me. Regrettably he drank a lot and had dreadful moods - which were of course unwelcome - but he never recovered from my mother's death and my older sister just reminded him too much of her. Carrie's attitude and behaviour towards him had been, in my view, unnecessarily vindictive. She always went too far and they both had evil tempers at times.

So, it was a great relief when Kurt burst into our lives and we certainly loved the spin he gave each of us in his fantastic sports car. Like his Ferrari, he was apparently like a whirlwind over the next few days, on a mission to get other branches of our family back together. Our situation offended the principles instilled into him by his own parents. Astonishingly, over the next month and a bit, he managed to reconcile Carrie and Dad, and then persuaded Grandpa and his second wife, Rosie, to get together with all of us. They proceeded to book themselves into the 'Grand' at Brighton for a week and their stay culminated in taking us to the races. To make up for not seeing Jo on her birthday they had already spent a good deal of the week in her company and she got on really well with them, especially Rosie.

How Grandpa had managed to get a box I don't know, but he was clearly more than very well off and no doubt he was able to pull a few strings. He seemed to know so many influential people, even minor royalty. An ex-officer in the Army, Bill had become first a royal bodyguard and then some sort of private secretary at Windsor. Rumour had it he also dealt very cannily with stocks and shares, but, however he had made his pile,

Charlie was absolutely right, he was certainly no miser. He refused to divulge much about himself though, giving his reasons as 'confidentiality and all that, my boy'. Now in his eighties, but looking at least ten years younger, he and Rosie led a very comfortable existence, but he obviously had a lot of regrets about my mother, as I was to find out one very sad day.

*

The vision before me was gently shaking my arm.
"Please fasten your seatbelt, sir. We're landing at Singapore in a few minutes."
"Oh, thank you, I'd nodded off."
"Best thing, sir, there wasn't a lot to see."
I looked out of the window and saw nothing but a dark void. Half an hour later I was investigating Singapore Airport, increasingly aware of the intense heat, even this late at night.
It wasn't long before I was aboard the connecting flight for Australia and finally on my way to Melbourne. But it was, literally, a long haul and after more food and a generous amount of wine I was soon dozing again.

*

"Bye, Grandpa, and thanks for a great day," I shouted over my shoulder.
I helped Josh, who was rather the worse for wear, into the house. Rosie drove off and I suspected Bill was out like a light too.
Dad had left the course at around six o'clock to get back for the animals. Kath had driven him and Charlie who was in his eighties now and rarely coped with nightlife. Meanwhile Bill and Rosie had taken Josh and

me for drinks, then a four-course meal, including a very large t-bone, followed by even more alcohol and a lot of catching up on family history.

Unbelievably it was gone two in the morning when I finally slumped into a chair in the study, having somehow managed to drag my brother to his bed. He was one and a half stone heavier, so just to get him to his room was exhausting. I dumped him on his bed as he was. No doubt he would sleep for about four or five hours and then be absolutely fine.

Sitting in the study was something I often liked to do when I'd hammered it a bit. I never liked going straight to bed and often didn't go at all. That early morning was such an occasion. I was thinking how remarkable Bill and Rosie were to be able to stay up so late at their age and handle the alcohol so well, when I felt my whole body tense. Suddenly I realised I was not alone.

Someone was there with me. And, astonishingly, it was my mother.

I froze in my chair. Then I thought that it must be the drink or.....

"Seth.....taxi.....Carrie.....stay awake."

Initially I was petrified. Stupid of course, being afraid of my own mother. But it was so eerie. We had lost her about eighteen years ago and I had virtually forgotten what she sounded like. But I knew this was definitely her voice. Yet, when I turned round, there was nothing, nobody.

"Bloody idiot," I berated myself, "drinking so much again. When will I learn?"

"Jo.....telephone."

That was certainly not my imagination.

"Mum? What's going on? Am I going mad, or what?"

"Stay up.....phone."

"Well I'm hardly likely to fall asleep now. This is such a shock, Mum. I mean.....well, what on earth is this about? Where are you? What.....what the hell's happening?"

Nothing.

I paced the floor, my initial fright now replaced with puzzlement and frustration. Eventually I sat down again and discovered I was shaking uncontrollably. My God, I thought, why.....?

When the phone rang I literally jumped out of my skin. I dumbly looked at it for several seconds then cautiously lifted the handset as if it were an unexploded mine.

"Er.....hello."

My voice was parched and the caller was obviously in great distress.

"Sorry, I can't hear you. Who is this, please?"

In a torrent of tears my sister Jo blurted out the horrific news.

"Seth, oh, Seth. It's Jo. Carrie's had an accident. We're in hospital now."

"Hospital?"

"She's in intensive care, Seth. She's going to die, I just know it."

I paused, simply unable to take in what I was hearing.

"Jo, whatever has happened?"

"She was hit by a taxi, Seth. A car accident, like Mummy. Seth, it's like Mummy, all over again....."

I began shaking all over.....

*

"Ladies and Gentlemen, for your information we are now beginning to fly over Australia and expect to land at Melbourne in approximately six hours time. Thank you."

The announcement woke me up with a jolt. Then for a long while I looked out of the window and, as I studied the cloud formation and marvelled at air travel, I thought again about my older sister.

*

Carrie was laid to rest in the Suffolk churchyard next to our mother.

It was the strangest and saddest of occasions and particularly poignant for Dad and Grandpa Bill, for quite different reasons. I have no idea how any of us got through it, in truth.

Dad had decided the location. He called the three of us into his study a couple of days after Carrie had finally slipped away. Jo had taken it very badly and the atmosphere was appalling.

"Like you, I daresay, sleep has eluded me these last few days," began Dad. "Carrie and I had a bad relationship of course, but this doesn't make it any easier. If I could change a lot of things I would."

"Daddy, please don't blame yourself, you mustn't. Carrie told me she was so delighted you and Kurt got on," interrupted Jo.

"I know, darling, and I'm pleased the last time I saw her was such a positive occasion. But there was also something about her mood that told me to be wary of her new-found contentment. She would have married Kurt I think, but she told me there wasn't enough time."

"You mean, you think she knew?" I asked.

My turn to interrupt.

"Quite possibly."

"But how come?" Josh asked.

"I think she just knew, Josh, let's just leave it at that."

Josh simply shrugged his shoulders, never one for digging too deep. Whereas Dad and I exchanged a fleeting, yet telling, look.

You see, I had actually experienced the briefest of one-way conversations from my mother the previous evening in my room.

"Carrie here.....you go.....Jo strong.....will cope....."

I had sat and puzzled for hours, especially over the words 'you go'. Go where?

But I ended up having to accept it was all beyond my understanding. Perhaps it was just my imagination after all. Who knows? Anyway I simply tried to convince myself she and Carrie were back together again. I found all that sort of stuff difficult to swallow but I had a hunch Dad might actually believe it.

"What I do know for sure," continued Dad, "is that Carrie would want to be buried with Mummy. Earlier today I therefore began making arrangements with the current Rector at Chesney and I believe we shall be able to conduct a private service there, and he thinks there is space next to Mummy's grave."

I rushed over to Jo, just beating Josh to it. She had collapsed in tears again.

"Jo," said Dad, as Josh and I consoled her, "it's tough, I know, and her funeral won't be easy for any of us. But I have insisted it remain private and I know the villagers will respect that. We have to be strong, Jo. So, I suggest it will be the four of us, Kurt of course, Grandpa and Rosie, and, I thought, Charlie and Kath. Are you all agreed?"

None of us questioned him further. We were all too numb and Dad had clearly given it a great deal of thought, whereas we hadn't. It all probably made sense really. And anyway, as Josh remarked to me later, did it actually matter?

*

It was a warm, sunny morning. Apart from Kurt, we had all set off early and arrived in good time for the midday service, Grandpa and Rosie pulling into the car park just ahead of us. Charlie and Kath arrived five minutes after us. To our surprise Kurt had already been staying in the village a couple of nights, and we discovered later he had spent a lot of time investigating the area in which we had all spent our early childhood. He had read an old diary of Carrie's and needed to see where she had apparently been so happy.

Kurt had, unsurprisingly, lost his spark and very much kept himself to himself that day. We all struggled through it of course but I couldn't help but feel most for Dad and Grandpa. For my father it was a reminder of our past here and for Bill a first opportunity to see his own daughter's grave, as well as witness his grand-daughter's funeral. His disciplined military bearing simply fell apart.

After the burial Josh and I accompanied Jo back to the car but, about halfway, I dropped back and turned round for one last look at the churchyard. Dad and Bill were literally propping one another up, both clearly shaking with grief.

"The worst day of their lives I should think," said Rosie, coming up to me and wiping the tears from her face. "I've never seen Bill like it. He's always been so strong, so dignified."

I couldn't respond, just gave her a cursory hug and returned to the car. Apart from my mother, in Bill's case, they had had no kids of their own, so I imagined Rosie found it all pretty difficult to comprehend Grandpa's level of grief. Inside me however I railed a bit at 'dignified', but I let it pass. I was too raw. No need for anger. It wouldn't help.

*

I came to just as fellow passengers were beginning preparations for us to land. I checked my watch and calculated I had been travelling, overall, for virtually a whole twenty-four hours. Astonishing! So far away from home already. Thousands of miles.

I felt a mixture of excitement and apprehension as I left the customs hall. I needn't have had any concerns though because, in time, everything turned out dandy.

*

My three years in Australia stretched to seven and it was to be 1998 before I set foot on English soil again. In that time I changed, apparently, almost beyond recognition. That country is amazing and I lived there in awe of its rugged beauty, soaking up every different exciting aspect of the place, never once regretting my grandpa's gift. And, for me, Australians were, without doubt, the greatest fun to be with. You had to work hard to be accepted, and any airs and graces were soon shot down in flames, but, on the whole, I was fortunate enough to live with, and meet, some really friendly people who soon made me feel very comfortable. Their hospitality was second to none, and, boy, could they drink! It didn't take me long to find that out.

*

"Hey, Seth, have another Red Banger, then I'll get Ty to knock up some burgers and we'll have a few beers. Chill a bit, yeah?"

"Thanks, Pete, I think I will. I don't know what your wife puts in these but they hit the spot."

"Vodka and stuff, I think. Oh, here she is, we can ask her. Jan, Seth here's wondering what you put in the Bangers."

"Well, vodka....."

"Like I said."

"Quite a lot, to be honest. Then a bit of this and that. Tomato juice, Worcester sauce. You call it 'Bloody Mary' in England, I believe."

"There is a similar drink, and it is called that. But blimey, Jan, these knock your block off. They're nothing like, really."

"Hey, who's beginning to talk like an Aussie then!"

Their daughter, Maddy, dropped into the chair next to me and clasped my hand.

"Whew, it's really quite hot today. Summer's on the way, I think."

"Quite hot? If this is quite hot I don't know how I'll cope in the height of summer."

"You'll be ok, mate," joined in Ty, as he popped open a beer and started preparing the barbecue, "the highest we go here's only the mid-thirties and then we just fall into the pool."

"Mid-thirties? What's that in English money?"

"You Poms," said Pete. However will you cope with the twenty-first century, I wonder? It's well over ninety, that's for sure."

"Jeez, I reckon I'll be permanently in the pool in that case."

"Not with my daddy about you won't. No chance. Bloody slave-driver."

"Now then, Ty, no need for that."

"Leave him be, Jan, I am what he says, but if I wasn't he'd only sit on his arse all day."

Everyone, especially Ty, burst out laughing.

"I'm doing him a favour, really."

"Well, you're certainly doing me one, Pete. You all are," I said.

"No worries, mate. When my great-uncle, or whatever he bloody is, first rang me, I must admit I had my doubts. It's rough out here at times, no argument, and, no offence, his description of you was a mite worrying."

"No offence taken. I understand. I just want to repay you all for the chance you're giving me."

"You're repaying me already, Seth. It's all hell here this time of year, what with the shearing and that, and you're doing ok. Just don't give me another bloody heart attack by shaving them too close that's all. Some of the poor little bastards, they'll be shivering for a week."

I reddened, although no-one could tell because of the tan I was already getting.

"I struggled back home when I first had some Jacobs. Didn't get close enough that time. Sorry, Pete."

"Always assert yourself. Don't let them get on your wrong side, mate."

Maddy and Ty gave me sympathetic glances and Jan mildly rebuked her husband.

"Seth's still learning, Pete. You're being a bit harsh."

"Course I'm harsh. That's how I've got where I am. Can't afford to be soft."

"Pete's right, Jan, and, honestly, I'm pleased I got a bollocking. It made the other hands realise Pete's not giving me special treatment. I don't want that. I need to be accepted by them for who I am, not who I know."

"He's right, Ma," said Ty, "and it's worked. Even Billy sat up and took notice. You got a lot of respect today, Seth."

"Well thanks, Ty. That means a lot."

"If that shit Billy Holmes respects you then you must have done well," commented Maddy, as she again put her hand casually and comfortably onto mine.

"Billy's ok, Maddy, he just likes a fight. You know that," said Ty. "Now, Daddy, are you up for one or two of these?"

"Two. Need you ask?"

I was only just getting used to Ty calling his father 'Daddy'. At home Josh and I might have thought it unusual, but somehow in this situation Ty made it sound perfectly natural.

"How about you, Seth? Same?"

"Please, Ty."

I glanced over at Maddy who was now helping her brother by heaping salad onto the enormous plates. 'My Little Beaut', Pete called her. And he certainly wasn't wrong there.

It was late October. I'd been here for over three months now, but I was still confused by the change in seasons. When I had arrived in July Victoria was experiencing one of its wettest winters for decades. But this pleased Pete. It ensured all his waterholes would be filled to the maximum for his cattle and sheep. To hear them talking now of summer approaching, just before November, was very odd, but I was slowly beginning to adjust.

Spring of course was time for sheep shearing. It was an important and hectic period for Pete and his family. I was therefore pleased to have first had a couple of months or so to get used to my new situation. Not that I had that much time to draw breath. Maddy and Ty drove me here, there and everywhere, so proud to show off their country to me. Driving long distances was nothing to them and on many occasions I'd been taken out well into the evening on some jaunt or other. They were so friendly and full of energy and it soon rubbed off on me too.

Pete employed shearers on a short-term contract. They had to get through close on one hundred sheep a day. That was what he expected, and demanded. In my first week I had barely got as high as forty. Fortunately I was ranked as a trainee and apparently this wasn't such bad going, although Ty had warned me his daddy would never tell me that. Ty managed well over the hundred each day and his burnished, muscular frame was testimony to that. And I knew he could put it about. Just ask Billy Holmes!

Ty was a year or so older than me and his sister just twenty. I gathered from Maddy that their parents were in their fifties, but she tipped me off never to ask. They all had given me a great welcome, even though I could see, right from the off, Pete clearly had his doubts, as he had freely admitted. His first welcoming handshake had nearly crippled me and he had obviously enjoyed that. But I respected him and was prepared to work my butt off to prove myself. This didn't seem to go unnoticed and, consequently, when we were not working he almost seemed to treat me as one of his own.

Pete often wanted me to sit with him on the veranda late at night and hear about his 'Mother Country'. He had never been there, nor had he got much interest in travelling. He just liked to chat, to learn about England. Occasionally Jan would join us but Pete was, it had to be said, rather chauvinistic, and it wouldn't be long before he'd be suggesting to Jan she might like to go and knock us up a brew. He seemed to want those moments with me to himself. And such moments became special to me too, as time wore on. Perhaps it wouldn't be long, I found myself hoping, before I could enjoy some similar moments with his 'Little Beaut'.

Maddy's hand-holding meant nothing to her, I realised that. It was just natural friendliness, like a sister I guess. But her touch often enflamed me. As I have indicated already my shyness made me hopeless in women's company, and Maddy sometimes had a disturbing effect on me. I never could tell if she realised. She certainly didn't seem to. I was just a second brother. And, along with her real brother Ty, they became my constant companions that first fantastic year.

By the end of July I had accomplished so many extraordinary things and the last days of my stay with Pete and his family were a sad time for me. On my final night with them they threw a farewell party and, fortunately, the wind and rain held off. A lot of the ranch hands, together with their wives and girl-friends, were invited along to wish me well. It was a great opportunity for them to pull my leg yet again as, one by one, they brought out their various oft-told tales about my rawness and naivety.

"Hey, Ty, you remember that day in the bush you nearly shot Seth's arm off?"

Les, their most experienced hand, started it all off.

"I never saw a bloke shake so much in all my goddamn life."

The other lads joined in the laughter.

"First live snake I'd seen close-to, Les. Nearly filled my pants."

"I know you did, mate, I was there. Ty and I watched it slide up on yer. Big fellah he was."

"You mean, you saw it and didn't warn me?"

"If you'd moved, boy, he would have got a little narked. Ty here always had him covered. Top shot our Ty. Although he had drunk a few tinnies that evening. Might have missed I suppose."

Everyone chuckled again.

"I don't know what was worse, discovering him next to me or eating him for supper."

"Yeah, well, I told Mac he'd undercooked it. Always ruins decent grub, don't you, Mac?"

Ty shouted over to a massive Scot who had been with us on that particular round-up.

"Och, the bloody thing was that thick. I canna always work miracles, you know."

"Yeah, well just once would be nice," said Les.

I got some brief respite while everyone turned their attention to ribbing Mac about all his ill-fated culinary episodes.

I glanced across to the house and noticed Maddy was alone on the veranda, gently rocking in her daddy's chair.

She caught my eye and beckoned me over.

"Do you fancy a ride out to Caley's Creek, Seth?"

"It's a great idea, but won't it look rude of me? They've all come on my account."

"No worries. They'll enjoy themselves whether you're here or not. Come on, we won't be that long anyway."

We saddled up our respective horses. Pete had let me ride a beautiful five year old colt from the day I had arrived. He had a white blaze and two white socks on his forelegs. Boy, could he fly. Like the wind he was, and would have made my dear old fellah back home look only fit for the knacker's yard. Maddy chose the younger of her two greys.

"Come on, gel, hup, hup, hup," and Maddy was away.

My mount needed no such encouragement and flew off in hot pursuit, very soon overtaking with ease. It was a bright winter's evening and the full moon helped us reach the creek in no time at all.

We dismounted, tied up the horses and found my favourite spot - a gnarled eucalyptus tree stump that conveniently provided sheltered seating for two, although this was the first time I'd been here with anyone.

"You like it here, don't you?"

"I like it all, Maddy. I'm sorry to be going, but I have to abide by my grandpa's wishes. I owe him so much."

"We've loved having you. Even Daddy. Never known him so sociable till you turned up."

"He's been good to me, Maddy. Helped me look at life in a different way. I was a bit scared of him at first though I must admit."

"Yeah, well, we've all been that over the years. Has to have things all his own way. Always the boss. We never dare cross him, even Ty, although he could clock him into the middle of next week if he had a mind to it. I've seen Daddy reduce him to tears many a time."

"And what about you, Maddy? You seem to be the

apple of his eye."

"That's true to a point. But he'll make sure he gets his own way with me too, don't you worry."

"What do you mean?"

She looked away and I could see her black eyes glistening in the half-light. I gently took her by the hand.

"Maddy, whatever is it? You can tell me."

Her look turned fierce.

"You know our neighbours, the Charltons?"

I nodded.

"Well, Daddy wants to go into business with them and get hold of even more thousands of acres. I'm part of the deal apparently."

"You're what?"

"Oh, Mum and Daddy have always assumed Harry Charlton and me will eventually get hitched. Suddenly, Daddy's applying pressure. Old man Charlton's hanging his boots up and Daddy sees this as his chance to totally rule the roost round here."

"You mean an arranged marriage? In this day and age?"

"No, Seth, it's not exactly that, but Daddy will get his way, no doubt. Always does."

"But it's not right, Maddy."

"Yeah, well, try telling Daddy that."

"And this Harry, do you, well, do you have feelings for him?"

"I do, yeah, but I'm just not sure I'm ready for the whole marriage thing. Mum hinted again last night and I lost it a bit with her."

"Then you mustn't let them persuade you, Maddy. I can't hear of you being bartered like this."

"Oh, Seth, you're so sweet," she said, taking my hand in hers. "My big English brother taking care of me. How I shall miss you being around."

My heart sank. So it was just fraternal feelings she

had for me after all. 'So sweet'. Story of my life.

Maddy kissed me lightly on the cheek and jumped up. "Beat you back."

And I let her win. I'd lost all interest in racing and partying, but I managed to go round saying cheerful goodbyes to all the boys before turning in for my last night at this amazing place. Despite not really wanting to leave them all I vowed to be positive and prepared myself for the next stage of my adventure. And it did actually turn out to be a very different experience.

*

Marnie had lost her husband three or four years ago and her sister Lil had lost her marbles.

That's how Ty began preparing me on the journey to their fruit farm which was a short distance from Melbourne. He referred to his aunts fondly however and assured me I would get along, despite Lil's problems.

"You just have to be ready for her to say outrageous things, mate. You'll get used to it. Oh, and she cackles a bit."

Ty explained that Marnie's husband, Blue, had run the place for forty-odd years and never did retire.

"Obstinate old bugger. Always refused to take on help and ended up collapsing amongst his blueberries one day. Heart attack, just like that. Marnie then employed a couple of blokes to run the place and they've been about ever since. They've got a cushy number, those two. Decent enough old fellahs, but lazy. Wouldn't last five minutes with my daddy. But Marnie ain't bothered. Never really been interested and likes their company I guess. Don't blame her at her age. She's over seventy. Besides, her older sister got ill a couple of years back, obviously couldn't look after herself, so Marnie moved Lil in with her."

"So who will I take my orders from?"

"Doubt there'll be any, mate. If I were you I'd case the joint for a bit, see what needs improving, then take the bull by the horns. The place needs sorting out. Potential there, but it's gone to rack and ruin. Blue would turn in his grave."

"Blue, that wasn't his real name I assume?"

"That's all I ever knew him as."

Ty turned off the highway a few miles before the outskirts of the city and drove his jeep down a narrow driveway.

"Here we are, Seth. This is 'Kookaburra'."

"Why 'Kookaburra'?" I asked.

"When Blue found the place it was renowned for all the birdlife. Sadly he didn't do some of them a favour, what with his pesticides and that. But there are still a few kookaburras about. The 'Laughing', you'll hear quite a lot of them. Always sound like they're taking the juice. The smaller 'Blue Winged' are a bit rare now. They make piercing noises like maniacs, so that's no loss. Bit like poor old Lil I guess."

Marnie was on the porch ready to receive us. She greeted me warmly and I could smell lunch on the go as she led me into her bungalow.

"You'll stay to eat with us, Ty? I've knocked up plenty of stew."

"Sorry, Marnie, love to, but Daddy wants me back pronto."

"Ah, that father of yours. Gives you all no time to breathe. I always tell him, that's how my Blue went, forever pushing himself. But of course what do we women know, eh, Seth?"

Marnie gave me a mischievous wink.

I smiled. I already sensed I was going to get on well with this lady.

"I must say Bill's description of you don't seem that

accurate. Bit puny, he said, in need of plenty of my home cooking. But look at you."

Marnie playfully squeezed my arm muscles.

"Plenty for a young Sheila to get hold of there and no mistake."

I blushed but took it in good part.

"To be fair, Grandpa was right a year ago."

"Yeah," agreed Ty, "we soon sheared his golden locks off, tanned him up and got him into shape."

"I've told you before, Marnie, never show tradesmen into your front parlour."

We had company.

"Lil, these aren't tradesmen. You know Ty here. Pete's boy."

"Just leave the carpet in the shack. We're not paying you to lay it as well."

Ty and I exchanged glances and I was mighty glad he had given me good warning. I did as he suggested and took the bull by the horn.

"I'm Seth, from England. Bill Tompkins is my Grandpa. I'm very pleased to meet you, Lil."

"Blimey, Marnie, did you hear that? This carpet's come all the way from England. You must give him some stew after such a long journey."

Ty and I did our best to keep composed.

"It's all sorted, Lil," said Marnie, as she guided her out of the room. "Seth will be staying to lunch. In fact he'll be staying a long while. But Ty has to get home."

"Oh good. I like that blonde fellah. The other one looks shifty though. Heh, heh, heh!"

Once they'd left the room Ty and I burst out laughing.

"See what I mean about the cackle? Anyway, you've made a good first impression, mate. No surprises there."

"Thanks, Shifty!"

We locked arms and said our goodbyes.

"You may see me on the odd occasion, mate, although

Daddy don't let me away for long, as you know. I'll probably have some more carpet to deliver in a few months!"

We both chuckled and he went on his way, while I looked forward to Marnie's cooking.

I was given basic but comfortable lodgings in a separate annex beyond their bungalow. It was effectively a bed-sit with a shower room and was more than adequate. A wood burner ensured I would never be cold, and it certainly could turn very chilly this time of year.

After lunch Marnie introduced me to her two hands and left me to get to know them and my new surroundings. In fact over the next few weeks I had a good deal of time to myself and this enabled me to give the place a thorough investigation in order to see if I could come up with some ideas on how to improve things. There was a lot of potential and I just needed some time with Marnie to discuss my thoughts. I didn't want to tread on anyone's toes and of course I had no idea what money, if any, was available. But I definitely couldn't see myself just sitting around doing very little, which, as Ty had suggested, was what everyone else seemed to do.

I got my opportunity one lunch-time several weeks later when Marnie had prepared a pot roast for Lil and me, and had also invited Buck to join us. Buck was in his late sixties I guess and obviously provided Marnie with occasional company and conversation. He lived just a couple of miles away and rolled up every morning - never that early - in a beaten-up Toyota truck. He was a retired farrier, a bachelor all his life and lived with his sister Yvonne in a similar dwelling, so this was home from home really (although Yvonne certainly didn't have Lil's problems). Marnie's other hand, Herbie, wasn't invited and I remarked on this as we sat down.

"Herbie won't be joining us then?"

"Never does, Seth. I always used to try and persuade him but he's never been able to eat like this. His aboriginal blood is pretty strong and he finds being contained in four walls like this difficult. Gets claustrophobia I think. So, much as I'd like him with us, I don't bother even trying anymore."

It made sense to me. I myself had tried to engage Herbie in conversation but he seemed to withdraw into himself. He actually resided about a couple of hundred metres from my quarters in a very ragged old tent that flapped about in the wind, on the odd occasion making it difficult for me to sleep. One night I got up and wandered outside. I glanced across to his tent and he was sitting with his back to me, crossed-legged on the damp soil smoking a clay pipe, then murmuring, apparently oblivious of everything going on around him. I could sense he was in a very different place so I respected that and returned to my bed.

"Herbie's someone you need a lot of time to get to know," said Buck. "Even now, having knocked around with him for a few years, I know nothing about him really. But he's harmless. He helps me with fruit deliveries to the city, and just keeps himself to himself the rest of the time."

"So you don't know anything about his family then?" I asked.

"Nope, nothing. What I do know though is that he holds this deep-rooted resentment about the downfall of his race and how he, and many other aborigines, feel the likes of us have usurped their sacred land over time and abused it."

"But he's happy to work here," I offered.

"Yeah, sure, and I've said that. But I think he sees Marnie's place as about the only sort of situation where he can work now. You see, none of us bother him. We let him approach us if he needs anything and we all tick along that way. There's not an ounce of malice in his body, Seth, but get him on the booze - which I don't let happen anymore - and all the bitterness comes out."

"They never can take the drink," said Marnie, "and it seems to affect them worse than most."

"Lazy bastards, all of them."

"Now, Lil, enough of that. They're just different, that's all," replied Marnie.

I had noticed before that her sister bristled at the mention of Herbie and often resorted to some pretty vitriolic language about them.

"You're too soft with him. Soft as shit."

"Well he's not the only one I'm soft with, is he? Now, I've made your favourite for afters, rice pudding, so pass your plate and I'll clear this lot up first."

"Here, I'll help you, Marnie."

"Thanks, Seth. Buck here can entertain Lil for a few moments."

"He's going to lay my new carpet for me, aren't you, darlin?"

"You mean the one Seth brought from England?"

Buck gave me a knowing wink.

"It's Axminster you know."

I gave Lil a sympathetic smile. I found it hard to join in any mickey-taking and Lil's outbursts troubled me at times. But I was gradually getting used to them. Later, as we finished our dessert, I took the chance to begin airing some ideas I had.

"Marnie, erm, well, I've been thinking."

"Spit it out then, Seth, I'm all ears. Got some ideas for the place I hope? I reckon it certainly needs a little spring-clean."

This encouraged me and I returned to the table.

"I don't want to make any suggestions out of turn but my grandpa hasn't sent me from England to, well....."

"Sit on your arse," interrupted Marnie.

Lil cackled and Buck smiled at Marnie.

"As you say, Marnie."

I smiled at her too.

"Come on, out with it, for goodness sake, Seth. I realise you're here to work and learn, so I can take advantage of that and get this place sorted a bit, with your help. But don't expect any of us to change our ways. None of us has got your strength and energy. So you just tell us your ideas, you do the work, and I'll find the money for everything. Blue left me loaded."

Very encouraged now I enthusiastically put forward my proposals. Ironically enough Buck was very supportive, despite my previous concerns, and actually seemed pleased to have someone like me coming up with fresh thoughts. I needn't have worried about stepping on anyone's toes as it happened.

Once I had briefly outlined my ideas to Marnie she left me to go into greater detail with Buck, having to attend to Lil who needed her. When she returned it was even more positive.

"Seth, just you draw up a list of what you need and I'll organise the money. Do it as soon as you like. It'll be great to see the place smartened up. My Blue would be delighted."

Fundamentally my plans were simply to update what Blue had begun to put in place all those years ago, and Buck was helpful. He undertook to show me how to hard-prune all the fruit trees and bushes that surrounded the small estate and had been ignored for so long; he also agreed that the blueberries could benefit from a change of location to a sunnier spot, and one that was wetter. Buck listened with genuine interest to my plans for the strawberries, but he clearly had few thoughts to offer himself because the growing method I talked about was rather foreign to him.

Blue had in fact begun to install a hydroponic system

of cultivating strawberries and even virtually sorted out the irrigation, so all I had to do was source the best possible plants and set them. Strawberries for Christmas! One of those strange situations I was now beginning to get used to.

*

Late winter and spring saw me putting my theories into practice and, on the whole, everything worked well, especially the strawberries. The blueberries seemed to benefit from being moved but only the taller varieties really flourished whilst some dwarf types that I tried were disappointing.

Come summer we were able to employ casual pickers and we bought a bigger and more suitable delivery truck which I drove daily to the city during the strawberry-picking season. These trips also enabled me to spend some time as a tourist. Unlike Pete, Marnie was most insistent that I took plenty of opportunity to see as much of the country as I could. So much so that, one hot evening in the New Year, she knocked on my door and invited me up to the bungalow for drinks.

"Haven't had a chance to thank you, Seth, for all your ideas and hard work," she said, passing me a can of cool beer.

"I've enjoyed it, Marnie, and believe me, it's not been such hard work. Compared to Pete's place this has been a holiday."

"Well, I'm pleased to hear it. Life's for living. I tried telling my Blue that. He wasn't quite as bad as Pete, but not far off. I just wish he was still here to enjoy my twilight with, but instead I'm stuck with....."

She paused and realised she probably ought not to say any more.

"Lil's pretty bad I guess, Marnie?"

"More than anyone else knows. And I'm not going to complain about her. It's not her fault. But she is bloody hard work and no mistake. I'm not really cut out for all this nursemaid stuff and the doc told me last week she's getting much worse and will soon need twenty-four hour care."

"Can you get her into a home?"

"Oh that's not a problem. I'll pay whatever it takes. But when I tentatively talked to her about it the other day she told me to eff off. It's going to be difficult but I know it's gotta be done, and soon."

"I don't know how I can help, but I will of course if I can."

"Thanks, Seth, you're a good man. But Buck helps me through really bad days."

She paused again.

"He, er, he's asked me to marry him. Can you believe that?"

"Why, Marnie, what a turn-up for the books! That's great, isn't it?"

"Yes and no."

"What do you mean?"

"Seth, it's good of the old bugger to offer but I'm too old in the tooth. And so is he. I mean, imagine me walking up the aisle at my age. Bloody laughing stock. Anyway there's only ever been one for me. My Blue was that special. No, I shall refuse Buck."

"What a shame."

"I shall tell him he can come and warm my sheets up for me sometimes though!"

We both burst out laughing and grabbed another tinnie.

"Now then, I nearly forgot," added Marnie. "What are you like underneath a car bonnet?"

"Pretty good really. I've worked on and driven all types of vehicles back home."

"Great, because I want you to renovate that old campervan in the garage. I'll pay for all the parts you need. Before summer is out I'd like you to have the chance to go off in it and tour for a bit. You've seen plenty of Melbourne, but you need to perhaps take off to more distant parts for a while, now things are quietening down."

"But how will you cope?"

"Same as we've always done. And anyway Buck's got second wind since he helped you implement your ideas. Got a bloody glint in his eye too. I'm going to have to hold on to my pants I think!"

I laughed with her again.

"Marnie, I'm sure I can repair it and have it running like new. I'd be delighted to do it and thank you for the offer of time off. I won't abuse your generosity though. I'll just take a couple of weeks."

"See how long the VW takes, then shoot off for a month, Seth. I can fend off Buck's amorous advances for that long."

She gave me a saucy wink.

"Well, let's see how I get on, shall we? I must say I want to travel the Great Ocean Road, as far as the Twelve Apostles at least."

"Do that. And this time of year Port Campbell's full of young guys like you. Plenty of pretty young Sheilas too. You should get yourself a hot-blooded Australian girl, Seth. Do you wonders. Strapping guy like you. Can't understand you not having a girl back home. You're not bloody bent I hope?"

I laughed and assured her I was perfectly normal, and we completed our evening in comfortable silence, until.....

"Marnie, where the hell are you? Marnie, come here. I've shit myself."

Poor Marnie dragged herself out of her chair to go and

tend to Lil. Turning round at the door she said:

"Seth, I really can't take this much longer. I just can't....."

She wiped away tears of frustration and went to mop up poor old Lil.

*

I had the campervan singing a fine tune by the end of January and, to my surprise, help had come from an unexpected source in the shape of Herbie. Apparently he'd got his name from mechanics at a garage he cleaned up at for a short while before coming to Marnie's. The garage specialised in VWs and Herbie picked up a fair bit of knowledge, even being allowed to work on an old Beetle near the end of his stay. He couldn't take the environment for very long though. The noise and commotion offended his deep spiritual nature. But he seemed to quite enjoy helping me and I appreciated his occasional tips and his spare pair of hands.

On what was to be the final day working on the vehicle I invited him to share some of Marnie's homemade lemonade in the middle of the morning. Up until then he'd always refused, going off instead to sip some water from his carrier. But this time he relented and shyly squatted down near me as I finished giving the VW a coat of wax polish and then got up to fetch our drinks.

As we drank I struggled to think what to talk about. I gazed towards the blueberries, set now in front of a fir spinney.

"It's wonderful here, Herbie, isn't it?"

There was no response. He stared out into the distance, his eyes vacant.

"I shall miss it all come winter. But my grandpa insists I move on again and I need to respect that."

Still nothing. Herbie just sat there, remarkably still

and upright. Then, at last, a response.

"It is not as it should be. Stolen goods, damaged beyond repair."

I had no idea what to say in reply. I knew exactly what he was getting at of course but any further words from me would be superfluous. It ran bitterly deep with him.

"One day my forefathers will be avenged."

A chill ran through me, despite the intense heat. Then, without warning, and to my relief, his mood lightened.

"But you, Seth, you are a kind friend. I thank you and will not forget you."

Before I could say or do anything he was on his feet and walking to his tent. I sensed it best to leave it all there. And I hoped he would one day find his real home.

*

I was away for the whole of February and returned in March to pitch into the apple harvest. Again casual pickers were on site and it was well into April before everything was into cold store.

As autumn led into winter it was again time for me to start thinking about the next, final leg of my adventure. In July I would be off to work for another of Bill's contacts, near Yering, on a thriving vineyard and winery in the Yarra Valley.

"It's beautiful there, Seth, you'll love it," said Marnie, on one of my last days with her. "Might even pop out and see you myself."

"Please do that, Marnie. Bring Buck here as well."

"No bloody fear. I shall need a rest from him, that's for sure."

We both laughed and Buck smiled.

"Can't help myself, Marnie, you're such a beaut."

"Oh, will you listen to him? Old charmer."

"Well, at least you won't have to worry about Lil," I said.

"No, and that is a relief. Didn't even recognise me on my last visit, so I have to accept she's in the right place. It's no use feeling guilty. I did what I could when I could."

This was typically matter-of-fact from Marnie but my mind had wandered ever since Buck had called her a 'beaut'. It reminded me of Maddy of course and I already thought about her quite enough. It had been just over a year since we had taken that ride to Caley's Creek and, despite her often being in my thoughts, I had resisted writing or calling in. I sensed it was not the time or place. Nor did I anticipate contacting her in the coming year either. From what Marnie had told me I was in for a pretty hectic time. And she certainly wasn't wrong.

*

My last port of call was, as Marnie had said, set in a simply beautiful environment, north-east of Melbourne. My new hosts were actually not related to me, even distantly, but had been recommended by Pete to Grandpa Bill. Ritchie and Marilyn Hall were in their fifties, and childless. All their energies had been devoted to expanding their thriving vineyard, located quite near to the famous Yering Station in the Yarra Valley, at Yarra Ridge. They were very good at what they did and had keen business minds, the pair of them. For all that they also seemed to be hospitable, although neither of them was particularly warm-natured in the way that Marnie had been. Brisk is how I'd sum them up, I guess. Brisk, but not necessarily brusque. At least, not all the time.

The set-up was very commercial and I benefited from being allocated a richly-appointed bungalow apartment overlooking the valley. This was one of six dwellings they would eventually be letting out to tourists, the other five being in the course of construction on my arrival. A real holiday setting maybe, but I knew, straight away, I would be required to work long hours again. As I've always said this never bothered me and I soon got back into the swing of things. Marnie had been overly generous to me really. This had included the parting gift of the campervan, which pleased me no end.

On my second evening Ritchie and Marilyn invited me into their luxurious ranch-house which was tastefully furnished, oozing quality, along with everything else they seemed to handle. Over a sumptuous supper they set out my terms of reference in a business-like manner and I was left in no uncertain doubt as to what was expected of me. One aspect was a pleasant surprise though and would enable me to make a certain amount of use of my previous experience with farm animals in England.

"So, Seth, Pete tells me that, a couple of years ago, you got quite handy with sheep?"

"Well, of a fashion. I think I gave him some anxious moments to begin with though."

"That's as maybe, but he assures me I could use you this time of the year to look after my small flock."

"Oh, I didn't realise you had sheep."

"Only about two hundred and fifty, but they still need caring for and I sacked my shepherd about a month ago."

"Right, well, I'll certainly give it a go. Why did you have to sack him?"

"I think that's my business, don't you?"

"Sorry, yes, of course."

"No worries. Now shearing time is round the corner so, if I show you the ropes tomorrow, I'll expect you to manage them the rest of your stay here."

"Might even expand the operation if you're good at it," suggested Marilyn.

"Yeah, well, let's not run before we can walk, eh."

Ritchie put his point firmly.

"Will I also get to working in the vineyard and winery?"

"Blimey, yes. A few head of sheep won't keep you occupied for long. I've told our manager Biff Simpson to take you under his wing from the moment shearing's over. Biff will make sure you learn as much as possible about grapes and wine during your time here."

Marilyn really came into her own at this point.

"We're nowhere near the size of places like Yering, but fifty-plus acres of grapes are still a hell of a lot and we know the direction we want to go. The future is about red wine as far as we're concerned, and we have plans to tap into the tourist industry big-time."

She clearly relished what was obviously her PR role in the enterprise.

"Pass the spuds would you, love," said Ritchie.

He continued.

"Mari's right. We do grow a few white grapes, but when people like you look for Australian wine on your supermarket shelves in England, it's more often than not you go for a red from this area. Your first choice used to be French, but we're muscling in and gradually increasing our market share, believe me."

"You're right. The number of bottles of Australian red has gone up a lot back home in the last few years."

Underlining my comment I finished off another glass, appreciating its full-bodied taste and texture.

"I know I'm bloody right. We've been to your country. You can't make decisions sitting out here, mate. Mari and I are often hopping over to England and other important wine-consuming parts of Europe. You find your market and you make sure you produce the goods to supply that market. That's how we operate here."

"But it's not just about producing wine. We want to provide much more," added Marilyn. "When we've completed the other holiday apartments we'll also be offering package tours. We intend organising more wine festivals and guided tastings. That side of the business only began to take off last year. We produced our best range of reds in ninety-one. That started bringing more than just the locals in."

"Yeah, with help from a young journalist we bumped into in London, Mari here produced a bloody fine brochure and catalogue, and soon your top-notch connoisseurs from all over were bombing in. We're looking at promoting helicopter flights this summer too. Some bloke we met in Sydney, he's a pilot and really up for it. So, Mari will be organising that soon."

"You certainly don't let the grass grow under your feet, either of you," I suggested.

"How old are you, Seth?"

Ritchie threw me for a moment.

"Er, thirty-one."

"Yeah, well, at your age I was going nowhere until I met this great girl here." He turned to Marilyn.

"Aw, now don't start to embarrass me, Rich."

"It's a fact. I met her, Seth, and for the next twenty or so years she has inspired me to work my butt off. This place was rack and ruin when we started on it. Now look at it."

"You have every right to be proud," I ventured.

"Have you got a woman, Seth?"

The inevitable question came from Marilyn.

"Not yet. Haven't found the right one I guess."

"Rich, we'll have to sort one out for him, won't we, love?"

"I'll leave that to you, Mari. You're the bloody matchmaker round here, not me."

"Well, I was thinking about that journalist you just mentioned, Clare MacIntyre. She's due here again in about a month on one of her whistle-stop trips. She'll be editing my notes for this year's article in 'Wine Today' magazine. Suitable for Seth, you reckon?"

"I'll say. She'll have the shirt off your back before you know where you are, that's for sure."

He smiled and supped more wine.

"Rich, no need for that, even if it is true!"

Mari giggled, showing me, for the first time, a more human side.

"I shall look forward to her arrival," I said, "but first I've got your sheep to shear, so it's just as well she's not arriving yet. Sounds like I shall need all the strength I've got."

The intoxicating red was clearly beginning to have some effect.

Ritchie and Marilyn both chuckled again and I was relieved they could actually relax a bit. I had begun to think I wasn't going to have much fun but this Clare sounded like good news, although of course I knew I would be nervous as a kitten in her company.

*

"Seth, this is Clare MacIntyre. Clare, meet Seth. He's shadowing our manager Biff for a few months or so."

"Lucky you. Hi, Seth. And you're from England I gather?"

"That's right. Brighton. Well, nearby."

"Hey, my boy friend Mitch hails from Lewes. Not that far away."

"Yeah, pretty close. And you?"

"Well, my name suggests I'm a diehard Scot but I'm sure you will have already picked up my private English education," she laughed. "I'm a Londoner really."

It was an attractive laugh and she was certainly a very attractive woman. About my age. Quite tall, slim, brunette, with deep brown eyes that set off her finely-chiselled facial features. Very, very good looking, with an infectious smile and a knowing presence. Oh yes, she was streetwise, and did indeed make me more than a little nervous. Pity about the boy friend, but best to know straight away I suppose.

"So, how long are you here for?"

"Sadly, Clare can only stop over the one night," said Marilyn. "She flies up to the Gold Coast late tomorrow to join Mitch at his brother's wedding."

"Yep, then it's a couple of days break before I return to London. My boss gives me little time to breathe these days I'm afraid. Sorry, Mari, but, knowing you, the article's all ready to hit the high street anyway."

"Well, possibly, but you know I value your input and I had actually hoped to enjoy more of your time."

"I should have explained properly before I came out here. The days of being able to spend weeks at a time on lovely projects like yours may have gone altogether it seems, although I have had a pretty tempting offer from a leading broadsheet back home. They want someone to pen food and drink articles for their weekend magazine. Might be worth a change. We'll see."

"If it means I shall see more of you, so much the better," said Marilyn.

"Tell you what. I'll say I will only take the job if my first article can be about you and Rich!"

"Done!"

"We'd better get on then, hadn't we? Nice meeting you, Seth."

She held out a slender hand.

"Good to meet you too."

She seemed in no hurry to release her gentle handshake.

"Say hello to Sussex for me," I said, feeling slightly awkward.

"I'll do that."

As she walked off I vaguely caught her saying a couple of complimentary things to Marilyn about me, but I chose not to place any importance on them. Throwaway lines no doubt. Besides, there was this Mitch. Lucky fellah. Lucky fellah indeed.

*

My year flew by and, shadowing the manager, I learnt so much in a very short time. There seemed to be nothing Biff didn't know about the husbandry of such a place. Only when it came to sheep could I hold a candle to him. But, not surprisingly I suppose, Biff's days at Yarra Ridge were numbered. He was, over spring and summer, head-hunted by a major vineyard a hundred miles or so away and the wooing process was such that, by autumn, he'd made his mind up. Ritchie and Marilyn told me the news one April evening as we drank wine on their veranda.

"We can't blame him for taking the job," said Ritchie. "We're not small anymore and have big plans, but Biff is ready for an even greater challenge. He's got a wife and three kids so he's got to think of their future."

"When does he leave?" I asked.

"End of next month."

"And soon after that we shall lose you, Seth," added Marilyn.

"Yeah, the time's flown and I must admit I haven't given a thought to what I shall be doing when I get back to England."

"You don't have to go back, mate," said Ritchie.

"But I've got to start thinking about a career. Quite what I don't know. I certainly don't want to just go back and do what I used to. It seems a pretty unexciting backwards move really."

Marilyn gave Ritchie a long, hard look and, almost

imperceptibly, nodded.

"Then don't go back, Seth," continued Ritchie. "Stay here with us. I've got work for you, I've got plans."

"Stay here? Are you serious? What work could I do? What plans are you talking about?"

"Jeez, I haven't had so many questions thrown at me since I proposed to Mari here."

"For goodness sake tell him, Rich," said Marilyn.

"Seth, stay with us, be our new manager, help us expand our flock, and help us take our vineyard into the twenty-first century. Make this your home, Seth. It's what we'd like, isn't it, Mari?"

"Absolutely. And, as a bonus, I undertake to find you a wife."

We all laughed and I hung my head in disbelief at the astonishing offer I had just received. I simply could not believe my ears. In fact, I was close to tears.

"Are you sure I'd be up to it all, Ritchie?"

"No doubt in my mind whatsoever. You're a hard worker, Seth, intelligent, with vision. What's more, you're modest, and I like that in a guy. You let your body do the talking. Can't stand boastful bastards. You go away and think about it, Seth. I realise you have to consider many aspects, especially things back home."

"We won't rush you," said Marilyn.

"No, tomorrow morning will be fine," added Ritchie, smiling.

"Rich, you told me you'd give him a couple of weeks."

"Oh, did I? Well, there you go, Seth. Two weeks today, give me your answer."

He picked up an envelope from the table.

"Mari's drawn up a contract for you. Similar to Biff's really. But, in your case, we've included a section to cover expansion of the flock. The sheep side of things will be hived off and costed as a separate entity from now on. That's of course provided you accept our offer."

"It's an amazing offer, thank you, and I assure you I shall give it all my thinking time over the next fortnight. I've never actually been employed before. It's a strange feeling. I'm so grateful to you both for having such faith in a novice like me."

"You're no novice, mate, you're a natural. I honestly believe that. But don't let that go to your head. I'm a real bugger to work for, aren't I, Mari?"

"And to live with!"

"Did you hear that, Seth? So untrue. I'm a pussy cat with her!"

"Tiger, you mean."

And Marilyn's comment told me it was time to disappear. They clearly needed to be alone, and I definitely had a lot of quiet thinking to do.

*

I was certainly grateful to have two weeks to think everything through. Ritchie told me to suspend all my duties and simply concentrate on deliberating over his offer. The contract seemed very generous to me and I could easily have said yes straight away, but I had a lot of things to consider, and people to consider. So, I packed up a few things in the campervan and set off towards Warburton Trail. I didn't need to travel far, just find a tranquil spot to fish and think. I soon spotted just the place.

For two or three days I pondered, chewing over everything as I caught crayfish. I made a list of benefits and drawbacks. There was really only one of the latter - folks back home. The postal delays would grant me no time to receive any responses from England so I knew I had to get back to Yarra and make an expensive, but necessary, phone call.

In the event I needn't have worried. It did of course concern me that it might be many more years before I saw Dad, Josh and Jo again. But Grandpa had been right. All my experiences in this country had indeed made a man of me. I was so much stronger, physically and mentally. Yes, I missed them on many occasions, particularly Josh. But he and Jo were forging their own lives now, just as I was mine. I was very comfortable in my own skin (except of course in the company of attractive, single women!) and, from correspondence I had received over the three years, it was clear that Josh was thriving on being the kingpin of the smallholding. He seemed to be expanding slowly but surely, and even getting the odd contract from a small local mini-market chain. Jo had recently finished a music scholarship at Birmingham Conservatoire and was clearly destined to play cello for a living, in some shape or form. An offer from a national orchestra had already apparently been received. So they both seemed well set.

And Dad? Well, I had nothing but positive assurances from him on the telephone that all was well. Whether it was or not, no-one was going to say, so I had to believe it. Anyway, the long and the short of it was that he felt strongly I should snap up the opportunity. And, once Josh had said what amounted to the same thing, I guess my mind was virtually made up. But I still had three days to meet Ritchie's deadline and I took all that time, just to be absolutely sure. We were, after all, talking about my whole future.

In the end I took the job.

*

I found it all hard to take in during that first year or so. Little old Seth Rayner, just thirty two years old and already managing an exciting business for two people whose ambitions knew no bounds.

After about eighteen months I had substantially expanded the flock; taken on responsibility for hiring and firing shepherds, shearers and hands; led the erection of endless lengths of fencing; negotiated contracts with city abattoirs; and covered at the vineyard for Rich and Mari during their not infrequent trips away. It was relentlessly hard work and I had no time whatsoever to do anything else.

Eventually, on New Year's Day, 1996, I allowed myself the luxury of a day off. As I have indicated this was my first full day of doing absolutely nothing since I had taken the job on and I almost didn't know how to relax. Even on other holidays, or weekends, there was always so much to be done, but I set out from day one determined to repay Rich's faith in me. Besides I knew he expected nothing less. He and Mari paid me very well, I had virtually no expenses to worry about, and my energy levels were at their peak. So, it was non-stop work.

To my amazement the campervan started immediately on that first morning of the year and I set off for Kilda Beach. St Kilda was, to my mind, a sort of Bohemian centre, the promenade stretching for a mile or so and along all of it countless stall-holders peddling works of art, trinkets, junk, whatever you chose to call it. I found the place fascinating and spent the whole day browsing, interspersed between some swimming and sunbathing. The town had a reputation of course. It seemed to be a popular hang-out for the gay community for example. In the past this might have troubled me but my new-found strength of character and strong physical presence had helped me dispel any such uncomfortable feelings by now.

I was still very shy of the so-called weaker sex though and I found myself colouring up on the three occasions I was propositioned that day. I say 'propositioned', perhaps that's too strong, and it was just that I couldn't handle any flirtatious advances or comments. I definitely had a hang-up and I was quietly ashamed and embarrassed because I still had not experienced having a girl friend, let alone sleeping with a woman - much as part of me wanted to. It simply hadn't happened, despite Mari's occasional efforts on my behalf.

Deep down of course I knew the source of my problem. And on my return home I received some sad news that would make me have to confront it.

Mari knocked on my door virtually the moment I was back.

"Mari, hi. Come in. I've only just got back."

"Hi, Seth, meet any nice girls today?"

"Plenty, but, you know....."

"Oh, dear, what am I going to do with our shy Englishman?"

"Just write me off as a hopeless case and consign me to a life of bachelorhood I think. My brother's just the same apparently."

"That's not what I've understood. Right playboy you've said in the past."

"Sure, but he won't ever settle down, mark my words."

"Well, Seth, coincidentally I've been talking to Josh today."

"Blimey, my twin brother has phoned? Wonders will never cease."

"Yes, well, erm, he had some bad news I'm afraid, Seth."

My mind immediately thought of Dad.

"Bad news? Is it my dad?"

"No, it's your grandpa. It's about Bill."

"Oh, I see. What's the problem?"

"He died yesterday, Seth. I'm very sorry."

Mari put her hands on mine.

"On New Year's Eve?"

"I guess so, yeah. I'm never quite sure about the time difference."

I tried to take in the news and realised what a shock it was really. But I decided to be as positive as I could.

"Let's hope he went out on a high," I said, trying to be cheerful.

"Well, according to Josh, that was definitely the case. Heart attack after a huge celebration. Didn't know much about it from what I heard. Went out with a bang apparently. Josh particularly wanted you to know that."

"Good, that's good."

I paused and there was an awkward silence between us.

"Well, thanks for telling me, Mari. Now, if you don't mind, I think I'd just like time out to take all this in."

"Of course. Can I knock you up a snack? Rich and I are just about to eat."

"No, no, thank you. I don't feel like anything right now. I think I'll just open a tinnie and quietly toast a great bloke. He gave me so much you see."

"Seth, you've repaid him ten times over. I've never known anyone work as hard as you have this last year or so. Well, other than that old man of mine of course."

"I'm still an apprentice compared to Rich," I replied.

"No, you're wrong there. He needs to slow down a bit now. This news has shaken him a bit. You see, Rich has had one or two little warnings. I must make sure he doesn't go the same way."

With that Mari left me to myself.

I suppose that last comment surprised me a little, although I had actually noticed one or two small signs that perhaps the years were beginning to catch up on Rich. Anyway, it wasn't Rich I wanted to think about.

I settled into my hammock on the balcony and spoke

to the silent hills that were settling to slumber beyond our vineyard. I gave humble and heartfelt thanks for a man I knew was sitting there in the distance listening to me. In no way was I a religious person, but I had a certain belief that the spiritual presence of someone significant in one's life could remain with you beyond their allotted time on this earth. Yes, he was there alright, and I just knew he would always be about to give me the odd bit of guidance. This knowledge gave me strength to ride out the sadness I naturally felt. It also helped me decide not to dash off back to England for the funeral. Bill most definitely wanted me to remain here to continue the important work he had enabled me to embark upon.

My decision not to go was underlined the next day when Pete rang from Warnock. As I have already said I had avoided contact with Maddy since leaving them. I had kept in touch only very occasionally with Ty, and hardly at all with Pete. But it was good to hear his gruff tones on the end of the line after such a long while.

"Seth, you haven't been to see me you miserable bugger."

A typical opener.

"Well, Pete, you know how it is. Never a minute I'm afraid. Working for you Aussies is bloody hard work."

"Thought perhaps we weren't good enough for you now. Vineyard manager. Blimey, you certainly landed on your feet, mate."

"I like to think I've earned it," I replied, determined to give as good as I always got from him.

"Don't doubt that, cobber, don't doubt it for one minute."

Well, well, seemed as though I had won that little contest anyway.

"Look, Seth, I just rang to say sorry about your grandpa. He was alright was Bill. We all got to like him whenever he was over."

"Thanks, Pete. I owe him a lot of course."

"Yeah, well, as I've always said, you have to put in if you are going to get anything out of this life. You do seem to have earned it I must say. I don't think you owe him as much as you make out."

"Maybe, but he gave me a wonderful opportunity."

"Whatever. Now look, Jan and I want to invite you over this Friday. It's your grandpa's funeral that day we've heard, and we'd all just like to take time out to remember him. Will you come? There's a bit of a celebration to be had as well, and we'd like to catch up with you anyway."

"Pete, that's really good of you. I'll think about that. Thank you."

"Jan's idea of course, not mine. I wouldn't have thought of it. We didn't know if you'd be flying back."

"No, it never seriously crossed my mind to be honest."

"Seems a bit pointless to me I must say. Don't think Bill would have thanked you for it. He'd want you staying here I reckon."

"I reckon."

I was briefly wondering what the celebration might be about, but didn't have any chance to dwell on it.

"Good, so we'll see you about, what, seven or eight? Ty will be doing one of his barbies."

As I recalled with Pete there was no further debate to be had. I would be going, because he'd made his mind up. Anyway it would seem churlish to refuse such a decent gesture.

"Sure, Pete. See you Friday. Thanks again."

"No worries."

And that was that. I guess this all meant I would see Maddy again, but then I would simply have to do my best to deal with it.

*

"Right, everyone, let's have your attention."

Pete was ready for one of his little family speeches.

"In England about now dear old Bill Tompkins is being laid to rest. We obviously can't be with him and," turning to me, "I know there's one of us would certainly wish he could be. But Seth here has gotten himself an Australian streak of practicality over these last few years and hasn't flown home, so I invited him to join us today in remembering a good Pom - if there is such a thing....."

"Now, Pete," Jan interjected, "there's also one right next to you," pointing to me.

"Oh, yeah, clean forgot."

Pete smiled and punched my arm. I didn't flinch.

"You've toughened up, boy. Now, where was I?"

"Rambling as usual, Daddy," said Ty, laughing.

"Yeah, well, I'm allowed at my age. Now, Seth, I thought you might like a word about dear old Bill before we stand silent for a bit."

"Thanks, Pete. I guess I would."

I paused to gather my thoughts. As I did so I looked round the little gathering: Pete, Jan, Ty and Maddy of course, plus some old friends of theirs I recognised. Then there was a small group of folk I couldn't place. I cleared my throat.

"I have come to realise that you don't have to necessarily know someone a very long time for them to become important to you. For example I only met you all about four and a half years ago and you immediately became like family. Thanks for that."

I hesitated again, not wanting to say too much yet hoping to find the right words.

"Some of you won't know that I actually only knew Bill for about a year before I came out here and met you. Yet in a very short time my grandpa changed my whole life - and for the better. So please join me in a short moment of silence to honour this very special and generous man. A man I shall never forget."

After a couple of very special quiet minutes, Pete spoke again.

"Thanks, mate. Now, everyone, we're also here for another very important reason."

He turned to Maddy who was standing next to a stocky, rugged guy.

"My lovely daughter here has, after a lot too many years, finally agreed to become Mrs Charlton."

I gasped, but no one heard. They were all cheering and hollering. I tried to look as though I was joining in, but felt wretched.

"It's not before bloody time, so, girls and boys, raise your glasses to Maddy and Harry."

"Maddy and Harry....."

An hour or so later I found myself on the veranda with Ty. We caught up a bit over a beer or two.

"Another tinnie, mate?"

"No thanks, Ty, I think I'll be getting back."

"Young lady to see?"

He nudged me knowingly and winked.

"No, no, just a lot to do early in the morning."

"Well, great to see you, mate. You might not have a Sheila lined up but I have, so I need to be off myself."

We bear-hugged and he sauntered off whistling cheerfully, just as Maddy came out from the kitchen.

"He seems full of beans," I said to her.

"Yeah, Ty's met a girl from Tasmania. Potty about her."

"And you, Maddy? Are you happy too?"

There was silence.

"Maddy?"

"Yeah, I guess."

"That's a bit subdued for someone who's just got

engaged. You don't seem too sure."

"I'm fine. Really. Just fine."

Maddy turned away slightly and I cautiously felt for her hand. She faced towards me again, her proud features smouldering as she slowly, but firmly, removed her hand.

"How dare you."

"Whatever do you mean?"

"How dare you pretend to care after all this time."

"But, Maddy, it's not pretence, I....."

"Three and a half years. Three and a half years I've waited. No letters, no calls, no visits. Now you think you can just drop right back in at the drop of a hat."

"Maddy, I wanted to see you, believe me, I really did....."

"Jeez, you've only been down the road. It would have taken no effort. But I obviously wasn't worth it. We weren't worth it."

"Maddy, listen....."

"No, Seth, you listen. You were the first man I ever really trusted. We were friends, very good friends, or so I thought. I confided in you for God's sake. You seemed to care about me, yet you just left me to become a bargaining tool for my dad, leaving me no one to turn to. Mum wouldn't even support me."

"Maddy, you can still say no to all this. I told you that before. Your life's in your own hands. Just go out and do what you want, not what your parents decide."

"Oh, yeah. Go out and do what? No, just like my mum before me, I know my place. And at this place it's a man's world. Always has been, always will be. You're alright. Look at you, sitting pretty, doing what you want. But then, you're a man. Men can do what they bloody well like."

She got up to go.

"Wait, please. Maddy, you're so wrong about me. You don't know how much I've been thinking about you all this time."

"Save it, Seth. You're too late. I can't trust you anymore, so don't waste your breath. I really don't want to see you again. Do you hear?"

She began flouncing off, stopped, turned around, and finally spat out:

"But that won't bother you, will it?"

I was left staring into the gathering gloom, utterly devastated. Yet again my pitiful lack of experience with women had let me down in a big way. I simply had no understanding of where Maddy was coming from.

When I got back home I sat out all night in a stupor, vacantly staring out towards those hills again. Sleep deserted me. I hoped Grandpa hadn't.

*

And he hadn't. It took me a while but I eventually pulled myself round and got back to doing what I did best. The next few months were a busy time at the vineyard and I tirelessly threw myself into my work.

On a wet, cold day in August I was more than assured Grandpa hadn't deserted me. Quite the opposite. Completely out of the blue a very formal thick piece of correspondence arrived for me from a solicitor in London. I was shaking as I read its contents and couldn't concentrate on my work for well over a week.

I knew my grandpa was wealthy of course, but just how wealthy bowled me over the morning I opened that letter. Bill had left Josh, Jo and me huge amounts of money. No conditions attached, other than the fervent hope we would all invest it wisely in our different future careers. I was dumbfounded and immediately delegated my jobs for the day before riding out to the Valley to try and digest it all.

I tethered my horse and walked up to the brow of

Doone Hill. The rain had desisted and a gentle warmth had actually settled by midday, so I simply spent the rest of the day in a trance, walking, riding, gazing and talking. Yes, talking. To Grandpa. Somehow I sensed he was there and I was able to thank him.

I honestly had never in my life given much thought to money. I'd never really struggled so I realised I was infinitely fortunate, but that was about it really. It had never bothered me at all. Now I just felt completely stunned. The sum of money we each had been bequeathed doesn't actually matter, but I reckoned it would be enough for me to buy my own ranch one day, and all that I desired to go with it - well, nearly all, but then she was way beyond reach now of course.

I returned home to be told by Rich that first Josh, and then Jo, had been trying to contact me. No surprises there. Eventually I managed to speak to them both and we were all agreed that it was too much to take in and each of us would be taking plenty of time to think through the immense implications of Bill's amazing gifts. Josh had some initial hare-brained idea of buying a racehorse and seeing his colours win the Derby, and I teased Jo she could now go to America and run for President (she was always writing to me about her disgust at the current incumbent's foreign policies). As it happened neither Josh's thoughts nor my teasing of Jo turned out to be that wide of the mark.

*

"So what do you say, Seth? Are you up for it then?"

"Well, I'm really not sure, Clare. It's not me."

"Oh, come on. I won't take up much of your time and it'll be great for Rich and Mari. Give their vineyard a real shot in the arm. My new journal has a huge following."

"Why does it have to be centred on me?"

"It's just a different and more interesting slant on what might otherwise be a pretty routine article about yet another thriving vineyard in this area. Be a sport, Seth. Please agree to it, if only for your bosses. They've worked hard and deserve good media coverage at this time. Say you will."

"Oh, go on then."

"Brilliant!"

"But I know I'll live to regret it. I prefer to hide my light under a bushel to be honest."

"It'll be sensational, trust me."

"Yeah, I think that's what I'm worried about."

We both laughed.

"I can arrive tomorrow evening and we can start work the next day. Then I'll set up a photo-shoot for, let's say, a week's time."

"That sounds ok. Meanwhile I'll delegate a few jobs so I can give you about an hour each day."

"An hour! You'll have to do a lot better than that. Now you've agreed I shall be wanting you full-time on this."

"Oh, come on! Surely not?"

"My sort of work is just as demanding as yours you know. It may not be physical but there's so much to get through before we can produce the finished piece. And it's going to be massive. You really won't regret the time spent. It'll be well worth it I assure you."

"Put like that, how can I refuse?"

"You can't, this call's been recorded. Bye."

"Until tomorrow then....."

I was going to say more but then realised she'd hung up.

It was late January 97 and, yes, Clare MacIntyre was back in the country. Her love for Australia's more reliable weather had finally seduced her and brought her permanently to Melbourne where she had landed a high-profile job with the 'Herald' Group as Editor of their monthly consumer magazine. The post with a London broadsheet had proved too restricting for her and lasted only months. The move to Melbourne had also been triggered by the breakdown of her relationship with Mitch.

Clare had always promised Mari she would do whatever she could to promote 'Wine World' - the new name of our vineyard - as much as she possibly could. I wasn't that comfortable about being so prominent but it was actually quite trendy to cover businesses by focusing on a leading figure within an organisation. So, for Mari's sake really, I agreed. Rich's health had been a bit up and down lately and this gave her something else to think about. I felt I could hardly refuse.

The next evening Mari prepared a lovely shellfish pasta for supper and we all washed it down with plenty of beer. I was surprisingly relaxed and found myself almost at ease with Clare. She looked wonderful in a very attractive pale pink dress that showed off her tanned figure to perfection.

I was pleased to see Rich more himself and apparently the medication he was on for his angina promised to have a good effect. But he was closely monitored by Mari and it wasn't too long before she hinted we should call it a day.

"Can I help with the dishes, Mari?"

"No, Clare, wouldn't dream of it. I'll just load them into the washer I think, thank you."

"Well, in that case, Seth, why don't we go up to your apartment and start taking notes?"

"Yeah, sure. I've got to co-operate eventually, so now's as good a time as any I suppose."

Clare and I rose from the table and bid Rich and Mari goodnight. We wandered to my lodge and I fixed some more drinks while Clare draped herself over one of the veranda loungers.

"God, it's so beautifully hot," she murmured as I put her glass down.

She stretched out and turned towards me, offering me her hands to be pulled up. Her touch sent me into meltdown, and she knew it.

"I don't think we'll bother with notes tonight," she whispered, "and that drink can wait."

I was on fire as she began gently stroking my back.

"I need you, Seth....."

*

So, at the ripe old age of thirty-five, I finally broke my duck. And Clare was just what I needed. I had a lot of lost time to make up and she expertly dealt with my lack of experience.

I had a really amazing week, and when she returned to her Melbourne flat I went about my daily routine in a bit of a fog for some while. In time we settled into a cosy pattern, with me visiting her about once a month for a long weekend - eating out, theatre-going and making energetic love.

I started buying her gifts. In fact, to be absolutely truthful, I showered her with expensive presents. And, by the end of July - just six months later - I was convinced I wanted to spend the rest of my life with her. Clare was intoxicating and I have to admit that I had become rather a pushover.

As more time wore on and I gradually got to know Clare's friends and colleagues, I mysteriously found myself retreating again into my old social shyness. It's difficult to explain because I actually thought I would grow in confidence as a result of being Clare's partner. But it was just the opposite. She was very tactile to everyone and I found myself resenting this, especially where other men were concerned - and there certainly seemed to be plenty around. During our periods apart I began wondering who she might be with and what they might be doing. Sadly I realised I was getting far too possessive and I didn't seem to trust her. Clare herself had not given me any real cause to think this way, but there was always an inexplicable air about her that made me feel I might not be a permanent fixture. I confess I was also becoming a bit tiresome.

Every February we hosted a wine festival and 1998 was no exception. Clare was in attendance on a professional level and I knew she was hoping to collar the French chef, Marcel Henri, who was planning to add to his considerable European chain by opening a very expensive restaurant and hotel on the northern outskirts of the city. Clare and I managed to grab a quick lunch together but it was not an enjoyable half-hour for me.

"So, you'll be stopping off for the night I take it?" I said.

"Sorry, you take it wrong, darling. I'm up to my eyes. This festival's bloody hard work for me and I need to justify my salary. According to my bosses circulation is down over ten per cent against last year and I've got to watch my back. I need to get behind a computer tonight and type up my monthly report."

Her response was a big disappointment to me. Our time together had dwindled of late and I was getting prickly about it.

"Surely one night wouldn't make any difference?"

"Oh, look, there's Marcel. I must catch his attention."

She completely ignored my comment and stood up to wave enthusiastically at the very handsome, sharply-dressed Frenchman who responded by joining us.

"Marcel, this is Seth Rayner. He manages this amazing place."

"Ah, bonjour, Monsieur Rayner. It is, how do you say,

very impressive, no?"

"Thank you. We think so."

"Now, Marcel, I really won't let you go until you promise me an interview. Our journal can do your restaurant no end of good. I'm sure we can help convince the planners to grant you the site you're after. So, when can I see you?"

"I fly back to Paris tomorrow so that only leaves tonight."

"Great. Come to my place and I'll fix you a steak. Won't be up to your standards of course but I've got a rather good red I could open, courtesy of this man here."

Clare pointed at me and I managed a tight smile. Then she gave Marcel a card and that was that. Deal done, and another quiet night for me.

"Shall we say eight o'clock?"

"Merci beaucoup, Clare. I shall look forward to it."

With that he excused himself and Clare checked her watch.

"Well, thanks for nothing," I said.

"Don't be a bore, Seth. My job's on the line. I need to land this Marcel, by hook or by crook."

"And what's that supposed to mean?"

"It means my work comes before even you, that's what."

"I just wondered what by hook or by crook entails."

"That's my business. I operate how I like to get the right result. If it means a cheap steak, a bottle of your free wine, and a bit of flannel, fine. I can live with that."

"Well just make sure it stays at that."

"Oh, for God's sake!" She stood up. "Give me a break and stop being so bloody pathetic."

With that she stormed off, leaving me feeling very unsettled.

The rest of the day was hectic for me and it was gone ten before I got back to my place. I tried Clare's number but, predictably, I just got the answer-phone. I left a message, more in hope than expectation, and, sure enough, I received no response.

I had a very restless night and in the morning my lack of sleep made me irritable towards some of my team who were only looking for guidance on where to store equipment used for the previous day's festival. Instead they received an uncustomary bollocking. After a slightly better afternoon I later apologised and at dusk I trooped, somewhat dejectedly, to my lodge. My answer-phone had one message. My spirits rose as I thought it must be Clare, but it was from Josh back home:

'Please ring urgently. I've got some news.'

I checked my watch and worked out it must be about mid-morning, so I gave him a bell.

Our dad had died.

*

"Whoever are all these people?" I asked Josh. "I recognise one or two but not many."

We had grabbed a couple of chairs in our lounge and were sitting out of the way in a corner watching Jo, Kath and Rosie busily serving hordes of folk refreshments.

"Well, Dad was actually very popular in the village and he also knew a few people in Brighton through Charlie," replied my twin.

"Pity about Charlie," I continued.

"You say that, but he seems happy enough, comfortable. Kath takes great care of him of course."

"Yeah, seems to be her calling in life."

"The amazing thing is Charlie has suddenly lost his stutter. I was round there a couple of weeks back, seeking some legal advice, and he talked non-stop without any impediment. I reckon it's some sort of compensation for his loss of hearing and failing eyesight."

"Could be I suppose. So, what were you looking for advice on?"

"Well, Seth, like you and Jo, I'm still reeling from the shock of all that money. The doctor had warned me Dad was not long for this life and it made me think what would I do? I've outgrown this place. Not sure I want to stay so far south and I might even consider moving back to Suffolk."

"To do what?"

Josh tapped the side of his nose. He still liked keeping me in the dark. But I had an inkling.

"It wouldn't have anything to do with horses would it?"

"That's the worst of being a twin," he laughed. "No secrets."

"Strange, isn't it? I've been away nearly seven years and yet I still know what you're up to."

"It certainly isn't something you can explain to anyone," agreed Josh.

There was a break in our conversation while we helped ourselves to more sausage rolls brought round by Jo.

"And you, Seth, you've had quite a time lately. Is she leading you a merry dance then?"

"Who?"

"I don't know her name, but I just know something big is going on for you at the moment. Yet you don't seem comfortable."

"Yeah, well, there has been someone lately. A journalist. Clare. She wrote a feature on our vineyard last year, written around me of all things."

"And business turned into pleasure?"

"I guess. But it hasn't been much fun lately."

"Cheer up, mate, I'm sure there are lots of other pretty little fillies over there ready to bite your hand off, especially when they hear about your fortune."

"Never could play the field like you though, fellah."

"Best way. Saves getting hurt."

"I wish I could be like that. Anyway, enough. You mentioned Suffolk. Jo was telling me last night that Dad's ashes are to be scattered in Chesney."

"That's what he wanted. In some ways a bit of a surprise, in view of his rift with the Church, but of course he'll be with Mum and Carrie. At least the rest of us will know they're all together."

"Do you believe in that sort of stuff now then, Josh?"

"No, you know I don't. I am sure you and I are tuned in to the same wave-length, mate. But none of them have really gone have they? I can already hear them having a laugh together. And Mum still looks after us all, you know....."

Josh was, to my utter amazement, momentarily overcome and, as I consoled him, I realised how much we had both changed in certain ways. Unbelievably I seemed to be handling this situation far better than him. He struggled to control his emotions, fiercely dismissing the tears, and after a moment or two he began to recover.

"I'm going to miss the old bugger. He drank himself to death in the end you know. Never recovered from Carrie-Ann. Nor did I for that matter. Think about her and Mum every day."

"I know," I replied.

"Dad admitted he initially wanted me to be the one to go to Oz, not you. But, after a while, we started to grow closer. We went out quite a bit together and he even nearly got his leg over a friend of mine's mother once."

We both laughed at the thought of it. Josh seemed to be pulling himself round with humour - always his antidote.

"Couldn't go through with it of course. Mum was too special."

"I know the feeling."

"You'll be fine, Seth, mark my words. She's probably pining for you right now."

"I doubt."

"So, when do you say you have to go back?"

"I can only stay another week."

"Well, once I've sorted everything out here, who knows, I may come over for a holiday."

"Josh, I'd really love that. And bring Jo if you can."

"Well, in that case, it will certainly have to be a couple of years or so. She's under contract to her orchestra for at least that long I think. Here, you won't believe this, but guess who she met in Italy last year when she was on tour?"

"An amorous Romeo or two no doubt. Look at her. She's so beautiful."

"She certainly is. Well, she bumped into Daisy."

"No!"

"I kid you not. And after seven years."

"Dear old Kurt. Carrie said he was always bumping into people. That's how she met him apparently. So, how is he?"

"Sadly, a complete shadow of his old self, according to Jo. Never has got over Carrie and never will, she thinks. Become reclusive apparently and that's why we've never heard from him."

"Poor bloke. Oh well, that's life I guess. Now, Josh, perhaps you'd like to introduce me to some of the people here. We're getting carried away a bit. Better not appear too rude."

"Yeah, sure. You're right. Come on then."

He put his arm round me and together we chatted to people whose names I would never recall, but who all, without exception, spoke warmly and glowingly of our father. And it actually became a surprisingly happy occasion.

But, after everyone had left, my thoughts turned to

home. Yes, 'home'.

It rather took me aback as well. You see, I no longer saw this place as home, and of course, to use a hackneyed phrase, home is where the heart is. My heart was now clearly in Australia. I already missed it, and of course I desperately wanted to be happily reconciled with Clare.

So, six days later, at Heathrow, I stood on English soil for what I genuinely believed might be the very last time.

*

The reconciliation with Clare didn't happen.

I was very slow getting back into work mode, the result of jet-lag and emotional fatigue I think. There were no messages from Clare so, after a couple of days, I took a delivery to Melbourne City Mall and then drove to her flat. I had my own key so I let myself in.

The place looked like a bomb had hit it, with remnants of what was obviously some sort of party the previous night. And in the bedroom I somehow sensed Clare might have had more than just company for dinner. No real evidence, simply a sickening feeling that developed in the pit of my stomach.

I returned to her sitting room. As I did so her phone rang and the answering service kicked in:

'Hi, baby. Hope you're up for more of the same tonight. Suggest my place. The bed's more comfortable. Bye.'

So, there we were. Absolute proof. I had been discarded for a new model.

*

It took me many months before I could really smile again. Mari and Rich were obviously aware of the situation and I told them quite clearly that it would not affect my work. They both knew that anyway. So I just did what was put in front of me and, slowly but surely, began the long, painful process of getting Clare out of my system.

Fortunately I had lost all my respect for her. That may sound like sour grapes but it was actually the case. And it was very important for my healing process. I would have respected honesty and openness from her. It would still have been tough to take, but a brief explanation would surely have been the least I could have expected? Therefore, in a strange way, to be binned just like a piece of unwanted rubbish was a good thing. It hardened me up and taught me an invaluable lesson. Better to discover the real Clare MacIntyre now rather than get in too deep. I had hoped to marry her, you see, and now I was bloody glad I never asked her.

*

About a year after my break-up with Clare we enjoyed a magical spell of warm, sunny weather from mid-February right through to the first week of March.

One February morning I was out rounding up some stray ewes when I noticed another lone horseman galloping towards me from Rourke's Ridge. As he drew nearer, waving and gesticulating like a madman, I began to realise who it was.

"Ty, you old son of a gun. What are you doing out here looking so pleased about?"

My pal reined in his horse creating a cloud of dust and whooping with delight. He had always been a vigorous rider but I'd never seen him like this before and I burst out laughing. Characteristically he joined in and we dismounted and slapped one another on the back.

"Whoo, what a day, Seth. What a beautiful day."

"It certainly is, but what's brought you out here like this, and how did you find me?"

"Well, in your usual efficient way, you'd left clear instructions back at the ranch on how to find you in an emergency."

"And what's the emergency then?"

"I just had to tell you, mate. I'm getting married."

"What?"

"My Cindy's agreed to be my trouble and strife."

"Ty, that's fantastic, but you could have just phoned. It would have saved you a trip."

We bear-hugged and laughed again.

"No, I wanted to see you. We've all missed you, mate, and I wanted to tell you face to face. Still can't be doing with that techno stuff I'm afraid."

"It's been a long time I guess. What? A couple of years?"

"More than that, mate. We call you Mr Three-Year Man back home."

"Well I get called a lot worse here," I chortled.

"Yeah, they seem a lively bunch. But you obviously manage them bloody well. I sensed a lot of respect in between the banter."

"Don't tell me. I can just imagine you stirring it up for me."

We sat in the shade of a tall eucalyptus tree which waved gently in the light breeze.

"Phew, it's hot. You got some water, mate? I've run out."

"It's all that excitement, Ty. Here you go."

"Ta."

"So, when's the big day?"

"Pretty soon. That's why I'm here. Fifth of May."

"Blimey, it could be chucking it down."

"No worries. We'll cope with the weather. Day after, guess where for the honeymoon?"

"Gold Coast?"

"No way, mate. Bloody England, that's where. Two weeks in London with Cindy's sis and then a European tour till the end of June."

"Fantastic. Well, I'm really pleased for you, Ty."

There was a moment of silence before he turned to me, looking suddenly serious.

"Seth, you'll be my best man won't you?"

The question rocked me. I paused in disbelief.

"What? Me? You're joking?"

"Not on your life. Say you will. Please."

"Look, Ty, I would love to, but.....well....."

"It's Maddy isn't it?"

I was again stopped in my tracks. I looked at him. Ty, so open, so totally honest. I couldn't even try and pretend to him.

"Yeah, mate, I guess it is. You see, the last thing she said to me was that she never wanted to see me again. So I just can't think how we can both be at your wedding. Maddy mustn't miss it for the world, so I don't see how I can possibly do it, much as I want to. But it's an honour. A real honour, mate."

Ty looked at his watch.

"Seth, I'd better be off soon. But, before I go, I want to say this. My Cindy and Maddy are real close and Maddy talks a lot to her. There are things you should know about my sis, but I'm not sure I'm the one who should be saying anything. She's just not the girl she used to be."

"Ok. I would really rather not know anyway. What's past is past. I've come to understand that in life, if nothing else. But I still don't think it would be a good idea."

"Seth, I always tell things as they are. You believe me, don't you?"

"Mate, you're one of the most honest people I've ever

known."

"Well, let me just say this then. I know for sure that Maddy does want you to be there, and, what's more, she wants you to be best man as much as me. Sleep on it and ring me next week."

"I thought you hated technology."

"Not in this case I don't."

And with that he cantered off, leaving me with much to think about.

I spent the next few days turning Ty's request over and over. In the end I felt I had no option really. Looking back on my first year in this land he and I had indeed become very close, full of mutual respect. So I decided to risk it, hoping Maddy wouldn't be too cold towards me.

*

"You bet I bloody do!"

"Er, just 'I do' will be fine, thank you, Ty."

"Sorry, padre, got a bit excited."

I barely contained myself. Only Ty could get away with that. I nervously felt yet again for Cindy's ring.

"Right, let's, um, stick to the script from now on, shall we?....."

Cindy's folk were city dwellers so the wedding reception was held at the Belvedere Hotel on the western outskirts of Melbourne. Remarkably, Maddy and I managed to carefully avoid one another until very late into the evening. We met at the bar and I offered to buy her a drink. Her response was a bit cool but I dealt with it.

"We don't have to pay."

"Oh, right. Well, that's good. I'll order a large one then."

She smiled and went to leave with her drink, but hesitated.

"Seth, thank you for being Ty's best man. It's what he really wanted."

And she gave me no chance to reply, hurrying off to chat to friends who were getting more and more drunk by the minute. I kept wondering where her Harry was.

Distance never being a problem to Aussies, Pete had paid for a bus to take a party of us back to his place, where I was to stay overnight, and the next morning I woke to rain lashing on the windows of my lodge. At about nine I ventured outside to find a rather damp note pinned to the door:

'BREAKFAST AT OURS WHEN YOU LIKE'

Typically kind of Jan and, although I wasn't that hungry, I braved the elements and ran down to the ranch-house. I hammered at the door to be welcomed by Maddy.

"Jan wrote a message about breakfast?"

"That was me. Mum and Dad have already gone to see Ty and Cindy off at the airport."

"Oh, right."

Yet again it struck me Pete was driving a lot of miles in a short period, but I remembered he always insisted he couldn't sleep in a foreign bed.

"Well, don't just stand there, come in. Breakfast's ready in the kitchen. Go through."

"Thanks."

So, it was just the two of us, something I hadn't been ready for at all. After toast and coffee, eaten in nervous silence, I plucked up courage to say something. The air needed to be cleared. I thanked her for breakfast and then, fearful at her possible reaction, I began asking the question that had been preying on my mind all night.

"Erm, I didn't see Harry at the wedding."

"No, well, you wouldn't have. He's not around anymore."

"Oh, right, so....."

"I did marry him. Should have listened to you though. It lasted less than a year."

"Maddy, I'm sorry."

"Don't be. I'm not."

"Can I ask what went wrong?"

"How about everything?"

"I see."

"Harry knocked me about, Seth. It started pretty soon after the wedding. I hid it from my family for as long as I could but Daddy walked in on one of Harry's outbursts one morning and tore into him. I thought he would kill him....."

"I would have done," I murmured.

"Yes, I believe you would. Anyway, I knew Ty was waiting outside in the truck. I raced out, yelled at him and he came and hauled Daddy off."

"Thank God for that."

"Yeah, just as well. To cut a long story short, I returned home with them later that day and I've been here ever since."

"Are you divorced?"

"It should go through this month hopefully. As you can imagine it's been complicated. Of course my dad can't stop blaming himself but he'll be ok. Seeing Ty so happy has cheered him up no end."

There was a long silence. Then Maddy smiled. It was the smile I had never forgotten, the smile I had fallen in love with all those years ago.

"Something funny?" I asked.

"I was just thinking about 'Mr Three-Year Man'. Ty's good with nicknames. Every three years we seem to have these little chats, you and I."

"The last time you said you never wanted to see me again."

"Don't remind me. We all make mistakes. I think that was my biggest ever."

Maddy smiled at me again and this time I suddenly knew all would be well. I held both her hands across the table and the tender look she gave me made me realise how much this beautiful young woman had always meant to me. This was our moment.

"I think I love you, Maddy," I whispered.

"And I love you, Seth. I always have."

*

We got engaged six months later and were to be married the first year of the new millennium. Everyone appeared to be over the moon for us, especially Pete.

"I just don't understand how I could have been so bloody blind," he said one evening as we all enjoyed the first barbie of the summer. "Looking at you now, it's obvious."

"Well, my darling," said Jan, "you spend so much time with those sheep of yours that you miss the important things."

Maddy got up and went round to her dad, hugging him.

"Don't worry, Daddy, you get there in the end. We wouldn't want you any other way, would we, Seth?"

"Sure, I'd agree with that. He's paying for the wedding, so I'll agree to anything."

"Cheeky bugger," laughed Pete.

He leant over the table and his eyes had moistened.

"You're going to be my second son, Seth."

Then, quickly becoming his old self again, he re-filled our glasses.

"Just make bloody sure I have plenty of grandsons."

*

The year 2000 was the most significant of my life. For, as well as getting married, I became the proud owner of the vineyard.

Ritchie's health had become a source of real concern and Mari made it very clear he had to sell up. They had no knowledge of my inheritance from Grandpa Bill and were therefore amazed when I asked to be given first refusal. They were really taken aback when I eventually met their asking price.

To cap it all, two or three weeks before the wedding, Maddy proudly announced our news that she was pregnant.

"What!" Pete exclaimed.

He pretended to be indignant, but we all knew he was delighted really.

"Jeez, you could have waited a few more months, boy."

"I've only done as you asked, Pete," I said, "and there'll be plenty more I can assure you."

"Oh, and do I have any say in the matter?" Maddy asked.

"Well, you certainly did with this one."

The next day I took off on my new chestnut, a wedding gift from Pete. I rode all day, just taking a short breather by the river. While my horse drank and rested I sat thinking just how fortunate I was, and how, not that far short of forty years of age, everything had suddenly seemed to click perfectly into place.

As I glanced along the river bank I noticed an old fisherman packing up his rods. He looked up, saw me watching, and waved.

"How you doing?"

"Couldn't be better," I shouted back.

"That's good. I'll be off now then. Cheerio, Seth."

"Bye, Grandpa, and thanks again. Thank you so very much....."

BOOK FOUR: TWIN OF THE NORTHERN HEMISPHERE

I switched off the mower's engine and stopped to admire the plethora of bluebells that engulfed the farmhouse at this time of year. My gaze switched to the new sign, erected in my absence during the recent trip to see my brother. I read, with a certain amount of pride and satisfaction:

'CHURCH FARM HOLIDAY LODGE'

However, as so often seemed to happen in my life, it was not long before my brief bit of peace was shattered. The outside bell began ringing insistently, which meant my secretary probably needed a cheque signed, or Susie had decided to shoot back to London.

It was the latter. But, by the time I'd parked the mower and sorted a couple of other pressing matters out, she was a puff of smoke. I waited with an expectant smile on my face, and was not disappointed to hear the usual squealing of brakes as she reached the junction of our lane to the high street. Always in such a blessed hurry that one, but I always made sure she never rushed me. Have me down the aisle in a flash, given the chance. That is, if I were to believe my secretary, Lizzie. And I never had any reason to doubt her judgement. Lizzie James was my rock. She knew everything, and everyone, in my life, and was indispensable, as well as being a very good friend to boot. But nothing more than that, I am sorry to say. I'd tried once with her, and got my fingers well and truly burnt. I secretly hoped she might melt a bit one day, but wasn't holding my breath. You see, Lizzie never mixed business with pleasure. Frustratingly, I was the business and her fiancé of three years, a dull but decent accountant, was the pleasure.

I entered the farmhouse and went into her office, which had been converted from Dad's old study.

"Ah, there you are. You missed Susie. She had to fly. Something about see you at the weekend and don't forget your dinner jacket."

"Oh, God, it's that bloody ball of her mother's. I'd clean forgotten."

"You certainly had. I've got you down for Sally Shaw's charity auction at 'Greenways'."

"Really? That's fantastic. Lizzie, you're a genius. You've just saved my life."

"Susie's not going to be amused, Josh."

"True, but.....well....."

"Do I sense yet another filly taking a tumble?"

"No.....that is.....well, perhaps. Oh, Lizzie, I just can't deal with her break-neck speed. Susie's great fun, but....."

"Thought so. Another one bites the dust then?"

"Yeah, looks like it. I know you think I'm heartless but I just can't seem to find the right one. Unless you've changed your mind and might be interested after all?"

I beamed my best smile at her.

"You don't want to find the right one, Josh, and anyway, I hardly think that Don would be very happy, do you?"

"Lizzie, come with me to Sally's. You'd enjoy it. Regard it as work if you have to."

"Is that an order, Mr Rayner?" Her turn to smile.

"Well, of course not, but are you busy Saturday night?"

"Going to the theatre. Sorry. Don's birthday treat."

"Well, even I wouldn't try and twist your arm in that case. Wish him 'many happy returns' from me."

"I will. Thank you. Now, if you remember, I've got the rest of today off, and all tomorrow. It's his actual birthday then."

"You know very well I'd forgotten."

"Of course. So, I've left a list of things you must do before next Monday, including a phone call to your brother. Your sister-in-law was due yesterday. You may be an uncle already."

"Knowing Seth he'd have rung me the moment she was born. I won't bother him yet."

"What do you mean 'she'? I didn't think they knew the sex."

Lizzie never forgot anything.

"They don't. But I know."

"Now I've heard everything. However do you know that?"

"Never mind how, Lizzie. I just know."

*

Patsy Ann Rayner was born three days later.

After I'd put the phone down from an ecstatic Seth on that Sunday evening I grabbed a beer and wandered outside to sit on Dad's favourite bench. It had been a beautiful day and, for early May, was still pleasantly warm. I raised my glass.

"Bless you, little Patsy!"

I could picture the three of them on their ranch and I recalled the wonderful trip my sister Jo and I had enjoyed last winter.

*

Seth had wanted me to be best man and Jo a bridesmaid at their wedding, and of course neither of us hesitated for one moment. A lot of changes had taken place in the two years since my father's death and I was only too happy to embrace a few months of complete change and relaxation. For Jo it was slightly trickier but, fortunately, her orchestra's European tour for 2000 ended with a final performance at London's Festival Hall in September. This enabled us to travel to Oz together in early October, giving us a couple of weeks before Seth's wedding. In fact we'd arrived just after Maddy's announcement about their baby.

I was lucky enough to spend more than four months with them all and I certainly came to understand why Seth was ready to live the rest of his life there. Quite a country. Not for me on a permanent basis, because I just knew I would miss England too much. But it clearly suited Seth down to the ground and I was so very pleased for him. Envious in a couple of ways, but I still firmly resisted the thought of settling down myself. As I have already intimated, Susie seemed to want that but, watching Seth and Maddy together on a daily basis, I had to admit I didn't seem to have yet experienced that very special bonding with any woman. Certainly not Susie. So it was destined to fall apart, just like the many others. And it was always my fault.

Jo had to report to the ESO during the last week of December, so she was over there with me for just over two months. Her orchestra had an important series of New Year engagements and she was committed contractually. This was still long enough for us to enjoy one another's company to the full, and we regularly took to borrowing a couple of Seth's horses, setting off for the day in just shorts and tee-shirts, and soaking up the Australian sunshine.

It was on one such occasion I learnt of her future plans and she managed to wheedle some of mine out of me. We had tethered the horses by a river, as instructed by Seth.

"Well, Sis, isn't this grand?"

"Fantastic, Josh. I love being here and I'm so happy for Seth."

"Yeah, me too. He deserves it," I replied.

"Now, Jo, let's hear about you. I keep wondering what my little sister's up to these days. No doubt constantly fending off the close attentions of all those trumpet players."

Jo laughed, but said nothing.

"Come on now, don't be coy."

I took her hand and gently squeezed.

"You're so pretty. You're not going to tell me there isn't anyone?"

"Oh, Josh, you just have to know, don't you?" She laughed again.

"I simply need to know you are happy and enjoying life."

"Rest assured I am both." She hesitated. "Although there is someone very special actually."

"Good. What instrument?"

"None at all. He's a politician."

"Good grief! Labour I suppose, knowing you?"

"Yes, of course. He's a very junior minister in the Home Office. And don't you start getting onto your high horse. Your lot ran out of good ideas years ago."

"To be fair I can't argue with that, but what I can't swallow is Labour's attempt to try and claim the centre ground."

"It's where all political battles are won, Josh. I'm not over the moon about it myself. Even Michael's ill at ease with some of his party's foreign policies, but of course he has to toe the line otherwise he puts his promising career in jeopardy."

"So, this Michael, has he captured my sister's heart?"

"Josh, you never let go do you?"

"I just care about you, that's all."

"I'm not the poor little young innocent you take me for, Josh. I can take good care of myself. Please believe that."

"Ok. But you know you can always count on me."

"Darling, of course I know that. But it's about time you looked after yourself, isn't it?"

"I'm fine, Jo, just fine."

We momentarily sunk into our own thoughts before Jo spoke again.

"I'm thinking of giving up the orchestra by the way."

"Oh, really? Well, that's a surprise. I thought you were enjoying it."

"I like it to a point, but living out of a suitcase in swish but impersonal hotel rooms can lose its attraction you know. A bit like all your lady friends that come and go."

"Now then, cheeky."

I paused.

"So, what would you like to do instead?"

"Well, promise not to laugh, but I actually want to enter politics."

"What?"

"Are you really that surprised?"

I sat and thought about it and realised it did make quite a lot of sense.

"No, I suppose not. I'm just initially a bit taken aback I suppose. So, how does one actually get into politics then?"

"The filthy lucre helps," laughed Jo.

"I guess it does. I hadn't really thought about that before. And dear old Grandpa has helped you consider it all I suppose?"

"Yes, he has. And Michael is, I admit, a big influence."

"Would I have heard of him? What's his surname?"

"Unlikely. The only pages of the newspaper you study are about horses."

"That's a bit harsh. I read about rugby as well."

We both laughed again.

"It's Michael Fairbrother and I cannot think you would have heard of him. He's a rising star, not an established one."

"No, you're right. So, how will you break into it then?"

"Well, I'm a member of the Party and I already have a few useful contacts, as well as Michael that is. In his case, for example, he eventually ran for three by-elections and got in at the third attempt up in North Yorkshire. Being a local helped. He's from Ripon you see."

"Hm, nice little racecourse there."

"That's right. But now he spends a lot of time in London. He works every God-given hour and is so passionate about it all."

"And this has rubbed off on you, I can tell."

"I think it has, Josh. I have a desire to do something about the welfare of the next generation, which will include my own kids, and I feel I probably ought to follow my instincts."

"Kids? Blimey! Does Mike know about this?" I smiled.

"No, of course not. I was just speaking hypothetically. But what else can I do with all that money?"

"Good point. You go for it, Sis. Use those contacts. Nothing wrong with that. It's the old adage of who you know, isn't it? I will be right behind you."

"Well, let's just see. I'll give it serious thought in the New Year. Now, what about your future? You've set Church Farm up wonderfully. I'm so impressed with what you've achieved and the opportunities you're creating for people."

I laughed.

"You sound like you're in the House already," I said.

"No, Josh, I mean it. Come on. You must also have plans? Don't try and tell me otherwise."

"Well of course I have. I don't deny it."

"Spit them out then. I deserve some information after spilling my own beans."

"True, I suppose. Well....."

I was still hesitant about saying too much so, before I gave Jo any hint about some of my own hopes and aspirations for the future, I went back over what had been happening at home and how, in essence, I was setting up a charity at Church Farm. I had only given her sketchy details in the past. So I explained that, if all went to plan, a situation would develop enabling disadvantaged people to live and work there, much as we had been allowed to. I talked to Jo for ages and she listened intently, genuinely interested.

Later on, alone in my room, I realised that, unlike Jo or Seth, my other plans didn't really include anyone else, but then I was different from them both in that respect. I admit I very much enjoyed the company and pleasure of attractive women but I was still very wary of sharing every aspect of my life with any of them. That might perhaps have excluded Lizzie James of course, but I was out of luck there, as I have already explained. She had been the one woman I felt I could completely rely on. Yes, Lizzie had helped me enormously in the early days of our charity, but then she had arrived with a lot of charitable and secretarial experience.

Prior to the establishment of the charity Charlie Youngman had also been a very wise counsellor, despite his very advanced years. He had helped me a lot when I first discussed my ideas with him.

We chatted in his conservatory one late September afternoon in 1996, a few weeks after I had inherited my little fortune, so I took the opportunity of floating the outline of my plans to him.

Basically, I had felt for some time that I wanted to move on. I had reached saturation point with the smallholding and, with Dad in a pretty bad way, I knew I needed to take steps to sort the future out. But it was complicated, and until Grandpa's astonishing gift came along my ideas couldn't possibly be considered. It was therefore an absolutely amazing piece of luck when I inherited so much. His gift enabled me to proceed, although the legal mechanics were a real nightmare and I didn't wish to set anything in stone while my dad was still alive. It would have seemed disrespectful somehow and I knew he was on borrowed time, so it really wasn't right.

Heeding advice from Charlie the eighteen months between receiving news of Grandpa's gift and my dad's death did however allow me planning time and a lot of fundamental issues were sorted out, albeit at substantial cost legally.

By the summer of 1998, six months after Dad had died, and with my brother's and sister's blessing, I had been given the green light to create a charitable trust. Now, nearly three years later, I was a few months away from leaving myself, hopefully enabling the charity to proceed with the important work I had envisaged.

As I have said the legalities were extremely complex and expensive but after a lot of researching I discovered an American charity that had an organisation in England called 'Opportunity Knocks UK', and I was eventually authorised to direct 'OK UK', as it had become better known, to effectively 'buy out' the Oak Apple Trust's tenure of Church Farm. The last-named had of course enabled our family to live there for nearly thirty years but they had been swallowed up by a larger environmental group about eight years ago anyway. See what I mean about legal complexities?

'OK UK' had a huge amount of investment capital set aside for projects such as mine. After many lengthy meetings, frustrating telephone calls and endless correspondence, over far too long a period for my impatience, the real work began and my hopes gradually turned into reality.

Renovations started, literally around me, to create suitable accommodation in the farmhouse for people who had special needs and disabilities. They would live there permanently and be looked after by skilled staff, who would live-in and supervise the running of the smallholding, with our guests working alongside them. The renovations also included a substantial extension onto Dad's study, which itself became an office. The work took the best part of two years to complete.

In 2000, alongside completion of the renovations, the Lodge was built and later dedicated to our dad. My intention had always been to create a holiday situation for disadvantaged families. I had never forgotten the fantastic holidays we had enjoyed as a family and I just wanted others to have the same chance, regardless of their low incomes.

It was at the beginning of this year that Lizzie had arrived, having been transferred by 'OK UK' from a similar project in Worcestershire. I was given an honorary position on the charity's council of management and more or less allowed free rein on how the project developed. But in truth it was Lizzie who ran the show and everyone knew it. And I had no problem with that. She knew exactly what I wanted and how to implement my wishes. My time there was limited anyway because I had agreed to be out by the end of the summer 2001. I would miss all the exciting hustle and bustle, and I would certainly miss working with Lizzie, but it was time to be off. You see, I had other exciting plans. Long-held dreams that dear old Grandpa Bill's generosity would now make reality.

So, returning to that conversation with Jo, I eventually summoned up the courage to tell her what I had done with a very large part of my gift from Grandpa. Jo was not going to let me off the hook you see.

"Right, Josh. You've updated me about the charity but what I really want to know is where are you going to be in a few months time? What are your personal plans? Knowing you, something exciting no doubt?"

"Ah."

"Well, don't just sit there. Tell me."

"Shouldn't we be getting back? It's getting late."

"Josh Rayner. You will tell me if we have to stay here all night."

I had no choice really. And so I gave Jo my news.

"I've bought some stables, along with training rights for horses belonging to about half a dozen owners, at a yard near Newmarket."

"Josh, that's wonderful. Oh, what fun."

"It's going to be a bit more than fun, Jo. I shall have to work bloody hard to make a success of it."

"But you will, Josh, you will. All three of us have worked hard throughout our lives and you're not going to change. I have total belief in you. You'll make a tremendous success of it, of course you will. And Grandpa just adored horseracing."

She hugged me and demanded more details. I gave her just enough information to satisfy her and then we headed back.

*

I suppose, looking back on that conversation with Jo, I avoided saying too much because I so wanted to make a success of something that totally stemmed from my own initiative. I couldn't bear the thought of letting Grandpa down. For me failure was not an option, but of course I was entering a very high-risk zone. And the agreement I had made was overly complicated I have to admit.

The Australians love their racing and I was lucky enough to have attended the Melbourne Cup with Pete and Jan - Seth's future in-laws - back in November. There I had bumped into Mike Wishaw, a mate of Pete's and a leading owner and trainer with a huge string of horses in Sydney. He also owned a very small but successful yard in England. We spent a great part of the day in conversation together and, later, a whole week at his family home near the New South Wales capital.

Mike was obviously becoming rather a victim of his own success. Supervising even a small stable in England was apparently taking its toll and he was looking to eventually offload the yard. As we talked, realisation dawned on me. It suddenly all came together in my head. I was never one to take too long to make decisions and, before you knew it, there I was the owner of a yard with two dozen or more stables and fifteen four-legged friends.

I was very fortunate because Mike, while wishing to be shot of it all, nevertheless happily co-operated with a complex arrangement that gave me the time I needed to break into this new world. I believe, from what he told me, it also gave him the ability to balance some delicate tax affairs.

Before being granted a licence to train, I had to be clearly seen as an Assistant Trainer in a yard recognised as being successful. Even though I was technically the owner of the yard and everything that went with it from Autumn 2001, I would be learning my new trade from the bottom rung, working for five years as assistant to Mike's English trainer, Freddie Watkinson. I had to ensure I didn't mess up on this. I had made this huge five-year commitment, but I was determined to make it work in return for my good fortune. It was going to be tough, I knew that. But I also believed it was the right thing.

So, how could I be so sure? Let's just say I'd had guidance, shall we, and simply leave it there.

*

By September I was beginning to experience such a crazy mixture of emotions. I was simply running on adrenaline. I wanted to train so much yet, during my last week at Barton Green, I felt pangs of sadness and not an insubstantial amount of raw fear.

Inevitably, one balmy afternoon just a couple of days before our departure, I wandered around Church Farm saying thank you to all its nooks and crannies and recalling so much. Yes, I did say 'our' departure. Susie hadn't fallen after all. She'd re-mounted and we were on course again. For how long? Who could tell? But I was mighty glad she was coming with me, I freely admit. Her bubbly nature helped make the tough changes just a little bit easier. I had become uncharacteristically unsure of myself lately and I appreciated her company.

That September afternoon and evening I needed to be alone though. I spent the majority of the time up at Field End, basking in the really warm sunshine, stretched out on my favourite recliner. I dropped in and out of thoughts about all the significant people from my past and my mother was right at the forefront.

I knew Mum of course for less than ten years and, no doubt like most people, couldn't remember much of the first four. So about five years are all I really had to look back on.

At the time, being a very lively twin boy, I didn't realise the hard work Seth and I must have been. Although I was always the noisy one of the two, Seth certainly had his moments too. We were forever getting into all sorts of scrapes. In those early days I was by far the stronger physically and at school frequently dispatched myself to sort out any of my brother's antagonists. The usual chain of events saw Seth losing his rag with someone, then taking them on at a physical disadvantage, before I popped up and laid into them. I was constantly getting hauled up in front of the Head and letters were often sent home warning my parents that my behaviour would not be tolerated. But that didn't stop me and I somehow survived all their disciplinary threats. All this before I was ten even!

Dad appeared to approve of my actions in one respect but nevertheless often gave me a very hard time for interfering. Like me he seemed to want to protect Seth but I realise now that he had hoped my brother would sort his own problems out. Well, he certainly would now! In Australia I had marvelled at Seth's stature and strength. When we were in our teens and playing rugby he'd always been stuck on the wing because of his light weight and speed, while I was a pretty strong prop forward. There would certainly be a role reversal now. He had made a complete mess of me arm-wrestling one evening at Pete's. I lost five-one and only got the one when Seth was momentarily distracted by Maddy. His strength was awesome and I was getting podgy.

So, as I say, during our early childhood we were bloody difficult, and yet I never once heard my mother complain. She was always positive, full of fun, loving and energetic, forever initiating games for us all and joining in with great gusto and laughter.

Laughter. That was it. Laughter. My lovely mum's middle name. Never one to be phased by setbacks, always looking on the bright side, and constantly hugging and kissing us all. And that's what I missed so much from day one of her tragic accident.

When my dad had finished trying to tell Seth and me she had been killed I remember the tidal wave of anguish and sorrow that swept over me. I was inconsolable at the news and not even Grandma Molly could do anything to help me for the rest of that day. Strangely I soon came to realise however that mourning publicly about it was not something I would be able to cope with. Besides, even at that young age I seemed to sense that Dad was going to need me to be strong and I therefore stubbornly took up that mantle. Until night-time, that is.

I always knew when my brother had fallen asleep and every night, for months on end, once he'd nodded off I took out my favourite photo of Mum from under my pillow and cried until I was exhausted into sleep. And, to this day, I don't think anyone ever knew. You see, I made sure I muffled the sound so nobody could hear. Of course Seth would have suspected. We were so close. But to his credit, if he did, he allowed me to suffer my private pain alone. I have no doubt he had his own way too. Mum was so special to us both and never treated one of us more favourably than the other.

*

Even in September the sun was quite scorching and, at around three o'clock, I felt for my cotton top and slipped it on. I went to the house, fixed myself a late sandwich lunch and returned to my recollections, also armed with a couple of beers.

As I ate and gazed at the landscape again I realised, fantastic as this place had been, it was certainly time to go. It had all changed so much over the years of course. And that was primarily down to me I suppose. I liked to think the changes had been for the better but the special people in my life were no longer about. The happiest times had, without doubt, been our childhood holidays here with Bertie and Glad.

I finished my beer and took my shirt off again. The sun was a perfect temperature now and I wanted to make the most of it.

Those family holidays were fantastic. Brilliant times we had. Days that would be forever etched on my memory. Indelible. And I could hear my mother shouting across the garden now:

"Josh, find Carrie please. We want to get to the beach while the sun's still out."

"Will do, Mum."

Then:

"It's ok, Josh, don't worry, she's here now."

I sat up, startled, and rubbed my eyes in disbelief.

"Mum? Is.....is that you? I mean.....no, I've obviously been dreaming.....stupid idiot....."

There was momentary silence, before:

"Dad's here.....and Grandma.....Bertie and Glad....."

My head was beginning to play tricks with me. Definitely too much sun.

"You go on without us, Josh.....you have so much to do.....we'll all catch up with you later.....get cracking....."

No, it wasn't the sun. It was definitely my mother. And I realised she was telling me to go ahead and do what I had to.

I looked around me, unrealistically hoping to catch a glimpse of her. Bloody stupid emotion of course. I lay back down on my makeshift pillow and wept like I used to all those years ago. I had never felt so alone and I confess it took all my strength of character not to go over the edge that day.

I didn't sleep much, but got up my usual time and felt astonishingly perky. It was as if my mum's unexpected presence the previous day had re-charged me during the night. From being completely at sea and out of it, I had again become my remarkably confident self although, naturally, I still felt a degree of apprehension. Looking back I guess it had been necessary for me to experience that brief period of desolation. But life is for the living. This was a phrase my Grandpa Bill had always used and I was determined to share that outlook. As far as I could see Seth and Jo were out there living it and now it was up to me to take the plunge and go for it as well. Thinking about it I had, perhaps surprisingly, been the least adventurous of all the four siblings. I had been the one to take the cosy, familiar and comfortable option. Well, now I needed to walk away from here and right out of my perpetual safe haven. There was a new challenge to meet and I gritted my teeth in readiness.

*

A constant feature of my life over the years seemed to be the very strong influence of a sort of elder statesman. Bertie, Dad of course, Grandpa, and dear old Charlie Youngman. Sadly, all of them had died now, including Charlie, who had quietly drifted away in his conservatory one Sunday afternoon about a year after I had left Barton Green. Kath had assured me he died a very happy man, having backed my five-year-old miler Red Rooster at 8-1 the previous day.

On cue, Freddie Watkinson, Mike Wishaw's trainer, had conveniently stepped up to fill the breach and continue my long line of wise counsellors.

Right from day one I had taken to Freddie and I like to think it was mutual. We got on well and I was to become very grateful to this blunt but kind man from the Midlands. His vast experience and intimate knowledge of horses, combined with my enthusiasm and my apparent ability to gather good people around me, was the foundation of what soon became an outstandingly successful stable.

It's a well-worn cliché, I know, but I owed everything to Freddie. Never once did he make me feel inadequate or out of my depth. The majority of trainers usually progressed from being jockeys, whereas I had no such experience to fall back on. Many people in Freddie's position would have been less than co-operative, cynical even, but I like to think I won him over with my positive approach and willingness to learn by getting my hands dirty.

The combination worked. As Freddie continually impressed upon me, you were only as good as your next runner, not the last winner. And we had plenty of those I can tell you, including two out of three in my first meeting at Nottingham. Not that I could take any credit for any of our early successes.

I remember Nottingham so well. We had travelled there towards the end of my second week, leaving Susie to put some finishing touches to our sitting room furnishings. We had spent the previous week getting settled in and now I wanted to crack on with the business in hand. As we hit the outskirts I asked Freddie if he thought I was completely crazy to be doing what I was.

"No, sir, why should I think that?"

"Now, Freddie, what's with this 'sir' business? Please always call me Josh."

"But I can't do that. You're the Gaffer, sir."

"Freddie, we all know that is only in theory. In my eyes you are the Gaffer and I shall make sure that all our lads clearly know that. So, please, do as I ask."

He thought for a moment before saying any more.

"Well, that is very generous of you. I really appreciate the gesture. Thank you.....Josh."

We exchanged smiles and never looked back.

"So," I asked Freddie a few miles later, "what are the most important things I should learn about this game then?"

"With due respect, firstly don't look on it as a game. It should be regarded as a serious business, Josh. Provided, of course, you always make it enjoyable for everyone involved."

"I'm sorry. Bad use of the word. I am very serious about it all, I assure you."

"I'm sure you are. The most important factor is good teamwork. Keep the lads working hard, noses to the grindstone, but in a pleasant manner, using humour when you can. Take an interest in their lives, their families, their hopes for the future. Make them always feel important - which they are. Don't mollycoddle them of course, but I always say a bit of genuine concern goes a long way. Better a carrot than a stick, eh?"

"Absolutely. And what about the horses? I mean, I've always ridden since I was a kid, but getting them fully prepared to run races and hopefully win for their owners. What's the secret?"

"Simple really. You've practically said it. Just take the word hopefully out. Proper preparation is essential and each of those horses must be absolutely ready. You see, I understand why racing has had its share of problems and critics throughout its history. And it will always be the case. Some trainers actually don't always send their charges out to win. I'm not criticising them. It's just not really my way."

He hesitated for some reason but then carried on.

"They may have good reason to instruct jockeys to coast but I feel the punters deserve a good effort from the stable every time. They put money on us trusting we are going to do our best. And that's what we should do. Every single time without fail."

"But surely there are times when you must know your horse can't win?"

He seemed to look wistful for a moment.

"Yes, but I only insist my jockeys ease up when they

know their mount has genuinely given their all. I won't ever allow them to be mercilessly thrashed."

And, with this sort of invaluable code of conduct, plus many other very impressive principles ringing in my ears, I set off on my long and, what turned out to be, very lucrative career.

*

Over the next five years I abided by Freddie's ethics, worked astonishingly long hours, and reaped the rewards.

By 2006 I had managed to gain some respect in the flat-racing world, proving that effort and enthusiasm could be part of a successful formula. But then I had been blessed with that extra magical ingredient of Freddie Watkinson.

Freddie retired soon after my five years' apprenticeship and we remained firm friends. It obviously gave him much pleasure to monitor my progress after his retirement and I didn't let him or myself down. Unbelievably I took fourth place in the trainers' championship for 2007 and my reputation quickly grew. I seemed fortunate enough to have the Midas touch and one or two very wealthy owners began transferring some of their horses to me, which meant I had to quickly improve the stabling.

I also began to benefit from my sister's newly-acquired fame, having successfully stolen a supposedly safe London Borough seat from the Tories in the 2005 General Election. Over the following two years she had made considerable impact at Westminster and, with my unexpected success on the track, we both had often found ourselves in the media spotlight, although Jo's was much higher profile than mine.

Astonishingly - in my case - we had even been invited to appear on a BBC news programme at the end of 2007.

The researchers had dug out Jo's maiden speech in the House of two years prior because they were now reporting on alcohol excess and abuse. Jo had made that the theme of her speech and it had impressed a lot of people. She had highlighted the negative impact of drink on our own family life so they thought it would be good to get me along there as well. I have to admit it was scary, but nevertheless it did both Jo and me a lot of good. Jo was outstanding and very feisty towards the interviewer, neatly fending off criticism of Labour's economic policies, while I was just there to make up the numbers really. But as a result I did get even more owners contacting me and work simply consumed me.

If only my private life had been as successful. Misguidedly I had long ago failed to put in the work and time needed to keep Susie happy. And, as a result of my continual neglect of her, she had confronted me one evening less than two years after our move from Sussex.

"Good day?"

"Yeah, thanks. I think we might have one winner at least this weekend."

"Josh, you know we're off to Edinburgh?"

"What? Surely that's not for a couple of weeks yet?"

"No. It's this weekend."

"Well, I'm sorry. You'll just have to postpone it. I can't possibly make it. I must go with Freddie to Newbury. We've got four runners and that includes Bernard Cole's promising two-year old. I have to be there."

"Horses, horses, bloody horses. That's all I ever hear about these days. Or Freddie this and Freddie that. What about me, Josh? What about us?"

Her voice had risen in anger - a very rare occurrence. I sat on the arm of her chair and tried to put my arm round her. She pushed me away and flounced over to the gin bottle.

"Oh, come on, old girl, don't be like that. Wrong time of the month is it?"

As soon as I had said it I bitterly regretted such pathetically misplaced and hurtful chauvinism. Especially when a glass came hurtling towards me.

"Hey, easy now!"

"How would you know what time of the month it is? Can you remember the last time? I can't. You even talk to me as if I'm a bloody horse. Perhaps if I got one of the stable lads to put a saddle and noseband on me you might begin to show some interest."

Susie leant against the sideboard and the tears started. This time she allowed me to console her and, for admittedly the first time in a long while, we ended up having a very early night. But it wasn't enough and we both realised that. A month later it was over. She packed her bags and left. This time for good.

In the end it wasn't as acrimonious as it could have been. But Susie was extremely cut up and I did actually feel very badly about the way I had treated her. As she said on our last evening together, I always got completely carried away with whatever my latest challenge was. She had apparently begun to feel this when we had been at Barton Green. And, in all honesty, I had no defence to offer. I never was intentionally selfish but I had to admit that the evidence suggested I usually was. She admitted she had hoped to become Mrs Rayner and have kids and I could only tamely say it was just not for me. Which was true. I was clearly married to my career and would only make a hopeless husband and father.

We made love one final time but she was gone way before I stirred the next morning. I didn't even hear her squealing brakes. Sadly, like Susie, they had lost their zip too.

*

As my experience in the racing world increased I went from strength to strength, even challenging for one of the top two Trainer's places at one point in 2008, only to end up third. Frustratingly the season turned sour at the Epsom autumn meeting. One of my best prospects, Action Replay, had been moved up to try a mile and a half on the actual Derby course. This turned out to be a bit of a disaster, the horse apparently outpaced by half a dozen others on the run down from Tattenham Corner.

I did however feel a need to speak somewhat sharply to Action's jockey in my office the following week. This was uncharacteristic of me but Freddie, whom I had invited to our box for the day, had muttered something during the final part of the race that had slightly troubled me. And, more puzzling, neither he nor my jockey seemed to share my bitter disappointment at the result. It wasn't a major race by any means but I was particularly fond of Action and his abject performance that day was hard to swallow.

There was a knock on my door.

"Come in."

It was my leading jockey, Ben Faulkner, responding to my request for a chat.

"Ben, sit down. Thanks for coming in early."

He looked sullen and was obviously ill at ease.

"Just thought we could review Action Replay's race on Saturday. It didn't go according to plan and naturally the owners and I were very disappointed. So, can I have your account of things, please?"

"I told you after the race," he gruffly replied.

This stung me.

"Ben, please don't take that surly attitude with me. We both know there was virtually no time to talk then and all you were able to say was that he ran out of steam when it mattered. That's just not good enough. I need to give the Raleigh Syndicate chapter and verse as to why the strong market favourite didn't produce the goods for them and the punters."

"You were there, Gaffer. You could see for yourself, surely? The distance was too much. He couldn't do the extra."

Ben was unable to maintain any sort of eye contact and I began to feel a mixture of anger and even suspicion.

"What I saw was a top-rate horse at the peak of fitness ridden by a first-class jockey and both of them, for some unknown reason, not performing well when it most mattered. We both know he most certainly can do the distance. We timed him on his final gallop here. It was quick, bloody quick, and he still had a bit left."

"So, what are you suggesting, sir?"

Ben's face was flushed now.

"I'm not suggesting anything. I'm simply trying to get to the bottom of it all. Ben, you know as well as I do that Action Replay was bursting with energy and fitness, yet you're trying to tell me he simply ran out of steam. I'm just puzzled. I'm also bloody annoyed actually. I clearly told you to keep him tucked in quietly down the hill until the final half furlong."

"Well, perhaps I tried to let him go a bit too early. It happens sometimes, Gaffer. We all make mistakes."

There was a pause.

"Ben, as you came out of Tattenham, I'm convinced Freddie said something that I can't for the life of me get out of my head. I'm sure he muttered 'now, Ben'. Can you throw any light on what that might have been about?"

I paused. Ben was looking down at my desk.

"What did he mean, Ben?"

"Well, knowing Mr Watkinson of old, I expect he just felt that's when I should have gone."

"And that's exactly when you did go. Against my orders. Much as I respect Freddie, it's what I say that matters now, Ben."

"But Action was desperate to go, sir. I could hardly hold onto him."

"Yet you said earlier he ran out of steam. Now you apparently couldn't hold him. Which is it, Ben?"

Stony silence. I sighed. This was all getting me nowhere.

"Ok. Have it your own way. But I'm not happy, Ben. I feel you blatantly disobeyed my instructions and I am wondering why. At the moment I want to give you the benefit of the doubt but if I ever have cause to suspect anything untoward going on in my yard, rest assured all those involved will be out of work and up in front of the authorities. Do I make myself perfectly clear?"

He said nothing, but gave me a murderous look.

"Ride Dawn's Gift out today. I want Abigail to give Action some very gentle work."

Ben almost snarled as he replied.

"Of course, sir. Whatever you say."

His final glance smacked of totally uncharacteristic insolence and he seemed to carry away with him a sense of relief, as though he'd got away with something.

Realistically I knew I could never prove anything. This sort of thing did unfortunately happen in the racing world now and then. And anyway it was always my policy to try and believe what people told me and to trust them. But somehow things didn't feel right. I knew I would be phoning Freddie at some point. I simply was unable to let this matter rest. I kept telling myself that Ben was right and Freddie probably did just feel he should have gone when he did. But why did Ben go against my orders? Surely Freddie wouldn't have interfered and countered my instructions? No, of course not. Too much of a pro to behave like that. Something wasn't right though and Ben's unconvincing version of events had unsettled me.

*

"Freddie, did you get back home in one piece?"

"Yes thanks, Josh. I don't like driving much these days as you know, but of course it's not far and I was home by eight. My Tam had some supper ready, bless her."

Tamara Watkinson was Freddie's only child and he absolutely idolised her. He'd married late in life but, like me it seemed, probably put horses before humans and his wife had actually left a few years back. At eighteen years of age Tam could see both sides of her parents' problems and had sympathised with her mother, but only to a point. She had inherited her father's love of horses, you see, and so she stayed on to look after him. Now, nearly twenty-four, Tam was a very promising rider amongst the up and coming breed of young jockeys. Yes, women were at last beginning to compete with men on the course, and why not? Unheard of a few years ago, but a welcome change in my view. Tam had ridden out for Freddie and me for years and her talent was obvious. She worked out regularly at the gym and was slowly gaining the strength in her arms and legs that would doubtless see her challenging the top male jockeys one day.

"Freddie, I need your advice on a couple of things. Can I treat you to Sunday lunch this weekend? Your local's pretty good, isn't it?"

"Well, yes, they do a half-decent roast I believe."

"Good. Let's see, I'll pick you up at about one. Is that ok?"

"Thanks, Josh. I'll look forward to that."

*

Freddie rented a very modest bungalow a few miles the other side of Newmarket from me and, unusually, I was a bit early arriving. He was still in his gardening clothes and made me a coffee before going to get changed.

I looked around the drab living room and was saddened. It seemed a very lonely place really. Then, as I unenthusiastically sipped cheap instant, the phone rang. I ignored it of course but my ears immediately pricked up when the answer-phone clicked in. I knew that voice very well.

"Freddie, they want one more big killing. Ring back today."

A few minutes later Freddie was back down and clearly looking forward to our lunch. I wasn't going to spoil it just yet.

*

"Another drink, Freddie?"

"Goodness me no, Josh, thanks very much. I can't possibly keep up with you."

"Guess I should stop too."

"Smashing meal, Josh. Very kind of you. Now, I expect you want some help in return?"

"Now, Freddie, put like that it sounds a bit harsh."

"But you said on the phone you need advice. So how can I help?"

I hesitated briefly but had already decided to go straight in. It was the only way I knew and that telephone message had simply fuelled my suspicions.

"I believe Ben Faulkner purposely lost that race at Epsom on Action Replay."

Freddie shifted very slightly in his seat but looked me

straight in the eye, saying nothing.

"He went totally against my orders and put the gas on almost as soon as they came out of the Corner. Ben was under strict instructions to hold Action up until well inside the final furlong."

I paused. Still nothing from my old mentor.

"It's so unlike Ben. He's my top man and always does his level best to follow orders."

"You quizzed him afterwards of course?"

At last Freddie spoke.

"Naturally, but it was all very unsatisfactory. Contradictory. First he was making out Action couldn't do the distance and then he tried to suggest he may have made a mistake and gone too early. Reckoned he couldn't hold the horse and that he was just bursting to go. None of what he said made any sense to be honest and it has cast doubt in my mind about Ben."

"Now, Josh....."

"Look, that horse was in perfect nick, absolutely ready for the race. Anyone could see that. I'm surprised I haven't been dragged up in front of the Stewards. He was 11/8 favourite and came in seventh of twelve for God's sake!"

"Yes, well, sometimes you just have to accept that favourites do disappoint."

"Or jockeys."

I looked at him hard and long.

"Or friends."

There was a very long, uncomfortable silence, which I eventually broke for his sake. After all I still couldn't be exactly sure of any involvement on his part. Truth be known, I was desperately hoping I'd got that bit wrong.

"Come on, Freddie, it's a shame to spoil our outing. Let's get you home. I just thought you might be able to help."

"Josh, I've known Ben a lot of years and all I can say

is it must be a one-off. He possibly made some bad decisions that day but don't punish him, or yourself, any further. Let it rest is my advice. You make a good team. No sense in spoiling it over one minor race."

I railed inside at what he said but I held back in public. I just couldn't leave it there. I had to solve this mystery, so I made sure I invited myself in for another bevvy. At his gate he obviously was hoping I would just drop him off, which was not a very good sign.

Eventually I was presented with another coffee, which I had no intention of drinking. As Freddie sat in his armchair I threw calm discussion out of the window and began fiercely interrogating him.

"You weren't at all surprised or disappointed by Action Replay's performance. Why not?"

"Well, too long in the tooth I suppose. Anyway, I'd had a good day."

"Made a big killing did you?"

For the first time that day Freddie looked distinctly ill at ease.

"Er, not exactly, no. But I had some luck in two earlier races and won a few bob."

"Why did you say 'now, Ben' as Action started coming down the hill?"

He was flustered now and reddened slightly.

"Did I?"

"You bloody well know you did."

"Well, er, I don't know really. Old habits die hard. That's how I always used to instruct for Epsom."

"Bullshit!" I exploded.

Freddie looked shocked and not a little scared. Then he jumped out of his skin when the phone rang to add to the tension.

"You'd better answer that hadn't you?"

"Oh, er, it can wait."

"Answer it!" I bellowed, leaping out of my chair.

"You never know, there might be another big killing to be made."

Freddie rose unsteadily to his feet, shuffled to the phone, and lifted the receiver.

"Hello."

I glared at him.

"Um, look, can I ring you back?"

Once more I gave him a hard look, but it was with a confused mixture of anger and bitter disappointment this time. While Freddie listened to the caller's reply I simply shook my head in disbelief and stormed out.

*

For the last few weeks of the flat season I simply got on with the job and, on the whole, managed to put the unsavoury Epsom incident onto the back burner. As a stable we managed two or three more winners, all with Ben Faulkner on top, and although he was wary of me, we rubbed along and he followed all my instructions to the letter. I didn't make any contact with Freddie though until after the last meeting of the season at Doncaster.

Ben and Tamara both had riding engagements with other stables down at Lingfield, so I took my young apprentice, Tom Mortimer, to the Doncaster meet. I confess that until Tom put me in the picture on the road, I had no idea Ben and Tam had been going out together for some time. But then I never was too aware of such matters.

We only had the one runner, for the financier, James Downing, but Tom did very well, holding tenaciously on to third place in a large field. Downing was pleased so it was well worth the trip, especially as it gave Tom a lot more confidence which I hoped would augur well for next season.

Our runner was in the third race and I wondered

whether to call it a day or not. I made sure our horse was safely back in his box and, deciding we'd watch the big race of the day - which was next - I went off to search for Tom. Suddenly a familiar figure appeared furtively out of a horse-box a short distance ahead of me. Freddie didn't spot me and was clearly hurrying back to the stands. I stopped dead in my tracks, absolutely horrified. Surely not? Not again! Please, not again.

The feature race simply passed me by. I found a corner of a crowded tea bar and studied my race-card for the fifth and sixth races. There it was, in the fifth, staring at me. The promising Masked Intruder. Trained by Martin Dawson, he had won four on the trot in good company at a mile this season, but today was stepping up to a mile and a quarter for the first time. It was a relatively low-profile race with pretty average opposition and he would go out a very hot favourite. His jockey, Willie Deans, had occasionally ridden for Freddie in my early years, but I refused to use him. I didn't like his overly aggressive riding style and I was always surprised when Freddie used him, albeit infrequently. I knew Martin and Freddie were good mates and so, for me, the outcome of that race was inevitable.

I watched the race through field-glasses and saw it unfold exactly as I feared. Intruder, backed down to even money, ran out of stamina in the closing stages, finishing a weary fourth. Punters would be surprised and disappointed, but no-one in authority would pick up on it. The plan was cleverly conceived and well-hatched.

I left for home feeling sick. I just had to do something about this for I couldn't, and mustn't, let it rest any longer.

*

"Let me top you up, Tam."

"Well, just one more then."

"Ben, another beer?"

"Thanks."

"Josh, look, I'm going to clear up the kitchen and then get an early night," said Ruth, my girl-friend at the time. "You three will want to talk horses as usual and that's not for me of course. So, night-night all."

"Thanks for the great curry, Ruth," said Tam.

"You're very welcome."

Ruth's lack of interest in my career might become a stumbling block in time, but there was a lot about her that appealed and she was a terrific hostess. Anyway we had pre-arranged all this. She knew it was business, not social, and she unselfishly played out her role perfectly.

"Now, you two, Christmas is around the corner, I've had a great season, I've just eaten well, and I should be in very high spirits. But I'm not. And you both know that. And you both know why. So, it's cards on the table time. I want total honesty and transparency and I give you my word that you have no need to hold back for fear of the consequences, because there won't be any that will adversely affect your future. That's, as I've said, provided you're straight with me."

Tam was the first to respond, as I anticipated.

"It's about my dad really, isn't it?"

I nodded.

"And Action Replay?" Ben added.

"Not just Action," I interrupted, "Martin Dawson's Masked Intruder as well."

"Intruder?"

Ben was clearly taken aback and looked at Tam, who shrugged and seemed equally surprised.

"Come on, Ben, you knew about this back in October. I was there when you rang Freddie."

"No, Gaffer, not Intruder. I didn't know which horse or stable, not even the meeting or race. I was just a messenger on that occasion. You must believe me, sir, I had absolutely no idea it was Mr Dawson's stable."

I sighed in exasperation and thumped the arm of my chair to let my frustration out. Tam wisely read the developing situation and took charge.

"Ben, the boss is going to have to know everything. Everything."

There was a long silence. Ben still looked very unsure but, eventually, he conceded there was no alternative.

"Let's have it then," I demanded.

"Well," said Tam, "it's quite a long story."

"We've got all night and Ruth cooks a mean breakfast."

By two o'clock in the morning first Tamara, then Ben, had told me the whole story. Tam was often tearful but I saw another side to Ben that night and he was there consoling her, before filling me in with more details until she had regained her composure.

When they had finally left - with a hug and a handshake I'm pleased to say - I re-kindled the fire in my study and sat by it deep in thought. Right until that breakfast.

*

Tam had explained that her dad had always struggled financially and things got particularly bad in 1994, just before she started at high school. She recalled her parents' endless rows over money, the cost of school uniform, the expensive extras needed so she wouldn't feel inferior to her peers.

Freddie got into gambling big-time and ran up crippling debts at a small chain of bookmakers in the North Midlands, run by one Eddie Savage. Out of the blue however, towards the end of 1995, all that had changed. The bookie's account was cleared in one fell swoop and bank loans were substantially trimmed. But at a price. An even more crippling price in the long run. Years later Tam found out Freddie had sold his soul under pressure from race-fixers. He had wrestled with his conscience for weeks on end after he had been approached, but the bank started putting pressure on him, then the bookie got nasty. He had to do it. There was no way round it. You see, the bookmaker and the race-fixer were one in the same, and Freddie was being blackmailed. The chilling threats concerning his daughter's future safety finally turned him.

In the earlier years he and Willie Deans would get the tip-off at a meeting about a week before the fix and afterwards collect payment from Eddie Savage's on-course bookie. When I came along Savage had to adjust things because Freddie was easing into retirement and was no longer a constant presence at the various racecourses.

For Savage I was a double-edged sword though because of course I was green as grass and he could take advantage of that. He dropped Deans and started using Ben during 2007, which was when he and Tamara got together. The choice of horse and stable got more sophisticated. Up until then Savage had never taken the risk of picking a horse from Freddie's own yard, but Action Replay changed all that.

I asked Tam and Ben no end of questions of course.

How did they all know that Savage would carry out his threats on Tam? When Freddie first hesitated in 95 Savage sent two of his bully boys round to persuade him. They broke three of Freddie's ribs and he lost a few teeth as well, just for good measure. Savage meant it all right. Savage by name and nature.

What sort of scam was it? The horse simply had to lose. Savage's bent betting ring would bet on it not to win.

Why did Savage enlist Ben? Obvious really. He was compromised once he started dating Tam. Then he received the same threat Freddie had got over ten years ago.

I also wanted to know how and when horses were selected by Savage. Apparently, in the early days, Freddie simply got an on-course tip-off about five or six times a year. Deans would then enact an old-fashioned but effective pulling back, using all his old guile and skill. But now, as I well knew really, a minor low-profile race was chosen, with a horse moving up in distance after a string of successes. There had however been only two or three races in each of the last two seasons, presumably because Savage wanted to lessen the risk of detection. Conversely Freddie stepped up the risk of his own choosing. Because, although he was fairly certain Ben would protect Tam, he knew Ben was young and headstrong on occasions. So, to make doubly sure, Freddie made it his business to sneak a bucket of water into the horse's box beforehand. It was an old trick, one that affected a horse's performance, but high risk, especially for Freddie. After all, I'd spotted him at Doncaster.

Finally I had wondered how Ben and Freddie got paid now. I was heartened to learn that Ben refused all payment, while everything Freddie had ever received still remained untouched in a separate bank account. He had never spent a single penny of it and vowed one day to send it all to the Jockeys Benevolent Fund. Eddie Savage cleverly operated a false punter's account in Freddie's name and electronically transferred varying amounts from time to time. All very plausible, all very clever, and extremely difficult to unravel.

Basking in his success, Savage had fairly recently opened up two or three casinos up north. Perhaps one day soon he'd push his luck a bit too far. I intended to be there when he did.

First I wanted to make peace with Freddie.

Then I might just visit a Labour politician I happened to know quite well.

*

"Now that's a first for me, Titch, seeing a Prime Minister in the flesh. Certainly in a rush though. Is he always like that?"

"Pretty much. He's gunning for my boss at the moment. Home Secretaries always seem to get it in the neck."

She stopped walking.

"Here we are."

We were in Portcullis House and she squeezed me into a very small office.

"Less an office, more a broom cupboard, but it's more private here than back at the Home Office. Now, my darling, how can I help? It's really great to see you but from your call it's obvious you're not here to compliment our government."

"No, you're spot on there. Anyway, you're not going to keep your job long, are you?"

"No comment."

We both chuckled.

We were three weeks into 2009 and on the previous Christmas Eve I'd apologised to Freddie, he to me, and we had polished off most of the scotch I'd taken round. Now I was hoping Jo could give me advice. I wanted to expose Savage and put a stop to Freddie and Tamara's hell. I was certain Freddie wouldn't be able to deal with it for much longer.

Encouragingly my sister was more than prepared to approach a Scotland Yard DCI she knew well, at least to see if the police had anything at all on Savage.

"Josh, it might take some while I'm afraid but we could strike lucky, you never know."

"Thanks, Jo, I appreciate that. I realise it may take months, even years, but at least I feel I'm doing something positive about it."

"Just don't hold out too many hopes is all I'm saying. I'm sure Bob Stapleton will want to get his teeth into this one though and I'll push it as hard as I can. Let's face it this is serious crime we're talking about."

"Yeah, it is. And it's certainly affected me. Ruth reckons I'm even more of a challenge lately!"

"Ruth's lovely, Josh. I bet she meets the challenge, and more."

"Oh, and what do you mean by that then?"

"You know what I mean. I just hope you don't ever panic and cut her loose."

"No, I really don't want to do that. It dawned on me over Christmas just how much she means to me actually."

"Good grief! Did I hear right? Is my Josh in love, or what?"

"Now, leave it out, Titch. That's a bit over the top."

"I know she loves you."

"I find that very hard to believe. I mean, I'm such a selfish bastard most of the time."

"If you were so self-centred you wouldn't be here now. Look, I've got to get back to the Home Office - there's an important meeting. I'll keep you posted."

"Thanks. Thanks a lot, Sis."

"Give my love to Ruth."

"I will."

"And give her yours as well. Ok?"

I paused and we exchanged smiles.

"Ok."

*

The next couple of months leading up to the new flat season were pretty hectic. With an increasing number of owners entrusting their horses to me I needed to continually upgrade stables and training facilities, which also meant employing more people. But top jockeys were hard to attract. I was becoming successful but not yet big enough to tempt them away from the best yards. I was therefore concentrating on a blend of youth and experience and I particularly wanted to use female jockeys on occasions. I had a theory that there were certain sensitive types of horses that responded better in their hands. Perhaps I was wide of the mark but, if Tamara was anything to go by, I thought I just might be right. It was doubtful that the likes of Tam would ever achieve champion jockey status in my time as a trainer but I reckoned she and a couple of other rising stars would be good for fifty winners or so in future years. In Tam's case, I hoped it would be for me.

All was quiet from Jo, but we'd agreed it would be a long process. As the season unfolded I could tell both Ben and Tam were working hard and riding well but I could also sense they weren't quite themselves. Freddie certainly wasn't. He looked ill and I realised he must be dreading a phone call from one of Savage's cronies.

Suddenly, one day in April, Jo rang asking me - well, telling me - to drop everything and meet her the following day in London to buy her and a friend some lunch. There was an element of subterfuge and I wondered what was going on.

*

When I spotted them with their heads close together at a secluded table near the back of a Greek restaurant in the

Strand I thought, blimey, she's got herself a new man.

"Josh, late as usual."

Jo pecked me on both cheeks.

"Yeah, well, I did have a bit further to come than you."

"You wouldn't have been on time if you lived round the corner. Now, let me introduce you two. Meet Bob. Bob, this is my horse-crazy brother, Josh."

Jo could tell the penny hadn't dropped, for I never could remember names, unless they were horses.

"Bob Stapleton, the detective I told you about?"

"Ah, of course. Good to meet you."

"Sorry, Bob, he's hopeless. He thought you were my new flame."

"You're not wrong."

I laughed, and they joined in.

Over lunch I was bowled along by developments. I had no idea Jo had acted so swiftly, although I should have known really.

I listened intently to Bob Stapleton and it transpired that Eddie Savage's casinos had already been under surveillance. Apparently drug dealers were operating there and Savage was doubtless involved and taking a cut. Once Jo had put Bob in the picture about the race-fixing he had sent a couple of his team in undercover to check out all aspects of Savage's various business ventures. In the past week one of this team had tipped Stapleton off that a fixed race might be imminent. Calls to and from Freddie's and Ben and Tam's landline phones were now being monitored by the police.

"Do they know? Didn't you have to get their co-operation?" I asked.

"No," replied Stapleton.

"I was only talking to Freddie a few days ago."

"I know."

"You know?"

"You're meeting him for a beer tomorrow at his local."

"Well I'm damned."

I shook my head in astonishment.

"I wish you could see yourself, Josh."

"I'm flabbergasted I admit. It's like something from the movies. So, Bob, what's going to happen now?"

"We wait. I'm sorry, but no more questions please."

"No, no, of course not. The less I know the better, I can see that. Just so long as Freddie and Tam are going to be safe."

"I can't guarantee that."

"What?"

"We shall stay close but successful arrests can only be made if your friends co-operate with Savage. That's why we don't want them to know anything. We want them behaving as Savage would expect. You must keep it all to yourself, Josh. One slip of the tongue could blow everything wide open."

I paused to let my slow brain take all the detail in. This was indeed serious stuff.

"Very well. I guess I set it all in motion when I asked for Jo's help. I told no-one then and I'd be absolutely stupid to let anything out now."

"Good. Well, Jo, I'll see you around no doubt. Thanks for lunch."

"Thank Josh. It's his tab."

"Thanks, Josh."

I smiled sheepishly as we shook hands.

"Phew, that was pretty mind-blowing! More coffee, Jo?"

"I think so. We've got another half an hour to catch up."

"Another of your meetings then?" I asked as I caught the waiter's attention.

"No, it's, er, personal actually."

"Oh, I see. There's nothing wrong is there?"

"Not really."

Her eyes welled up.

"Whatever's up, Titch?"

"Josh, I can't have kids."

Jo wept briefly, pulled herself together as the coffee arrived, and put a brave face on it. Throughout all this I was as useless as my father had always been when it came to dealing with tears and emotion. Eventually I muttered how sorry I was but Jo was coping again by then.

"That's ok. I had another miscarriage not long ago and now I've been seriously warned that, at my age, we really mustn't try again. I've got to see my doctor again this afternoon. I think Mike's secretly relieved. He was worried I might insist on marriage with a child in the offing."

She managed a brave smile and I knew not to pursue the subject.

"Well, I reckon our Seth's making up for both of us, Sis."

"Yeah," she laughed now. "He's certainly not been holding back has he? I talked to Maddy the other day and this fourth one of theirs could even be twins."

"No! That would be, what, five in about ten years?"

"Well, nine to be precise. So, I think I'll just stick to being Auntie."

I gently held her hands in mine and we let silence say the rest.

*

By mid-summer all thoughts of race-fixing, Eddie Savage and DCI Stapleton were virtually banished from my mind. I still cared about Freddie and Tam's welfare of course but I had to leave it to the professionals and leave everything to their judgement.

My concentration needed to be centred on Hip Hop, the exciting Derby prospect who had an outside chance of providing me with my first classic success. Sadly he was well beaten, along with the rest of the field, by the hot favourite, who just flew. But Hip Hop got very close to the runner-up and I was happy to settle for third in the end.

Then, just over a week later, came the thunderbolt.

Newspaper reports in the national dailies informed me of Eddie Savage's arrest, together with three accomplices. My heart missed a beat at 'three accomplices' but Freddie, Ben and Deans weren't mentioned. The reports actually referred to some of Savage's stooges. The police had thrown the book at him and he was confidently expected to go down for a very long time.

That same morning I received the briefest of calls from Jo saying firmly that I must never divulge anything on the whole matter. And that, of course, was how I would play it. I would be an absolute idiot to do otherwise.

Astonishingly, a couple of weeks prior to the Derby, in a minor race at Haydock, Ben had pulled my own six year old, Bayonet, and I hadn't even twigged. Admittedly he had been expected to win but was pipped at the post. I subsequently studied that race time and time again and had to hand it to Ben. He'd completely fooled me. He was beside himself with remorse when it all came out, but I assured him he did the right thing.

In July Freddie was rushed to hospital following a heart attack. After-shock I expect. Mercifully he survived but was never quite the same again. Savage's trial later that year nearly finished him off but, at long last, he had the shadow of Eddie Savage removed from his life when that Achilles Heel was given the maximum sentence.

Further enquiries into other aspects of his business dealings were ongoing which meant he would never be bothering anyone again.

Then, early in the New Year of 2010, I was pleased to be a best man again. This time to Ben. And there was never a prouder father than Freddie Watkinson as he tottered up the aisle to give away his Tam.

Ben and Tamara weren't the only ones to tie the knot that year. Jo and Michael were to be the only witnesses at my marriage to Ruth one sunny October day in a quiet civil ceremony near Newmarket. Well that, as I understood it, was the original plan until, literally seconds before the nuptials, the hotel room door burst open and there was my brother beaming from ear to ear. I stood rooted to the spot, glanced at Ruth, Jo, and then Mike. They were all smiling and obviously in on the secret.

"Hey, Josh, that's not much of a greeting, mate," Seth shouted.

I mumbled apologies to the Registrar and rushed to my twin, tears simply streaming down my face. There was nothing I could do about them for I had never quite experienced such emotion before.

It must have been nearly ten minutes before I had calmed down, after a stiff drink at the bar, sandwiched between two trips to the Gents. Fortunately the Registrar, although very busy that day, had allowed extra time at Ruth's request.

After that very patient man had completed the ceremony the five of us enjoyed my favourite rack of lamb in the hotel restaurant.

"However did you get away with it, Seth? All those little ones back home and it's your busiest time on the ranch."

"Well, mate, there's a chance I might not have made it if I didn't have a couple of reliable foremen working for me. I realise that Jason's only one but he'll be ok. And as for the rest of the kids, well, Maddy's got Jan and Cindy on hand to sort them all out. She'll be fine. Anyway, I wouldn't miss this. Never thought I'd see the day."

"They won't even realise he's not there, will they, Jo?" Ruth piped up, digging Seth in the ribs. "It takes us women to cope with children, doesn't it?"

Jo laughed, nodding in agreement, but putting an arm round Mike as she did so. I fleetingly thought how painful talk about kids probably was for her. Perhaps I should have put Ruth in the picture.

"So how long are you over for, fellah?" I asked Seth.

"I fly back the day after tomorrow."

"That soon?"

"Lots to do back home, mate, and anyway, I don't think Titch and Mike could stand it for too long. Our Sis has got a country to help govern and, as you've said, I've got a ranch to run."

"Not any more, Seth. I'm in opposition now."

"Oh yeah, of course. I forgot. Must be jet-lag."

Back in May Labour had suffered an election defeat although Jo had remarkably retained her seat, bucking the trend with an increased majority. She had been rewarded with a senior post shadowing the Treasury.

"Yes," said Mike, speaking for the first time, "it's time for your brother's lot to have a go again, Seth."

"Well hardly, Mike," I responded. "It's going to be a nightmare having to work in a Coalition. We'll get nothing useful through."

Mike had actually lost his seat and was now a director of a successful wind turbine company.

"Now then," complained Ruth, "I refuse to listen to any more politics on my wedding day."

"Mmm," I murmured, "I wonder how Comfort Zone's getting on at Windsor?"

"Nor horses."

"It's going to be a very quiet afternoon then."

I couldn't have been more wrong. Gradually, over the rest of the day, friends from far and wide arrived. For Ruth had arranged a big party.

The next day - well, half-day, for we all rose late - Mike stayed behind at ours with Ruth because they both insisted Jo, Seth and I spent the afternoon out together. It was special and we walked and reminisced for hours.

*

If I had been surprised to get married at forty-eight then it was a greater shock to find myself a father at fifty and, two years later, a father again. Ruth produced Henry first, and then Evie. It was at this point I realised just how Freddie felt about his Tam. To me, Henry was absolutely great, but I confess I was utterly besotted with my daughter and I boringly told anyone who cared to listen she would go on to be the first-ever female champion jockey.

And yet I really shouldn't have been unprepared for either marriage or fatherhood. You see, I'd had a visit from my mother prior to our wedding.

Significantly I was in Sussex, stopping for one night in Church Farm holiday lodge, following an important charity council meeting. I was sitting in the garden that evening with a cold beer trying to get my head round the numerous plans Lizzie James had for the charity over the next few years. In the end I gave up. I'd stick to horses. So I wandered down the path to the old five-bar gate to take in the familiar landscape.

"We're proud of you, Josh.....you're doing so well....."

Strangely I wasn't that surprised to hear my mum. I'd almost half-expected it I think, although I wasn't ready for what she said next.

"Marry Ruth.....loves you so much.....you won't

regret....."

"But, Mum, you know I'm too unreliable. She deserves better than me. All of them do. I let women down."

"Boy and girl....."

"Now hold on a minute, me a dad? Is that what you're saying?"

"Ruth....."

And that was it. She was gone. Cupid disappeared off the radar after that and, nearly four years later, as I recalled that day's one-way conversation, I smiled to myself. She never seemed to get much wrong, my dear mum. She only ever made one mistake - she couldn't control that car.

*

So as I've said, in 2014, approaching fifty-two, suddenly there I was a husband and father. I doted on both the kids if I'm honest, spending as much time as work allowed with Henry after Evie was born. Ruth was struggling to get her to breast-feed but persisted determinedly. This made Ruth permanently exhausted. Luckily Tamara was often about and became a great help to her. Also luckily, for me, Tam was not yet planning on having kids of her own and therefore became a very important rider for our stable.

As I had forecast, she had been riding plenty of winners and we were all excited at the yard since she was going to be on board my best filly, Birdsong, for the Oaks at Epsom the following month. This horse was a little temperamental and usually nervous going down to the start but Tam always talked her gently through it all. She was unbeaten in both her races of the current season and had been defeated only once in five starts the year before. So this lovely animal really could possibly be my first classic winner, and plenty of other people thought so too - she was ante-post favourite.

On the day Birdsong didn't disappoint and came home brilliantly to win easily by two lengths. I was overjoyed and Tam was beside herself. We all celebrated well into the night and I got home rather late, having consumed far too much champagne at the racecourse.

It didn't help when I discovered Ruth propped up in bed, frustrated with Evie who wouldn't co-operate with feeding yet again. Selfishly all I wanted to do was keep celebrating and I ranted on about Birdsong until Ruth simply couldn't take any more.

"Look, Josh, I'm genuinely pleased for you, really I am."

"You don't give that impression."

"I'm sorry. It's just.....I can't....." and she burst into tears.

Not my strong point, tears, as I've said before, but this was so very unusual for Ruth so I had to sit up and take notice.

"Ruthie, I should be the one to apologise," I said, gently taking Evie from her. "I just didn't appreciate how much all this has been getting you down."

"I wanted to be with you today, Josh, I really did. I know I don't understand your world very much but I do always want to share your successes. I don't like it when you have to celebrate without me. But our babies need me here at the moment. It's how it must be. I've.....I've missed you so much today....."

More tears flowed.

"Ruth, I shouldn't have stayed out so late."

"I watched the race on tv and was so excited. Then I waited and waited for you to come home so I could share it with you....."

Evie had dropped off so I lowered her into her cradle and eased myself into bed. My head was banging intolerably.

"We can share it tomorrow, love. Come on, time for some shut-eye. You're all in."

She got herself comfortable and felt for my hand.

"Everything's going to be ok, isn't it, Josh?"

"Of course."

"You've seemed so distant these past couple of months."

"Well, I have had a lot on, what with the Oaks and a couple of new owners."

"I just want us to be a family and spend time together."

"Ruth, we are. Believe me, nothing matters more to me than you and the kids. Nothing."

"Not even Birdsong?"

"Not even Birdsong. Now, let's stop this nonsense. Look, we'll have a day out tomorrow. Perhaps a picnic on the Heath?"

"That'll be nice. I'll take her bottle. I've decided to give up on these."

She snuggled up close beside me and both of us must have dropped off to sleep straight away.

We did have a very happy day, although the picnic was predictably hit and miss with two little ones and our two dogs. Nevertheless it was, I thought, a turning point for Ruth. I certainly hoped so.

I was enjoying a whisky in my study at the end of that day. Ruth had retired early, much happier though. I realised that I had managed the situation rather like my father had all those years ago when Mum died. He had been fine with one-offs when it came to entertaining his offspring. I reckoned the same could probably be said of me. I loved my two children. I was proud of them. But, like Dad, it had all come so late in life to me and I was often a somewhat reluctant father. Fortunately, unlike Dad, I still had my wife and I was sure this blip in our hitherto cosy existence was only temporary.

And so it proved. Gradually we got back into the swing of things and, nearly a year later, Ruth seemed to be coming right out of what Jo had suggested to me was possibly a period of post-natal depression.

*

Jo herself had an incredibly hectic and astonishing 2015. The Government had somehow stuttered to complete its full term and a general election was called in April. Jo was, perhaps surprisingly, Shadow Chancellor at the time. I joked about it to her saying I knew learning how to take £1 per dozen for egg sales at our farm gate all those years ago would pay dividends one day. She had also shadowed Northern Ireland prior to her current role, so she was now regarded as quite a political heavyweight. What's more, by all accounts she was becoming a very tough opponent to deal with, especially in the House.

However, as much as I respected her, I'm pleased to say a Conservative government was returned.

Jo wasn't surprised at the result. Again she retained her seat, although the Greens had contested the seat for the first time and remarkably came second, albeit a long way behind Jo.

At the time I doubt anyone could have forecast that a few months later Jo would become Labour Party Leader. Yes, Labour elected a woman to lead them for the first time in their history and, to my amazement, it was my little sister!

On the day of the General Election in May, Ruth and I had supported Jo - despite my political colour - travelling in her wake as she tirelessly toured her constituency to persuade last-minute floating voters. It was actually a quite extraordinary experience for us. Ruth's mother and Tamara were in charge of the children at our place and we were to have our first-ever night away from them. All day long, and into the evening, Ruth kept fiddling with her mobile but after a couple of drinks at the post-election party she started to relax more.

"Who is that striking young woman with Jo and Mike?"

"Can't remember her name."

"Well, why am I not surprised? Actually I should have said 'what is she?'"

"Works for Jo in some shape or form."

"Personal Assistant?"

"That's it."

"Very pretty. You've obviously impressed."

"How come?" I asked, not really interested.

"Well, she keeps glancing over here."

"Old enough to be her father."

"That's the attraction I expect."

"Well, you're the attraction for me and to be honest I'd be more than happy to leave now. We don't have to wait for the result and that king-sized bed in our hotel room looked very comfortable."

"We'd better go and try it out then, hadn't we?"

Ruth's eyes sparkled and we quietly slipped away.

*

To my disappointment Ruth was unable to join me in the autumn at celebrations following Jo's election as Labour leader. They took place at a Premier Inn in Birmingham city centre near the conference hall, and of course the media smartly latched onto 'Premier'. It guaranteed Jo almost blanket coverage in the press the next morning.

Henry had a filthy cold so Ruth understandably stayed at home to look after him. I was saddling two or three runners at Wolverhampton the following weekend -

dependent on the going - so Ruth had persuaded me to travel to the Midlands earlier in the week on the day of the vote. I certainly wasn't too enthusiastic about attending a Labour Party event but in the end Ruth got me to go for Jo's sake. I arrived in the conference hall just as the result was announced and, despite myself, I couldn't help feeling a great swell of pride. Jo had won comfortably and I was glad I had listened to Ruth.

At the celebrations in the evening however I felt very much the odd man out. I already missed Ruth and I didn't really enjoy being at social events without her these days.

I had found a reasonably quiet little bar and was just about to call it a day when I was joined by a very attractive member of Jo's campaign team. I vaguely recognised her from the General Election as Jo's P.A. I was checking my watch as she hopped onto the bar-stool next to me. She gave me a wide smile and confidently ordered a drink.

The barman served her a very large glass of wine and she knocked some of it back greedily.

"Phew! Didn't I need that," she declared, turning to me.

I smiled.

"I'm Beth Farraday by the way."

"Good to meet you, Beth. And I'm....."

"Josh Rayner, the famous racehorse trainer."

"Well, I'd hardly say 'famous', to be honest."

"That's just what your sister says you are."

"Famous?"

"No, honest."

I smiled again and looked into my empty glass.

"Let me order you another pint, Josh."

"Thank you, but I'll buy it."

"No need. All mine are free you see."

She caught the eye of the barman again.

"So, what's it like working with my sister then, er....."

"Beth."

"Yeah, sorry. Hopeless with names."

"I know. Jo's told me that too."

"It's going to be a challenge discovering something about myself you don't know by the sound of it."

She laughed.

"What's amusing?"

"You. Jo says exactly that. You're amusing, and in a way you don't always seem to realise. She says you've got a very special sense of humour but you're often shy to bring it out."

I have to admit I was a little embarrassed by the personal way the conversation had taken off, but my beer arrived and I was able to take a long swig and regroup.

"Thank you for this," I said.

"Cheers."

I looked at my watch again.

"I calculate that, in less than five minutes, I must have learnt a great deal about myself. So much so that, if we continue at this rate, by the end of the evening I'll be able to go on 'Mastermind', specialist subject Joshua Rayner, 1962 – 2015."

I could see I'd amused her again.

"I don't believe you're that old. Sixty-three? Come on!"

"I'm not sixty....."

I had started to correct her maths then twigged she was doing a double-take. It was my turn to laugh.

"Nearly had me going for a minute there."

"Anyway, in answer to your original question, it's brilliant working for Jo but she is a taskmaster. I have to deliver, or else. It's pretty knackering."

"And what do you have to deliver? I'm sure it's not her mail or her weekly shop."

"No." Another smile. "Her schedule. I'm her Girl Friday I guess. The job title is 'Trouble Shooter', but if I don't arrange each day's timetable precisely I'm the one in trouble and in the firing line."

"Jo never suffered fools gladly and she's certainly a perfectionist. I suppose that makes your job that much harder."

"Sure, but it's not all bad. Jo's very kind to me and we have so many laughs when the pressure's off a bit. She's always telling me about the antics you and your brother used to get up to."

"Oh, we're back there again are we?"

"And Jo loves your amazing impersonations."

"I think 'amazing' is rather too generous."

"Do Freddie the Frog for me."

"What?"

"Do your Freddie Frog song."

I hesitated, shaking my head.

"Go on. Please?"

She wasn't going to let it go so I duly obliged and she creased up.

"Oh, that is so hilarious!"

Another more familiar voice thankfully rescued me from having to do an encore.

"I'm glad my brother is such good company, Beth."

We both turned round to greet my sister who was beaming.

"Oh, Jo, you're so right about him."

"He's not been doing 'Old MacDonald' just yet I hope?"

"No, but tell me more."

And with that Jo happily recounted more moments in her childhood when Seth and I entertained her.

An hour and three pints further down the line, Jo and Beth were dragging me to the centre of the gathering, announcing it was cabaret time. There was no way I could have done it without plenty of alcohol inside me, but everyone else seemed to be in a similar state of bonhomie and I was cheered generously at the end.

So, my dull evening actually ended on a rather bright note. Or rather, on a moo-moo here and a moo-moo there.

*

Looking back, I confess young Beth Farraday turned my head a fraction that day. Oh, not in any inappropriate way, though she was certainly attractive enough. I simply found myself thinking about her on occasions and it brought a smile to my face. Her own mischievous smile, her bubble-bath personality, her child-like awe of my very ordinary jokes and impersonations, her friendly and easy-going manner. And, in my perhaps too open and honest way, for a while I had talked about her rather a lot to Ruth, especially one day as we washed up.

"Made quite an impression on you this Miss Farraday. I presume she's single?"

"Yeah, she's engaged to some actor. Well, I guess we just clicked like father and daughter really."

"Now they don't necessarily click, as you put it. You should know that well enough."

"True, I see what you're getting at."

"Do you, Josh?"

"Well, you mean about Carrie and my dad."

"Yes, but what I'm really trying to say is, be careful."

"Oh, Ruth, now come on, please give me some credit. Beth's my sister's employee and we just met at Jo's party and had fun. That's all."

Ruth put her hand in mine and gently touched my cheek with the other one.

"I know that, Josh, but people sometimes misinterpret your friendliness and you've admitted in the past it's unwittingly got you into a bit of a hole. I realise where you're coming from. Just so long as she does. That's all I'm saying."

"Ruthie, thanks for pointing these things out but believe me that young lady is very street-wise. People like me pop in and out of her life but are soon forgotten. Anyway, I'm just a clown. You know that."

"Performing for laughs. I know. Come on, these dishes can drain overnight. Let's get to bed."

"Now that's more like it."

We smiled knowingly at one another.

I was getting one of her irresistible looks and further talk of Miss Farraday, or anyone else, was dismissed instantly.

*

One morning a few months later, as spring flowers were saying farewell, Beth popped briefly back into my life. Ruth had taken the phone call and was just finishing the conversation as I walked into the kitchen.

"Oh, hold on, will you? He's just come in. I'm sure he'd like a quick word."

'Who is it?' I mouthed.

Ruth handed me the phone and just smiled, so I had to take the call.

"Hello?"

"Hi, Josh, it's Beth."

"Beth?"

I noticed Ruth smiling again at my awful memory as she picked up Evie.

"Beth Farraday, Jo's assistant."

"Oh, right. Sorry, my head's full of horses, feed and stable-lads this morning. Beth, how are you?"

"Good thanks. But up to my ears as usual."

"I'm glad to hear my sister's still cracking the whip."

"You are full of horse-talk, aren't you?"

"I thought you were going to say horse-shit for a moment then. Anyway how can I help?"

Ruth arched an eyebrow quizzically as she changed Evie. I shrugged my shoulders while Beth burst out laughing.

"Look, I've given your wife the details. But briefly Jo's in East Anglia for two days next week and rather hoping you can put her up overnight."

"Scheduling you call it, don't you?" I said.

She laughed again.

"Yep, that's about the size of it. Anyway, your wife's going to get back to me when she's talked to you. Other phone's going. Absolute madhouse! Must go. Sorry. Bye."

I looked at the dead phone in a bit of a daze.

"Girl in a hurry," Ruth commented.

"Whirlwind."

In the event it was I who later made the return call. Ruth had put me in the picture over lunch and I realised I was down south for the same days as Jo's trip. It was an important three-day meeting at Ascot but Ruth would put Jo up. They would have fun.

"Josh," shouted Ruth.

I was in the yard with yet another feed rep. I excused myself and left him with my Head Lad.

"Darling, I've got to collect Henry from Playgroup. Can you look after Evie, please?"

"Of course."

Ruth reached the back door and shouted again.

"Oh, and I haven't had time to phone that Beth Farraday back. Will you do it?"

"Sure. No problem."

First I checked Evie was still asleep then I hunted for Jo's direct number. Eventually, under invoices for hay and straw, I managed to track it down, making a mental note to try and improve our filing system one day. I dialled.

"Beth Farraday."

"Oh, Beth, it's Josh Rayner. I had hoped to get Jo."

"Sorry, she's out all day. If it's about her trip to you I can help."

"Yes it is. Please tell her it's absolutely fine for her to stay but I won't be there. Ruth will love entertaining her though."

"Ok, it's programmed in. She'll contact your wife once she's on her way."

"Programmed in? It makes us sound like computer software."

"Just all part of the jargon here."

"Well I'm glad I deal with people face-to-face and not have to live in your world, I must say."

I think she might have picked up my slight irritation because she slowed down a bit and seemed to want to make amends, prattling along about when we met at Jo's party. Apparently she had since heard from Jo about the many comedy sketches Seth and I had enacted.

"But she wouldn't tell me the punch-line about Happy and Grumpy."

"Ah," I said, "Jo always giggled at that."

"So?"

"No, no, I have to be in party mood. Anyway I think I hear my little one stirring and I'm in charge. Look, why don't we meet up sometime next week when I'm down?"

"That would be very nice."

"I'll give you a call perhaps and we could have a bite somewhere. Bring your boy-friend along. I don't really meet many actors."

"Right, well, I might be hearing from you then."

"Take care now."

Evie was rather damp and I was only just finishing sorting her out when Ruth got back from the village with Henry. He wanted to show me his latest picture of a horse. More like an elephant really.

"Did you make that phone call to Jo's office, love?"

Ruth asked.

"Yes. We're all programmed in. So bloody impersonal."

"Not everyone is as easy with people as you are."

"Oh, we chatted for quite a while in the end. Beth could tell I was a bit narked with her cold efficiency."

"She's a busy person, Josh."

"So am I. So are you. But we always try to give people time."

"I think we're too accommodating at times."

"Not a bad fault. Anyway I might be meeting up with her and her fiancé when I go to Ascot. Should be interesting meeting him."

"You've always found actors dull and pompous in the past."

"Oh, you mean old Charlton Nesbitt. Well, yes, he's certainly a boring old fart, and what a name for pity's sake. But I just ask him about his latest play, press the button, and off he goes. A small price to pay for his two cracking mares."

"Here we go again, Henry," said Ruth, hugging our son, "it all ends up with horses with your daddy, doesn't it?"

"And you're following in my footsteps, aren't you," I added, as we lovingly watched him starting to draw another elephant.

*

After the second day of Ascot we had already saddled three winners, two seconds and a fourth, and I was feeling very chipper. I sensed this could be my year. It was unusual for us to get off to such a successful start. We were usually always playing catch-up. But it was different this time and we all felt very positive about the season ahead.

I was therefore in very good humour by the time I had dinner with Beth Farraday. Apparently her fiancé, Tom, was busy rehearsing for a new production at the Old Vic. 'The Tempest' I think.

Anyway conversation and wine flowed and we chatted comfortably enough on a wide range of subjects. The whole of the restaurant enjoyed my Grumpy story because I was getting somewhat raucous.

Over coffee in the hotel lounge we both became a bit more subdued and I asked her about her family. Big mistake. It changed the whole tone of the evening, which had been fun up until then. Beth simply clammed up and I just assumed she found relationships difficult. Rather like my sister, Carrie, I couldn't help thinking. Then I recalled Ruth's intuitive comments in our kitchen. So I switched to asking Beth about her fiancé's career and although she opened up a bit more it all still seemed uncomfortable territory for her. I happened to glance at her left hand and wondered.

"I take it you two are still engaged? I notice the ring's missing."

By her look I guessed I'd put my foot in it again but she did reply eventually.

"I only wear it when Jake and I are out. I don't do jewellery to be honest. Anyway he insists I wear it when we socialise. He just likes parading me in front of his lovey-dovey acting pals."

"You don't approve I take it?"

"They make me cringe. So false. Always acting. You can't trust anything they say."

"Well, we all act up sometimes. Look at me earlier."

"Yes, but that's so different. You simply responded to my request. Anyway so many of his so-called friends are such creeps, whereas I feel comfortable with someone like you."

"Oh dear, it's very sobering to know I'm nice and

safe. I was hoping I might score tonight."

"I hate that expression."

"Sorry, it was just my joke, Beth."

"Maybe, but I don't like it."

I got touchy now.

"There's no 'maybe' about it, young lady. It was a joke."

She gave a wan smile and the atmosphere had noticeably chilled. No matter how hard I tried I seemed to have unwittingly spoilt her evening with my crass remark.

"So," I said eventually, in an attempt to rescue things, "what has Jake got lined up this year?"

"After the Old Vic's run he's got a slack period, but then, believe it or not, he's off to America filming."

"Exciting. Will you be going over there with him at any stage?"

"He expects me to drop everything and go with him and a part of me wants to, but....."

"Which part?"

"The part of me that wants to be with him I suppose."

"Then for goodness sake go, Beth. And make sure you stay with him, if he's the one you want. I was given similar advice once and the best thing I ever did was marry Ruth."

She started gathering her things together to go.

"Yes, well, who knows? I might go or I might not."

I stood up to say goodnight but the whirlwind was back.

"Thanks for dinner, Josh. But it's been a long day."

And, without a backward glance, she hurried out leaving me to wonder, not for the first time in my life, why I always managed to put my foot in it so often. God, I thought, some women can be such sensitive creatures. I never had understood them and I reckoned I never would.

*

I was really pleased to get home to my family and share the success of Ascot with Ruth. Unbelievably we'd saddled two more winners on the final day.

In fact the whole of that season was fantastic and I ended up Champion Trainer. Not only that, I was fortunate enough to repeat the feat the following year too.

I never did hear from Beth Farraday again. Quite soon after our dinner-date I gathered from Jo that she'd suddenly left her employment to work abroad. Well I hoped she had joined Jake in America and that he would eventually have the good sense to marry her. Sensitive she may be, but in the very short time I'd got to know her she seemed to me to be a good person, decent. What was so interesting to me was that her super confidence in the workplace veiled a distinct lack of it in her personal life. Yet another example of the contents being disguised by the packaging.

*

At the end of 2017, with two seasons as Top Trainer under my belt, I learnt to my immense surprise that I had been recommended for an MBE. I had to keep it all hushed up of course until the New Year's Honours List was published. This was difficult because I was over the moon.

What pleased me more than anything was that there were two reasons for me getting a gong. Obviously, by now, I was very much in the public domain as a successful trainer. But of greater importance and significance to me was that the accolade had been made for services to horse racing and to charity. The latter was clearly in recognition of Church Farm and that gave me the most satisfaction.

At the ceremony in the Palace I received the MBE from His Majesty and afterwards, over a cup of tea, Ruth, Henry, Evie and I were joined by the Leader of the Opposition and her husband.

"Congratulations, Bruv."

"Thanks, Titch."

My sister hugged me.

"I'm so proud."

"Yes, well done, Josh."

"Mike."

He shook my hand warmly.

"I don't suppose I'd have got it if your lot had been in power, Jo?"

"No chance. You just squeezed it in time."

"So, we should believe what all the political pundits are suggesting then?"

"They can't hold on much longer," said Mike, "and they're still so divided over Europe."

"I don't know what to say, Mike. I'm Tory through and through but now there's a part of me that wants success for Jo here."

"Early days, Josh," said Jo, obviously keen to change the subject.

"Now," she continued, "I've booked a table at that Greek place I know you like. They're happy to take little ones so what are we waiting for?"

"Lead on, McDuff," I cheerfully shouted.

"Your daddy should have been on the stage, Evie," Jo said, taking her by the hand.

"Will there be crinkle-cut chips?" Henry asked, grabbing my hand.

"Well, possibly," said his mum, "but I'm sure there'll be some amazing ice-cream for afters."

"Nice one," replied Henry.

"Dear, oh dear," I said, "not even six yet. Wherever do they get these phrases from?"

*

That year was momentous for the Rayner family and none more so than for Jo. Her husband had been right at my investiture. The Conservative government couldn't hold out, Europe divided them yet again, and Labour came back to power a few months later in a landslide victory.

My sister, the Right Honourable Joanne Rayner, became the first female Labour Prime Minister in the history of Great Britain.

It was a strange sensation being brother to the Prime Minister, although it hardly affected my daily life of course. What was interesting was my reaction to her Premiership and the policies she doggedly pushed through. Naturally I was proud of her but Labour had such a huge majority in the House that they soon seemed to have virtually demolished most of the good measures I and many other people I knew felt were worth keeping in place.

I saw in Jo, as Premier, those same tough, uncompromising traits she often portrayed as we grew up together. And it has to be said she doubtless made a lot of enemies over the next few years, some of them dangerous even. One formidable lady. As Ruth confided in me one day, Jo was, as a sister-in-law and her children's aunt, thoughtful, kind and generous but she would never want to get on the wrong side of her.

As time passed I often thought about Jo and concluded that there had also been a noticeable change in her over recent years. And I actually felt I could trace it all back to that time she first told me she couldn't have kids.

*

My own career was busy and very successful. It was in fact probably the most satisfying period of my life, workwise and personally too. Between 2018 and 2021 good fortune was my constant companion and I managed to enjoy two more seasons as Champion Trainer, although 2022 was disappointing. Early on there was severe coughing in our yard and my string of horses never really got going all season. But I was philosophical.

That year, in July, Seth and I became sixty. At the time of course I was snowed under, but a great celebration was on the horizon. In October, together with Ruth and the kids, I was to fly out to Australia, leaving the yard in very capable hands. The trip would finish just after Christmas and we would be home for New Year. We were all very excited. Henry was ten now and Evie would be eight while we were out there. Ruth and I therefore thought this was the perfect time for them so that it wouldn't interfere with high school education. I quietly felt it was the best possible education for them anyway. Besides, we all needed a good holiday.

*

Well, what a reunion! What a time we had!

I thought I could knock the beer back, but the way those Aussies drank, especially Seth's brother-in-law, Ty. It was something else, and something Seth admitted to me he had never quite got used to himself.

Wherever we travelled the scenery was spectacular and, just as I'd thought on my earlier trip, it truly was a magnificent country Seth had chosen.

Our children were in paradise with five cousins to entertain them. Yes, Seth had managed yet another one. Henry and Evie revelled in their company and not even Ruth had any qualms about the two of us taking off for a few days together in Sydney at the end of October.

Views from the Harbour Bridge were simply breathtaking and our visit to the Opera House awesome. We were particularly lucky for the Moscow State Ballet was touring at the time, and we watched a lavish production of Prokofiev's 'Romeo and Juliet'. The experience was unforgettable.

A big attraction at Seth's ranch was their new pool. Every evening - I don't think we missed one - we gratefully had a dip and the kids were often in and out all day long while their cousins were at school. After just a few weeks they were already getting a beautiful tan and this was only Australia's early summer really.

One evening, the second Sunday of November, we all had a particularly long swim and the kids were shattered. We had finally popped them into bed at nine. Seth's Jason, now just thirteen, was a bit awkward about going at this time, but he had school the next morning and one sharp look from Seth had been enough. Seth and Maddy's youngest, Shane, had been born the year between our two so was quite happy to be bundled along with them, although he too had to attend school of course.

"Maddy had her way with the names for your two youngest then, Seth," said Ruth.

We were relaxing in their massive sitting-room with Seth and his older children.

"Afraid so, but there you go, Ruthie. I had a pretty good say with these three, so fair dinkum."

I looked at each of them in turn. They certainly were great kids: Patsy, now unbelievably twenty-one and a real stunner, just like her mum; Eleanor was already nineteen and very pretty too - a little like our sister, Carrie, I thought; and Will, sixteen, named after his English grand-father, our dad of course. He was very like Seth, quiet, thoughtful, but very interesting to talk to when you could get him on his own.

"Oh, my God! Seth, come quickly! Quickly!"

Maddy had suddenly screamed from the kitchen.

"Jeez!" Seth exclaimed. "Might be another spider. Can't be too careful. You guys sit tight."

He rushed out of the room.

A couple of minutes later he trudged disconsolately back, an arm round Maddy, who was visibly trembling.

Seth and Maddy slumped onto a sofa before Seth eventually managed to tell us in a strained, broken voice.

While she was clearing up a few bits of washing Maddy had put the tv on and the programme had been interrupted for a news-flash.

Our sister, Jo, had just been shot at the Cenotaph in London as she laid a wreath on Remembrance Sunday.

*

Seth and I each held one of Jo's hands as we sat either side of her hospital bed. Detectives guarded her room and aides buzzed in and out from time to time.

"Shouldn't they let you rest?" I protested. "It's been less than a week and you've only just come out of intensive care."

"The country still has to be run, Josh," she weakly replied, "and all they usually need is my signature. Michael checks the detail before I sign."

"My God, Sis, you always were the stubborn one," said Seth.

"Well it's what has pulled me through."

"But you're still seriously ill and you need to rest," I said.

"I am tired. Very tired, I have to admit. The pain doesn't help."

"Look, we'll be off now. You get to sleep and we'll pop in again tomorrow."

"I will, Josh, and thank you both so much for coming.

But then I knew you would."

"See you tomorrow, Sis," said Seth, bending down to kiss her cheek.

"No, Seth. Look, listen, both of you. Josh must go back with you, and you must all finish your holiday together."

"Well, Jo," I said, gently squeezing her hand, "you just let us be the judge of that."

"No, I insist. I'll be fine in time. Lovely as it was of you to come, neither of you can do anything here. Besides, I've got Michael and the best doctors to take very good care of me. Now, go. Please. Go back to Australia and complete your holiday."

Walking to the station, Seth and I agreed it was difficult to argue with Jo. We had seen her come out of immediate danger and her husband was constantly with her. But we were both still unsure about leaving the country just yet so the next day we took the opportunity to hire a car to Suffolk and visit Mum, Dad and Carrie's resting place at Upper Chesney.

*

We stood graveside, arms locked and heads bowed, as England's winter made its brittle presence felt. Then, thankfully, the fierce wind dropped and a period of relative calm ensued.

"Go back.....Jo fine.....has Michael.....finish your holiday."

Our mother was there, reassuring me. I glanced at Seth, wondering if it was just me she had spoken to. Had he heard anything?

We remained in the churchyard for a while then, as the wind got up again, my brother turned to me.

"I guess we go back then, Josh."

BOOK FIVE : A MUSICAL PREMIER

As I knelt down I was aware of what seemed to be a distant gunshot, accompanied by searing pain in my left hip. Then I received what journalists later described as a ferocious rugby tackle. I staggered forwards as another shot rang out, and blacked out as my head hit one of the Cenotaph steps.

The human avalanche was my bodyguard. He saved my life that day. That same day he lost his.

My potential assassin was also killed. Somehow he had managed to infiltrate complex security arrangements. From an office window on the top floor, very close to the Cenotaph itself, he had unleashed the first shot, just as I bent to lay the wreath. The pain was excruciating but, luckily for me - and tragically for my bodyguard - his second effort hit Matt Lancaster in the back as he dived on top of me.

I vaguely regained consciousness many hours later. I drifted in and out for over three days and was only released from intensive care on the fourth day.

It transpired that the gunman hailed from Belfast, but thorough investigations suggested that the young Irishman had no affiliation to any group. Rightly or wrongly, it was concluded, in time, that he was working on his own. He had a history of mental illness, but I would never know what actually drove him to want to kill me. Although he had managed to get into the building he had completely misunderstood the office exit code and became trapped as armed police cornered him. I'm told he was shot because he threatened to endanger them too.

I had to believe that.

On the Friday morning, nearly a week later, my brothers arrived from Australia. I knew they would come. They both needed to actually see me alive and kicking. Well, alive anyway. Kicking might be out for some while. I insisted however that they booked a return flight as soon as possible to resume their family holiday together. Of course they protested, but I really saw no point in them having to hang around unnecessarily on my account. They dropped in again three days later on their way to the airport.

"Now you're sure about this, Titch?"

"Oh, Josh, of course. I'm through the worst. Don't you read the papers?"

"As you've always said, only the back pages," he replied.

"Honestly, Seth, I'm headline news on a daily basis and still he doesn't notice."

They both chuckled, but my feisty conversation seemed to convince them they could consider flying back now, especially since Michael had hardly left my side for a week. He, along with the Deputy Prime Minister, Jonathan Petchey, vetted all my papers for signature, and helped enable the Government to get through the immediate crisis. Jon's role was a new one, because of course I had, in my efforts to streamline the way we governed, ironically knocked that particular post on the head.

"Off you go, both of you. I'm out of danger now and your families need you. Besides I've got to get plenty of sleep."

*

It did take a lot of sleep over the ensuing weeks, initially on my hospital bed and then at Number Ten.

For the most part I had the most vivid and detailed dreams. I literally found myself re-living the most significant moments of my last twenty-five dramatic years. Of course I was on the strongest imaginable painkillers and they certainly would have contributed to everything tumbling back with such clarity.....

*

"First in, last out again, then?"

"Yes, Jack, it looks like it."

Our driver carefully eased the cello out from the belly of the coach and kindly strapped it to my instrument carrier.

"Thank you, but I could have done that."

"It's my pleasure. Now you go and enjoy the break. You'll love it here."

"I'm sure I shall, but everyone else is probably already in the pool by now. Perhaps I should have learnt to play the piccolo like my mum."

"Well, not everyone," said Jack, nodding knowingly at a familiar figure as he sauntered towards us.

"Come on, my sweetie, you're missing the party. Here let me help."

It was Gabriel Morgan, the orchestra's brilliant leader. Everyone, even the blokes, was 'my sweetie' and I noticed Jack smile to himself as he went off to tidy up his beloved wagon.

"No need, thanks." I quickly replied. "Jack's sorted me out. I can manage perfectly now."

"I was thinking that perhaps you'd like to join a few of us at Lake Garda tomorrow. Some of the other strings are already coming. The hotel always allows us access to one of their mini-buses for local use."

Gabriel had toured many times with the European Symphony Orchestra, whereas this was my first trip. He was like a fading matinee idol really, but harmless fun. Anyway, his experience of where, and where not to go, was useful to the novices like me. So I agreed.

"Is it far from here?" I asked as we walked to Reception.

"No, no. It's about halfway to Brescia. That's towards Milan."

"I shall look forward to it. But just at the moment I can't wait to get into that pool. Catch up with you later."

I guided my cello to the lift and soon found my room on the third floor.

I was relieved to discover I was still sharing with Samantha Bennett, a quiet and studious viola player, with whom I had begun to strike up a good rapport. She was from Maidenhead and one of surprisingly few English string players in the orchestra. Our section seemed to be dominated by Dutch and Germans.

"Goodness!" I exclaimed. "What a view!"

"Beautiful, isn't it," said Sam, as she emerged from the shower. "Apparently that's Verona in the distance."

"Well, I'm certainly looking forward to this part of the tour, especially the next few days. I want to make the most of our break. Today's Tuesday, isn't it?"

"Yes, although it's hard for me to keep track."

"So, no more work until Saturday. Fantastic! Are you coming on Gabriel's little outing tomorrow?"

"I'm not sure. I've got so many cards to send home."

"Well I'm keen to see Garda but I must admit I wouldn't mind some solitude either. Perhaps there'll be a chance to slip away for a while when I get there."

"Just watch out for those charming Italian men if you do," laughed Sam.

"I've grown up with two older brothers, so I think I'll cope. Now I really must have a swim."

*

It was the beginning of May 1997 and it could be fairly said that I seemed to have landed on my feet. At the end of last year I had signed up to a five-year contract with the ESO, following a couple of years with an English national orchestra.

Following months of intensive rehearsals we had embarked on tour mid-April and had so far performed in Rotterdam, Frankfurt and Salzburg. During May we would still be travelling, but less intensively, and we were touring Italy for the whole month. After Verona and Lake Garda we would be moving on to Bologna, then Florence, and, finally, Milan and Lake Como.

Admittedly I was at the age when such excitement was mind-blowing and head-turning, and sometimes I simply couldn't believe my good fortune. How lucky was I to be seeing so many amazing places? After Italy we were to travel to engagements in Lyon, Paris and Brussels, arriving home towards the end of June, just in time for my twenty-eighth birthday. Although a very European mix, the orchestra was based in London and this was also a bonus. It was sensational and I would be foolish not to make the most of every moment.

Life certainly hadn't always dealt me such a good hand however. My dad often used to say it wasn't the cards you were given, but the way you played them. While I could see where he was coming from there had definitely been times, particularly in my teens and very early twenties, when I had my doubts.

I never knew what it was like to have a mother of course. I was still only two when mine had her fatal car crash. And I suppose my sister, Carrie, was the closest I ever got to having one, in the early years anyway. Certainly Carrie and Dad behaved like a married couple sometimes, constantly bickering. I hated it. Fortunately my twin brothers always managed to put a smile back on my face whenever I was upset, especially Josh.

Without doubt, the worst moment of my life had been experiencing the tragedy of my sister, following my twenty-first birthday celebration. And yet, in that strange way fate has of tweaking one's life, conversely it turned out to be the beginning of a really positive period for me.

My hitherto uncertain career suddenly clicked into place and took off. You see, after leaving high school at eighteen, rightly or wrongly, I didn't really want to leave home. Perhaps I was just scared to. It was the only security I'd known, difficult as it had been without another woman around. In the last few years I suppose it was fair to say I had taken on my mother's role, in a strange sort of way. Carrie never came home and I slipped into looking after three men. I took various part-time jobs after I'd left sixth-form college, but just for pin-money because I was certainly kept busy on the smallholding. Besides, having only 'A'-level Music, I wanted time to get further qualifications under my belt. So, as I have intimated, Carrie's death was in fact a prelude to happier times.

In September 1990 I was accepted onto an extended four-year Music Performance degree at the Birmingham Conservatoire. Looking back, I wouldn't have been ready any sooner. As it was, at twenty-five years of age, I left Birmingham highly qualified and much more equipped to deal with what life had to offer. I was tougher mentally - I certainly had never lacked physical energy - and my self-belief grew in abundance. So much so, I then landed that first orchestral job I referred to earlier.

Dad and my brothers had insisted on me pursuing my degree. They all felt it would help to gradually ease the grief of losing Carrie. I was a little concerned about them, for they had all been battered by it too, but plenty of people offered to clean and cook, so I knew they wouldn't starve. There was also a momentary concern in my mind a few months later, when Seth left for Australia, but this was soon dispelled by Josh who was adamant I saw it through. I did suspect, however, that his and Dad's meals were becoming more and more liquid each day.

After two years in my first job I began to get itchy feet and had decided, if I could, I would move on to pastures new. I had become rather a Europhile and began looking for work that might take me abroad. Then, in August, I received the same incredible news from Grandpa Tompkins' solicitors that my twin brothers had each received.

The huge windfall, whilst genuinely appreciated by me, was, at the time, something I couldn't quite cope with. I admit I went straight out and bought myself a little sports job, and I also invested in a cello, the quality of which I could never have before contemplated. Other than that, I stuffed it all into a building society account and tried not to let the worry of it weigh me down. That possibly sounds odd, condescending even, but, when you have grown up used to just having enough, large sums of money thrown at you can actually muddy the water a bit. Nevertheless it was of course really good to know I had it there for the future.

*

"Hey, Jo, why don't we take a boat out round the lake after coffee?"

"Sounds inviting, Gabriel, but I'm more inclined to go for a quiet meander, if you don't mind."

"That's fine, sweetie. If you want a splendid lakeside walk, one starts across the road beyond that news-seller over there."

"I might just take your advice. Thanks."

"We shall stay based around here. They do superb

sea-food lunches."

"Sounds good to me."

I put on my sun-hat and glasses.

"See you in, what, a couple of hours, say?"

"Sure. We won't be far away. Ciao!"

I started walking in the direction that Gabriel had pointed. Oh dear, he really was persistent at times, but I'd managed to fend him off so far.

As I crossed the road and approached the news-stand, I became conscious of a noisy fracas going on a few metres away. A gesticulating policeman was trying to explain to a very frustrated tourist that he couldn't park his Ferrari where he'd left it.

Suddenly, I stopped in my tracks, absolutely shell-shocked. Surely not? It couldn't possibly be! I studied him for another moment, and then he shouted again at the officer. I wasn't dreaming, for the voice was unmistakable. The colour and model of the Ferrari had changed, but it was definitely him.

It was Daisy.

I found myself in a quandary. Should I greet Daisy and risk the further wrath of the already irate officer, who clearly had not appreciated being shouted at? He was now issuing a ticket, while a fuming Daisy paced up and down. On the other hand, I was concerned he might leap into his car and roar off, never to be seen again. There was no alternative.

"Kurt?" I shouted. "It is you, isn't it? Kurt Nielsen?"

He turned to face me, as though he had perhaps half-recognised my voice. Then I realised I had sun-glasses on, so I removed them.

"It's Joanne, Carrie's sister."

"Jo? It cannot be so!"

He took the papers from the officer, stuffed them into his jacket pocket, and very politely thanked him. The bemused policeman stalked off, muttering angrily and shaking his head in exasperation.

"Dear Joanne! How wonderful! What a surprise!"

He proceeded to hug me for so long I feared he might get fined again, but he eventually released me and, as he did so, I could tell his eyes had welled up.

"Hadn't you better move your car?"

"My car? Oh! Yes, yes, I think perhaps maybe."

He searched for his keys.

"But, I am thinking. Have you time on the hands?"

I smiled at his characteristic grammatical slip, something that had always endeared him so much to all of us.

"Well, yes, all morning really. Perhaps longer even."

"Jump in. I take you to the north of the lake, yes? It is even more beautiful."

I explained my situation, so he parked again - legally this time - and we walked back to find my orchestral colleagues. Kurt waited for me while I went and spoke to Gabriel.

"I've bumped into an old friend and he wants to spend some time with me. I hope you don't mind, Gabriel? Would it be rude of me?"

"Don't be silly, sweetie, of course not. I see what you mean by 'old friend' though."

"Well, he's your age actually," I twinkled back at him.

"Ouch! I deserved that."

"He was my sister's partner when she was killed."

"Oh, I'm sorry. Then you most certainly should go. We'll meet up again later, or back at the hotel tonight. Now off you go."

"See you later."

"Have fun."

*

Remembering Kurt as I did, I certainly thought I

would have fun, but he had changed dramatically. Oh, it was lovely to see him again, don't get me wrong. We had a deliciously lazy lakeside lunch, and enjoyed a long walk amongst olive groves. But he was a broken man really. After his initial excitement at meeting me, he became melancholy, and my heart went out to him. In nearly seven years he had become a shadow of his old, vibrant self. Now forty-six, he still dressed sharply, but the previously upright figure was noticeably stooped. It was as if his spirit had withdrawn into itself, leaving a shell of a man.

I learnt that he'd left Ferrari about five years ago to set up a separate sports car company in Milan, developing his own prototype. Apparently it was a considerably cheaper car, aimed at the young executive market, and sales were beginning to lift off. However his business success clearly failed to make him content and, of his own admission, he had lately started to become somewhat reclusive.

"You still drive a Ferrari yourself then?" I asked over lunch.

"Oh, yes. There is no substitute."

"And how come you're here in Garda today?"

"It's just a very rare day out, Jo. So, you see, it was fate, no?"

I smiled.

"I brought Carrie-Ann here once....."

I took his hand.

"You haven't kept in touch, Kurt."

"No, I apologise. But please understand. You did nothing wrong. No. It is all just too painful."

"I'm sorry."

"One year. That's all we had together. But that year, it was perfect."

"Kurt, I'm sure there'll be someone else for you one day again."

"Oh, Jo. So kind you are, trying to cheer Daisy up. But, no. Like my car, there is no substitute."

I squeezed his hand and he raised mine to his lips, brushing it lightly with an affectionate kiss.

"Forgive me. I have been very poor company. Let us walk now."

We had a lovely meander and then he drove me back.

"So, it is the end of the month you arrive in Milan?"

"Yes, we have two concerts, one by Lake Como."

"Ah, now it is clicking with me. The ESO, yes?"

"That's right."

"And you are playing one of Bach's Brandenburg Concertos, I believe?"

"Yes, number five."

"The harpsichord. My mother's favourite. I like it too. Perhaps I will get a ticket for Como. I live in nearby Bergamo."

"That would be great."

"Well, we shall see. We shall see."

We had arrived at my hotel.

"I do hope I'll see you in Como, Kurt, and thank you for a lovely day."

He opened the car door for me. I got out and then he tenderly held me by the shoulders.

"It hurts, seeing you, Jo. The memory of my Carrie-Ann, it is so hard....."

"I understand. Well, er, I'd better be off. Goodnight then."

"Goodbye, Jo."

I didn't see Daisy at the concert, and I never saw him again. That, I guess, was how it had to be.

It had still been light when I got to my hotel room. Sam was out on a walk apparently, so I sat by the window. As dusk fell, I wept for Kurt, and I wept for Carrie. Sometimes, when I was upset like this, my mother was there to console me. Even though I couldn't possibly remember her I knew that voice – it had to be Mummy.

"Wipe those tears.....enjoy life.....put sadness away now.....James is waiting....."

She was right, my boy-friend back in England was probably expecting a call so I went in search of a phone. James was my present, possibly my future even, but certainly not my deep past. That needed to be buried now.

*

The tour was an amazing experience and the concerts, with the exception of Bologna and Lyon, were very well attended.

Soon after my arrival home James took me out for my birthday and we walked on the South Downs. It suited me to be based at Barton Green when I wasn't involved with the orchestra since I could catch up with everything at home. And it didn't take me very long to realise that Dad's health was taking an alarming tumble.

I had tried to share this with James over supper in Brighton, but he seemed very on edge and I didn't seem to be getting through to him. Suddenly, I realised why. Like a rabbit out of the magician's hat, he produced what worryingly looked like a ring. He opened the box and wished me happy birthday again.

A ring is exactly what it was, and I certainly hadn't been prepared for this moment.

Now I never had been someone who could pretend and act up, so I'm afraid he saw my look of panic straight away. He had indeed intended that we got engaged that evening, but, faced by my response, he realised it was all rather premature. We spent a long time discussing it and, to his credit, in the end he accepted that I just wasn't ready. And I wasn't. By a mile. He must have been hurt, I suppose, but in practice it changed nothing in our relationship, and he perked up when I agreed to wear it, albeit not where he'd hoped to see it.

A few months later, just as I felt most things in my life were beginning to move in the right direction, we lost Dad following a short illness. On reflection it was no surprise. He was only in his mid-seventies, but continual and excessive alcohol in his bloodstream led to his demise.

I was extremely upset of course, but not that shocked because I had received one or two hints from the usual quarter. So I had been braced for it and therefore able to contain my grief.

On the day of the funeral there was much to be done, which helped, and I bustled around making sure the multitude of mourners was fed. Seth had flown home and that was emotional of course, but I got through it all pretty well.

I had arranged with the undertakers that we would collect Dad's ashes at the end of the week. Before Seth flew back to Australia, he, Josh and I would be scattering the ashes up in Suffolk, near Mummy and Carrie's graves.

The rain was persistent but eased at around noon, long enough for us to wander down to the wildflower meadow abutting the church graveyard. There we left Dad, back where we believed he'd want to be, despite his struggles of the past. The boys propped me up, for I cried copiously. Not just for Dad, but for Carrie and for Mummy, whom I never remembered, yet seemed to know so well. And, finally, if I'm honest, I cried for myself. I felt so alone again, for some strange reason.

However, as had happened more than once in my life already, this feeling of adversity somehow strengthened me.

After Seth had gone, and Josh had got back into his routine, I resolutely vowed that the past was not for dwelling on. And I clung to the hope that I would one day find some lasting stability in my life.

Several months later, in the autumn, I met the Labour MP, Michael Fairbrother.

*

One Friday evening, having finally completed a rather ragged rehearsal in York Minster, I felt I wanted to grab a break from orchestral colleagues. The Musical Director had been tetchy all afternoon, complaining that the acoustics of the Minster were troubling him. However hard we tried there was no pleasing him that day. But I wasn't keen to get embroiled in a chorus of negative moans that would inevitably spill out at the hotel bar afterwards. As far as I was concerned he had always been an outstanding conductor and he just probably wasn't having a very good day. It happened to us all. He'd certainly frustrated me, but I tried always to respect his extremely high standards.

Anyway, I'd noticed on arrival in York that morning that there was to be a party-political debate in the city on a subject very close to my heart. On the poster the motion suggested parallels could be drawn between the increasing levels of alcohol consumption and domestic unrest.

I found use of the word unrest interesting. The usual theme was violence and perhaps then I might not necessarily have given the debate a second thought. Somehow this alternative wording struck a chord and rather intrigued me.

I walked into the hall a little late and sat towards the back. There was a reasonable attendance but numbers were less than had been hoped, I learnt afterwards, because of another meeting taking place over at Burnley, where the BNP was gathering momentum at the time.

A Liberal Democrat was first to speak, playing on the heart-strings of the audience, as was her apparent habit. This was nothing, however, to the Conservative MP who followed. Typically virtuous and pompous, he harped on about the need for greater abstinence and the importance of society returning to a complete family circle status. He stressed the damage to the next generation of the fallout from the single parent situation. It was outrageous. What neck he had, for, just six months earlier, I recalled that this family man had been caught by the tabloids with his trousers down. He'd been captured on camera drunkenly leaving a night-club in the early hours wrapped round a rising soap-star. His wife, at home with three kids, was not too impressed.

The Labour MP stood up and I fully expected him to make a cheap party political point by raising the Tory's sordid little affair, but I was pleasantly surprised. Michael Fairbrother simply, and rather cleverly, opened by saying how 'interesting' he had found his colleague's remarks. He made no accusations - and most in his position would have done. Instead he paused sufficiently to let the audience draw their own conclusions. A clever technique indeed. He went on:

"I suspect, ladies and gentlemen, that the actual motion will be easily carried because it would seem that all speakers here tonight are, by degrees, persuaded that there most definitely is a close link between excessive drinking and problems in the home."

He turned to the fourth speaker.

"I certainly don't wish to pre-empt Fiona Grayson's contribution, but I know her well enough to say that with confidence."

M/s Grayson nodded.

I began wondering if I could stay awake much longer.

"Where I differ from my parliamentary colleagues who have already spoken is on the subject of this so-called happy family circle. How trite!"

At this I sat up, for, in all honesty, I had so far found his bland, rather lugubrious northern delivery rather dull.

"Yes, trite."

He turned round to quieten the Tory, who was attempting to voice disapproval.

"For I come to this subject from a different angle. The angle of domestic unrest, which I believe is at the very core of this motion.

"Since Victorian times, generations have subsequently played out this hypocritical farce. Oh, as long as everything looked alright on the surface, subservient wives would turn a blind eye to the heavy drinking and philandering. The marriage had to endure at all costs."

Oh dear, my eyelids were feeling heavy again.

"Not so with many mothers of today though, who, I suggest, are made of far sterner stuff, and who refuse to allow continual domestic unrest to de-stabilise their children's lives."

Now, that's much better.

"Let me give you an example:

"A few months ago, a devoted young mother visited my surgery in Ripon. It could be argued perhaps, in hindsight, that she needed a social worker more than me, but I do actually look back believing I put her on the right track that day.

"You see, she was at her wits' end. Her husband, whom she still clearly loved, had taken to regular, heavy drinking and could hardly put two coherent sentences together most nights. He never hit her, or violated her in any way, but, when sober, used sarcasm as a weapon, particularly at the weekends and in front of their offspring. Gradually she was losing her sense of self-worth and the kids, a girl of fourteen and son of eleven, were becoming deeply affected. All three of them started experiencing unrest. Domestic unrest. Domestic unrest fuelled by excessive alcohol.

"Those children feared that, one day, their father might suddenly assault their mother. Or them. A man that, deep down, they loved, and to whom they looked for love in return. And this fear of theirs, along with that of the mother's, was mixed with shame. The mother found herself ashamed of him in front of their own children, and the kids, especially the daughter, felt nothing but acute embarrassment whenever friends were round.

"Is this a healthy environment for our children to grow up in? Of course not. But, sadly, this lady's case is increasingly common-place, although I happen to know that she is getting a divorce, albeit with much regret, and has already moved with her children to a separate flat.

"We, as a government, must be there to support victims like her and her kids. The father too. Perhaps him even more so.

"Yes, we all agree that there is a link, alcohol to unrest. It's not rocket science. But it's how we deal with it. My honourable member of the Opposition here will try to sweep it all under the carpet in, perhaps, a genuinely laudable attempt at family reconciliation. However, left to fester under the surface, I believe unrest can only inevitably lead to violence.

"Your Labour government will do all it can to protect family values and try to keep families together, but there is a limit, and I unashamedly applaud the action this lady has taken. Fuelled by high levels of alcohol her husband brought worrying unrest to the family home. We cannot let such cases develop beyond the danger level. Somehow - and all parties need to work together on this - we must stamp out the increasing problems excessive drinking is creating for us all. Thank you."

He sat down to generous applause and I was moved to join in, but rather mildly. He had of course hit a very raw nerve for me.

I had fully intended shooting straight off after the meeting, but rather needed some caffeine. Do you call it fate, or what? In front of me was Michael Fairbrother. He'd requested a hot chocolate and caused the ladies serving to panic a bit. He turned to me to apologise.

"Sorry to hold you up. Can't help myself. I'm a chocoholic in every possible way, I'm afraid."

"Better than being an alcoholic," I smiled.

He looked at me and nodded thoughtfully.

"Without doubt. But I'm not too sure it does my waistline much good."

"Nor does booze."

He looked thoughtful again.

"Very true."

"And at least people know what to buy you for Christmas."

He laughed.

Eventually a flustered lady returned with a steaming mug. He thanked her and then, turning round to me as he wandered off with it, suddenly asked if I might like to join him at an empty table he'd spotted.

And so, that's how our friendship started - over a romantic cup of hot chocolate. By the end of the evening he had decided to attend our concert the next day and thought he might also bring his sister, Polly, who was apparently a talented and successful illustrator for children's books.

I returned to my hotel room that night and confess that I didn't return my boy friend's call. I really hadn't felt that good about the relationship for a long while and, for some reason, tonight had helped to make my mind up. I knew I would call it a day. It was really only several months later before I fully appreciated why. James was exactly my age, too keen to settle down, very predictable and totally lacking any ambition. I, however, had no wish to give up what I had. I still enjoyed the excitement my orchestral career offered, and, additionally - perhaps most significantly - I found myself rather attracted to a man nearly fourteen years my senior.

*

Michael and I pursued our separate careers and simply met when we could. It worked well since neither of us was in any sort of hurry.

Nevertheless, about eighteen months later, there I was in Australia with Josh, admitting to him that Michael was a bit special, that I was becoming quite influenced by him, and that I was even considering quitting the orchestra for politics. I realised, rather surprisingly at first, that after nearly four years, the gloss of the ESO was already fading. I couldn't realistically see me carrying on beyond the end of my contract at the end of the following year. So, it looked as though I could be leaving the music world behind at only thirty-two, whereas I genuinely had imagined it would be a lifetime's commitment. But then something very deep down was clamouring to come out.

Finding myself temporarily out of work at the beginning of 2002, I soon managed, admittedly with Michael's help, to land a job with the Labour Party, working in PR, helping prepare press releases. It was rather mundane but at least I had entered the political arena.

Later that year Michael and I rented a small London apartment together, but both of us had made it crystal clear that marriage was not on the table. For Michael in particular it seemed totally inappropriate. He was so busy, away a lot, and had intimated a disinterest in ever being a family man. And as for me, marriage didn't seem to hold much attraction. I was perfectly happy as I was, with the freedom to come and go as I pleased. Children? I didn't really think so.

The previous year had been especially hectic for Michael, a year in which Britain experienced a great deal of unsettling activity, politically and otherwise.

In the General Election Labour was returned with a similar majority in the House and Michael increased his personal majority by about a thousand votes. In between concert engagements I had occasionally managed to support him and thoroughly enjoyed the political exchanges on the road.

After his re-election Michael was switched to the Ministry of Trade and Industry. It was a turbulent time in other parts of the World however, so I was quite relieved it hadn't been the Foreign Office. This relief was misplaced.

In September I was staying at Barton Green for what I had supposed would be the last time. Josh was leaving for Newmarket with Susie in a couple of days and I had wanted to say goodbye to the place. On 11th September the World turned upside down, and my world did too.

Josh and I watched tv in horror as news came through of two hi-jacked planes crashing into the World Trade Centre. I was devastated because Michael was there - actually in the building at the time. He had been part of a British delegation attending a conference to find ways of assisting the poorer coffee growers of the Third World. He was determined to try and create a fairer bargaining position for them.

If I hadn't had Josh, and later Susie, with me, I think I may well have gone completely over the edge that day.

Josh and I sat sickeningly spellbound as we watched trapped and desperate people hurl themselves out of office windows. Every time another limp body dropped, like a puppet, to its inevitable end, I uttered a strangulated cry and I panted raggedly.

"No, no! Please, God, no!"

Josh put his arm round me.

"He's probably fine, Jo."

"But you can't know that. Look! That could be him." I wailed uncontrollably. "How can anyone survive that? It's impossible."

"Jo, he might. You have to try and believe that."

*

Michael did survive. And yet, in a way, he didn't. He was indeed in the building at the time of impact of the first plane. The noise and ensuing chaos was apparently indescribable. Fortunately Michael's group was very quickly marshalled out to safety by an extremely alert security guard. In the weeks that followed, after attempts to track the man down and thank him, Michael learnt he had later been killed, getting trapped and overcome by smoke as he scaled some stairs to try and help others on higher floors. This news deeply affected Michael for a very long time. And in truth he never did fully recover from the horrendous experience.

What really hit Michael for six was what had most shocked and upset me, and probably everyone else witnessing it or watching on tv. People jumping. One night, soon after our reconciliation at his flat, he broke down in my arms as he emotionally recalled bodies tumbling from the sky.

He experienced frequent nightmares of the same scenario for years after. Often I would wake to discover him saturated in sweat, as if in a fever.

Despite this devastating experience Michael worked, if anything, even harder, and with a fiercer intensity. He continued to travel widely and, as I have mentioned, we began living together.

The following year Michael was one of many Labour MPs who argued strongly against our country going into

Iraq. His own diplomatic sources were certain it was unnecessary and the electorate had its doubts too. This was reflected in the ballot box in May 2005 when we got back with about one hundred less seats.

However there were also a few new Labour Members of Parliament elected, and I was one of them.

The previous year I had entered politics seriously. Again with Michael's help - and I am shameless about this - I was successful at the interview for candidature of a safe London borough seat. Well, as it transpired, it wasn't that safe, but I managed to scramble in by just over four hundred votes. It all proved just how unpopular our intervention in Iraq turned out to be.

A life-changing moment of course. At thirty-five I entered Westminster.

I had also experienced a life-changing moment of a different kind early in 2004. A miscarriage. And when it occurred I realised that, although children hadn't been planned, I had actually started to look forward to it.

I felt totally unbalanced for a long while but it was something I just had to get through. I certainly wasn't going to sit back and feel sorry for myself for too long so I guess that was when I finally decided I would have a crack at trying to get elected to Parliament.

Despite what I have just said, I admit I was very down for many weeks after I'd lost the baby, particularly when Michael was away. But, eventually, I managed to get over it, with help.

I was in our London apartment early one summer morning with the french windows open. Michael was in the West Country. We lived on the ground floor and had the benefit of a small, but private courtyard. A pleasant breeze rustled the curtains I had made and hung only two days earlier. And although I had opened the windows the drapes were still drawn. I studied them critically before finally congratulating myself on a job reasonably well done. Now perhaps my imagination went absolutely haywire for a few moments, but I know what I saw, what I sensed, what I heard. I had sat down to study the newspapers and the next time I looked up those curtains were drawn back. And she was there.

"No more moping.....people need you.....follow your political ideals....."

It was at that exact moment I knew the path I was being directed onto.

*

I found being an MP so rewarding and very exciting. For most of that Parliament of course I was going to be feeling my way. A maiden speech, delivered at the end of 2005, seemed to go well, although I confess it was very much taken from Michael's model that he used that first time we met in York, but personalised to my experiences. There had been a debate about how young people, often under-age, had far too easy access to alcohol, via supermarkets and off-licences, where a blind eye was turned for profit. I therefore grasped an opportunity to chip in. It was well received, so much so that, two years later, a keen young researcher for the BBC had found the speech and I was invited to be part of an item on teenage binge drinking. My brother Josh was also on the programme. He was in the public eye too at the time and the Producer thought it would be effective to have us both on board. Josh modestly felt he was only there because of me, but he spoke really well, though taking rather a back seat.

During the programme I had my first experience of journalists moving the goalposts when you were off guard. Suddenly the interviewer switched from the subject and decided to shift the spotlight onto our government's rather shaky situation. She heavily criticised the PM, which was fashionable at the time, but Josh assured me afterwards that I had defended my boss stoutly with devastating effect. Apparently it was quite scary for him witnessing me lash back! I was a bit argumentative that night I must admit.

To my surprise, after a couple of years concentrating on local constituency work, I followed Michael's early path in politics and became Junior Minister at the Home Office.

Several months later MPs from both sides of the House, and the Lords, became embroiled in fallout from the Expenses Scandal and Michael and I were no exceptions.

That year I had been pleased to help Josh out with his race-fixing problems, and by April the Met were on the case. Then, in May, the 'Daily Telegraph' published the first details of how MPs were supposedly fiddling certain of their expense allowances. As it happened I was mentioned, but fortunately it was a very minor mistake on my part, for which I simply got a mild rap on the knuckles. We employed a lady to do the cleaning, simply because we were both so busy. To claim for her hours was not seen as a problem. Rather stupidly, however, I also submitted bills for cleaning materials that she'd given me. These were not regarded as allowable. Maisie had already paid for them so I simply paid her back with her wages and it all got logged as wages. Silly mistake. Anyway, it was accepted as a genuine oversight, I paid it back, and that was that.

Sadly, for Michael, it was nowhere near as straightforward. And, looking back later, I am convinced the episode ultimately cost him his seat.

Up in Ripon he had continued to utilise a former baker's shop as his surgery and constituency office, the same premises that he'd had when I first knew him. Being very well-meaning, yet perhaps, in hindsight, rather thoughtless, he let his sister, Polly, use a back room for her work on children's books. She couldn't concentrate at home with her teenage daughter studying to a continuous background of heavy metal! Where Michael came unstuck was claiming all rent, and other expenses relating to the premises, failing to remember making an appropriate deduction for the room occupied by her.

Polly had become even better known for her children's illustrations and was in Harrogate attending a high-profile launch of Monica Seagrove's latest book, 'Christmas Is For Kids'. The timing of the launch would doubtless make both of them a bob or two. An alert 'Telegraph' reporter had tracked Polly down and soon tripped her up. He had received a tip-off from a local paper and became suspicious.

Danny Glover only asked the one question: 'Where do you actually work on all your illustrations, then?'

Being the open lady she was he got what he wanted and skipped back to London.

It was of course, as with my error, a slip-up by Michael, nothing fraudulent, but the local press in Yorkshire particularly gave him and Polly a very hard time.

We all got through it. Michael quickly put the matter right and submitted a new claim. But damage was done. And I felt sad that such an earnest and hard working man should be pilloried the way he was, but it was a lesson learnt. And, as I have said, a contributory factor to Michael losing his seat. Added to that was another miscarriage and so life certainly had its difficult moments.

To my relief Michael moved on quickly and positively from his election defeat and was soon offered a plum job with 'Wind Force', a highly regarded company with government contracts in the order book for offshore wind turbines in the North Sea. He had always been adept at making the best possible use of reliable contacts and it wasn't long before he began to excel in the position of Marketing Director.

I astonished myself by getting back with an increased majority. This bucked the national trend, so I was pretty pleased with that.

Again to my surprise I was subsequently rewarded with a senior post shadowing the Chief Secretary to the Treasury. I really had better watch out for those cleaning bills now! It was to become a challenging role because, of course, the new Government had to pick up the pieces regarding the national deficit and we were being blamed for the dire financial straits our country was in. Such criticism was, frankly, very often difficult to defend. So I was battling away with my back to the wall right from the start, often unable to constructively oppose what the Chancellor and the Treasury were trying to do.

I was therefore pleased in late autumn to enjoy some welcome light relief with my family. Michael and I took a short break in order to attend Josh's marriage to Ruth. And Seth was coming. He would be staying with us for a short while before and after the event, and I was so looking forward to it.

*

"Do you fancy a hot chocolate or coffee?"

It was six-thirty on a rather frosty October morning. Michael and I were in Arrivals at London Heathrow waiting for Seth's plane to land.

"Oh, chocolate, I think."

Over the years he had converted me.

"Are you hungry?" I asked.

"Famished!"

"Yes, well, stupid question really. In that case I'll

have a croissant and apricot jam as well, please."

"Right."

"And you'll have that outrageous looking 'Breakfast Blowout' with just about everything but the kitchen-sink no doubt?"

"Of course."

I smiled. No surprises there. Michael adored food, especially the first meal of the day, and was eagerly anticipating it all as he perused the menu. He marched off beaming to get our food while I checked the flight information screen. We had managed to find a small table near one that I could just about read if I squinted. I made a mental note to book an appointment with my optometrist.

I glanced up at the screen again. Good. The Qantas flight had landed. At last. Forty minutes late, but Seth was here now and he should come through the gate in about an hour. Well the delay had pleased Michael. It meant he could eat. But I did have concerns about his weight and normally I made sure we both ate sensibly whenever possible. The next few days were a holiday for us though and so caution was thrown to the wind until Seth's departure on Monday. He'd stay with us for two nights before we all travelled up to Newmarket. We were booked in for Friday and Saturday nights at the hotel where Josh and Ruth would get married. Josh had no idea Seth would be there. He thought Michael and I were to be the only witnesses. He knew nothing about the party afterwards either, which all added to my excitement.

*

Tears streamed as I greeted my brother.

"Hey, Sis, what's all this? I thought you'd be happy to see me!"

"Oh, Seth, I am, I am. I'm so pleased, but it's been ten

years and I've missed you.....so much....."

And the tears flowed again.

Eventually I let go of Seth, remembering Michael, who had considerately waited in the background.

"Seth, come and meet Michael."

I tucked my arm in his as he picked up his luggage with the other hand.

"Is that all you've brought?"

"Well, yeah, travel light, that's me. But, blimey, it's bloody cold here."

"Michael, this is my other brother you've heard so much about."

"Seth, good to meet you at last."

"You too, Mike. You're a lucky fellah you know landing our lovely little one here."

"I can't argue with that."

"You'd better not," I laughed.

The two men wandered off together as if they'd been buddies all their life, leaving me in their wake thinking 'ten years and after a couple of minutes I lose him again.'

But I did get him to myself the next day. He'd crashed out in the late afternoon on that first day and I heard him wandering about soon after midnight. The flight had certainly disorientated him. Later, over breakfast, we started catching up. Michael had arranged to spend some time with his sister, who was also visiting London.

"Now, Seth, I've got you at last, so tell me all about the family. First, how's Maddy?"

"Oh, yeah, she's fair dinkum."

"But pretty worn out with all those children of yours?"

"She thrives on it, Titch. Absolutely loves it. It's all she wants. The kids are her life. Well, and me of course!"

I swallowed hard and kept smiling.

"That's good. And tell me about those nieces and nephews of mine. The last pics Maddy e-mailed me made me want to see them all so much."

"We're all of us so busy though, aren't we? Now, the kids. Let me see. Patsy's nine, Eleanor seven, Will four, and of course Jason's just one. They certainly are all a handful, but they're absolute beauts, just like their mum. Oh, and me, in the boys' case."

We laughed.

"And you, Sis, you've not had any? But then I guess you have your reasons?"

I sighed.

"Sorry, Titch, none of my bloody business."

"Let's just say it's not meant to be, Bruv."

"Sure."

"Anyway, I'm forty-one now and got a very demanding career."

"Forty-one!" He whistled. "Jeez, I suppose you must be. Josh and I are knocking on fifty."

"You don't look it. Nowhere near. That country's clearly been the making of you."

"It's Maddy. She keeps me young."

"But look at you. Not an ounce of fat or a single grey hair."

"Well, it's true I never need to go down to the gym. Every single day I'm working full-on, round the clock even."

"Hard work has never fazed either of us though, has it?"

"Nope, and Josh neither by all accounts."

"He does work hard, very hard. But, like Michael, the middle-age spread is beginning to make its presence felt."

Seth chortled.

"Too many pints in Josh's case, I expect."

"Yes, and too many hearty breakfasts in Michael's."

We both laughed again.

"Now, tell me about this politics lark, Jo. Any chance you can get me a peep into the House of Commons while

I'm here?"

"Well, I could fix something, I suppose."

*

"Hey, Josh, that's not much of a greeting, mate!"

Yet again I couldn't fight back the tears as I witnessed the twins' emotional reunion. Dear Josh, his jaw dropped to the ground as Seth burst in on our brother's wedding day.

It was an unforgettable moment, as time seemed to momentarily stand still.

Later in the afternoon, as Ruth's party got into full swing, Michael and I spent some time sitting with Josh's jockeys, Ben and Tamara, who had of course got married themselves earlier in the year. Ruth was here, there, and everywhere, excitedly greeting even more friends as they dropped by, while Josh and Seth were inseparable. Josh tirelessly trawled our brother round each table introducing his 'Australian' twin and proudly telling his guests about his vineyard, his ranch, his Maddy, his kids, his horses, his sheep, his everything!

Josh was like a young child, unable to contain himself. Seth's presence had literally put the icing on the wedding cake for him. It was so heart-warming for me.

"The Gaffer's certainly enjoying his day, Ben," observed Tamara.

"Well, I guess he wants to make the most of his brother. Jo, they don't look twins really. I mean, yes, they certainly look alike, but....."

"Seth looks younger?"

"Yes. It must be all that sunshine."

"I think that has a lot to do with it, but then your boss doesn't get the physical exercise Seth does."

"But he works damn hard, Jo," said Michael.

"Of course he does, but he also likes the good life."

We all smiled and seemed to agree on that.

"He's a fabulous man to work for," said Tam.

"Really? Well, I'm pleased to hear that."

"Yes," agreed Ben, "he's the best. For someone who came to the game late he's remarkable really. Got a natural gift."

I smiled again. Hearing such praise was very satisfying. I knew that the race-fixing episodes had affected Josh. He'd taken a big jolt. It was good to know he was held in such high regard.

"Well, thank you for that, Ben, and for what you said too, Tam. I've never actually been allowed to know too much detail about either of my brothers' work."

"That's because you're too wrapped up in your own, let's be honest," said Michael. "Now, Tam, let me get you and Ben some wedding cake."

"Well, very thin pieces then, thank you. We have to watch our weight."

"You're not the only ones," I said, playfully poking Michael's midriff.

"Back to the salad diet on Monday. Promise."

I raised my eyebrows to Ben and Tam, who both smiled.

"Now, tell me some more about this horse-mad brother of mine and what he's up to. He never will, that's for sure....."

The next day was memorable. None of us stirred early of course, and Seth for one was struggling from the previous day's celebrations. But after checking out of the hotel we drove over to Josh and Ruth's place for a very light, and very late, breakfast. I drove. Michael was also a bit the worse for wear and I hadn't drunk any alcohol. Then I rarely did.

In the afternoon Ruth and Michael sent Josh, Seth and me packing while they organised supper.

Josh, almost as if he was flying in the face of my

comments about his developing paunch, took us on a vigorous seven-mile circular hike on the Heath. We had three amazing hours together, laughing most of the time, and all of us agreeing how lucky we had been with our respective partners.

"Ruthie's fantastic, mate," said Seth, while I gratefully rested between the twins on an old fallen beech, overlooking some gallops. "A real stunner. No wonder she stopped you in your tracks. It needed someone to."

"Well, I guess I've got Jo here to thank for that. You remember, Sis? You were the one who opened my eyes."

"I do remember. And I'm glad you did open them. Seth's right, she's beautiful."

"And so are you, Sis," said Seth. "Michael's a really lucky guy too."

"I'm the lucky one," I replied.

"That's good to hear. Well, Josh, seems like we've all struck gold then, us Rayners."

"Certainly have, Bruv."

"Well, half the Rayners," I sighed.

The two men looked at one another knowingly and each instinctively put an arm round me. Then, after a short silence:

"The other half are all together, Titch," said Josh.

"Yeah," added Seth, "they've got one another, just like we have."

*

I waved to Seth one more time then headed for the car park. Strange, I was always so emotional at any reunion, yet perfectly calm at the goodbyes. I suppose it was because Josh, Seth and I all managed to move on to the next thing in our lives and it was almost as if our very brief periods together were just enough to inject sufficient adrenaline until the next time. As soon as I started driving my mind was in political mode once more.

There were many frustrating moments for me in Opposition and I soon realised that I much preferred it when we were in power. But the next few years turned out to be of immense value to me in my development as a more rounded politician. Yes, I did hanker for government again, yet I knew deep-down I needed to gain more experience in different spheres. To his credit, our new party leader certainly ensured I switched areas of work whenever appropriate. By no means was I successful in every situation and in one post I actually became rather a controversial figure. But more of that later.

Firstly the main thrust of my work was to become very focused on the 2012 London Olympics. The majority of people - myself included - were looking forward to the spectacle, but the ever-escalating costs were, quite rightly, beginning to concern us all.

By the previous December, a very tough financial time for so many people in Britain, pre-Christmas seasonal goodwill had not been in abundance by any means. The man in the street, struggling to ensure his family could enjoy the festivities, was understandably angered by some Games statistics released at the turn of the year. Talk about bad timing!

Well before the Government's latest figures were released I had already dug deep to find out about the increasing costs and they made for disturbing reading. Although I had always been an Athletics fan I was very dismayed at where the costs were actually going. Along with our Shadow Sports and Olympics Minister, I became more and more vociferous with my protests in the House. So much so I found myself suddenly in great demand by the media. I appeared on tv and radio, as well as attracting substantial press coverage in the build-up. In general the reporting was fair and accurate, but then of course I was on pretty solid ground, for more of the electorate had similar views than not.

*

"My second guest this morning is the Labour Shadow Secretary to the Treasury, Joanne Rayner."

John Deakin turned from the camera to welcome me.

"It's fair to say, I think, we are all rather reeling as a result of recent Government figures from the Sports and Olympics Minister."

Deakin then did me rather a favour and summarised the main financial details that had so shocked us all. Initially all I had to do was sit tight and look suitably stern. I could do that, no problem.

"There are countless statistics being bandied about, but basically the National Audit Office is warning that the £9.3 billion budget for the Games is in grave danger of being exceeded. Now I know, Joanne Rayner, you have made it your job to scrutinise the detail. Can you please enlighten our viewers? Wherever are we going on all this?"

"Well, the Government's sailing very close to the wind and the boat could easily capsize. Frustratingly, the prophets of doom when London's bid was successful may just have been right after all."

"And were you one such prophet? You became an MP that year, I remember."

"That's right. No, I wasn't. I admit I was excited by the prospect. But the estimated total cost then was £2.4 billion. Now, as you said, it's £9.3."

"So it's virtually quadrupled in, what, seven years?"

My heart momentarily sank because, too late, I realised I had made a careless mistake and possibly given him an opening. I had allowed my nervousness and excess adrenaline to take over and forgotten the costs had actually begun spiralling wildly while we had still been in power. I reckon he knew that, but luckily for me he seemed to be fiddling with his earpiece and he unwittingly let me off the hook. I quickly continued, vowing not to slip up like that again.

"These are numbers that are difficult to get our heads round, so let's look at component figures that make for easier understanding. Firstly, security and policing.

"The security bill alone has doubled with the introduction of sophisticated x-ray machines and metal detectors, as well as miles of security fencing. The ordinary working man has every right to scratch his head in puzzlement. It has no bearing on his everyday life whatsoever. But he'll have to pick up the bill."

"Surely you must agree that these measures are essential? I mean, already it has been suggested that they have been undertaken in the face of a very specific security threat."

"No. You and I know this is probably conjecture or a convenient excuse to justify more expense. Besides, the figures I have mentioned don't even include the vast amounts already spent on security of the various venues during construction. And furthermore, of even greater significance, overall policing costs have now been set at £475 million. That's a huge amount of money for just two and a half weeks."

"Your point being?"

"My point being that we can always seem to stump up for lavish one-offs, but not for vital routine scenarios. We need these levels of investment for ordinary day-to-day policing throughout the UK."

"Presumably then you won't be overjoyed at the increased cost of staging the ceremonies either?"

"Well I'm hardly doing cartwheels."

He smiled as I continued.

"Suddenly the Government has found enough to double the original budget, a budget that was always going to be met by the Games' privately-funded organising committee. Now public money has entered this arena."

"As with all such major projects though there is of course a Contingency Fund which, you must agree, the Government can always call on?"

"The Fund stands at a mere ten per-cent of its original amount. It hardly seems adequate at this stage of the game."

"Or Games?"

He couldn't resist the pun.

"Joanne Rayner, thank you for joining us."

He turned to the camera.

"So what effect will all this have on you, the taxpayer? Our reporter Matthew Wilkes has been to see the Whitehall spending watchdog....."

*

Afterwards, over coffee, I took the chance to thank John Deakin.

"You missed tripping me up early on I think."

"I did. My producer was gabbling in my ear and I lost an opportunity, I admit. But anyway, thank you. It went very well."

It had indeed gone well and I was pleased with my performance. Less so however five days later when I was part of another debate on the radio.

*

".....and she is considered to be one of the brightest rising stars on the Opposition benches.

"Our final panellist really needs no introduction. Matthew Crowther. Matt won five medals of course at two successive Olympics more years ago than perhaps he'd care to remember. He is currently Chairman of the sports consultancy, 'On Track'."

I had been introduced to the famous athlete before we went on air and found him to be suave and charming. Back in the eighties I had been a great fan, but I allowed all this to temporarily cloud my thinking at the beginning of the programme. It was one of those embarrassing moments when my heart stupidly ruled my head.

"Our first question, please."

"I'm Paula Wood. When we won the Olympic bid in 2005, did we in fact lose?"

There was much audience reaction.

"Grant Nolan."

The Tory predictably defended the figures and I got ready to respond. The Liberal Democrat was allowed his say and then it was my chance. But my notes went out of the window when the Chairman rather changed my script.

"Joanne Rayner, we know you are particularly unhappy about the latest projections, but surely, at the end of the day, they'll be forgotten as the splendour of the whole thing unfolds? I know you're a keen follower of Athletics."

"Well, yes, I have certainly enjoyed the sport over the years....."

"And do you remember Matt Crowther here winning a gold medal?"

"Yes, I do. I was fifteen at the time and recall jumping up and down with excitement as he crossed the winning line."

"How about that, Matt, we've unearthed an unlikely secret fan."

There was laughter from the audience before he turned back to me.

"And no doubt you had a poster on your bedroom wall as well?"

Further laughter, with other panellists joining in this time. I was angry. Angry with myself. I was coming over as a dumb bimbo and I needed to repair the damage.

"And who adorned yours, I wonder?"

This response got only token applause so I was aware I had to return to the question, and quickly.

"Paula Wood is absolutely right to ask if we've lost instead. I want you all to consider this winners and losers scenario. For each single winner of a gold medal, whatever the sport, remember there are numerous losers. And that is exactly how the Games will reflect on society after the event. There will be winners, service companies awarded lucrative contracts for example. But far more losers. To millions of people, especially those in, or near, poverty, the Olympics will be beyond their reach, unattainable, in a totally different world from theirs. Except that they, along with everyone else, will be paying off the new deficit - the Olympic deficit - both directly and indirectly. And it will doubtless be the most vulnerable in our society who will suffer the most when it's all over. They will be the biggest losers. The Sports Minister keeps harping on about the lasting economic legacy the Games will leave. I fear the economic legacy will be even more debt. Lasting debt."

The warm and prolonged applause did go a little way to appeasing me. I felt I was slowly winning with the audience now, but I certainly hadn't won myself over. I must ensure I never exposed myself like that again.

*

The negative financial implications of the Olympics were resoundingly banished from everyone's minds once they started to take place and I didn't meet anyone who wasn't inspired by the uplifting spirit of the Games. Yes, there were inevitably one or two initial hiccoughs, but the whole country was bowled along by the outstanding performances put in by our country's athletes. Our high medal tally was unprecedented and the numerous successes certainly surprised me. Michael and I had managed to get tickets for the first Saturday. The electric atmosphere in the Olympic Park and the friendly cheerfulness of all the helpful volunteers made it an experience I would never forget.

*

I continued my financial role within the Shadow Cabinet until the middle of 2013. I think it surprised me how absorbing I found the post and I was rather frustrated with the position I got moved to in a fairly major summer re-shuffle. And this was despite assurances from our leader, Graham Thorne, that it was designed to broaden my horizons.

"Jo, you're aware I'm tinkering of course. I've been really impressed with your work and I'm following your career very closely. Now I want to hand you something a little bit different, a job that still requires a high level of tact and diplomacy. Northern Ireland."

"Northern Ireland?"

My disappointment must have shown.

"I had a feeling you wouldn't be best pleased."

"Well, I'm not. You've always said I struggle to be tactful and you know very well I must be the least diplomatic of all our senior colleagues."

"Precisely. So, you need a challenging opportunity which should introduce such skills to your armoury."

"But Ireland's hardly a challenge anymore."

"Certainly it's nowhere near experiencing the problems of the past, but you'll be well aware that several recent outbreaks of violence and bombings are warnings not to be ignored."

I didn't respond immediately. Instead I tried to think how I could wriggle out of this one.

"I've got no alternative?"

"Jo, I'm pretty adamant. I hope you'll take it."

His response made it rather difficult for me to refuse. I was in a tight spot. Perhaps I'd thought all I had to do was object vociferously enough and he'd immediately capitulate. He clearly wasn't going to, and it was I who eventually gave in.

Possibly my strongest argument had been that there was hardly a job. Back in 2010, as we finished being in power, the Northern Ireland Office transferred policing and criminal justice to the Northern Ireland Assembly and Executive. Power sharing in the country was working. Yes, perhaps it was still a society deeply divided, but the different identities and aspirations of Ireland's two main communities were being skilfully managed at Stormont. The Belfast Agreement had finally brought Unionists and Republicans to the conclusion that neither majority rule nor unity by force was an option for the future of the Province. I therefore almost saw no need for a Secretary of State, let alone someone shadowing him.

I returned home quite down and Michael tried to be positive about it all with no success. He took Graham's line, and that annoyed me even more.

"It's toothless. The job has no real worth. There's nothing for me to do, Michael. I'm being shunted into the sidings."

"I can't believe that. Complacency on Ireland is dangerous. Look at those riots last month. And there could easily be a lot more."

It was certainly a possibility, but I just wasn't in the mood to be placated. So we had an increasingly heated exchange, I was pathetic because I was disappointed, and it took me the best part of a week to grudgingly accept the situation.

I was eventually persuaded my new job might have some worth after all when, a few days later, a whole series of cynical car bombs near Belfast killed four policemen and injured innocent bystanders, including children. Threats were issued - from unnamed sources - suggesting this could signal a new wave of violence. For well over ten years there had been relative calm, despite the occasional rioting and bombing. These latest atrocities however were serious and both the First Minister and the Deputy First Minister condemned them. Similarly alarm was expressed on all sides of the House at Westminster. The Secretary of State, up until now, of necessity, nothing more than a pen-pusher, was clearly rattled. He returned to his official residence at Hillsborough Castle, even though it was the recess, and I was also sent to the Province to show cross-party support.

I spent the next three or four months carefully researching the troubles over the previous forty years. I found myself able to sympathise with both sides' views on certain issues but, like the majority of people, I couldn't possibly condone the horrific violence. Not at any level. Gradually however I was judged – unfairly - to be rather too sympathetic with the Nationalists. Furthermore, two incidents in November caused me embarrassment, as well as giving both our Party and the Government a few headaches.

At the beginning of the month I had hinted, only hinted, during a press conference in Belfast, that perhaps the Northern Ireland Executive had shown some weakness and complacency in policing the Province of late. Yes, they were expressing condemnation of atrocities, but it didn't seem to be converted into effective action.

I considered my criticism to be very mild but the Irish press tore me to pieces. It was nothing to the dressing-down I received from within my own party though. I was summoned back to London and roasted by Graham Thorne in very uncharacteristic fashion. Once he'd finally calmed down I tried to put my perspective on it all.

"But, Jo, you can't just go waltzing over there telling them they're not running their country as they should. They've done an unbelievably good job in trying circumstances and your comments have rocked the boat. Now, please, we need to maintain a really good relationship."

We talked for another hour and I was sent back, rather with my tail between my legs.

A week later I felt moved to attend a Remembrance Day ceremony in Ireland, before I was due to return to London. I genuinely wanted to show the people of Belfast that day just how much I cared about all those lost over the years on both sides. Without giving it a second thought I quite naturally wore a red poppy, and then I was in trouble again. You see, I'd forgotten that poppies were controversial, being seen as somehow representing support for the British Army. So, again I was criticised, but I think I just about managed to explain myself to the media this time.

Similarly, although displeased, Graham was more understanding when I got back this time.

"I hope you realise now, Jo. Their troubles will probably never go right away, much as we would all love that."

"I hadn't done enough homework had I?"

"No, but you're learning. Now do you see why I gave you this role?"

God, he could be so patronising at times.

I would possibly have continued with the Ireland job

until the next election. However two dramatic events took place in a short space of time which soon changed all that.

Michael and I had just finished supper one evening and he offered to wash up. As he got up he crashed back down onto the floor.

In retrospect the heart attack - thankfully minor - came as no surprise. All his life he had been on the heavy side, he loved his food, and exercise was minimal. Now all that had to change. He would soon recover but his lifestyle needed to alter substantially.

Naturally, for a few days, I took leave to care for him, but fortunately the attack was very mild and a serious warning more than anything else. He was put on strong medication and seemed to recover very quickly, all things considered.

A couple of weeks later I was told to report urgently to Graham Thorne's office. It transpired that a bombshell was about to be dropped. Our Shadow Chancellor had got stupidly involved in a public spat and was going to have to stand down. Apparently his youngest child was the victim of cyber-bullying at school and the main antagonist was the son of a rather brash businessman in the City who usually had plenty to say for himself. Both sets of parents had been summoned to the School Head, and in the hall afterwards, in front of a couple of staff and some students, the boy's father started calling our colleague all the names under the sun. One taunt tipped Ian too far and, in a moment of madness, he decked him.

"Now, Jo," asked Graham, after he'd put me in the picture, "how's Michael?"

"Recovering well, thanks. But it's been very frightening."

"Of course. That's another reason I want to relieve you of Northern Ireland."

"But I won't let my work suffer any more, Graham.

His doctor has said it was a warning, he's on the right medication, and he'll be fine now."

"I appreciate all of that, Jo, but you have to be away a lot. Better if you're London-based again, I feel."

"You said 'another reason'. Did I miss the first one then?"

He smiled and acknowledged my sharpness.

"Jo, how does Shadow Chancellor appeal to you?"

*

Michael had prepared supper the following Sunday and popped a bottle as I sat down.

"Whoa!" I protested. "What's this about?"

"Time we had a little celebration I think."

"Well, just a small drop then. And don't you get too carried away."

"Jo, for pity's sake! I refuse to make life miserable. I shan't go overboard, don't worry. It has been a shock and I'm going to be sensible in the future. But I can't go from one extreme to the other. Life's a question of balance, isn't it?"

"Yes, of course. Sorry. You know I don't want to be a kill-joy. I simply hope you can stay well, that's all."

"Look, the ball's in my court. You can support, but you can't do it for me. Now, here's to the new Shadow Chancellor. Amazing! I'm so proud."

We clunk our glasses and drank.

"Mm, nothing but the best then?"

"Naturally."

He started serving the food.

"You know, the surprising thing for me in all this is how quickly Ian went. I mean plenty of others have got into little scraps in the past, especially during elections."

"Well, Graham actually told me a bit more than I've let on, darling."

"Oh?"

Michael stopped pouring the sauce.

"Unfortunately he didn't just knock his antagonist over, he then apparently uttered several expletives himself. I'll leave you to imagine the sort of thing. Suffice to say there may be charges brought and Ian's certainly in very deep water."

"I see."

He finished serving and sat down opposite me.

"Well, let's not worry about Ian. Always been a bit of a hothead. He should have controlled himself, whatever the provocation."

He re-filled his glass and toasted me.

"Here's to you, love. Now, enjoy your meal. I've been slaving for hours!"

*

As it happens I held the post for only six months, so it was difficult to achieve too much. The whole country had known there would be an election in 2015 and it was just a question of when it would be called.

Between us, our Leader and I decided it would best serve me in particular not to get too distracted by day-to-day matters. Instead Graham wanted me to concentrate on all the financial aspects of Labour's manifesto. This task alone made huge demands on my time. Anyone could slate a government's policies. Easy. But the electorate wanted to see some credible alternatives.

Right up to the Election all of us on the Opposition benches struggled to ignite people's interest. At the beginning of the month leading up to the polls, we still only had a slender one or two-point lead. And in surveys on who would make a better Prime Minister the Tory incumbent was way ahead of our man.

During the campaign we had plenty of fodder to throw

at the Government yet, on the doorstep, I got the impression that voters were either uninspired by our policies or perhaps found some of them too radical. It also has to be said that, although I publicly backed him to the hilt, privately I had become more and more dismayed at Graham Thorne's lethargic leadership as Election Day approached.

Nevertheless, I always relished the chance of a good fight and was especially looking forward to a televised debate which involved two leading Tory and Lib-Dem politicians and me. This was going out live a week before polling day, chaired by Caroline West.

By this time I had become extremely confident in front of cameras and behind microphones. I revelled in it all actually. The first bit of good fortune I had that evening was that, for the opening question, I spoke last. A further slice of luck was to witness the other two tearing into one another from the very start. Over the five years of Coalition they had always maintained an uneasy alliance. This rift played into my hands, so I felt I was winning even before I had started.

"Joanne Rayner, I imagine you see the latest unemployment figures as good news?"

God, she could be a bitch.

"Good news? If you think I welcome such appalling figures then kindly think again. It's certainly not good news for hard working men and women looking over their shoulders fearful they may be next. It's hardly good news for school-leavers either, is it?

"And all my parliamentary colleagues here can engage in is cheap political in-fighting, pathetically scrapping with one another. Where's their sense of collaboration now I wonder?

"No, these figures are disastrous and a wake-up call to us all. Let me remind our viewers of them because of course those two haven't. Three point three million unemployed! Over three quarters of a million more than when they took office five years ago. Even worse than that, the percentage of young people unemployed - sixteen to twenty-four year olds - is up to twenty-eight. Well over a quarter of the next generation. It's shameful.

"Ok, I can appreciate what many of you will be thinking. Can Labour do any better? Yes, I really do believe so. To successfully kick-start the economy we need to produce. To produce goods and to provide effective services. Only then can we begin to get on top of this disastrous employment situation.

"Traditionally Labour has tried to preserve the highest possible standards in public services and....."

Both my adversaries started shouting and heckling.

"Now don't you try your bully-boy tactics out on me, lads. You know from bitter experience it just won't wash."

The audience clapped and cheered.

"Please allow her to continue," said the interviewer, quite unnecessarily in my view.

"Oh, don't worry, Caroline, I can look after myself perfectly well, thank you."

She glared. Then we had never got on.

"This government, as in the past, has systematically decimated public services which have always been a major contribution to fuller employment. And private enterprise, in a suppressed economy, has sadly failed to combat that. Enough about them though, because you want to know what we intend doing about it.

"As Shadow Chancellor I know money's tight. Of course it is. But, like your personal household budgets, it's how we allocate what little we have got. Yes, we will endeavour to inject all we possibly can back into public services, but we are also urgently concentrating on how our young people can be confident there will one day be work out there for them. Not just any work. Worthwhile jobs that will restore their self-esteem and make them want to get up in the morning. Work that will ensure they can cover the cost of basic essentials.

"We have therefore drawn up measures whereby the pay package will include benefits-in-kind for fundamental necessities. And they will receive in-post training from older, experienced people. In other words, full-time, meaningful on-the-job apprenticeships that will inject hope into young people's lives."

I could see from the interviewer's stance that my time was up for this one and I knew attempts to try and take this further would be blocked, so I wrapped it up.

"Draft proposals, entitled 'Learning to Work', are on our campaign website. Please have a look at them. Yes, they are radical. But fresh ideas are what we need. A completely new way forward."

I got a good reception and had performed well that night. Sadly, come Election Day, it all went terribly wrong. I really had thought we might win after all, but no. The Conservatives had a late surge and won outright power. Although I achieved personal success, many respected colleagues departed. We had a bad night in truth and I was bitterly disappointed. The Lib-Dems had a catastrophic time, but it gave me little comfort.

*

"Never mind, Titch," said Josh over lunch the next day, "my man will lead us all to the Promised Land!"

"He's certainly good at making promises."

Ruth put a conciliatory arm round me.

"We had a brilliant day yesterday, Jo. I don't know how you do it."

"Thank you, Ruthie."

"Look on the positive side, love," said Michael. "People are sitting up and taking notice of you now. Your future's really bright. I'm sure we'll win next time."

I thanked them for all their support on the road the day before, but I couldn't mask my frustration. I was deflated at the thought of being in opposition again. And I wasn't sure I shared Michael's belief. The 'next time' seemed such a long way off and I might not have any more fight left in me. But of course I was mentally and physically drained.

After a busy week or so sorting out correspondence and e-mails, Michael and I took a long weekend break. I wanted to go to Suffolk. We found a charming converted blacksmith's forge with views across the estuary at Orford, close to the castle. I wanted to visit the old churchyard and talk.

*

"Oh, Mummy, what do I do now? I've got nothing left to give."

My mother had been resting here in Chesney for over forty years and Carrie for virtually twenty-five. So long. So long since I had shared any sort of close relationship with another woman. Selfishly I felt cheated and sorry for myself and I pleaded with Mummy to comfort me. But an oppressive silence lay like a blanket and nothing penetrated it. So I gave up, kicking out angrily at some shingle on the path as I traipsed dejectedly back down the lane. On the way I met a lady I vaguely recognised from my early childhood.

"Good morning," I said, trying to appear cheerful. "Very peaceful here, isn't it?"

"The castle's full of people though," she replied, passing on.

I had intended taking Michael to the castle the next day so I thought I'd take a quick look now in case there was a special event on he might enjoy.

On arrival, contrary to what I'd been told, I found it deserted. Not a soul. Yet it was half past eleven on a Saturday morning in May. Puzzled, I shrugged my shoulders and took a path down to a sheltered grassy knoll I had spotted. Sitting against a boulder I nodded off in the warmth and was only woken by the church clock chiming twelve.

*

Many people were beginning to enjoy their picnics. Mummy was unpacking a hamper, while Dad held Carrie's hand as she tottered uncertainly after her red setter puppy. Dad lifted Carrie up and returned her to Mummy. Retrieving the dog, who had begun making a nuisance of himself, Dad noticed me and waved. He said something to Mummy who turned round and also waved. Then she got Carrie to do a pretend wave. I rushed down towards them, past a courting couple and another young family. But, by the time I'd reached the spot, they'd disappeared. I looked in every direction. Gone. Everyone gone. It was deserted again. I stood rooted to the spot, tears of frustration welling up.

I trudged disconsolately back up to the road. As I continued walking a very pregnant woman was coming from the opposite direction. She recognised me and stopped.

"You're Joanne Rayner the MP aren't you?"

I nodded, not wanting to get dragged into any conversation.

"Well, you'll become Labour Leader now. It's your time, you mark my words."

Then she was swiftly gone. I looked back, and only then was it that I noticed the dog on a lead. The same young red setter.

*

Graham Thorne, if not much else, was dogged in defeat and he was obviously going to try and cling on to his job. I had lost my patience with him, as had most of my party colleagues. I didn't join in the clamour for his resignation though. I felt that sort of behaviour simply made us look divided. But I certainly hoped he would step down because we needed a new leader who could inspire and unite. And Stephen Moorcroft was perfect for the job. Well, that was my opinion, until he sounded me out one September afternoon.

"You've been very quiet on the leadership, Jo."

"Well, best we wait and see what Graham does."

"He's quitting. Tomorrow," replied our Deputy Leader.

"Tomorrow?"

"Yep."

"With dignity, I hope?"

"Totally."

"Mm, well, that's good news then. You can step up and replace him, Stephen."

"Not me."

"Oh come on, don't give me all that coy stuff. Save that for the media."

"Jo, I'm serious. I will not stand."

"Why ever not, you dope."

"Because at best I would be a long way second."

"Nonsense! Who to? There's nobody to touch you."

"Oh yes there is."

"Who?"

"You of course."

"Me?"

"Everyone that matters wants you. Mark and Jeremy might put themselves forward but are no threat."

"But I'm a woman."

"So? What's that got to do with it?"
"I really don't think I'm up to it, Stephen."
"Come on, Jo. It's your time, you mark my words."
Now where had I heard that before?

*

As it transpired Stephen was spot on. Graham did resign and, to my amazement, Conference later elected me as their new Leader. 'By a distance' as Josh typically described it at a celebration in the Premier Inn afterwards.

The next morning I excitedly read every newspaper account. Many headlines were encouraging, but one tabloid stood out: 'Jo's Premier Party'. It was corny of course, but I confess I rather liked it. Tacky, but prophetic perhaps?

*

I certainly experienced a remarkable first two and a half years as Labour Leader. For some inexplicable reason virtually everything I touched seemed to bring success right from the word go, while, conversely, the then Government's position seemed to weaken rapidly. Policies were not working and their popularity nose-dived. At one point, a couple of tabloid newspapers, who survived on sensational journalism, even suggested we were heading for anarchy.

In all my political jousting with the PM I always avoided blaming him and his Party for the economic situation. I considered this futile and unfair since it was a global problem and had been for years. I would never assume our policies would turn it around, and I concentrated instead on areas where I did have total confidence we could change things for the better.

Following on from our defeat and my leadership election, I gathered around me a team of men and women I knew I could trust to do an effective job in what I had picked out as key areas. It was a small team, far smaller than most shadow cabinets historically, and I fully intended never to shuffle them around in the future. Once chosen, I left them to get on with it and slowly grow in the belief they would each one day govern in their specific field of expertise. I never once interfered at departmental level, but then I had made it perfectly clear from the onset what I expected of them. And I knew they would deliver. Leaders couldn't be expected to do everything. It was a team game and the captain didn't need to be everywhere on the pitch. When giving someone a job to do, a role to play, so many people just couldn't help themselves. They had to stick their noses in. And this so often led to their downfall as well as everyone else's. I never understood why they did it. A sense of insecurity perhaps?

Primarily we put the bones on our 'Learning to Work' programme. By the next General Election unemployment was at three and a half million. Young people were losing heart and none more so than in Northern Ireland where over a third of the working population under twenty-five were jobless. This factor was contributory to the increasing amount of protests, riots and general unrest in the Province.

Our manifesto prioritised getting people into work. It was both the centre and the cornerstone.

All leaders were granted a lot of media air-time and I took full advantage of this to get our objectives across as clearly as possible.

*

"Tonight it is the chance for the main Opposition to explain as much of their manifesto as time allows. Jo Rayner, Labour Leader, is with me."

John Deakin turned to me.

"Of course, I've had the pleasure of interviewing you many times over the last few years. Your rise has been meteoric, but that's not a surprise to most of us. I personally recall first throwing questions at you just before the London Olympics."

"And you've clearly not lost any of your old charm, John."

"Well, it's never succeeded with you."

"True, but keep trying. I rather like it."

He chuckled, and the audience enjoyed it too. I was flirting with him, but more than ready to move on to the serious stuff.

"Now, 'Learning to Work'. We've had a long time to consider this paper, which is your jewel in the crown, wouldn't you say?"

"It's probably the most significant part of our manifesto, yes."

"But vouchers? Can they really work? I mean, I remember my old man getting some way back for his lunches. Whatever happened to those?"

"Employers stopped issuing them."

"So won't this happen again? And it's not just lunches this time, is it?"

"No. But it isn't just employers this time. We envisage a tri-partite arrangement between the employer, the Government, and major players in industry and commerce."

"So cost will be shared equally?"

"Shared, certainly."

"But not equally?"

"Possibly. Possibly not. I refuse to try and persuade the public with pre-election promises I can't guarantee to keep. That's where I differ from many other politicians. However, what I can say with conviction is that our radical proposals do stand a good chance of creating significant job opportunities."

"But you'll be scrapping the minimum wage?"

"Not for existing jobs. We won't punish those already in such a scenario. However I struggle to support such a concept any longer."

"Now the idea seems to be that the basic wage will be low and supplemented by trading vouchers which can then be exchanged for food, fuel, IT, that sort of thing?"

"The basic needs, yes. And, John, before you liken it to the post-war ration books of last century, I will do that for you. But only to a point. The number of vouchers will be geared to the basic wage and adjusted regionally. People residing in East Anglia will, for example, need more car fuel vouchers than, say, Londoners, who obviously enjoy better public transport facilities. This is where we look to major oil companies to play their part."

"The success of the whole scheme seems dependent on many companies playing ball. What if they don't? After all, it's sponsorship by the back door, isn't it?"

"I am encouraged by all my talks with various captains of industry in many different fields and therefore I'm certainly not prepared to countenance failure before we have even tried. What do you want me to say? That we'll wave a magic wand and jobs will appear from nowhere? Come on. Ok, this is unconventional and I, more than anyone, will acknowledge its possible pitfalls. But it has more to commend it than not. And to continue as we are offers no hope at all."

The audience applauded warmly.

"Now, there are other aspects to the proposals, aren't there?"

"Yes, of course. Training for starters."

"Let's talk about that then. You aim to fast-track

school-leavers into teaching, the emergency services and even medicine?"

"Yes, but that is nowhere near an exhaustive list. On-the-job training, with a basic wage and vouchers, but learning from top, experienced professionals."

"Glorified work experience."

"Oh dear, you really are being cynical now. No, not at all. We have had decades of successive governments extolling the virtues of further education, university, etcetera. Mis-guided. To begin with, tuition fees lead to more debt. If I may give a very personal example, both my brothers actually learnt how to do a job by getting stuck into it in the actual work-place, and this was the recipe for their success. Students have no idea how to do anything by dozing off in a lecture. That's if they've even bothered to show up."

There was tumultuous applause at this point.

"Half the degrees dished out today are worthless."

"So you'd presumably bring these now redundant professors out of university into the work arena?"

"Some perhaps. But of course university still has a vital role in society. However, we've gone from intellectual elitism in the fifties to the present unworkable concept of university for all. It doesn't suit all young people. It's not appropriate for everyone."

The audience clapped even more loudly.

"Now, I'm getting noises in my ear-piece," said John, "so I think....."

"Tinnitus?"

Much laughter.

"Or perhaps you need to see a shrink?"

The interviewer could contain himself no longer and joined the audience in appreciation of my wisecracks.

"I walked right into that one. And it's not the first time you've done that to me."

He wiped his eyes.

"I reduce them all to tears in the end. Family trait."

"I wish we had time to discuss your family background but it's fast running out and I'd like to touch on your taxation proposals. Radical again?"

"Radical again."

"In particular, food waste and water."

"That's right."

"But let's take the old potato first. Alcohol."

"We shall tax it really heavily and restrict availability to those who are under-age. Substantial fines will be introduced, and strictly imposed, where traders break that law. Zero tolerance. I believe the whole country knows where I stand on alcohol."

"Food waste then."

"We somehow have to come to grips with over-production, banning devious marketing ploys like 'two for the price of one'. To combat the obscene dumping of huge volumes of food deemed to be past the sell-by date we shall appoint Waste Inspectors to monitor supermarket stock levels."

"And finally water. What is your thinking here?"

"It is an increasing view that the next war may well be over water. I don't discount that at all. Climatic conditions over the past two decades have meant our long-term water reserves are being rapidly and seriously depleted. The majority of countries have the same problem. And, despite the warnings of very wise scientists, nobody is doing anything about it."

"But you can't tax water on top of the rate, surely?"

"Probably not, but I don't entirely rule that out. However we can certainly take a very hard look at the taxation for bottled water. It appals me how casually bottled water is consumed these days. And with such irreverence."

"Irreverence?"

"Well, have you not watched sports events, marathons

and football matches in particular, where only half-empty bottles are thrown around? Now kids are copying it in the school playground. It's a disgrace. And that's why we would start taxing it. Then it would be in people's interest to conserve more. We need to understand as a society that water is so precious. It's literally the fountain of life. Without it, we're all dead."

"I'm afraid I have to wrap this up, but, in one sentence, can you summarise your proposal on paid military and social service?"

"Phew! No, is probably my answer. Let me see. Well, it's basically an option for the long-term unemployed when all else may have failed for them. But please, as I always ask, read the detail on our website. I really can't do it justice in one sentence. Sorry."

"Fair comment. Joanne Rayner, thank you very much."

*

My election campaign manager was beside himself the next morning.

"Jo, you were terrific."

"Thank you, Tommy, I really enjoyed it."

"So did the audience, and the press. Already most pundits say we'll get in comfortably now. Your performance has really swung it for us."

"Easy now, please. There's nearly a week to go yet."

"Jo, you don't understand. It could be a landslide."

I was getting cross. I liked optimism but I kept remembering three years ago.

"Look, if and when the current PM concedes defeat, then, and only then, will I allow myself to start thinking about moving into Number Ten. Until then, kindly bottle it, and simply ensure the momentum is sustained."

I stormed out.

Tommy hadn't deserved that. He was just excited. But for me complacency couldn't be an option and Tommy would just have to put up with me being a tense old bat for a little while longer.

He wasn't the only one. Michael and I had long agreed our relationship was becoming spectacularly tossed around. But we were still just about managing short, precious moments together most days. People like Tommy, a diehard bachelor, simply didn't realise that I had to ensure Michael never felt left out in the cold. I hoped he never did, but I suspected there were many occasions when he bit his tongue. Whatever happened though, he was my rock and always would be.

*

"Tommy was right then, love. A landslide."

Michael eventually managed to find the bedside light-switch and the master bedroom at 10 Downing Street was drowned in darkness.

"He was, bless him."

"I must say it feels very strange going to bed with the Prime Minister."

"Well this PM is also a woman, so come and give me a hug."

"Are you sure there's not a policeman listening at the door?"

We laughed and snuggled up.

"No, I think, in these times of austerity, we're only allowed the one out on the street by the front door."

"Honestly, what is this country coming to? Economies wherever you look."

"What indeed."

*

As we drove through the gates of Buckingham Palace I tensed up and my hands became clammy. Michael patted me on the arm.

"Don't worry, old girl, he'll love you, you'll see."

"I've suddenly lost all confidence. And less of the 'old', thank you."

"Fifty next year."

"You beast!"

"That's better."

"What do you mean?"

"I want you sparky when you meet him."

"I wonder what you'll be doing?"

"Who knows? Tea with his missus? No. With his valet, more like."

"Well don't eat too much cake, that's all."

The limousine came to a halt and I took a deep breath.

*

"Your Majesty."

I curtseyed and the King invited me to sit down.

"Welcome. And my warmest congratulations on your election victory."

"Thank you, sir."

"Now then, would you prefer Joanne or Jo?"

"Well, Jo, please, sir."

"Good. Jo it shall be then. And, please, no more 'Majesty' or 'sir'. In future we are always going to be alone for our weekly meetings and so no-one ever knows what's said at these things. Remember, I have a christian name too."

"Thank you. I really appreciate that."

"Let's face it, we all arrive in the same way on this earth and depart in similar fashion. It's the awkward bit in between that's so darned confusing, isn't it?"

"You sound like my dad."

"And his name is?"
"Was. Will."
"Ah, a fine name."
We exchanged knowing smiles.
"Of course I'm not really the one who should be talking to you now. I'm only the night watchman."
"You never know, you might surprise everyone and score a century."
"Heaven forbid! I hope not. I get muddled enough already."
He fiddled nervously at his shirt-cuff.
"Now, I'm nearly as new to all this as you, but I do know we have to get a little bit of red tape out of the way first. So, we'll do that and then I want to hear about your family and talk to you about your fascinating proposals on Youth Unemployment."
"Thank you. I had to quickly read up on the history of your work with young people, so I know how far back your interest goes."
He obviously found this all very amusing and then I realised I had probably done my usual and been too open.
"Sorry, I didn't mean....."
"Please, don't apologise. I like honesty. I think we're going to get along very well, Jo. I liked the last chap, I really did, but....."
He thought better of it and then mischievously added:
".....you're rather better looking than he is!"
I blushed, but only slightly. He'd made me feel completely at ease and I found his charm a very attractive quality.
"Well, thank you, but I'm getting on a bit, as my husband reminded me on the way here. Fifty next year."
"Marvellous! We must ensure we have a meeting on your birthday then. We'll have cake, candles, the lot."
We both laughed.
"Only one candle though. Think of the economy."

"Oh, right. Of course. Dear me, Jo, I can see I'm not going to get away with much when you're around, am I?"

"I'd like to think it's unlikely."

We laughed again as he turned to some papers.

*

During the weeks leading up to the General Election I had set aside an hour or so every day specifically to consider what the basic elements of my governing style might be. I didn't wish to presume in any way, but, equally, I wanted to be well prepared should we win. I knew I needed to be comfortable in my own skin as Prime Minister. To begin with I intended to discard all the stuffiness and pomposity that I felt still went with the job. I was also particularly keen to ensure that the expertise of ministerial colleagues would always be put to best use and that they got their fair share of the limelight. I believed too many Premiers had allowed themselves to be drawn into commenting far too freely on contentious issues that really needed the relevant Secretary of State's grasp of the important detail.

This meant that I had to totally trust every single one of my senior team. It would be essential that I backed them one hundred per cent once Cabinet had agreed their recommendations. Historically I knew that division in any party eventually culminated in defeat. Of course I was strong-willed and I had very definite views on a wide range of subjects, but, if I ever sensed I was rowing against the tide, I knew I had to concede gracefully. No one person should ever be in a position to dominate and manipulate - and that applied to everything in life, not just government. I knew myself well enough to acknowledge this would be hard. When I privately disagreed with something I realised I would struggle. But there was really no alternative. I acknowledged that I would have to concede to good old-fashioned democracy. Fortunately I also knew my weaknesses. I might be confident on Home Affairs, but I recognised my experience abroad was not as strong as it should be. So, without hesitation, I appointed Stephen Moorcroft as Foreign Secretary, and, in years to come, his name was to become significant.

By the time it came to my first press conference as PM, I was therefore able to face the media with confidence.

*

"Good morning, everyone, I hope you haven't guzzled all the hot chocolate."

Friendly banter ensued, which was just the atmosphere I wanted.

"Now then, Harry, let me squeeze in between you and Catherine here."

"Excuse me, Prime Minister, but we'd like you sitting at a table if you don't mind. Our cameras can't pick you out too well there."

"Now then, Rupert Meadows, isn't it?"

"Yes, ma'am, Channel 4 News."

"And very good you are at your job too."

"Thank you, ma'am."

"But you really haven't worked this one out at all, have you?"

Much laughter followed from many of the other journalists sitting in the room.

"Firstly, Rupert, no more 'Prime Minister' or 'ma'am', please. It's Jo. And before anyone suggests I'm cosying up to you all, just for good press, you're absolutely right. Why else do you think you're getting so well looked after?"

More amusement.

"Look, everyone, please let me get this straight. I want this informal setting. It's much more civilised than having me perched up behind mikes. You will still get serious answers to serious questions, but let's all relax a bit, shall we?"

There was a general muttering of appreciation.

"Anyway I'm not so naive that I believe it's going to get you all on my side. My aim is simply mutual respect. And honesty. In my case, honest answers; in yours, honest reporting. Now, that's not too much to ask, is it?"

Again, common assent.

"Thanks, Jenny."

I acknowledged my PA as she handed me a mug of steaming chocolate.

"So, first question then. Oh, and Harry, if I ever have to sit next to you again, must you suck those dreadful lozenges?"

"Sorry, Jo, bit of a sore throat."

"Honey and lemon in future. Jenny, please could you add that to the menu?"

"Thank you. Most kind. Now, I do have a question. Northern Ireland."

I groaned inwardly, but then I wasn't surprised. It was beginning to worry everyone again.

"Your first weekend as PM saw widespread riots in the Province, especially Belfast, and it would appear that British soldiers are in danger of becoming targets of resurgent extreme nationalist groups. Yet, at the same time, you seem to have diminished the importance of Ireland to the UK by making the position of Secretary of State obsolete. Why?"

"I have consciously reduced the size of the Cabinet to make for more effective government. In the case of Northern Ireland, the existence of the Assembly at Stormont has increasingly made a Secretary of State less pertinent, so I'm simply channelling the Province's affairs through the Home Office."

"But surely you agree our troops are indeed under increasing threat?"

It was the BBC's Northern Ireland correspondent, Adrian Coyle, who had intervened.

"I understand the concerns and the Home Secretary, Hugh Napier, will be making a statement next week."

"Will he be condemning the 'Honeypot' tactics against army personnel?"

"As I vowed in my election campaign, I shall never pre-empt or undermine any of my ministers. Hugh will be giving you plenty to write about, rest assured."

"And what does that mean exactly?"

"It means Northern Ireland is very much on our agenda, and it means Hugh Napier will deal with it next week. Next question, please....."

The 'Honeypot' to which Adrian Coyle had referred was an alarming increase in situations where young women appeared to be getting into British army barracks on the arms of officers and NCOs and proceeding to their quarters, where they certainly weren't playing ludo. In Cabinet Hugh had used powerful and effective rhetoric to persuade all my colleagues that it was time to strongly and publicly condemn nationalist groups who were considered to be at the bottom of it all. I had argued that it would be a much better way forward to tighten our own ship, with more stringent security and a foolproof system of passes. But, at the table, I was in a minority of one and I therefore had no option but to back our Home Secretary. It had been the first challenge to my democratic resolve, but it was backing of course that was to cause me untold personal problems.

*

"So, Titch, here's to you. Happy Birthday!"

"Thank you, Josh. What a lovely surprise."

"Well I have to say, Sis, if I'd known just how much hassle it was all going to be to get you to this place I might not have bothered. But then I thought, damn it, I won't be beaten."

We all laughed.

"You rarely are these days," said Michael.

"Well, I don't know about that, but there was no way Jo's fiftieth was going to pass us by."

"Pity about those two, though," said Ruth, referring to my bodyguards sitting discreetly at a distant table.

"I'm working on it but getting nowhere. They could be home with their families."

"You have to realise, darling, you're a high security risk," said Michael.

"Who would have thought it, eh? My little sister high risk....."

We were celebrating my fifty years at a favourite London restaurant of mine. The first year of my premiership had gone quite well and there were encouraging signs of slight recovery in the economy. Furthermore there had been heartening movement downwards in the latest unemployment figures. I had suffered plenty of setbacks, but I was determined to learn from them and move positively forward.

*

And for just over three more years I did just that. We continually fine-tuned our policies as we became more experienced and, albeit at a slower rate than I would have liked, unemployment returned to far more acceptable levels and the economy became less stagnant.

But it was gruelling work. My patience often wore thin and it was Michael who kept me going when I was down. Yet I knew it was all very difficult for him too. I got very tired and irritable and he got it in the neck constantly. I'm sure the majority of men would have given me up as a bad job long ago. Not Michael. He was fantastic and I began to think I owed him.

So, in early autumn 2022, I was actually beginning to harbour thoughts of stepping down the following year. We would be calling an election, one we were expected to win comfortably, but perhaps five years at the very top were sufficient. I hadn't appreciated just how tough and lonely it would be. However, they were only thoughts and always when I was feeling particularly drained.

There were also times when I wanted to go on and on, but around the middle of November, standing at the Cenotaph, I wasn't given much choice and the decision was made for me in a very painful way.

The drug-induced wanderings of my mind, recalling all those years of my life, abruptly and violently ended with my head smacking against that Cenotaph step. As I blacked out I was of course unaware of my bodyguard lying dead beside me as he courageously saved my life on that Remembrance Sunday.

*

Following hospitalisation I simply couldn't stop thinking about Matt Lancaster's widow and his young son. What a horrendous experience they had suffered. They had apparently been watching on tv and it must have been appalling. There had of course been endless airtime devoted to the assassination attempt. I watched footage many times over, including slow-motion replays, and it was difficult to take in that I was the one at the centre of it all. I saw it more as a film drama. As Michael assured me one day in the New Year, doubtless it wouldn't be too long before such a film was in fact made. More agony for Sarah Lancaster was all I could think.

That woman was amazing. So stoical throughout the aftermath of the horror. We actually became good friends, but her husband's death would haunt me for the rest of my life. And I wanted nobody else to put themselves on the line for me again.

As the year unfolded I tried to concentrate on the immediate future. For the sake of the nation I needed to make the correct decision about where everything went from now. Towards the end of January it became obvious, after numerous consultations with doctors and Michael, that I simply couldn't continue as Premier. In fact, my health was such that, like it or not, I was going to have to face up to early retirement from politics - and possibly from anything else.

My previous sharp brain was befuddled; my memory kept letting me down; and I was still far from mobile. One dismal evening, as dusk fell, I turned to Michael from my wheelchair and admitted defeat:

"Michael, it's all over."

With typical stubbornness I insisted that no-one else was to know of my intentions until two days later, when I would hold a short cabinet meeting and then make my first appearance in the House since the shooting. It would also be my last. And the statement would be brief.

The next day Michael helped me compile my farewell speech. That evening we released a non-committal press announcement and speculation was rife when I attended a hastily organised cabinet meeting the next morning. There was only one item on the agenda. Colleagues were genuinely devastated, but each of them had realised that my forced resignation was inevitable from day one. Nevertheless, many tears were shed.

*

I wheeled my chair down the newly-installed ramp

outside the door of Number Ten and became blinded by the flashing photography and deafened by the cheers of journalists as I approached their cameras and mikes.

"How are you now, Jo?"

"Great to see you back!"

"Are you off to see His Majesty?"

"Will you be going to the House?"

"Have you got to resign, Jo?"

I appealed for silence and to their credit they immediately ceased their incessant clamouring to listen respectfully.

"Now, who was it mentioned resignation?"

An embarrassed voice confirmed my guess.

"Harry, do you not like my honey and lemon anymore then?"

"Very much! That's why I don't want you to go. None of us do."

There was a chorus of agreement.

"You are all very generous. Now, let me make a few things perfectly clear. No, I am not going to see the King today; yes, I am off to the House; and, as for resignation, I will only ever let you hear that dreadful word when I'm good and ready. Not before."

The ensuing cheers did my heart good, although I felt a little guilty at my mild deception. However it was of course only right and proper that I delivered in the House, not on the street.

*

The astounding reception I received as I hobbled into the Commons on my crutches was the most poignant of my political life. Everyone, from all sides of the Chamber, stood cheering and applauding. It was humbling.

With assistance I eased myself into the special seat

that had been positioned directly down from the Speaker's Chair. For two or three minutes I sat engulfed by a cacophony of affection, and I really had to struggle to keep my emotions in check.

"Order! Order!"

The poor Speaker had no luck with her first attempt.

"I shall have order!"

They quietened a little.

"The Prime Minister will make a statement."

More wild cheers.

"I said 'Order'!"

Then she looked directly at me and smiled.

"Prime Minister."

A hush finally fell.

"Thank you, and forgive me for remaining seated. I am overwhelmed by your astonishing welcome and humbled by the multitude of good wishes I have received over the last two months or so, from every imaginable source. I have had messages of support that have touched me deeply. Generous words from royalty, trusted colleagues, respected opponents, world leaders and, perhaps most significantly of all, from members of our great British public."

Huge cheers again.

I then went on to read from my prepared notes.

"Earlier today I had the opportunity to speak to His Majesty the King on our special multi-functional link-up that has been operational at Number Ten ever since I left hospital. With deep sadness I tendered my resignation as Prime Minister."

Absolute chaos broke out, with cries of 'no' and 'shame' ringing out from both sides of the House.

Eventually some sort of order was restored, but the atmosphere was highly charged now so the rest of my statement was deliberately brief.

"My state of health is such that I can no longer do the

job justice and the election process to appoint my successor will begin tomorrow."

There were more disappointed cries and I raised my hand again.

"Please give that person the support they will need and deserve. It is a tough job. A lonely job. And, in dark times, a thankless job. But let me say that, despite the pain of recent weeks, I would not have missed doing it for the world. It has been an immense privilege.

"I am grateful to every single one of you - and to past members - for the most wonderful eighteen years. Thank you. Thank you so very much."

I left the House to tumultuous applause, never to return again.

As I sank into the back of the limousine I dissolved into floods of tears. For it indeed was over. And it hurt. It hurt more than that damned bullet.

*

It took over two more years before my mind and body had fully come to terms with one another. It seemed I had to put up with the intermittent memory loss. It was frustrating, but even more so for others, especially Michael. Gradually, however, following several operations and endless physiotherapy, the jigsaw puzzle that was now my hip became more or less complete.

I was determined that one day I would walk and swim normally again, and not even the meccano pieces in my body were going to stop me. It was a very painful process but, by the summer of 2025, I had persevered and virtually achieved that goal.

In October Michael and I took a two-week holiday with Josh and Ruth on a beautiful Greek island, during which we would celebrate Michael's seventieth.

The day before his birthday, our first full day at the

resort, we were all lapping up the warm sun by the hotel pool, as it dried off our latest dip.

"So, Ruthie, the kids are full-time boarding now?"

"Yes, Jo, and they love it, although Evie's only been there six weeks."

"And what about their mum? Is she happy about it?"

Ruth glanced over at Josh who was miles away, as he and Michael both waved to the bikini-clad French beauties we'd met at dinner the previous night.

"In their dreams, eh, Jo?"

We both laughed.

"Am I happy about boarding? Oh, well, I deal with it. But I do miss them and I admit I've struggled a bit."

"And what about Josh?"

"He's always been for it. Thinks it's important for them to be able to appreciate the family home but not be totally dependent on it."

"Yes, well, I see where he's coming from, but I also feel for you."

"Oh, Jo, don't worry about me. I mean, I'll get used to it. Besides, Josh and I have such a full life. It's great. I've nothing to complain about."

"Well, I'm glad to hear that, my love," said Josh, turning towards us, "because if they weren't boarding we wouldn't be here."

"So, you're back with us again then?" Ruth replied.

"Don't know what you mean," he twinkled.

"Oh yes you do, Bruv. But you haven't managed to bring Michael with you yet."

"Nonsense!" Michael exclaimed as he rolled over onto his spare tyre, "I was just admiring the view."

We all smiled.

"I wondered why he was studying a French phrase book in bed last night when we're in Greece."

"Perhaps we'd better chat up some local male talent, Jo. Pity you don't still have a bodyguard. That last one was rather a hunk."

I fleetingly thought of the Lancasters and of course they all realised Ruthie had been a bit clumsy.

"Oh, gosh, Jo, I'm so sorry. I only meant....."

"No, please. You're right. He was rather a good looker, wasn't he?"

"I shouldn't have brought that up. It's just....."

"Ruth, it's ok, really. I can talk about it now. It still hurts, but I don't want you clamming-up all the time to spare my feelings. It's best out in the open."

"I'll get some more drinks," said Michael, squeezing my arm as he bent down to collect up the glasses.

"So," said Josh, "you got your way in the end, Sis? No gong, no title, no bodyguard? No memoirs even?"

"Well, Bruv, one honoured person in the family was enough, I thought."

He smiled.

"It was such a battle to persuade the powers that be though. They simply would not listen at first. In the end I believe it was the King who intervened and persuaded the Government, especially on the bodyguard issue. He hates having them himself."

"He appears to be a good bloke. Is that actually the case?"

"Yes. He's such a sensitive man too. Anyway I've survived nearly a year without protection now and I just try and put all that sort of thing behind me."

"This Stephen Moorcroft though, Jo, he seems rather dull for PM, especially after you," said Josh. "I reckon we'll be back in again before too long."

"Well, that's as may be. Not my problem, Joshie."

"And definitely no memoirs then?" Ruth asked.

"No. Far too painful."

Michael returned with more exotic drinks.

"God, I could murder a pint," said Josh. "These fruit salads are quite tasty, but a bit tame."

"Well, the barman was telling me about an English-style pub just down the road....."

"Oh, here we go," I said.

"I was only thinking about my birthday tomorrow," Michael retorted.

"Yeah, come on, Sis, at least let the old boy off the leash one more time before he has to settle down."

The men exchanged winks.

"Jo, you haven't told me anything about these retirement plans of yours. When are they all going to happen?" Ruth asked.

"Well, it's very exciting. The doctors have done all they can now, which means we can escape from London at last. Michael has spent five years on his energy consultancy, as you know, but I've finally persuaded him to move to Sussex."

"Back home, Sis."

"Pretty much, Josh. We've bought a lovely top-floor flat overlooking the sea near Hove. That's until we find something more permanent. A little cottage perhaps."

"But we'll still keep the flat on," interjected Michael. "You'll be able to stay there for holidays. It's got three bedrooms."

"All this will set you back a pretty penny," suggested Josh.

"But that's one area where we've always been so fortunate. There's certainly no shortage of funds."

"We've all been very lucky, Sis, that's for sure. But if anyone deserves their creature comforts it's you after all you've been through."

"Thank you. But I'm not going to cosset myself like a china doll. In fact, I might even start looking for some work. Voluntary of course."

"Hey! Now there's an idea! Why don't you contact Lizzie James? Church Farm always needs volunteers and it'll only be a few miles away."

"Now, why hadn't I thought of that?"

I beamed at Josh. He looked bemused, then realised I was doing a double-take.

"I think she's one step ahead of you, mate," said Michael.

"She always has been."

"You're easy meat when it comes to keeping up with us women, isn't he, Ruth?"

"Putty in our hands. And he loves it."

The whole holiday continued as that first day. The weather, the island, the company. They were all perfect. How I enjoyed it. How I had needed it.

*

We moved to Hove early in December and spent the next few months house-hunting. But to no avail. There simply wasn't anything on the market that attracted us. So we decided to stay put in our flat and not worry about further accommodation for the time being.

As midsummer approached I started exploring clifftop walks with my new baby - a beautiful black labrador called Solly. He was barely two and I had spotted him in an animal welfare centre outside Worthing. It was love at first sight - for both of us I think. Michael was often playing golf - the one sport he'd mildly dabbled at over the years - but he seemed far more interested in the beer at the club-house than anything else. And as for his self-powered caddy, well!

On one such walk I let Solly off his lead and gazed out to sea. We had recently discovered this isolated little cove quite by accident. The descent was via a tricky and narrow path, but well worth the effort. It was a place where I felt able to start thinking about the future without too many distractions.

For the first time in many years I sensed my mother's

presence again. All through the years of the Labour leadership, and then my premiership, there had been nothing. She knew I needed to be left alone to get on with it. Even through my very dark journey.

It was now, when I stood at a new, unfamiliar crossroad, that I really needed her. She realised that.

But it was by no means clear to me what she was trying to suggest that day.

"Lizzie.....Weatherall.....husband.....wife.....cliffs....."

As it happened I had already planned to contact Lizzie James again next week. We had spoken earlier in the year and she seemed very keen for me to get involved with Church Farm. But Jimmy had been long gone, together with his cows. Whatever was she on about? He was pre-historic! Then I started giggling at the absurd thought of Lizzie and Jimmy being husband and wife.

"Mummy, you're back again! Oh, it's been so long! I just can't work out what you're saying though."

"Trustees.....you.....and.....Josh.....not.....Josh.....not..... you.....Solly.....care.....walkers....."

"He's lovely, isn't he? And of course I'll take care of him. But you do seem a confused old thing after all this time."

I waited for a few more moments but that was it. Possibly the oddest contact I had ever experienced from my mother. Yet, as always, it did at least tell me something. I would therefore make Lizzie my first port of call and take things from there. Past experience of my mother had taught me that all would eventually be revealed. I just had to forget about it all for now.

*

"Lizzie James?"
"Speaking."
"It's Jo Rayner."

"Jo, hello, it's good to hear from you again. How are you?"

"Really well, thanks."

"And Josh?"

"He's being typically Josh, his wife tells me. But he's fine."

"Good. Now, I was hoping....."

As a result of that phone call I started doing a bit of gardening at Church Farm. It was certainly a very odd feeling at first, fifty years on from my childhood. So much had changed from when we had lived there of course, but there were many happy memories to recall.

In September Lizzie announced that she would be retiring in the following March after twenty-five years at the charity. She had remained with her partner, Don, and they were moving to Tuscany. So the charity needed to find a new Chief Executive and a new Trustee as well. But the latter was manipulated by Josh. He made out that, with Lizzie leaving, he felt it was also a suitable time for him to call it a day. I knew him too well and suspected that he wanted to give me a new challenge because he had made it very clear he wanted me to succeed him. Anyway, he got his way. But then he usually did. For some reason I had a few doubts, but took it on nevertheless.

During the next six months, as Lizzie worked out her notice, Josh and I served on the charity's Council of Management together. Over this period there were two particularly significant developments.

At the October meeting the Finance Director announced that, despite planning permission having been granted for conversion of the old cowsheds to a single-storey dwelling, the charity no longer felt there were sufficient funds to actually proceed with the creation of further accommodation. Even the coffers at OKUK were not, it appeared, as healthy as in the past. Furthermore, it being such a valuable, extensive and sought-after site, Council was asked to rubber-stamp the proposal to sell. This situation had obviously been shrewdly anticipated since the charity had somehow managed to obtain full residential planning.

"Please don't put it on the market," I said. "I'll buy it. I'll buy it at the full market value and cover all legal costs so that the charity incurs no expense whatsoever."

I was absolutely astonished at myself. It simply came out of the blue. Josh had a knowing look on his face and gave me a warm smile.

"Madam Chairman," he said, "obviously I cannot possibly have any say in this matter, much as it would please me no end if Jo bought it. Perhaps my sister and I should retire while the rest of you discuss the matter more fully?"

Council actually took very little time to decide and readily accepted my proposal.

I couldn't believe I had made such a bold statement without reference to Michael - the words were out of my mouth before I could stop them. Fortunately Michael was genuinely delighted. But then it was an amazing location, and that did rather help.

"Well," said Josh after the meeting had closed, "whatever would dear old Jimmy Weatherall have made of it all, eh?"

Jimmy Weatherall? Then the penny dropped. Of course! Lizzie James, Jimmy. Our mother had done it again!

*

The second significant moment was in December, when we interviewed candidates to succeed Lizzie. I was on the panel, along with the Chairman and two other members of Council.

One candidate stood out from everyone else. Robin Henshaw had immense charitable experience and clearly knew where to look for grant money. He also seemed to have detailed knowledge of government spending priorities in the realm of social services.

At interview he presented a new vision and direction for our work. His ideas included converting the holiday lodge into an alcohol and drugs rehabilitation centre, which of course made me sit up and take particular notice. His confident style and fresh ideas won him my vote, and indeed everyone else's.

Accordingly, Robin took over from Lizzie at the end of March 2027, and Josh retired as a Trustee. In an unexpected way, and one that was difficult to explain, I was significantly affected by these changes.

After only a few weeks of Robin's tenure, it occurred to me that he represented the start of a totally new era at Church Farm, which was necessary for the charity, yet tricky for me. Josh had set the charity up, along had come Lizzie to take the helm, and now here was I actually feeling slightly out of step. I was part of the old order and, as much as I applauded the new appointment, something niggled away at me about it all. Robin was extremely commercial and the warmth he displayed at interview soon melted away. He was without doubt what the organisation needed, but the charity was losing that special 'Rayner' factor, despite my presence. Lizzie had always respected this and carefully nurtured it. In fairness Robin couldn't possibly be expected to maintain that but without it I began to lose enthusiasm.

I therefore eased myself off Council in the autumn, citing - quite reasonably - our impending house move as the main reason. In the end, I had thought it best for everyone that I didn't run the risk of standing in the way of necessary change. Far better to be around as a friendly neighbour.

I privately shared my concerns with Robin, explaining that I felt the charity would be able to move forward more positively without me.

*

Michael and I always seemed to choose the festive season to move, but this time we had certainly cut it a bit fine. The last pair of curtains got hung on Christmas Eve! The conversion had been a brilliant success and the standard of workmanship was outstanding. We had been extremely fortunate in so many ways, as Michael and I agreed, sitting in the cosy conservatory on New Year's Day.

"Penny for them, love?" Michael suddenly asked.

"Jimmy's cows used to be milked right where we're sitting now."

He guffawed.

"It's true!"

"I don't doubt you for one minute," he replied.

"We are so lucky, Michael. Not only do we own this beautiful place but we still have our lovely flat as well."

"I couldn't agree more. But I can't quite see Bluebell and Buttercup managing that lift, can you?"

I laughed at the thought of it.

"Let's catch the news," suggested Michael.

But I still preferred to avoid bulletins. Too often they represented my past and I really didn't want to go there anymore. So I padded into the kitchen to prepare supper.

Michael joined me later, informing me as casually as possible that there had been further unrest in Northern Ireland. Commonplace as this had become, and as warm as my new kitchen was, a shiver nevertheless cut right through me and I sunk into a rather depressed state.

At around ten o'clock neither of us felt tired but Michael decided I needed cheering up. We had purchased some very clever television technology that enabled us to link up with other domestic installations worldwide, provided they had the facility too. Luckily Seth and Maddy did have it, so Michael input their code and the screen indicated they were receiving our call. Then, magically, an excited Maddy appeared and the 3-D effect made it seem as though she was actually in our room. Amazing!

It was early morning in Australia and the sun was already shining. Maddy and I were on-line for the current maximum of twenty minutes and her bubbly chatter made me feel so much better. I told her of our plans to visit the following Christmas and she couldn't wait to tell Seth when he got home from town. I gave her a guided tour of the house and rambled on about my plans for the garden. Then we had to disconnect.

In fact I'd asked a local gardening contractor to pay us a visit the very next day. It didn't take me long to establish we were on the same wave-length and he undertook to start the work in mid-February.

Once the gardener had completed his work I started to spend many happy hours toiling away and by the end of May I felt pleased with the outcome. Solly was quite a nuisance sometimes, but then dogs could often be frustrating in a garden. Consequently I had continued to take him for a long walk every weekday afternoon on one of the many coastal walks we had discovered a couple of years back. We could scramble down to the lonely cove where Solly ran in and out of the waves while I sunbathed against a group of rocks. The end of the walk conveniently came out near our flat.

*

It was on such a walk, later in July, when I first started meeting them.

A married couple, I guessed. A couple anyway, perhaps in their early fifties. Presumably they were on holiday.

On the first occasion I called Solly and put his lead on. He could be too boisterous for some people. As they approached the woman smiled and thanked me. He just nodded. Judging by his equipment they were bird-watchers.

Just two days later we met again, almost at the same spot. Again the man barely acknowledged me, but this time she made a real fuss of Solly.

"He's a lovely boy. I bet he keeps you on your toes. Full of energy is he?"

"Never seems to get tired."

"Like Trouper," she said to her husband.

She turned back to me.

"Our retriever. Pulled my arms off he did. Well, until our son died that is. Pined away for him after that."

"Oh, I'm very sorry."

I began to feel a little uncomfortable, as I often did once complete strangers started coming out with personal stuff like this.

"So, when was that?" I asked, more out of politeness than anything else.

"Nearly six years ago. Our boy was killed in action, you see."

"That must have been tough."

Solly was straining at the leash now, so I was able to excuse myself and continue our walk. Phew! Some people could be astonishingly open about private matters. The man had just stood back looking out to sea. Probably embarrassed.

Another few days later we met yet again.

Within moments she had asked a question I was still getting frequently asked by many people. I'd got used to it and accepted they just couldn't help themselves.

"Do you mind me asking? You wouldn't happen to be Joanne Rayner, would you?"

"Yes, that's me."

"The former Prime Minister, that is?"

"Afraid so."

"Only we just wanted to be entirely sure. Forgive the intrusion."

"Please don't worry. I get used to it."

We went our separate ways.

The next day was very warm indeed and, after walking down to what I had now secretly regarded as our private little beach, I was almost tempted to go in for a swim. But I decided not to risk the current, seeing as it was so isolated. I did strip down to my swimsuit though, and lay down on two towels while Solly went to cool off in the water.

As the sun beat down I became quite drowsy and only a barking Solly prevented me nodding off completely. He was having a tussle with a large piece of seaweed on the water's edge.

I hitched myself up and made myself comfortable again, this time leaning against a smooth rock. I smiled to myself as Solly got frustrated with the seaweed and began barking at it. That lady was probably right yesterday. She'd said dogs were as noisy and hard work as children. I couldn't really comment of course but I agreed that Solly was certainly demanding.

I closed my eyes again and found myself thinking a little more about the couple. He'd never said a word whenever I'd met them. But then she was hard to compete with I guess.

What was it she'd said about her son? Killed in action nearly six years ago. Middle East, perhaps? And that would have been round about the time of the Cenotaph shooting.

Whew! The sun was really hot today. I'd better not

stay out in it too much longer.

For the life of me I just couldn't quite place her accent. A very gentle lilt. Irish maybe? Yes, that was probably it. Quite pronounced when she'd said 'Rayner'.

Solly was beside me now, shaking himself dry and spraying me with salt water.

"Oh, Solly, you rascal."

He ran off again and I began dabbing myself dry. Glancing up at the cliffs I noticed something metallic glinting in the sun. It was probably someone bird-watching.

As the shot rang out my whole body froze while my mind instantly returned to six years ago.

To my horror Solly lay sickeningly still a short distance away. I ran towards him screaming, virtually blinded by tears. He was lying in a pool of sand-tinted blood.

I knelt beside him sobbing and waited for the second bullet while my mother put her arms around me.....

Tommy is a Storyteller who captivates but frustrates everyone he meets.

Look out for **DENNIS KING's** latest fascinating character in:

TOMMY TCHAIKOVSKY TELLS TALES

Nobody knew Tommy Tchaikovsky. A lot of people had met him but were never given the opportunity to get to know one jot about his past. To a point they could see for themselves his present situation and as for his future plans, well, even Tommy had precious little idea about them. For he led a nomadic existence, moving on when he sensed the time was right, always alone, but never lonely.

Whenever asked what his trade was he would reply, "Storyteller. I tell tales. But only to them that wants to listen."

Now his name was always the subject of much debate. Tommy he most certainly could be, but how plausible was Tchaikovsky? In truth that was a nickname, bestowed upon him by an ardent admirer many moons ago after he had intoxicated her in his caravan one night with breathtaking stories, cheap plonk and a liberal dose of the maestro's first piano concerto. Tommy had always adored Tchaikovsky's music and was therefore more than willing to utilise the name to his advantage. In fact he found it all rather amusing. And so Tommy Tchaikovsky was born - or, more accurately perhaps, invented.

(Due for publication later this year).